A Step in Time

The Complete Series

Second edition

Stacey Broadbent

A Step in Time (2nd Edition)
Published by Stacey Broadbent
Copyright © 2021 Stacey Broadbent

First published 2018

Licence Notes

Proofreading by Spell Bound
Cover image from Deposit Photos
Cover Design by Stacey Broadbent

ISBN: 978-0-473-58321-7 (paperback)
         978-0-473-58322-4 (MOBI)

Contents

Stacey Broadbent

Dancing Through the Storm

A Step in Time book one

Salsa is Sacha's life, and she will do anything to keep her place at the top. Even if it means the end of her and Dane.
In a bid to get over a breakup, Maddi joins the salsa scene and quickly becomes the sweetheart on the dancefloor. She's got the moves, she's got the talent, and now, she's got the man.

Bitter rivalry, deception and a desire to win

Who will come out on top?

Chapter 1

Sacha swung her leg over Dane, straddling him as he lay on the bed with his arms behind his head. She licked her ruby red lips seductively, as she ran her hands up and down his strong, muscular chest. There was a mischievous glint in her eye. Dane laughed, circling his hands around her waist.

"What?" she asked innocently.

"You're up to something. I can see it in your eyes." He grinned. "What do you want?"

"Who? Me?" She pointed one perfectly manicured nail at her own chest, eyes wide and virtuous. Dane pulled her towards him, lifting his head to meet hers before planting a kiss on her lips.

"Yes, you, little Miss Innocent." He kissed her again, wrapping his arms tighter around her waist. She unfolded her legs so that she was now lying on his chest, her legs intertwined with his. The kiss deepened, and Sacha let out a low moan as she ran her fingers through his hair. Dane's hands made a slow track down her back, his fingers easing under the waistband of her jeans. His arousal was obvious as she moved her hips against his, teasing him. She smiled against his lips.

"I think I might go," she whispered, pushing herself up off the bed. It was one of her favourite things to do to him; get him all riled up and then pretend she was leaving. She liked to be in control and have him beg her.

"You've got to be kidding me!" he whined as he sat up on his elbows, looking at her with hooded eyes. "Come on, it was just getting good, baby," he crooned, reaching for her.

"Mmm? It was, wasn't it?" She arched her back, stretching her arms above her head. Her already short top lifted, exposing her midriff. As expected, Dane lurched off the bed and sank to his knees in front of her, planting soft kisses on her bare stomach. His hand reaching around to cradle her behind as he did so.

"You… are… so… sexy." He kissed his way up her body as his hands slowly slipped her top over her head. With his chest pressed against hers, he whispered, "Please don't go."

"Well… seeing as you asked so nicely," she purred in his ear, her tongue darting out; something she knew drove him crazy. He cupped her behind in his hands and lifted her into his arms, his mouth crushing hers as he carried her towards the bed. "I guess I can stay a little longer," she murmured.

"What time did you wanna head down to the studio?" Sacha asked as she sauntered back in from the shower, wearing only a towel. Ensuring the knot was secured, she bent down to sift through a pile of clothes on the floor.

Dane had given her a drawer to use when she moved in, but she preferred a bit of chaos.

"You know, you're really gonna have to stop wiggling your arse at me if you want to get to the studio." Dane watched with a grin as she deliberately bent down even lower.

"I don't know what you're talking about it." She winked before selecting a tight red tee with a low-cut neckline, some jeans and red heels to match. With a look over her shoulder, she lifted her arm and dropped the towel, walking away from him with a smirk. She giggled at his sharp intake of breath.

"You're really not helping the situation by parading around like that," he groaned, flopping onto his back.

Sacha shimmied into her jeans, peeking back over her shoulder. "Come on, get ready!" She pulled her top over her head and fluffed her hair as she turned to face him. "I wanna get my groove on!" She wiggled her hips provocatively.

"Alright, alright." Dane pushed himself up off the bed and loped over to his drawers, pulling out a black shirt and some jeans. It was Thursday; dance night. Without fail, every week, they would drop everything to go to their studio, Latin Flava, and then on to Feeney's Bar afterwards for a night of social dancing.

They had both started dancing salsa a year ago and had had an instant attraction to each other. Sacha had a sexy, sassy way of moving; and Dane couldn't help but watch her every move. With her curvy figure and fiery attitude, it was clear to see she was born to salsa. There was a natural chemistry between them when they danced, and it hadn't taken long before they were more than just partners, both on and off the dancefloor.

If Dane was honest, he had started dancing to pick up chicks, and lucky for him, he happened to be good at it. Sacha was a firm believer that you could tell how a man was in the bedroom by the way he moved his hips on the dancefloor, and Dane's hips didn't lie. She was drawn to him like the proverbial moth to a flame. He towered above her tiny five-foot frame, but her attitude more than made up for her small stature. They made quite the striking couple really; she with her jet-black hair and pale complexion, and he with his olive skin, hair the colour of chocolate and eyes to match. It was no wonder they were the 'it' couple.

Both as dedicated as the other, they breezed through classes, practising at home and out at Feeney's. They lived and breathed dance.

Their teacher, Rachel, had suggested they work towards entering the Nationals at the end of the year. Competitive by nature, they jumped at the chance to show off.

Dane had been working on a choreography he was sure would 'wow' the judges. He had been watching a lot of lessons online, learning lifts and dips that they could incorporate into their dance. Sacha was more than happy to let him do all the hard work; she just had to make it look good, which happened to be her forte.

As with any collaboration though, they had their fair share of heated discussions, and both being just as stubborn as the other, neither one was willing to back down.

Sacha enjoyed antagonising him. She found it thrilling to see the fire in his eyes when they fought—it made the make-up even better.

"Hey, did I tell you I invited my mate Jessie along tonight? He's going to meet us at Feeney's to have a look," Dane said while ruffling a hand through his hair to give it that messy look.

"Jessie? Have I met him?" she asked, knowing all too well that she had.

"He was at that party we went to a few weeks back."

"Hmm. I think I know who you mean. Is he looking to pick up?"

Dane laughed, "Yeah, he's been going through a dry spell. I told him dancing is a great way to meet chicks, so he thought he'd tag along." He came up behind her, wrapping his arms around her waist and planting a kiss on the back of her neck. "It worked for me, didn't it?" His lips brushed below her ear.

"Sure did, babe." She spun around in his arms, stretching up to caress the back of his neck before pulling him down to kiss her again. "You ready?"

"And willing," he replied, grabbing his leather jacket from the coat hook. "We should make it in time for the advanced class. A bit of a warmup before Feeney's."

"Perfect."

Down at the studio, Sacha strutted in as if she owned the place, dropping her bag in the corner and jumping to the front of the line for warmups. She motioned for Dane to join her up front.

"You know all these moves. Let someone else get up front," he whispered, taking her hand and attempting to drag her away.

"I'm just giving them another style to emulate." She winked. Dane smiled and shook his head. Being one of the better dancers had given her quite the ego—not that she didn't already possess a rather large one. She oozed confidence in everything she did. And Dane had a thing for women with confidence.

Looking around the studio, he could see that she actually had a point. Some of the other girls in class were watching her every move and trying their best to copy her. He couldn't blame them; she did have an amazing style all of her own. No matter what she did, somehow it always looked effortless and sensual. It was no wonder the other girls wanted to be like her. There was something so intoxicating about her—girls wanted to be her, and guys wanted to be with her. He saw the way they looked at her, undressing her with their eyes. He knew she loved the attention too, and sometimes she did get a touch flirty on the dancefloor, but it didn't really bother him, in fact, he liked knowing they all wanted her, so long as he was the one who got to go home with her every night.

The combo they were being shown this evening was simple but beautiful. Sacha added in her own personal styling, making it her own. After the lesson, when music was playing in the background, they had a friend film them dancing the new combo. Dane knew others were running for their phones to secretly film them too, but he just grinned and put on a show, like always. Dane was nothing if not a performer at heart.

They danced as if a spotlight was on them, and everyone faded into the background. It wasn't until the song ended that they came up for air and realised a circle had formed around them. Their classmates clapped and cheered, egging them on. Dane grinned, spinning Sacha out to take a bow, then he followed suit. Anything to keep an audience entertained.

At Feeney's, later that evening, Sacha and Dane joined their friends at a table near the dancefloor. While Sacha changed her shoes, Dane went to get them some drinks from the bar. He was still buzzing from their mini performance at the studio, and it only spurred him on to complete their competition routine. He couldn't wait to see how people reacted to what he'd come up with. If his classmates thought what they did tonight was good, they were going to be blown away at the comps.

Leaning against the bar, Dane gazed around the room, checking out who was already here. A few new faces, but mainly all regulars; typical of a Thursday evening.

He caught site of a familiar face walking through the door and, with a grin on his face, he raised his hand to wave and catch Jessie's attention.

"You made it!" Dane called, slapping his friend on the back as he led him back to the bar. "What are ya drinking?"

"Jack and coke." He reached for his wallet, but Dane waved it away.

"On me, man." He paid for their drinks and they made their way back to the table.

"Hey, everyone, this is Jessie. He's come to have a look at what we do." Dane made the rounds, introducing him to everyone. "You remember Sacha?" he asked as he moved to stand behind her.

"Yeah, of course. Nice to see you again." He nodded in her direction.

"You too. So, you're gonna be one of us then?" she asked, a glint in her eye.

"Ah, yeah maybe. I saw you and Dane dance at that party. It looked pretty hot." He grinned. "If I could get a hot chick like you to dance with me like that, I'd be in heaven," he joked.

"Well, you never know. Your wish just might come true," she purred, watching him take his jacket off.

"Here's hoping." He winked, pulling a seat out to sit down. His eyes seemed to soak in his surroundings as they followed a couple out onto the dancefloor.

"Hey, you wanna dance?" Dane offered his hand to Sacha. "We can show him a couple things?"

"Sure thing, baby." She took his hand and they made their way to the floor. The tempo switched from a fast-paced salsa to a sensual bachata—exactly the kind of dance Sacha shined in. Dane circled his arms around her waist, pulling her in close as they started to move their feet and hips in sync. She wrapped her arms behind his neck, leaning her head against his chest as they moved. Dane lowered his hands to her hips, slowly pulling her closer so that her body was rolling towards his with every step. He changed his grip ever so slightly, giving the signal for her to twist her body side to side with the beat. They continued this flawless, and somewhat erotic dance around the floor. Every step he took, she mirrored. Every move followed to perfection. Slowly bringing her hands up above her head, he trailed his fingers down her every curve until they landed on her hips again. With a flick of his wrist, she spun between his hands until her back rested against his chest, and they continued to sway like this until the last notes of the song rang out.

"Wow." Jessie stared, his mouth agape. "I couldn't take my eyes off you guys. That was… amazing! Damn sexy too! You're one lucky guy, Dane." He slapped a hand on Dane's shoulder as he joined him at the table.

"Yeah, I know." He threw his arm around Sacha's shoulders.

"You wanna give it a go?" Sacha asked Jessie with a lopsided grin and a quirk of her brow.

"I don't know. I don't think my hips can move like that."

"Sure they can." She grinned, leaning into him. "Trust me." She took his hand and gently pulled him up out of his seat. "Just put your hands here." She placed his hands on her lower back. "And step in close so you can feel my hip movement." Jessie looked to Dane as if asking permission.

"Go for it, man! I trust you." Dane laughed.

Sacha put her hands on Jessie's shoulders and shuffled in close so that their thighs were touching, she nudged his knee out with hers, slipping her leg in between his.

"We stand this way so that we don't knock knees," she said, looking up at him as he laughed nervously. "Now, you're going to step sideways, starting with your left leg." She moved slowly, saying each movement aloud. "Step, together, step, hip." She flicked her hip up to one side then back down again. "And then we go back the other way. Right, together, right, hip." She pulled back, smiling. "See? You *can* do it. You just did the basic bachata step."

Jessie huffed out a breath. "Well, that wasn't nearly as scary as I thought it would be." He chuckled, bringing his hand up to rake it through his hair. "Can we try it again?"

"Sure. Go side-to-side a few times, get a feel for it." She counted the steps as they went, emphasising the hip movement, so he could feel the way to do it.

"The guy's a natural!" Dane slapped his friend on the back. "The great thing about bachata is that you don't even need to know lots of fancy steps. You can just go around the dancefloor doing those basic steps, feeling the music and it'll still look great." They took a seat back at the table, Dane grabbing Sacha and pulling her onto his lap. "Not to mention, you get to dance up close and personal with the ladies." He winked.

"You should come around sometime, we can show you some stuff," Sacha suggested.

"Yeah? I'd like that." Jessie grinned, swiping a hand across his brow. "Are you free this weekend?"

Chapter 2

Dane rolled over, his body searching for the warmth of Sacha's. Wrapping his arm around her middle, he pulled himself in closer, snuggling up against her back. His fingertips lightly brushed her stomach, tracing circles over her bare skin. His hands trailed down and around her hips, over her waist, and up to her shoulder, before making their way back down her arm, to her stomach once more. Her breath quickened as his hands slowly wandered over her body. She gently arched her back as he began nuzzling her neck—the part of her that was extremely sensitive. He kissed and licked a trail from her shoulder to her ear, making her wriggle.

"Good morning," he whispered as he continued his slow torment.

"Mmmm," she murmured, arching her back further, pushing her body into his with more intensity. Unable to contain himself any longer, he gripped her hip and rolled her towards him, lowering his lips to hers. She raked her hands through his hair and down his back, digging her nails in. Wrapping her legs around his waist, she pulled him on top of her.

"God, I love you," he said, looking into her eyes as he positioned himself over her.

"Back at ya, baby," she said with a grin as she lifted herself up to kiss him again.

"You're so damn beautiful."

"You're not so bad yourself." She leaned in to whisper in his ear. "Now stop talking."

Sacha sat on the side of the bed, blankets draped casually around her middle. She stretched her arms above her head, loosening her muscles before getting up. Glancing over her shoulder, she could see Dane peacefully snoring. Grabbing her silk robe from the back of the door, she slipped it over her shoulders and padded to the bathroom. She loved nothing more than a little morning action but lazing in bed afterwards was not really her thing. She splashed some cold water on her face to freshen up before changing into leggings and a singlet, ready for a run. Keeping her body curvy and toned didn't happen by itself. It required a rigorous exercise regime. Sure, dancing helped a lot too, but there was something to be said about being out in the fresh air.

Switching on her iPod, she peered into the bedroom to check if Dane was still sleeping. As suspected, he was out to it. *No stamina, that guy.* She grinned to herself as she grabbed her keys and headed out the door.

Running was like breathing to Sacha; it came naturally. She liked that she didn't really have to push herself to keep going, she just did. Always had, in fact. It made it easier for her to let her mind wander. She did some of her best thinking while pounding the pavement.

Today was no different. Jessie was coming over tonight, and there was a lot they had to get done before then—neither of them were very domesticated, so a mad dash clean-up normally ensued when visitors were expected.

She made a mental list of chores: wash last night's dishes, wipe down benches, vacuum lounge, prepare a salad and get some sausages out of the freezer. She wasn't much of a cook; sausages, chips and salad—that was the extent of her culinary skills. Dane didn't seem to mind though. What she lacked in domestic skills, she more than made up for in other areas.

In her mind, men were simple creatures; keep them happy in the bedroom, have beer in the fridge and snack food readily available, and they were sorted. Of course, it helped to have a great rack too. Sacha was well aware of the stares she got from men. And women for that matter. In fact, she quite enjoyed it. If showing a bit of cleavage was going to get her what she wanted, then why not flaunt what she had? If there was one thing her dear old mama had taught her, it was that seduction is the key to everything.

"Baby, you can work hard every day to make piss-all money, like all them other mugs out there, or you can use what the good Lord gave you and get everything your little heart desires," she'd say, while puffing on a cigarette and taking a swig of bourbon. *"See, honey, men? They're stupid. Don't think with their brains, they think with their dicks, and that's a fact. You, my girl, have been blessed with boobs and a booty that men will find irresistible. Show 'em a bit of skin, a good time in*

the bedroom, and you'll want for nothing, I can promise you that."

She had been only too happy to share her 'tricks of the trade' with her, and Sacha had been eager to lap up her words of wisdom. It wasn't long before dear old mama was also benefitting from the exotic looks of her daughter; their weekends were spent parading around bars, looking for men to approach. Sacha would distract them with her 'charms' while Mama would empty their wallets. But when Mama started trying to pimp her out, she'd decided it was time to go out on her own.

She refined her skills to acquire more than just pocket change, without having to 'go all the way'. She was pretty good at it too. There were various degrees to her seduction techniques—depending on what she wanted out of it. A little flirting to get discount in a store, a show of cleavage to have her drinks bought for the night.

With this mastered, she hadn't really had to work a day in her life. Men would fall over themselves just to buy her a drink. As if *that* would make her go home with them. Please! They'd need to do a lot more than buy a drink to get into *her* pants. No, she just made them think they stood a chance, until she got what she wanted. Contrary to popular belief, she hadn't been around the block with every guy in town—only the ones she could benefit from.

Dane was no exception. She could see his potential instantly and knew they could go far in the dancing world—the fact that he was hot was an added bonus. He'd been lured in, like so many others before him—

flash him a smile, laugh at his stupid jokes, and wiggle her arse in his direction—it had been all too easy. Now, he would do anything for her. Hell, she practically lived with him, rent free. He was just as big a schmuck as the rest of them.

To be fair, he did treat her like a queen, so she didn't really mind doing extra things for him. Not to mention, the sex was pretty good. Truth be told, she had grown quite fond of him. Originally her intentions had been for them to be together long enough for her to get to the top. Now, however, she was reconsidering this. He had made the fatal mistake of introducing her to Jessie.

Ah, Jessie. Now there was a beautiful specimen of a man. Tall and muscular—it was obvious he worked out—with piercing green eyes and sandy blond hair. She had definitely noticed him at that party they had been to, and now he was coming to their place—dangerous territory.

She could've forgotten about him, had he not shown up at Feeney's. Like Dane, he too had potential and she was good at bringing that out in men. There was no doubt in her mind that she could do the same for Jessie.

Dane was a brilliant dancer, but he held no challenge for her anymore and boredom was something that didn't sit well with Sacha. She needed the excitement. The thrill of the chase, so to speak. Dane had been a worthy opponent for a while at least. Plus, he had completely choreographed their routine, so she had barely had to lift a finger. But the spark had gone. She had just been going through the motions to get them to the comps, and then she had planned on ending it. Jessie was like the light at the end of the tunnel, and she *had* to have him.

Chapter 3

Sacha sauntered through the door, completely unaffected by her run. Not a hair out of place, or a drop of sweat to be seen. Sometimes Dane wondered if she was actually running at all. Not that he was one to talk. He had never been much of a fitness junky; he was lucky enough to have a fast metabolism, so found weight was never really a problem.

"Coffee?" he asked as she breezed past.

"Just gonna jump in the shower, but I'll have one when I get out, thanks."

Dane took another bite of his toast before flicking the switch on the jug and grabbing two mugs from the cupboard. He scooped coffee and sugar into both cups, then retrieved the milk from the fridge. As soon as he opened the lid, the stench of stale milk hit his nose.

"Ugh, that's nasty." He threw on some trainers, then knocked on the bathroom door. "We're out of milk! I'm just gonna shoot to the shop!"

"Okay!" Sacha yelled back.

"You need anything else?"

"Nah, I'm good, thanks!"

Shovelling the last of the toast in his mouth, he grabbed his keys from the bench and jogged out the door. The dairy was only a five-minute walk from their place, which was handy for times like these.

Armed with his bottle of green-top milk and a newspaper, Dane made his way to the counter. There was a leggy blonde standing in front of him, trying to choose between a Picnic bar and a Snickers.

"Just get both," he said with a grin.

"Huh?" She looked up.

"Oh, I said, just get both. You'll regret it if you don't."

"Hmm." She looked back at the bars before grabbing one of each, nodding to the cashier and handing over her cash. "Thanks," she said as she passed Dane.

Glancing back over his shoulder, he saw her eyes flick to his before she went out the door. She had given him the hint of a smile. He stepped up to the counter to pay for his things.

"Oh crap!" the cashier said. "She left her keys here."

"Hey, no problem, I'll go call her back." Dane jogged to the door. "Miss!" he called. "Excuse me!" He ran after her. She quickened her pace.

Really?

He reached out and tapped her on the shoulder. She spun around, her hands balled into fists.

"Whoa." He held his hands up. "I'm not going to hurt you. You just left your keys back at the shop." He pointed his thumb back.

"Oh. Well, that's a little embarrassing. I'm so sorry I freaked out. I just heard you running towards me and panicked." She giggled nervously.

"Hey, it's all good. It's good to be cautious." He smiled. "Come on, I'll walk you back."

"Thanks." She clasped her hands in front of her as she bounced towards the store. Dane couldn't help but notice how beautiful her smile was. In fact, he had to admit, she was quite stunning. Not that he would ever do anything to jeopardise what he had with Sacha. No other woman could compare. That didn't mean he couldn't admire another woman's beauty though.

"Found her," he announced when he walked back up to the counter.

"Thanks so much," she said to the cashier. "I'd forget my head if it wasn't screwed on." She laughed and turned to leave. "Thanks again. Maybe I'll see you around." She grinned, and then bounced out the door once more.

Sacha was out of the shower by the time he got home, and dancing around the lounge with music blaring. She was wearing the tiniest pair of denim shorts and a figure-hugging singlet. Definitely a sight to behold. He sure was a lucky guy.

"You took your time!" she yelled over the music, shimmying her way over. Dane loved it when she was playful like this.

"Had to help a damsel in distress," he said, wrapping his arms around her waist and pulling her gyrating body into his.

"Was she pretty?" She pouted.

"Not as pretty as you," he answered, kissing her softly.

"That's alright then. Am I still getting that coffee?"

"But of course." He went into the kitchen, adding the milk to their cups and re-boiling the jug.

"What time is Jessie coming over tonight?" she asked, kneeling on the couch in front of the breakfast bar so she could watch him.

"Around seven, I think. What are we drinking tonight?"

"Whatever you're buying." She grinned.

"Oh, it's like that, is it?"

"Yup."

"You might have to pay me back in other ways then." He winked.

"Whatever do you mean?" She blinked, an innocent expression on her face.

"I'm sure you can think of something," he teased.

"Hmm." She climbed off the couch, walking behind him. "You mean, like this?" She snaked her hands around his waist, unbuttoning his jeans.

"Mmmm, that could work," he said, closing his eyes as she began to stroke him.

"You like that?" she whispered.

"Mmhmm," he murmured.

"Well…" She removed her hand and slapped him on the arse. "You'll just have to wait till later." She grinned, grabbing her coffee off the bench, and stepping out of reach.

"Oh, really? Two can play at that." He lunged for her.

"Uh-uh! I've got a hot drink in my hand!" She squealed, holding her cup up for him to see.

"You'll just have to stay still then, won't you?" He ran his hand down her back, cupping her behind.

"We'll never get anything done at this rate!" She giggled.

"Cleaning is over-rated," he said, lowering his head to nibble her ear.

"Okay, okay! Let me put the coffee down first." He lifted his arm, giving her space to reach through to the bench before throwing her over his shoulder. She shrieked, giggling, as he carried her back to the bedroom.

Their morning was spent in various stages of undress, until Sacha finally dragged herself to the bathroom to shower once more. She didn't fancy being caught in the act when Jessie arrived. It would hardly help her cause.

Dane was busy washing dishes when she traipsed back to the bedroom, wrapped in her towel. She carefully selected the right outfit. Something that looked casual but at the same time, showed off her curves. A pair of faded jeans with rips down the front that moulded to her perfectly formed body, paired with her favourite vintage tee. She slicked her hair back into a ponytail, put a pair of hoop earrings in and slathered on some ruby red lipstick.

She could hear Dane starting up the vacuum cleaner in the lounge. She had trained him well. A little bit of horseplay and she barely had to lift a finger. She sashayed into the lounge.

"Thank you, baby." She winked as she walked through to the kitchen. The sausages were still thawing on the bench, so she put them in the fridge to finish off. Pulling open the veggie drawer, she grabbed a lettuce, capsicum, tomatoes and cucumber. She retrieved a chopping board from the cupboard, and slowly began slicing and dicing the veggies before adding them to a bowl.

"I'm going to head down to the liquor store before Jessie gets here. Any preference?"

"I always like bourbon, but whatever you want, baby," she cooed as she continued dressing the salad.

"Okay, won't be long." He gave her a quick kiss and grabbed his keys from the bench.

"I'll be here," she said. She wrapped cling film over the top of the bowl and put it back in the fridge. Looking around, she could see that Dane had pretty much done all the cleaning. With no plans of doing any more work, she switched her iPod on again, and made a playlist for the evening.

She was happily sitting on the couch with her feet up, flicking through a magazine when Dane came back, black bags in hand.

"You look busy." He grinned.

"Always." She put her magazine down. "What did you get me?"

"Bourbon, of course."

Sacha clapped her hands. "Ooh thank you, baby." She stood on tippy toes to kiss him. "I've got the salad and sausages in the fridge. I'll start cooking just before seven," she said, swiping the bag from his hand and pulling the bottles out. Twisting the cap off, she tipped it towards him. "You want one?"

"Sure, why not?"

"So, what stuff did you want to show Jessie tonight?" she asked as she stuck her head in the freezer to find the ice cubes.

"Maybe a little more bachata, a bit of salsa. We'll just see how he goes."

She topped the glasses off with cola. "Okay, good idea. He did seem quite keen on the bachata."

"Who wouldn't be, dancing with a hot thing like you?" He pulled her onto his lap, sloshing the drinks over her hands.

"Hey! You're making me spill the drinks!" She laughed, holding her hands up high and licking the liquid trickling down her wrist.

"You know? I really don't care." He grinned, finding the ticklish spot between her ribs. She squirmed away from his wandering hands, giggling and squealing as she did.

Chapter 4

"Mate, come in!" Dane held the door open for Jessie. "Welcome to our humble abode." He rolled his arm in the direction of the lounge.

"Thanks, man. I wasn't sure what you were drinking, so I brought beer and bourbon." Jessie held up his bag of goodies.

"It's gonna be a good night!" Dane laughed. "You hungry? Dinner's just about ready I think."

"Sweet. I'm starving." The boys walked through to the kitchen, putting Jessie's beer in the fridge and popping one open. "You want one?" he offered.

"Sure," Dane said, helping himself to one. "How 'bout you, babe?"

"Yeah, sure, why the hell not?" She grinned. "You boys want eggs with your sausages?"

"Oh, I don't mind. Whatever you guys want."

"Ooh, I could really go for some eggs actually, babe. Fried?"

"It's the only kind I make." She laughed. "You wanna get the plates out, while I cook 'em up?"

"But of course, m'lady." Dane stooped into a low bow before going to the cupboard. Jessie stood at the breakfast bar, watching with a smile on his face. "What?" Dane asked.

"It's good to see you happy, man. Sacha's good for you."

"She sure is." He planted a kiss on her cheek before setting the plates down on the bench.

"Oh crap."

"What's up?"

"I broke the egg yolk."

"Eh. It's all good. It's gonna get all mushed up inside anyway," Dane reassured, giving her a pat on the behind.

"Yeah, it's actually the way I like my eggs. Yolks are so over-rated," Jessie quipped while Sacha flipped the eggs over. She gave them a few seconds before scooping them onto the plates and dishing up the rest of the food.

"Whatever. You're just being nice." She looked up at Jessie with a smile. "Thanks."

"No really. It's just like my mum used to make." He took the plate from her hand. "Thanks for cooking."

"You're welcome. I don't do it often, so you better enjoy it while you can," she said before taking a large gulp of her beer. "Oh God. That's awful." She laughed, wiping her mouth with the back of her hand. "I don't know what you guys see in this shit. Gimme a bourbon any day." She offered the bottle to Dane.

"It's not for everyone I guess." He chuckled. "Here, I'll make you a drink. You sit and eat." He jumped up from his seat and poured her another bourbon and cola.

"Now that's a drink." She took a sip and sighed contentedly. "So, Jessie, what have you been up to today?"

"I spent the morning in the gym. Not much after that, I'm afraid."

"Ah, you're a gym nut. I thought you might be." She made a point of checking him out. "I like to run myself."

"Yeah? What about you, Dane? Does Sacha drag you out too?"

"Me?" he scoffed. "That'd be the day!" He patted his stomach. "This body of perfection you see before you is all thanks to good genes and dancing. I'm one of those people you love to hate." He laughed.

"Bastard!" Jessie and Sacha said together.

"Hey, it's not my fault I'm so damn hot." He held his arms out, strutting about the room like Mick Jagger.

"Poser."

"You love it."

Sacha rolled her eyes, laughing. "If you say so."

"So, are we gonna dance or what?"

"You up for it, Jessie?" she asked as she cleared the plates away and poured herself another drink.

"Sure, I'll give it a crack."

"What do you want to do? Salsa? Bachata?"

"I did really like that one we did the other night at Feeney's."

"Yeah, it's our favourite too, eh babe?" Dane said, grabbing her hand and pulling her in to a closed position. "This is your basic hold—it's the same for most dances. You want to have your hand on her shoulder blade, so you can lead her, like this." Dane gently but firmly, placed pressure on Sacha's back, signalling for her body to turn in each direction. "So, the basic step for bachata looks like this. Step left, together, left and hip. Then, right, together, right and hip." He demonstrated both by himself and with Sacha. "Now you try."

Sacha stepped in close, placing her hand on his shoulder.

"Ready?" she asked, looking up at him.

"Yup." He stared down at his feet as he began to move. "Left, together. Left and hip," he said under his breath. "Right, together. Right and hip."

"Good, now try doing it a little more fluidly. Not so much of a pause in between."

"Okay." His gaze went back to his feet as he started to move.

"Hey, I know I've got great boobs, but maybe you could try looking at my face instead." Sacha grinned.

"What? I wasn't!" Jessie's face turned a lovely shade of red.

Sacha threw her head back, laughing. "I was joking!" She looked up at him with a sly smile. "Of course you can look at my boobs."

Jessie's jaw dropped. He looked at Dane, who was trying hard not to laugh.

"Come on, I'm having fun with you." Sacha playfully patted his chest.

"You'll get used to her," Dane said, amused. Sacha's way of relaxing people was to flirt. He had seen it all before. He wasn't bothered—if she was going to cheat on him, she'd hardly do it right in front of him now, would she?

"I think he could do with another drink." Sacha made her way to the fridge to retrieve some more beers.

She topped up her glass while she was at it. "You gotta try not to think about it too much, and just feel it. Here, I'll show you." She put their drinks down and grabbed his hand, placing it on her hip. "Feel the movement of my hips." She slowly went through the steps, accentuating the hip movement for him. To her glee, his eyes never left her hips. "It's just like at the pub."

"Okay, I think I got it now." He took up the closed position again and started to move."

"Good!"

"You wanna try it to the music?" Dane asked, flicking through the playlist on the iPod.

"Good idea. I'll count you in." She waited for the music to start. "Ready?" He nodded. "Okay. Five, six, seven, eight."

Jessie had great timing; normally one of the hardest things to teach. Sacha was right in her assumption—he had potential.

"You're doing great! Now try sliding your right arm down hers, to an open position," said Dane. Jessie obliged. "Now if you want to turn her, you raise your hand on the hip step, that's her signal that she will be beginning to turn."

"Okay."

"Not too high, just slightly above my head." Sacha corrected his positioning before turning herself. "You can turn me in either direction, just use the opposite hand to signal."

Jessie did a few basic steps before attempting to lead her through some turns. He was picking it up quickly.

"Are you sure you haven't done this before?" Sacha asked. "You're very good."

"Ah, thanks. Fast learner I guess." He chuckled.

"And he's got a great teacher." Dane gestured towards Sacha.

"*Teachers*. You guys are awesome," Jessie said. "You couldn't give me another demo, could you?"

"Yeah, of course. Any excuse to dance with my lady." Dane selected what song he wanted before offering his hand to Sacha. Taking full advantage of Jessie watching, she decided to play it up and make it as sexy as she could. She wrapped her arms around Dane's neck, her body pressed in close. Any chance she got, she would roll her hips in Jessie's direction. When Dane turned her so that her back was up against him, she slowly writhed her body up and down, holding eye contact with Jessie as she did so.

"That was hot!" Jessie clapped with enthusiasm. "You gotta show me how to do that!"

"Stick with us and we will." Sacha winked, as she ran her hand down his arm. "We can show you *all* the tricks."

Several drinks later, Sacha and Dane had shown Jessie the basic salsa and bachata steps—he really was a fast learner. The more drinks he had, the more he loosened up, and the more Sacha put her skills to use. She was careful not to be too obvious in front of Dane, not that he would notice—she flirted with other men all the time and he never batted an eye. She had to play this one smart though. Jessie was Dane's friend. She would have to work on him slowly, until he could no longer resist her. It would happen. Eventually. She always got what she wanted.

"Guys, you have been fantastic, but I really should be going," Jessie said.

"Aww, you sure? We were just getting started. You can always crash here, eh babe?" Sacha pouted.

"Thanks, maybe next time." He smiled. "I'll just call a taxi."

"Sure thing, mate. Phone's up there." Dane pointed to the kitchen wall. "I think the number's on the fridge. Hang on." He staggered over, staring at the various magnets cluttering the front of the fridge. Grabbing one shaped like a car, he held it up, triumphant. "Here 'tis," he slurred.

"Thanks." Jessie made his call and gathered his things, ready to leave. They walked him to the door. Sacha held her arms out to him.

"Bring it in. We're huggers here." She pulled him down to meet her, so she could wrap her arms around him tightly. Her face in the crook of his neck, she brushed her lips lightly against his skin—soft enough that it wasn't obvious, but that he would question whether it had happened or if he'd imagined it. She pulled away, catching his eye. "Will we be seeing you in class?"

He held her gaze for a beat. "You know? I think you will. I had so much fun tonight."

"Yeah, me too." She smiled sweetly.

"We should do it again nex' week!" Dane chuckled. "It was good ta see ya again, man. I'm glad you came."

"Yeah, me too. Flick me a text when class is on, and I'll be there. I think it's fair to say I'm hooked now." He grinned, looking over his shoulder towards the road. "Sounds like my ride is here. Thanks again, guys." He jumped down the steps and jogged down the drive, giving a wave before climbing into the taxi.

"That went well," Sacha said as she closed the door.

"It sure did." Dane circled his arms around her waist, kissing her cheek. "Thanks for making him feel welcome."

"Don't mention it." She smiled, turning to face him. "It was my pleasure."

Chapter 5

Rory sat back and looked over her creations. Tan square; her secret recipe that had been passed down from her grandmother to her mother, to her; chocolate-chip cookies, and a two-tiered red velvet cake with cream cheese frosting. Not bad for an afternoon's work, even if she did say so herself. She couldn't think of a better way to spend her Sunday afternoon than cooking up a storm. She was more at home in her kitchen than anywhere else in the world.

She carefully manoeuvred the red velvet onto a cake stand, covering it with its glass lid so Maddi would see it when she came home. It was her favourite flavour, and Rory really wanted to cheer her up. She hadn't been herself since the break-up with Ty.

They hadn't been together long, but she had been smitten with the guy. Poor thing was devastated when he told her he was moving away and thought it best if they saw other people. Translation, "I want to sleep around."

It was week two of heartbreak city, and Rory was doing everything in her power to keep her best friend's spirits up. Every day seemed to be a little better than the last.

The two had been friends since the age of three. Rory had watched as another kid had made it their priority to pick on the new girl. After Maddi had been shoved by said kid, Rory had stepped in; if there was one thing she couldn't stand, it was a bully. She had taken an instant dislike for anyone who preyed on weaker/smaller people than themselves. It had become somewhat of a mission for her to stand up for the 'under-dogs' of the school yard.

Maddi and Rory had been thick as thieves ever since that day in kindergarten. Complete opposites of each other—sweet, shy girl Maddi, with her locks of golden curls, and confident, tom-boy Rory, with her peroxide-blonde pixie cut—together, they were the complete package. You couldn't have one without the other.

When they had reached high school, and started getting interest from guys, they had relied on each other's opinions. If they didn't pass the 'best friend test' then they were tossed aside. Some guys weren't so keen on the set-up, not wanting to have the 'third wheel' hanging around so much. Others tried to use it to their advantage, seeing if they could charm them into a threesome. Those guys never got very far.

As far as Maddi was concerned, sex was off the cards. She had been tempted, but there hadn't been anyone special who really made her feel that it was the right time. Until that day came, she would remain pure.

Rory on the other hand, was a little more open to things. She didn't sleep around, but if it felt right, then she was up for anything. Except a threesome with her best friend, of course.

She admired Maddi's self-control. It wasn't one of Rory's strongest qualities. She tended to get caught up in the heat of the moment.

Somehow, Maddi was able to stop herself from going too far. It was quite impressive. Rory had witnessed the frustration on Ty's face as Maddi sent him packing each night, all hot and bothered. The poor guy. You couldn't fault him for trying though. Maddi was gorgeous. She was one of those girls who was oblivious to her looks. She didn't even have to try. Long, lithe legs, bouncing blonde curls, piercing blue eyes and full pouty lips. She was tall and slender, but not without curves. She even woke up fresh-faced every morning; unlike Rory, who would have hair sticking out in all directions and eye liner smeared down her cheeks. Yep she certainly was a sight to behold.

To top it all off, Maddi was the sweetest, most down-to-earth girl you would ever meet. She really did have everything going for her. It was no wonder so many girls were threatened by her. If they only took the time to get to know her though, they would fall in love with her too.

Rory hung up her apron and switched the jug on to make herself a coffee. She put a slice of tan square on a saucer, then added a cookie too. She grabbed her favourite cup down from the cupboard and scooped in some coffee and sugar before getting the milk from the fridge. Hearing the front door open, she smiled.

"You're just in time. Wanna cuppa?"

"Sure!"

"Ooh, somebody's happy." She spun around to face her friend. Maddi had a huge grin plastered on her face. "Alright, spill."

"I've found something I think will be fun for us to do."

"Sounds intriguing. Tell me more."

"Salsa!"

"Salsa?"

"Salsa." She nodded. "I saw a poster advertising this studio called Latin Flava. They have these free beginners' classes starting tonight. You wanna go?" She clasped her hands together as if praying. "Please!" To really drive it home, she batted her eyelashes and pouted her lips.

Rory couldn't help but laugh. This was the most enthusiastic she had seen Maddi since Ty left. "Of course! Sounds like fun."

Maddi clapped her hands gleefully. "Yay! Thanks so much!" She raced over to hug her friend. "Do you think we need to dress up?" She pulled away, clutching Rory's shoulders. "What are we going to wear?"

"Whoa there, Nelly, it's just a class. I doubt they expect us to dress all Latina." Maddi's face dropped like a child who'd had their favourite toy taken away. Rory quickly added, "But I'm sure we could spice it up a bit. We'll have a fashion montage like they do in the movies. I'm sure we can find something hot to wear."

"Thanks, Rory. I really need this. And I've always wanted to try it. It's so sexy!" She wiggled her hips towards the kitchen then spied the baking on the bench. "Is that? Is that red velvet cake I see?"

Rory nodded with a grin. "All for you."

"Oh my God, you are the best friend a girl could have!" She flung her arms around her friend before carefully lifting the lid, running her finger through the frosting and popping it into her mouth. "Mmm… so good!"

"Okay, how about, we have a coffee and some cake, and then we can do our montage." She took a bite of her tan square.

"Deal," Maddi said, as she sliced herself a sizeable chunk of cake.

Chapter 6

After trying on every outfit in their wardrobes, Rory and Maddi finally decided on something to wear to their first-ever salsa class. Rory had opted for sheer black tights and denim shorts over the top, with a cute crop top that hung off her shoulder. A myriad of silver bracelets adorned her arms and hoop earrings for her ears.

Maddi, not wanting to draw too much attention to herself, had gone for some black leggings with cut-outs down the sides, and a tight pink singlet. Going for a more simplistic look, she chose to wear just the one leather bracelet and matching necklace.

They walked the few blocks down to where the studio was situated, a nervous excitement between them. Rory was secretly hoping for some hot guys to be there. As far as she was concerned, there was nothing hotter than a guy who could dance. She was always drawn to them when they were out at the pubs. Of course, they were normally there to dance anyway, so if anyone was going to catch her eye, it would be someone on the dancefloor.

A hot dancer would be a good distraction for Maddi too. Something to get her mind off Ty.

She wasn't disappointed. The studio, to her surprise, was filled with guys. She had expected to see a room full of women and barely any men, but it seemed to be the opposite. There were more than a few potentials in there. She looked at Maddi with a gleam in her eye.

"Look at how many men there are," she whispered loudly, a grin spreading across her face. "I wonder how many were dragged here by girlfriends, and how many are here to pick up chicks." She craned her neck, checking out every last corner of the studio.

"Wow, there's a lot more people here than I expected," Maddi said, wiping her hands down her thighs. "I didn't realise how popular it is."

"Well, *Dancing with the Stars* has probably had a hand in that."

"Yeah, I didn't think about that."

"You okay? You still wanna stay?"

Maddi took a deep breath. "Yeah, I wanna stay. It'll be good for me. I haven't been to a dance class in years."

"I'll be right here by your side, bumbling my way through." Rory gave her hand a squeeze. "Come on, let's go sign up."

They walked up to the counter where a bubbly redhead took down their details. Class would be starting in five minutes, and she pointed them to the open area in the centre to find a spot to stand. Lines were beginning to form already, so they tagged onto the end of one near the front.

The redhead walked up to the stage and turned her headset on.

"Welcome, everyone, to the free beginners' salsa class! I'm Rachel, and I will be your instructor this evening." She smiled, her eyes lighting up. "Tonight,

I'm going to show you some merengue moves which will get you dancing and shifting your weight properly for the salsa steps that we'll do at the end of the class. Don't worry if you haven't got a partner, we will move around the circle, that way everyone gets to have a go, and you will actually learn faster." She paused, pushing some buttons on a remote she had in her pocket. The studio was filled with music. "This is a merengue beat." She started to move her feet. "Left, right, left, right." She switched the music off again. "Not so daunting, is it?" She grinned, looking around at the eager faces. "Okay, so the movement is like climbing stairs. Left, right, left, right. Now, ladies, I know it's tempting to try and push those hips out like you see the pros do, but you will get into bad habits if you force it. Just focus on your feet first, and the hips will follow." She began marching on the spot. "This is how it should look."

"This is fun!" Rory whispered.

"I know! I love it already!"

"Alright, everyone, I'm going to put a song on for a warm-up. Just follow me!" Rachel turned the sound up and started calling out different directions for them to step in. Before long, they were all keeping in time and there were smiles all around.

"Okay, I want you to make a circle now. Grab a partner, or if you don't have one then you can slot yourself into the gaps." She waited as everyone began to organise themselves into a rough circular shape. Moving into the centre of the circle, she grabbed one of the spare bodies to partner her. She showed everyone how to get into a closed position and got them doing some basics on the spot. "Alright, now high five and moving on to the next person!" she called out.

There was light chatter as people introduced themselves to their new partners. Slowly, Rachel showed them a simple merengue combo, breaking down each step. They rotated around the circle after each section of the move.

"Alright, we'll do it one more time slowly, and then we'll try it to music. I'll get you all to move around once more."

Maddi stepped up to her new partner.

"Hi, I'm Jessie. Is this your first class too?" He smiled down at her.

"I'm Maddison… Maddi, and yeah it is. Does it show?" She giggled, her nerves getting the better of her.

"Not at all, Maddison Maddi. You make it look so easy!"

"Thanks." She blushed. "I've always wanted to try it."

"Well, it suits you." He pulled her in to the closed position, waiting for Rachel's instructions. Maddi looked over at Rory, who was giving her the thumbs up and mouthing, *Go for it! He's hot!* She stifled her giggle as she turned back to Jessie with colour in her cheeks.

"Friend of yours?" he asked, smirking as he watched Rory.

"Ah, yeah. I dragged her along with me. Excuse her. She doesn't know the meaning of the word subtle."

Jessie laughed. "You've got that right. I'm flattered, actually."

"Oh?"

"Well, clearly she thinks I'm worthy of you. I'd be lying if I said I didn't find you attractive." He smiled easily, his eyes searching hers.

"Oh, um, thanks?" She giggled again. "I don't really know what to say."

Jessie chuckled. "You don't have to say anything, let's just dance." He winked at her, before pulling her through the move as if he'd been doing it all his life.

"Now who's the natural?" she asked.

"I've got friends who dance. They showed me a few things in the weekend. They were meant to be meeting me here tonight, but I haven't seen them yet."

"You're so lucky! I'm definitely going to have to join classes I think."

"Yeah, it's pretty fun, eh? I'm sure Sacha and Dane wouldn't mind an extra person to teach, ya know, if you wanted to join me some time."

"Oh, ah, yeah, maybe."

"It's okay, I'm not a serial killer or anything." He winked again.

"It's not that. I'm just not really, ready for…" She stopped herself, pulling her lip between her teeth, worried she'd gotten the wrong idea.

"Oh no, of course, I mean, we just met. I just thought, ya know, you dance really nicely, and I'd like to dance with you some more. No pressure."

"Thanks… Um… Can I think about it?"

"Yeah of course." He spun her out, sending her on to the next guy in the circle. "See you around, Maddison Maddi." He grinned.

After class, Rory came bounding up to Maddi.

"So?"

"So what?"

"So, did you ask him out?"

"What? I just met the guy!" She laughed. "He did ask me to practise with him though," she said, as she turned to grab her gear, trying to hide the smile on her face.

Rory squealed. "That's awesome! He's so gorgeous!"

"Yeah, maybe a little," she teased. "Alright, maybe a lot."

"Speak of the devil," Rory said, making herself scarce.

"Hey, ah, here's my number, in case you want to go over some stuff." Jessie handed Maddi a piece of paper. "Ya know, if you want." He ran his hand through his hair before putting his jacket on. "It was nice to meet you."

"Yeah, you too. And thanks." She smiled.

"Hey, there you are! I thought you guys were coming to class with me?" Jessie said as he spied Sacha and Dane walking through the door.

"You didn't tell him, did you?" Sacha frowned at Dane.

"I must've forgot, sorry. We don't normally come to the free beginners'. We thought you'd probably want to stay on for the next class though."

"Oh, okay. Will I be able to do it?"

"Of course, babe, we wouldn't suggest it otherwise." Sacha winked at him as she shrugged her jacket off. She sat down, retrieving her dance heels from their bag. "It's still a beginners' class, just a few lessons in. I'll talk to Rachel and square you a spot."

"Thanks, Sacha." He smiled warmly.

Dane pulled him aside and asked, "So, did you pick up?" He grinned. Jessie laughed, kicking his toe into the floor but not saying anything. "You did, didn't you?" Dane slapped him on the back. "Smooth operator, you are."

"Bit of a stud, are we?" Sacha drawled. She stood up and touched his arm. "Don't be too hasty."

"Hey, us guys have needs." Dane smirked, planting his hand on her backside for emphasis.

"Don't I know it," she sneered.

"I'm not in any rush. She just moves well, and I thought it might be good to practise with her. I'm picking she won't be without a partner for long."

"That good, huh? You wanna snap her up then, mate."

"Yeah, that's what I was thinking. I already gave her my number."

"Well, until then, you are more than welcome to use me as a practise buddy," Sacha purred, rubbing his arm.

"Thanks, Sacha."

"Best way to fast-track your dancing. She'll whip you into shape, no worries."

"And you don't mind me stealing your girl all the time?"

"Mate, of course not. I trust you."

Chapter 7

"Oh my God! That was so much fun!" Maddi danced around Rory as they walked back home. "I'm definitely going back for more. How 'bout you? Did you like it? What did you think?"

"Yeah, it was pretty cool. I could go again." She smiled. "On one condition."

"Anything!"

"You have to ask Jessie out." She grinned, a mischievous glint in her eye.

"Oh, so you're gonna play it that way, are you?" Maddi smirked. "Well, joke's on you, I was already thinking about doing that anyway." She stuck her tongue out at Rory.

"Wait, what?" Rory stopped her. "You're gonna do it?"

"Mmm. Maybe."

"That's a yes."

"No, it's a maybe."

"It's a yes." Rory giggled. "You like him," she sang as she began skipping along the road, dragging Maddi with her.

"Alright, alright. Maybe I do like him." She held up her finger and thumb. "A little." She beamed. "He *was* pretty hot. And man, he could move."

"Mmhmm. The perfect combination. I mean, you know what they say about men who can dance."

"Um, no, what?"

Rory waggled her brows. "Got moves on the dancefloor, got moves in the bedroom."

Maddi shook her head, laughing. "Of course they do."

"Hey, they don't call it the horizontal tango for no reason."

"All sorted." Sacha smiled at Jessie as she sauntered back over. "She is happy for you to join in tonight and for the rest of the term if you like."

"That's brilliant! Thanks, Sacha."

"Don't mention it," she said. "You ready to get your dance on?" She grabbed his hand and dragged him out to the dancefloor. "We'll have a little warm-up while everyone is getting ready."

Wrapping her arms around his neck and pulling herself in nice and close, she waited for his lead. They swayed side-to-side to get the beat, then he started to move his feet.

"Good. Don't be afraid to hold me tighter. You won't break me, I promise." She winked. "I need to feel your leads, so really hold me." His grip tightened. "Now use your hand to direct me. Put pressure on your palm to move me this way, then with your fingertips, to move me that way."

Jessie did as she asked. He carefully manoeuvred her around the floor, while she writhed her hips against his, all the while, staring deep into his eyes.

"Everybody, gather round! Class is about to start!" Rachel called out as she made her way to the stage once more. Jessie blinked, breaking his gaze and stepping away from Sacha. His cheeks flushed red.

"You look like you're getting the hang of it," Dane whispered, as he joined them.

"Ah, yeah, I think so," Jessie stammered, suddenly feeling very self-conscious. He hadn't meant to get so caught up while dancing with Sacha, she was just so mesmerizing. The way she moved, the way she looked at him; like he was the only one in the room. If he didn't know any better, he'd swear she was flirting with him. But that wasn't possible, she was his best friend's girl for Christ's sake.

Sacha was pleased. She had seen the look in his eyes when they danced and when he pulled away. She had him. Now to reel him in.

"I thought maybe I could dance with Jessie tonight, while you dance with some of the other beginners. Share our knowledge around." Sacha smiled at Dane. A good stroke to the ego never hurt.

"Good idea. We can be good Samaritans for the night." He chuckled. "He's doing really well, don't ya think?" He nodded at Jessie.

"Yeah, he is." She looked over at him, smiling sweetly as she gave him a little wave. "Maybe while you're having a dance with the others, you could suss out a good match for him."

"Hmm. Not a bad idea. Though I think he was keen on dancing with that girl from earlier."

"Yeah, but we don't even know if she's going to stick around. Plus, he's new to this. You can get a better feel for their talents."

"Yeah, you're probably right. I'll do my best."

"Thanks, baby." Sacha gave his arm a squeeze before brushing past him and over to Jessie. "Hey, handsome, you're dancing with me tonight." She took him by the hand. He laughed uncomfortably.

"No, really, you don't have to give me special treatment. I can move around the circle like everyone else. You go dance with Dane," he offered.

"Nope. It's a done deal. You're stuck with me." She ran her tongue over her lips.

"Oh, okay then." He sighed, shuffling his feet.

"Don't be too excited there, cowboy," she said, sarcasm oozing.

"Sorry. It's not you. I just don't want Dane to get the wrong idea, ya know?"

"And what wrong idea would that be?" she whispered, looking up at him through her long lashes.

"What? I mean… ya know, like… I was into you, or something," he stammered, his cheeks turning a brighter shade of red.

"So, you're not into me?" she asked, pushing her hips into his and stroking her hand along his neck.

"I… ah." He pulled back a bit. "Of course I am. Look at you." Sacha beamed at that. "But that doesn't mean I'm going to act on it. You're my best friend's girl."

She pulled his head closer to hers, her lips brushing his ear. "What if I want you to act on it?"

"What?"

"You heard me. We'd be good together."

"But, Dane?" Jessie pulled back, frowning.

"What about him? He's a big boy, he'll get over it."

"What?"

"It's not really working out between us. It's run its course. He's not what I want anymore. And *you* are." She flicked her tongue into his ear before pulling away.

"… and cross body lead into a right turn for the ladies!" Rachel's voice came over the speaker.

Sacha led herself through the combo, letting her proposal settle with Jessie. His eyes kept darting between her and Dane, as if weighing up his options.

"Less thinking. More dancing." She grabbed his chin, making him look at her. "Focus."

"Easier said than done. You just dropped a bombshell on me."

"Don't act like it hadn't crossed your mind. I've seen the way you look at me."

"Again, I had no intentions of doing anything about it."

"Well, now I'm offering you a chance to get what you want. You know it would be good." She licked her lips provocatively.

"I don't doubt that. But Dane's my friend. I can't do it to him."

"Okay, I get it. You're loyal, I like that. But don't expect me to give up. I can be *very* convincing when I want to be." She rubbed up against him before spinning herself out to join the rest of the circle.

"You're looking awfully smug," Dane said, giving Sacha a gentle squeeze as she spun into his arms.

"Just thinking about how well Jessie is doing." She looked across the room to where he was. "He's quite the natural."

She watched as he tried to distract himself. It was obvious he was trying to avoid her; clearly, she had gotten inside his head, and she loved it.

"He's got you to thank for it. You've been really good with him." He pulled her in tightly, tilting her chin upwards. "Thank you." He bent down, kissing her sweetly.

"Anything for my baby," she cooed.

Dane smiled, rubbing his nose with hers. "I love you," he whispered.

"Back at ya," she offered, reaching up to plant a kiss on the tip of his nose. "Shall we go?" she asked, risking a glance around him to see if Jessie was watching.

To her delight, he was. A fire danced across his eyes before he looked away, brooding. She smiled to herself, satisfied with her evening's work. It wouldn't be long before he was hers.

"Sure. I'll just go say bye to Jessie." He trotted towards his friend.

Sacha turned to retrieve her shoes and jacket, all the while, keeping her eyes on the interaction between the two.

"Hey, man." Dane clapped his hand with Jessie's. "We're about to head off."

"Oh, okay cool. Thanks for coming down."

"Anytime. You're doing really well, ya know. We were just talking about you." Dane motioned towards Sacha. She wiggled her fingers in the air.

"Thanks, man. I'm really enjoying it."

"You should come around again this week, we can go over some more stuff."

"Oh, I don't know. I don't wanna impose…"

"Mate. You're not imposing. We live for this stuff." He nudged him with his elbow. "Come on, it'll be fun."

Jessie stole a glance at Sacha. "Yeah, of course. Sounds great." He gave a tight smile.

"Excellent! We'll see ya later then." Dane slapped his friend on the back before walking back to Sacha.

"Ready to go, babe?" He offered his hand.

"Sure am." She let him pull her up, lacing his fingers with hers as they walked out of the studio.

Jessie watched them walk out together, holding hands, bodies pressed close. He hated himself for feeling jealous. Dane was his friend. He shouldn't even be thinking about Sacha that way, but now that she'd revealed herself to him, he couldn't get her out of his head. Damn her!

She was enjoying watching him squirm too, he could see it in her eyes. They sparkled whenever she caught him looking at her. He had tried so hard not to, but something about her drew him in. It was like he was under a spell.

He heard her voice ringing in his head. *"He's not what I want anymore. And* you *are."*

He shook his head. She was playing with him. She had to be. He had just watched her kiss Dane.

And leave with him.

It couldn't be real.

He had to get her out of his head. He couldn't fall for his friend's girl. It just wasn't right.

Chapter 8

Maddi spent the next few days practising the steps she had learned. Every time a song with an eight count came on the radio, she would break into dance. The rest of her spare time was spent YouTubing salsa moves. She was hooked.

A timetable of all the classes available hung on the fridge for all to see. Maddi checked it every day, even though she practically had the thing memorised. She had circled all the beginner classes so that she didn't miss one. Tonight, there was another free one that she was wanting to go to.

She knew it would probably be the same moves repeated, but she didn't care, she just wanted to be there. It made her feel good. The music was so upbeat and happy that it was virtually impossible to stay in a bad mood.

It was an added bonus that she happened to be good at it.

And then, of course, there was Jessie. She knew it was silly to think that she had fallen for him after their brief encounter. No, he just made her feel good about herself. Made her feel as though she was worth the effort. It was a nice change.

Not that Ty had been a bad guy. He had just been very intent on getting into her pants, and every time she resisted, she saw the resentment in his eyes. She wasn't stupid, she knew it was why he left. It saddened her that he couldn't see past that—see that she was more than just a body. She knew she deserved to be treated better, but it still didn't stop it from hurting.

Salsa was the first thing to make her feel like her old self again after he'd left, and Jessie was a part of that.

She hadn't called him, even though Rory had been rather persistent. She figured he would be at the classes too, if he really was as keen as he said he was. It would be nice to have a dance partner to practise with though.

Rory was pleased to see her friend back to her happy, bubbly self again; even if she was being stubborn about Jessie. She'd never liked Ty, and Jessie seemed like a much better fit for Maddi. He seemed like a genuinely nice guy. It would be good for her to get back on the horse again. Nothing like a new love interest to ease a broken heart.

Rory had hoped to join Maddi at the next dance class to give her a much-needed push in the right direction, but duty called. She was a casual for a catering company and she couldn't turn down the chance to work. Maddi would just have to fend for herself this time.

"How do I look?" She came out, giving a twirl, her chiffon skirt taking flight.

"Ooh pretty!" Rory grinned. "Is that new?"

"It might be." Maddi giggled. "It was on sale and I couldn't resist it." She brushed her hands down the front of her skirt. "I fell in love with it. I thought it would look cool on the dancefloor."

"It's awesome, it really suits you." Rory dried her hands, walking around the counter to join her friend.

"I wish you were coming with me."

"I know, me too. But you know how much I love my job."

"Yeah, I know." Maddi smiled. "I'm just a little nervous going by myself."

"Are you kidding? You were amazing. You're gonna be just fine on your own." Rory placed her hands on Maddi's shoulders. "You and those hips were born for this."

"Thanks."

"Just promise me something."

Maddi rolled her eyes.

"Don't do that! You haven't even heard what I'm going to say!"

"Sorry. Go ahead, I'm listening."

"Promise me you will at least talk to him? You don't have to ask him out, just be friends if you'd rather. I just have this feeling he would be really good for you."

Maddi sighed. "Alright."

"Good." Rory beamed. "You'll thank me for it."

"Yeah, yeah." Maddi grinned. "Well, I guess I'd better head off. What time will you be home?"

"It's only a few hours so I should be home about nine. If you need me to be later though…" She winked. "Just flick me a text."

Maddi laughed. "Don't go getting ahead of yourself. I said I'd *talk* to him. I'm not about to jump his bones."

"We'll see." Rory grinned mischievously as she walked out the door.

Down at the studio, Maddi was standing quietly in the corner, trying to find a familiar face. She had been to plenty of dance classes as a child, but her confidence had waned somewhat over the years, and she wasn't as good at meeting new people as she used to be. Everyone seemed to be in groups already and she wasn't sure where she would fit in.

"You look lonely," Jessie whispered as he sidled up next to her.

"Oh, hey." She smiled, feeling her cheeks redden. "I was just thinking that I didn't recognise anyone here."

"Well, now you know me." Jessie chuckled. "But yeah, I guess this is a whole new group of people than the other night." He scanned the room. "Maybe we're the only insane ones who came back to repeat a basic beginners' class."

"Yeah, you're probably right." Her eyes sparkled as she let out a soft laugh. Jessie had a way of putting her at ease with only his presence.

"What do you say? Shall we team up tonight?" he asked, nudging her with his elbow.

Her lips curled into a smile. "Sure."

He grabbed her hand and led her out to the front of the studio. No one else had ventured away from the outer edges of the room, instead waiting for others to make the first move.

"Best spot in the class." He winked.

The chatter began to die down as Rachel took to the stage.

"Gather round, everyone! Make some rows and we'll rotate back to front so that you all get a chance to see." She began running over the same merengue moves they had done for a warm-up last time.

"Ready to look like pros?" Jessie whispered, winking. Maddi giggled.

"Hardly!"

"Compared to these newbies, we are." He grinned, taking her hand. "We got this."

The music started, and they ran through the warm-up before forming a circle. Jessie pulled her in to his side, making sure she stayed with him.

"Have you been practising?"

"Guilty. I can't help it! Every time I hear music, I find myself counting the beats to see if I can salsa to it." She laughed. "I think I may have an addiction."

"I know what you mean. I do the same thing." Jessie chuckled as he gave her a spin. "I think we have a problem."

"Hmm, you could be right. I wonder if there's a cure," Maddi joked. "Not that I want there to be. It's too much fun!" She rolled her body towards Jessie, his eyes widening.

"Where did you learn that?" he asked, a wide grin spreading across his face. "It looks *really* good."

Maddi beamed. "I used to dance when I was younger. That, and I may have been watching a bit of YouTube." She chewed her lip, looking up at Jessie.

"I'm obviously gonna have to do some of that too if I'm going to keep up with you."

"I seem to recall you having private lessons. I think you'll be fine."

"Yeah, I don't know how much longer I'll do those though. I mean it must suck teaching newbies when you've got your own stuff to practise."

"I guess. It's probably a nice change for them though. I'm sure they wouldn't offer to teach you if they didn't enjoy it."

"Yeah, you're probably right." He bent down to whisper, "It's more fun this way though." When he pulled back, his eyes glistened with mischief.

Maddi couldn't help but grin up at him. "Aww, you're sweet. It *is* pretty fun dancing with you."

"Why, thank you." Jessie smiled, a thoughtful look on his face. "I hope we can do this some more."

"Me too." She bit her lip, suddenly all too aware of their close proximity. He really was a good-looking guy.

It was still too soon though. Ty had only left three weeks ago, and she wasn't in any hurry to jump straight back into another relationship. Someone needed to remind the butterflies in her stomach of that though; they flittered about like crazy whenever Jessie looked at her with that lazy grin of his.

"You up for one more dance?" he asked, snapping her out of her thoughts.

"Huh? Oh, yeah sure," she said, pushing aside any feelings for him. "Lead away."

Chapter 9

After class, Rachel asked Maddi to join her for a chat. Jessie looked on with raised brows.

"Somebody's the teacher's pet," he joked.

"I doubt it. I'm probably in trouble. I haven't actually signed up for any classes yet. Maybe she wants to tell me not to come to the free classes if I'm not paying for the other ones." She frowned, running her hand through her hair.

"Are you serious? You won't be in trouble! She can't offer free classes and not have people come along. I bet she wants to tell you how good you are."

"I don't know."

"Maddi, listen to me. You. Are. A. Star. Everyone can see it." He motioned around the room. "You can dance circles around anyone here."

Maddi sighed. "I hope you're right."

"I know I am." He ruffled her hair. "You just need to believe in yourself, kid."

She batted his hand away, laughing. "Enough of the 'kid' talk, thanks." She grabbed her gear and rocked back and forth on her toes. "I guess I should go see what she wants."

Jessie put his hands on her shoulders, turning her to face Rachel. "Go get 'em!" He gave her a gentle push. She stepped forward, peering back over her shoulder at him. *Go*, he mouthed, waving her on.

She took a deep breath and walked with more confidence than she felt.

"Rachel? You wanted to see me?"

"Yes, Maddi, isn't it?" She smiled, bringing a rush of relief to Maddi.

"Yeah, ah, yes, it is."

"I couldn't help but notice how fast you are picking up the moves. I wanted to let you know that we have a girls' dance troupe if you're interested in some solo work."

"Oh, really? That sounds great."

"Yeah, it's a small group, but we get together on Saturday mornings for an hour or two. We're working on a new routine so it's the perfect time to join." She smiled. "I think you would fit in really well."

"Wow, I wasn't expecting that at all. Um. I'd love to join."

"Great. Here are the details," she said, handing her a card. "If you have dance shoes then wear those, otherwise I have some spare pairs that would probably fit you."

"No, no, I've got some I can wear. Will jazz shoes be okay?"

"They'll be fine. If you decide you want to pursue dance further, you'll need to get some heels, but we can look into that later." She looked down at her desk. "If you're interested, I could use some help behind the desk some nights. It would mean that you could watch the other classes and join in on some too, if you like. Free of charge."

"Seriously?"

"Yeah, if you're interested. I mean, I hope I'm not overstepping here."

"No, I'd love to help out! Any excuse to immerse myself in dance." She couldn't believe her luck. And to think, she had thought she was going to be told to leave.

"I'll let you get back to your friend, but we should catch up for a coffee one night. We can go over the timetable."

"Thanks so much, Rachel. Honestly, this means so much to me." She rummaged in her bag for a pen. "Here's my number, let me know when you want to meet up. I'm free anytime." She spun on her heels and skipped back to where Jessie was waiting.

"You look happy with yourself. I told you it was gonna be good news." He grinned.

"She wants me to join her dance troupe!" she said excitedly. "Can you believe it?" She bounced up and down, her cheeks flushed. She very nearly threw herself into his arms, she was so excited.

"Wow! That's better than good news, that's fantastic! Congratulations!"

"Thanks. I can't wait to tell Rory."

"Ah, yes, your really subtle friend. Where is she tonight?"

"Yes, that's the one." She laughed. "She had to work."

"So, you're going home by yourself?"

"Yeah, I only live around the corner though."

"Can I walk you? Just to make sure you get home safely?"

"Sure, that would be nice."

"Great." He offered his arm for her to grab onto. "Let's get you home."

They made their way out the door and down the stairs to the ground below. The lights of the surrounding stores and bars twinkled brightly, lighting their way. They walked in a comfortable silence, arm-in-arm, Maddi pointing out the direction of her house.

"You know, my friends live near here. The ones I was telling you about."

"Oh yeah? I've probably seen them around then. It's quite a busy wee area."

"I can see that. I guess having a shopping area so handy keeps it alive."

"Mmm," she agreed. "I like it. It's like having our own wee town inside this big city. Reminds me of home."

"You're not from here?"

"Well no, not really. I lived here when I was little, then my Dad got offered a job in a place much smaller than this. I moved back here earlier this year with Rory."

"Ah, I can see why you find it so daunting then." He smiled.

"Yeah, it takes a bit of getting used to."

"Well, I'm always just a text away if you ever need a friend."

"Thanks." She paused at her driveway. "This is me." She waved her arm towards her little house. "Did you want to come in for a coffee?"

"You know, I would like that." He nodded, following her up the steps.

She unlocked the door. "Rory?" she called out. Silence. "She must be still at work." She walked through to the kitchen and switched the jug on. "How do you have it?"

"Huh? Oh, just milk please," he answered as he wandered around the room, looking at the photos on the wall. "Is this you and Rory?" He pointed at a picture of two kids no more than four years old, covered in ice cream, with big grins plastered on their faces.

"It sure is. We've been friends a long time." She smiled, handing him his cup. "That was after a trip to the zoo. We had begged our parents for an ice cream the whole day."

"You look like little trouble-makers."

"Yeah, sometimes." She paused. "Well, Rory was anyway." She laughed.

"Why doesn't that surprise me?" He laughed with her.

"Hey, you hungry? Rory baked me a cake the other day and there's still some left."

"Ooh sounds good. I do love cake."

"Rory is like the best baker in the world. Seriously, you won't want any other after you try it."

"Wow, that's high praise. It must be pretty damn good. I can hardly pass up a slice of cake that'll make me forget all other cakes now, can I?"

Maddi grinned, bounding back to the kitchen. She pulled the cake out of the cupboard, holding it up triumphantly. "Ta da!" she sang.

He whistled. "Now, that's a cake."

"I know, right? I'm always telling her she should be making money out of this. It's like, her favourite thing to do." She cut two hefty slices, placed them on plates, and then ran her finger down the side of the knife to scoop off the icing before popping it into her mouth. Realising he was watching, she quickly removed her finger. "What? Don't judge until you've tried it. I bet you'd do the same." She waggled her finger at him.

"I don't know, you've talked it up a lot. I have high expectations now."

"And it will still blow those expectations out of the water. Trust me," she said knowingly. He grabbed his plate, and they sat on the couch.

"Alright, here goes." He took a large bite and as he began to chew, his face said it all. "Oh…My…God…" he mumbled.

"It's good, right?"

"That's the understatement of the year. It's the best cake I've ever eaten." He shovelled another piece into his mouth. "You know you've ruined all other cake for me now."

"I know." She smiled happily. "But it's so worth it." She tucked her legs underneath her as she too bit into the moist cake. They both sat there, nodding and chewing, unable to talk as they devoured the deliciousness.

"I think I just had a foodgasm," Jessie said, leaning back in his seat, rubbing his stomach. Maddi giggled.

"Yeah that happens a lot around here." She smirked. "I'll tell Rory she has a new fan."

"You do that. I'm gonna have to run home to burn this off."

"Like *you* need to worry about that."

"Oh yeah? Been checking me out, have you?" He chuckled.

"No!" Maddi's cheeks burned with embarrassment. "I mean…"

Jessie laughed. "It's okay, Maddi. I was just joking." He stood. "I really should get going though. I promised Dane I'd stop by after class."

"Oh, okay." Maddi stood and walked him to the door. "Well, thanks for the walk home."

"Anytime. Thanks for ruining cake for me."

"Anytime."

Chapter 10

Jessie walked the short distance to Dane and Sacha's, hoping their little encounter would be forgotten. If it had been up to him, he would have avoided going there at all, but Dane had been asking, and he couldn't keep putting it off any longer; not without it seeming suspicious.

Sacha had made it pretty clear that she intended on having him, no matter what the cost. Maybe if he told her he'd been with Maddi this evening, it would put her off, at least for a while. He knew that theirs was just a friendship, but Sacha didn't need to know that.

He let himself in through the back door.

"Hello?" he called out.

"In here!" Dane's voice came from the lounge.

"Hey there, handsome." Sacha sauntered out of the bathroom to his left, wearing only a towel.

Jessie's mouth went dry. "Oh, hey. Sorry, I didn't know you were in there," he said awkwardly, averting his eyes.

Sacha let out a sultry laugh. "You don't need to be embarrassed. You know I did this for you, baby," she purred, brushing herself up against him seductively.

"Come on, Sacha. I told you," he glanced down the hall, "it's not happening." He pushed past her, through to the lounge where Dane was seated.

"Where've you been, mate? I thought you were coming after class?"

"Yeah, sorry 'bout that, I should've text." He looked to see if Sacha was in earshot. "I was with that chick I was telling you about. Maddi."

"Oh yeah? Good for you, man!" He slapped his friend on the shoulder as he joined him on the couch.

"Yeah, I really like her," he said pointedly, watching Sacha as she walked through to the other room, a sour look on her face. "I walked her home and she invited me in for coffee."

"Nice." Dane drew the word out. "You should've brought her here for a dance."

"Yeah, maybe next time. I didn't wanna just invite her to your place unannounced."

"Hey, man, mi casa, su casa, you know that."

Jessie nodded, so far so good. Dane jumped to his feet.

"Right, wanna get started?"

"Sure." Jessie stood, removing his jacket and throwing it on the couch behind him. "What're we doing tonight?"

"Well, I thought seeing as you're taking classes for salsa, we could go over some more bachata. You seem to be getting the hang of it pretty quickly."

"Sounds good."

Dane pushed some buttons on a remote, turning the T.V. off and the stereo on. He had a playlist ready and waiting.

"Let's do a warm-up while Sacha is getting dressed." He began stepping sideways to the beat. "Once you've got that basic beat down, try switching it up a bit. Like this." He changed his footwork, adding a fast two step in place of the hip flick he had shown Jessie the first time.

Jessie watched, counting the beat in his head until he was sure he had it. He closed his eyes, concentrating.

"That's it!" Dane grinned. "You've got it. So you can flick between each of those steps in your basic partner work too. Once you get more comfortable, you can change it up even more."

"Sweet. I think this is enough for now though."

"Yeah, absolutely. Hey, babe. Look, I showed him a bit of flare to add," Dane said proudly as Sacha joined them.

"Yeah, I see that." She smiled, planting a kiss on his cheek. "You ready for me?" She turned to Jessie with a smirk.

"Ah, yeah, sure," he said casually, trying his best to remain calm. She certainly had a way of getting under his skin. The way she held his gaze with a knowing look, or the way she pursed her lips before speaking, the intoxicating smell of her perfume. Everything about her drew him in, no matter how hard he tried to fight it.

She stretched her arms up to wrap around his neck and pulled him in as close as she possibly could. Resting her forehead on his chest, she began to sway to the music, her body rubbing against him sensually.

Jessie swallowed. He had to get a grip. Putting his hands on her hips, he gently eased her body away slightly as he started to move. He was not going to let her make a fool of him in front of Dane.

Attempting to keep his cool, Jessie walked through the basics they had taught him previously, throwing in the new steps he had just learned. Sacha took every chance she could to pull herself back into his embrace, rolling her body in every seductive way imaginable. Flashes of her glistening body covered only in a towel kept popping into his mind. It took every ounce of his concentration to keep it professional.

"Mate, I don't know where your head is at, but keep it there. You're rocking out moves we haven't even shown you yet!" Dane stood watching them in awe. "That's amazing!"

"He sure is a natural," Sacha purred, her eyes locked on Jessie.

"It won't be long before he's teaching us!" Dane joked. "Oh, that reminds me, I was gonna give you a DVD with some moves on it, so you can practise at home."

"Oh, thanks, man, that'd be great."

"I'll just go grab it. I think it's in the bedroom." He jogged down the hall to their room.

Jessie dropped his arms from around Sacha's waist, taking a step back. She quickly followed him, her arms still curled around his neck.

"Where're you going?" She licked her full lips, pushing up against him. "You can't fight it, I know you want me," she whispered.

"Sacha, please," Jessie stammered. It was hard to think straight when she was so close to him. She took advantage of his weakness and, running her hands down his arms, she gripped his wrists, bringing his hands to rest on her behind.

"I'm yours, baby. You just have to say the word," she murmured in his ear, her breathe warm on his neck. "I can do things you've only dreamed of," she whispered before darting her tongue into his ear.

Jessie let out an involuntary moan.

"Found it!" Dane called as he padded back to the lounge. Sacha grinned up at Jessie, holding a finger to her lips.

"Shhhh," she said, winking. Turning her back to him, she met Dane in the doorway. "I was thinking, we should copy some of our music for him too," she said so innocently, as if she hadn't just been all over Jessie.

"Yeah, I was thinking that too. Don't suppose you have a USB stick on ya?" he asked Jessie, who stared blankly back. Dane waved his hand in front of his face. "Earth to Jessie." He grinned. "I think we've overloaded his brain."

"What? Sorry, yeah, I guess it has been a long night. Maybe I should head home for some shut eye."

"No worries, mate. Here, take this with you at least." He handed the DVD to him. "I'll upload some songs for you and give it to you next time."

"Thanks, Dane."

"Hey, what are friends for?"

Jessie managed a smile even though the guilt was eating him up inside.

Chapter 11

Maddi climbed the stairs to the studio bright and early Saturday morning. Her stomach was churning, a mixture of excitement and nervousness. She hoped the other girls liked her. It would be nice to have some friends at the studio.

Standing outside the door, she brushed her hands down her clothes, smoothing out any non-existent wrinkles. Taking a deep breath, she pushed the door open and cautiously stepped through.

Rachel was behind the desk and gave her a warm smile.

"Maddi, you made it." She waved her in, walking out to meet her. "Come, I'll introduce you to everyone."

The girls gathered in a circle, eager to see who the newcomer was.

"Alright, guys, I have a new dancer to join us." She smiled. "She's only been to a few classes, but I can see she has real potential. I'd like you to meet Maddi."

Maddi stepped forward, giving a little wave. Sacha folded her arms across her chest, pushed her hip out and raised her brow in interest. The other girls barely noticed, welcoming her with open arms.

"It's lovely to meet you all," Maddi said, her unease washing away as she peered at the group of smiling faces. "I can't wait to see what you've been working on."

"Pay close attention. We don't have time to break it down for you. We have a performance coming up in a few weeks," Sacha said abruptly. She spun on her heels and stalked across the room.

Maddi was taken aback. How had she gotten off on the wrong foot already? This girl didn't seem very happy to have her on board.

"Ignore her," the girl beside her whispered. She had red hair that floated about her pale face and a dusting of freckles over her nose. "She just gets territorial whenever a new girl comes along. She's kinda the leader of the pack."

"Oh, I thought Rachel was."

"Well, yeah, but she pretty much lets Sacha do whatever she likes." She stopped, lowering her voice even more. "I hope for your sake, you learn fast. Try to get as much as you can, and then after class I can show you some more. If you don't keep up, she'll make your life a living hell." She grinned. "Speaking from experience." She bounded over to the rest of the group, doing some final stretches before they got started.

Could this be the Sacha who is teaching Jessie?

"Let's go!" Sacha called out. The girls scattered into position. Once they were ready, Rachel pressed a button on her remote and the room was filled with music. The girls all spun into various poses before strutting to the front in a V shape. The choreography was tight, and Maddi was impressed.

When they had finished, she clapped eagerly.

"That was amazing!" she gushed. "You guys are great dancers."

"Yeah, we know. That's why we're here," Sacha said dryly. "Are you in or not?"

"Absolutely. Where do you want me?" She walked over to join them. Sacha pointed at a spot to the far right, furthest away from her. Maddi swallowed back the hurt she felt from having this girl she had only just met, treat her so rudely, and walked with her head held high to the spot she had been designated.

Rachel started the music again, and Maddi followed along as best she could, having only seen it once. The start was easy enough but the further they got into the choreography the more lost she became. Some of these moves she had never seen before today. She would have a lot of work to do to get up to scratch, but she was determined to prove her worth to Sacha.

"Not bad, newbie. You got a long way to go, though," Sacha said when the music stopped again.

"Ah, thanks? I'll get it, I just need to see it a few more times I think."

"Well you can sit and watch, or you can join in and just do it. Your choice," she said, turning back to the others. Maddi had the feeling she was being tested. She knew she would learn more by watching it again, but somehow, she didn't think Sacha would approve.

"You ready?" Sacha looked at Maddi. She nodded, taking her place.

They ran through the song another five times before taking a break. Maddi was puffed but exhilarated. She was slowly getting the hang of it.

She jogged to her bag, retrieving her water bottle and taking a long drink. The red head wandered over, taking a seat beside her.

"You're a fast learner. You'll fit in well." She smiled. "Sacha will warm up to you, don't worry. We all had to go through this in the beginning. She thinks she's God's gift," she joked. "She is a bloody good dancer though."

"Yeah, I like her style. She almost glides along the dancefloor. I bet she gets a lot of attention from the boys," Maddi said.

"Mmm, she does, but they all know she's with Dane. They're like the power couple of the dancing circle here."

"Oh yeah? I don't think I've met him yet."

"Stick around long enough and you will. They're everywhere." She took a swig of her own bottle. "How 'bout you? Any fella out there you can dance with?"

"No, not really. I mean, there's this one guy, Jessie. We've had a few good dances together, and I think maybe he likes me."

"Oooh hold onto him then. The good male dancers get snatched up pretty quick." She snapped her fingers.

"Good to know." Maddi smiled. It was nice to have a friendly face to talk to. "Have you got a dance partner?"

"Me? Nah, I just dance with anyone and everyone," she joked. "Bit of a social butterfly." She winked, nudging her with her elbow.

"Alright, enough chit chat, let's get back to work!" Sacha called, clapping her hands together. "We've only got two more practises before our show at Feeney's. We need to be flawless." She looked Maddi up and down. "Think you can master it by then, newbie?" She almost spat the last word, as if it left a horrible taste in her mouth.

"Yeah, I think I can have it down in time," Maddi answered, her chin raised in defiance. She walked over to her starting position. Rachel gave her a little nod of encouragement.

"From the top!" she said, pushing play.

The girls rehearsed for another hour straight, going over every little move with a fine-tooth comb. Maddi had to admit, Sacha had a good eye. She picked up on all the minor details that they were missing. No wonder she had the ego she did, she was a force to be reckoned with.

When they decided to call it quits, Maddi grabbed a quick drink before running over a few of the moves in the mirror. Rachel gave her a few pointers, but most of the moves she had down, it was just a matter of perfecting them.

The others had all taken off straight after class, leaving only Maddi and Sacha. She stood by with a critical eye, calling out commands.

"Raise your arms higher in the spin. Sharpen up your hand movements. Smaller steps. Were you paying attention at all?"

Maddi had had about all she could take for one day. She spun around to address her.

"What is your problem? You've done nothing but criticise me since I walked in." She stood, hands on hips, waiting for a response.

"*You're* my problem, newbie."

"What did I do to piss you off? I've done everything you've asked me to do!" She slapped her arms down to her sides, frustrated. "I don't know what you want from me," she said more quietly. Her burst of courage was starting to fade, and unease was settling in the pit of her stomach. "I'll just go." She walked to where she had left her bag. Sacha stuck her foot out as she was walking past. Maddi stumbled but regained her balance.

"Oops," Sacha said sarcastically.

"You did that on purpose."

"What you gonna do about it? Go crying to Jessie?"

"Jessie? That's what this is about?" Maddi asked, stunned. Of all the reasons for her attitude, this was far from what she had suspected.

"Yeah, that's what this is about."

"But, aren't you with Dane?" she asked.

"So what if I am? Jessie is mine, and you need to stay away," Sacha said, her voice full of menace.

"You're laying claim on both of them?" Maddi asked. She couldn't believe what she was hearing.

"You can have Dane for all I care, but Jessie is off limits. Got it?"

Even though they had only met that day, Maddi could tell Sacha was not to be messed with. There was something about her that told her she always got what she wanted. Maddi was not about to get stuck in the middle of a love triangle.

"Sure. No problem. He's all yours," she said, grabbing her gear. "You might wanna tell him that though."

Chapter 12

"So, I just had the weirdest conversation," Maddi announced as she walked through the door, dumping her bag in her room on her way past.

"Ooh do tell," Rory said, flicking the jug on in preparation for a chat.

"There was this girl at training, Sacha, she's kinda the big star of the group."

"Mmm."

"Straight away I could tell she had it in for me. She was real snarky and rude to me. I've never met anyone like her."

"Sounds like a bitch." Rory screwed her face up in disgust. "You want me to sort her out for you?"

Maddi laughed. "No, no, it's alright. I think I can handle her." She walked into the kitchen to start on the coffee. "I haven't even told you the weird part yet."

"Sorry, carry on."

"So, at the end of practise, I was going over some of the moves in the mirror and she just stood there, yelling at me. I called her on it and, get this… she told me to stay away from Jessie." She raised her brow and pursed her lips.

"What's up with that? I thought he was single?"

"That's the thing. I'm pretty sure he is. She's with this other guy, Dane. She was all 'back off, he's mine,'" she mimicked, snapping her fingers in front of her face.

"Seriously? What's her deal? Stringing her man along until a better one comes along? What a cow!" Rory said angrily. How dare she threaten her friend. "You sure you don't want me to sort her out? It would be my pleasure." She punched her fist into her hand.

"Believe me, it's tempting. But I'd rather leave them to it. Jessie and I are just friends, it's not like anything has happened," Maddi said, handing Rory a steaming cup of coffee.

"Still. It's not right. Surely Jessie can't be interested in someone like that."

"We don't really know him that well. And you haven't seen her. She's gorgeous. Petite with dark hair and pale skin. She's got this exotic beauty. And you should see her dance. She's amazing."

"Ah, have you looked in a mirror lately? Girl, you're hot as hell." Rory licked the tip of her finger and held it to her skin making a hissing sound. "Anyways, beauty means nothing when you have the personality of a wet rag."

Maddi just shrugged. She secretly hoped that Jessie would turn her down, but knew it was unlikely. Girls like Sacha don't get turned down.

Jessie and Dane were busy going over some men's footwork when Sacha came marching in from practise.

She dropped her keys on the bench and threw herself on the couch, stretching her legs out.

"What are you two up to?" she asked.

"Thought I'd show him some shine steps, spice up his solo stuff," Dane said, leaning down to kiss her. "How was training?"

"Not bad. I met your *friend*, Maddi," she said, screwing her face up in disgust.

"Oh yeah?" Jessie had been so happy for Maddi when she was asked to join the group, it had never crossed his mind that Sacha would be there too. He hadn't wanted them to meet like that, not without him warning Maddi about her first.

"Yeah. She seems… nice enough, I guess. Not exactly who I would have picked for you."

"What is that supposed to mean?" he asked.

"She just seems so… plain." She tucked a stray hair behind her ear, looking up at him through her dark lashes.

"They can't all be stunners like you, babe," Dane said, winking. He made his way into the kitchen to pour himself a glass of water. "Want one?" he asked Jessie, holding the glass up.

"Nah, I'm good. Thanks though." He turned his back on Sacha and went over the moves Dane had shown him.

"Do we have anything to eat?" Sacha asked over her shoulder. "I'm starving."

"I'll have a look." Dane went to the fridge. After staring into its depths for several minutes he declared it to be bare. "I can run down to the shops and grab some ham and salad for sandwiches if you like, babe."

"Would you? That would be great. Maybe some eggs too."

"Of course, my love. You guys can carry on without me." He grabbed his wallet and walked to the door. "Back soon!"

Sacha turned her attention to Jessie. She watched the muscles moving under his shirt as he practised. Her eyes wandered appreciatively up and down the rest of his body.

"Looking good, baby," she purred.

"Don't," Jessie snapped.

"Don't what?" she said innocently.

"You know what."

Sacha stood up, moving closer. "I'm not sure what you mean. Don't do this?" She ran her hand down his back, pressing her body against him. "Or this?" She snaked her other hand around his middle, finding her way under the waistband of his jeans. Jessie grabbed her hand, pulling it away.

"I said don't," he stated, less convincingly. She pouted.

"I know you don't mean that." She walked around to face him, trailing her hand around his shoulders and up his neck to rest at the nape. "I know you want me too," she whispered, standing on her toes to kiss his neck. She could feel his body responding which made her want him even more. She began to kiss and lick her way up his neck, gently pulling his face down to meet hers.

Jessie hated that his body was reacting to her touch, but he couldn't fight it anymore. She was so damn sensual. "Sacha," he said, his voice hoarse.

"Jessie," she breathed. She nibbled his lip, wanting to draw it out. Looking at him with hooded eyes, she pressed her lips to his.

With a growl, Jessie gave in, wrapping his arms around her waist and lifting her into his arms. She swung her legs around his middle, pulling them in tight. She needed to be as close to him as possible. She had thought of nothing more than this moment since that first night at Feeney's. It was better than she had imagined.

Jessie collapsed on the couch, taking her with him. She pulled her top over her head, grinning at him.

"I knew you wanted me too." She crushed her lips to his once more, rocking slowly in his lap, tormenting him. Her hands found the buttons on his shirt and started ripping at them, desperate to touch him. She arched her back as he began to kiss down her neck, tasting her. She sighed.

His hands gripped her behind, pulling her flush with his body. She ran her hands up his neck and cupped his jaw, bringing his mouth back to hers.

"What the fuck?" Dane dropped the bags of food he had been carrying. His hands balled into fists.

"Jesus, Dane!" Jessie sat forward, lifting Sacha from his lap. He stood, raking his hand through his hair. "It's not what it… Shit. I'm so sorry. I don't know what came over me."

"Sit. Down," Dane demanded. "I go out for five minutes, and I come home to find you fucking my missus? What kind of a friend does that?"

"We weren't fucking," Sacha said, holding her hands up and inspecting her nails as if it was an ordinary day.

"Close enough," he spat, turning his attention back to Jessie. "Do your damn shirt up!"

Jessie looked down, fumbling with his buttons.

Dane began pacing. "How long?" he demanded, waving a finger between the two of them. "How long has this been going on?"

"This is the first time, I swear," Jessie said, holding his hands up, palms out. "Jesus, I'm so sorry, Dane."

"Save it." He continued pacing. "After everything I've done for you. This is how you repay me?"

"I never meant for this to happen."

"Oh no, of course not. She just slipped and fell into your lap without any goddamn clothes on!"

"Dane…" Sacha started.

"Don't. I thought you loved me." He looked at Sacha, angry tears in his eyes.

She had the decency to look ashamed. "I know. I'm sorry."

It wasn't the response he had expected. "You're sorry I thought that, or you're sorry you got caught out?"

"Both, I guess," she said, holding his stare defiantly. "We were never going to be a forever thing."

Dane couldn't believe what he was hearing. Had she been toying with him this whole time? Was it all just a game to her?

"Well, I guess we both had different views of what *this* was," he said, before walking out the door, slamming it behind him.

Chapter 13

"Shit!" Jessie stood up, pacing. "Shit!"

"Calm down. He's a big boy, he'll get over it," Sacha said, stretching her arms above her head.

"Are you serious?" he asked incredulously. "Don't you feel any remorse? You just broke his heart!"

"I think you had a hand in that too, don't you?" Sacha smirked.

"Yeah. I know. I'm an arsehole." He rubbed his hand across his face. "Goddamn it! I'm such a shitty friend." He pounded the counter with his fist. Sacha sighed.

"Don't be so dramatic. He *will* get over it. I promise." She joined him at the bench, running her hand down his back soothingly.

"Please don't," he murmured.

"I'm not coming on to you. I was *trying* to console you." She touched his face, turning him to look at her. "I *am* sorry you got stuck in the middle of this." She peered up at him. "I know you probably think I did it on purpose, but I didn't mean for him to find out this way. I would've ended it with him eventually." She took a breath. "Can you forgive me?"

Jessie let out a long breath. "Of course I can. It wasn't exactly one-sided. I just…" He shrugged. "Dane was my friend. I should never have let it get that far. I should've had more self-control."

"But you do like me, don't you?"

"You know I do." He cupped her face in his hands. "More than I'd like to admit."

Sacha smiled at that. For a second there, she thought she may have lost him.

"We should probably get out of here before he gets back. I doubt he's going to want to see us anytime soon."

"About that." Sacha wrung her hands together, hoping he would agree to what she was about to propose. "I couldn't stay with you, could I?" She peered up at him through her lashes. "Just for a little while. I don't really have anywhere else to go."

"I don't know. Is that really a good idea, considering?" He waved his hand around the room. "It's not going to look good, us shacking up straight after. He'll think we planned this whole thing."

She nodded, lowering her eyes. "I know. I wouldn't ask, I just don't have anyone else I can turn to." She bit her lip, tears welling in her eyes. "In case you hadn't noticed, I don't really get along with many people. They were all Dane's friends at Feeney's. One guess as to whose side they will be on."

Jessie searched her face, knowing he couldn't say no to her, not when she was so vulnerable. He had never seen this side of her before. She'd always seemed so confident, so aloof. Turning her down would only make them both feel worse.

He brushed a finger under her eye, catching the tears before they fell.

"You can stay. I can't have you being homeless now, can I?" He smiled. "Go and grab your things. Just don't take too long. I don't want to upset Dane any more than we have already."

"Thanks, babe. It'll just be a few days, I promise." She stood on tippy toes to plant a soft kiss on his lips before jogging to the bedroom to pack her few belongings.

Jessie went to the window, watching for any signs of Dane's return. The last thing he would want to see when he came back home, was Jessie escorting his ex-girlfriend to his place. He knew it was a big mistake to let her stay, but what else could he do? When Sacha had said she didn't have anyone to turn to, there had been so much pain in her eyes. She may act like a tough, sassy woman, but deep down, he could see she was really just a scared girl who was desperate for acceptance. Somehow, that made her more alluring. He felt the undeniable need to protect her, and he would.

Now, if only he could keep his friendship with Dane intact too. That would be the real challenge.

Chapter 14

Maddi had been working for Rachel for a week when she asked her to go out for coffee. Recently single herself, Rachel had noticed that Maddi seemed a little distracted.

"Is everything okay, hon?" Rachel asked as they walked to their table.

"Yeah, everything's fine." Maddi smiled, pulling her seat out.

"Are you sure? You seem preoccupied."

"Oh sorry." She sighed. "I've just been thinking a lot. I'm a bit confused."

"About what?"

"Well, there's this guy."

"Of course there is. It's always a guy." Rachel smiled.

"Yeah," Maddi agreed. "He just seems to have disappeared off the face of the earth."

"What do you mean?"

Maddi stirred the foam around her cup before answering. "One minute we were having a good time, dancing and hanging out, the next minute, he vanishes. I haven't seen or heard from him."

"That's odd. Who's the guy?"

"Jessie. We were in beginners' together. I thought we had a connection."

Rachel pursed her lips.

"You know something, don't you?" Maddi leaned forward.

"I do." She nodded, frowning.

The penny dropped. "Oh… It's Sacha, isn't it?"

"I'm afraid so. I didn't realise you and Jessie were…"

"Oh no! We weren't. But I thought maybe we might. He seemed pretty keen. At least, I thought he was. I obviously read that one wrong." Maddi shrugged. "Well, at least now I know. I just wish he could've told me. Why would he just avoid me?"

"Your guess is as good as mine." Rachel took a sip from her coffee. "You know what? I have something that'll make you feel better."

"What's that?"

"A party! One of the guys is throwing one tonight. You wanna go?"

"I don't know."

"Come on, it'll be fun! We can let our hair down and forget about boys. What do you say?"

Maddi couldn't help but grin back at her new friend. A party did sound like fun.

"Sure. Why not?"

"Great! I'll let them know we're coming."

Dane had spent the days after walking in on Sacha and Jessie in a daze. He had never thought either one was capable of hurting him so much. How wrong he had been.

To make matters worse, he was pretty sure they were actually living together. Sacha had never really had any girlfriends to call on, and when he saw all her things were gone, he just knew that's where she'd be.

After a week of seeking solace in the bottom of a bottle, Dane had decided he needed to do something with friends to get out of his funk. A problem shared is a problem halved, or so they say. He had sent a bulk text out to all his dancer friends, inviting them to his place for a party.

He was several drinks in when he noticed a familiar face walking through the door. She was tall and slender, with bouncing golden curls. He couldn't quite put his finger on where he knew her from, but he knew he had definitely seen her before. You don't forget a face like that.

He watched as she quietly followed Rachel around the room being introduced to the others. She looked out of her depth, and he couldn't really blame her. It would be more than a little intimidating, walking into a room filled with half-drunk people that you had never met before.

Deciding to take matters into his own hands, he approached her.

"What are ya drinking?" he asked, plastering a grin across his face.

"Oh, ah, I brought a bottle of wine. I just need a glass if you have one, please," Maddi said, holding up her drink.

"One glass, coming up!" he said, pulling open a cupboard. "I'm Dane, by the way. I'm not sure if we've met before. You seem familiar, but that could be the booze talking." He chuckled.

"Oh, *you're* Dane," she exclaimed nervously. She hadn't expected to meet him here. "Um, it's nice to meet you. I'm Maddison." She held her hand out to shake, but Dane just grinned.

"You're with dancers—we're huggers here," he said, pulling her in for a big bear hug.

"Oh!" she said again, letting herself be pulled into his embrace.

"You'll have to get used to that, we all do it." He smiled, waving his arms to include the entire room. "Let me help you with that." He took the bottle from her hands and expertly removed the cork. "You've got some catching up to do. I've been mixing up cocktails for everyone all night. You have to try one. It's kinda compulsory." He winked.

"Sure." Maddi smiled, sipping her wine, already feeling more at ease.

"I see you've met Dane," Rachel said as she joined them. "This girl is one of our up-and-coming dancers. Definitely one to watch." She beamed, throwing an arm around Maddi's shoulders. "She's even joined the ladies troupe."

"That so?" Dane asked, his interest piqued. "As it happens, I'm in the running for a new dance partner. I'll have to give you a spin later."

"I'm just a beginner. I bet there's other girls who would love to partner you."

"Did I just get shut down? I'm crushed." Dane pretended to stab a stake through his heart.

"I didn't mean it that way!" Maddi laughed. "I just… I've heard how good you are. I'm not really up to your standard."

"I'll be the judge of that." He smiled, holding his hand out to her. "Come on, let's see what you can do."

Maddi looked at Rachel, who just smiled and pushed her forward. She took his hand and followed him to a clear spot on the lounge floor. He grabbed the iPod and flicked to one of his favourite salsa tracks.

"This is a good one," he said, tapping his feet. He tugged on her arm until she stepped forward enough for him to slide his other arm around to her back. Smiling down at her, he began to move his feet in the basic step. "I have had a few, so excuse my lead."

"I think I can forgive you." Maddi grinned, happy to be dancing. She was most at ease when moving her body to music.

Dane led her through several basic combos before throwing a few together at once. To his pleasure, Maddi followed perfectly.

"You know, I think Rachel might be right. You *are* good."

"Thanks, but forgive me if I don't believe you until you've danced with me sober," she joked. "You may find you have a completely different opinion then."

"I doubt that. I know a good dancer when I see one."

Maddi looked at her feet as she felt her face redden.

"Not good at taking compliments, huh?" Dane chuckled. "That's something else you'd better get used to. You're one of us now." He spun her across the floor, into the arms of one of the other men.

"Oh!" She giggled as he continued the dance before spinning her back to Dane. "That was fun!"

"It's a little trick we like to call 'hi-jacking'." He lowered her into a dip to finish the song. "I think it's time for another drink, don't you?"

"Sure," Maddi said breathlessly. She skipped back to the kitchen to retrieve her wine. Dane busied himself with cocktail mixing.

"You look like you're having a good time," Rachel said, a glint in her eye.

"Yeah, I am. Thanks for bringing me. It's just what I needed.

"What do you think of Dane?"

"He's great fun to dance with." She beamed.

"Well, yeah of course. But I mean, what do you *think* of him?"

"What?" Maddi frowned before her eyes lit up and she covered her mouth with her hand. "Oh! No, he's not really my type. He seems really nice though."

"Oh, that's a shame." Rachel pouted.

"Get these into ya, ladies." Dane appeared with two tall glasses filled with an amber liquid. "It's got vanilla Galliano, vodka, peach schnapps and orange juice in it."

"Mmm, that's delicious!" Rachel said.

Maddi nodded in agreeance. "Yeah, it really is. Are you a bartender?"

Dane laughed. "I wish. Nah, I just like to experiment." He raised his glass to the two of them. "To new friends." They each clinked their glasses together.

"To new friends!" they chimed back, laughing.

Chapter 15

Several drinks and dances later, Dane finally remembered where he had seen Maddi before.

"Snickers!" he bellowed with a grin.

"Excuse me?" Maddi asked, nearly choking on her drink.

"That's where I know you from! You were the girl who couldn't decide which chocolate bar to buy." He chuckled. "I knew I'd remember eventually."

"That was you? That's a little embarrassing."

"Why? Because you thought I was a stalker?" he joked. Maddi couldn't help but giggle.

"All I could hear were these heavy footsteps getting closer and a man yelling out to me. Can you blame me?" She laughed.

"Heavy footsteps? What am I? An elephant?" Dane put on an unconvincing hurt expression.

"You know what I mean!" She giggled again.

"I might have to teach you a lesson for that." He leaped up and scooped her into his arms, making her squeal.

"Put me down!"

"I can't hear you!" He swung her up and into the air, passing her onto one of the other guys there.

She shrieked as she was thrown from guy-to-guy around the room. This was the most fun she had had in a long time.

Once she was back in Dane's arms, he placed her gently down on the ground with a huge grin on his face. She playfully swatted his arm.

"I can't believe you just did that!" she said, pretending to be cross.

"Didn't you enjoy being thrown around like a rag doll?" he asked, smirking.

She thought about continuing the charade of being upset, but the smile spreading across her face betrayed her. "Actually, it was pretty fun," she admitted. "I can honestly say I've never been thrown around a room before."

"Glad to entertain you." He bowed down before her.

"That looked interesting." Rachel joined them.

"Yeah, you could say that." Maddi chuckled. "Quite exhilarating actually."

"You're very trusting to let a group of drunks throw you about." She laughed. "I would've been afraid they'd drop me."

Maddi's jaw dropped. "I didn't even think about that!" She swatted Dane again.

"Hey! We would never have dropped you!"

"Hmmm." Maddi pursed her lips. "I'll let it slide… this time." She pointed a finger at him. "But only because I'm having so much fun."

"Good to hear it. Must be time for another dance then." He grabbed her hand before she could turn him down, pulling her out to the centre of the room. He leaned in to whisper in her ear. "You know what?" he asked.

"What?"

"I think we make a great team."

"Oh really? What are you basing this on?"

"Well, I helped you with your chocolate buying, we dance well together—even under the influence, *and* I can throw you around without dropping you." He winked. Maddi laughed.

"That makes us a good team?"

"Yep. Think about it. If we can dance this fantastically while drinking, we will be even more amazing when we're sober," he said matter-of-factly.

"I have to admit, that's a pretty good argument. I see a flaw though."

"What's that?"

She leaned in. "Maybe we just *think* we're dancing fantastically, when in actual fact… we suck." She tilted her head, brows raised, waiting for his response.

"I cannot believe you just said I suck at dancing," Dane said in mock outrage.

"Wait, that's not what I said. I said *we* suck." She pointed her finger between the two of them. "Us together. Under the influence. Not you by yourself. You're great!" She rushed the words, trying not to offend him.

"So, you admit it then?"

"Admit what?"

"That I'm great." He smirked.

"You, are just twisting my words!" She laughed. As much as he wasn't her type, she was having a great time hanging out. He had a magnetic quality to him.

If she was completely honest with herself, she agreed—she did think they made a good team. She just hoped that he would still feel the same once he had sobered up. Having Dane as a dance partner would be a lot of fun. Having someone to practise with regularly would be good for her dancing too. Not to mention the added bonus of getting back at Sacha for the way she had spoken to her, and maybe for taking Jessie from her. Not that he was 'hers' to be taken in the first place. But she did feel as though she had lost a friend.

"What's going through your mind right now?" Dane asked, poking her nose. "You look all serious all of a sudden."

"Nothing important." She smiled. "Must be time for a top-up." She wiggled her glass in the air.

"Your wish is my command." He took her glass back to the kitchen to mix up yet another cocktail.

Maddi pushed thoughts of Sacha and Jessie to the back of her mind. Tonight was about feeling good and forgetting the bad. She stood on legs that were more jelly than she had anticipated and wobbled her way into the kitchen.

"How strong are you pouring these?" she asked, leaning against the bench for stability. "If I didn't know better, I'd think you were trying to get me drunk." She grinned.

"Ah curses! She's onto me!" He winked, handing her another drink.

"Wait, I can't tell if you're serious or not," she said, confused.

"Relax, Maddi. I'm not gonna jump you. I prefer my women to be of sound mind." He grinned.

"I don't know if I should be offended by that or not!" She laughed. "But I'm going to choose to believe you mean you wouldn't take advantage of a drunk." She swirled her straw around her glass before taking a sip. "Ooh that's good! This is definitely my favourite," she said.

"I bet you say that to all the boys."

Chapter 16

Maddi stumbled back home in the early hours of the morning. She tried hard to conceal her giggles as she knocked the coat rack—and by some miracle—managed to catch it before it crashed to the floor. She did, however, smack it into the wall and drop half the coats. Shushing herself, she stooped down to pick them back up, bracing herself against the door frame.

"Having fun?" Rory asked, tying her robe as she padded out of her room.

"Oh-my-gosh! Sssorry! I dint meanto wake you," Maddi slurred, a drunken grin plastered across her face. "I might've hadda bit-too muchta drink." She giggled, collapsing in a heap on the coats.

"Come here, you big dork. Let me help you up." Rory smiled, happy to see her friend had had a good night.

"Bending is hard." Maddi frowned before erupting into yet another fit of laughter. Rory grabbed her hands and pulled. Maddi folded in half, which made her laugh even more.

"You have to help too! Plant your feet!" Rory laughed.

"Okay, sssorry. I'mma try this time." Maddi put on a serious face, pulling her knees in. She managed to get to her feet this time, and with the help of Rory, she made it to her room. She plonked down on the edge of her bed, flopping backwards. "Bed is good."

"Yes, it is. Are you going to be alright? You need a bucket?"

"Huh?" Maddi said, her eyes already beginning to close.

Rory pulled her shoes off and rolled her under the covers as best she could. She went to the kitchen and poured her a glass of water to leave on her nightstand. Smiling, she switched the light off before heading back to her own room.

The next morning, Rory was busy in the kitchen when a squinty-eyed Maddi made her way out to join her.

"What time is it?" she croaked.

"Eleven."

"You should've woken me!"

"Why? You got big plans today? You got in pretty late last night, I figured you could do with the sleep." Rory grinned.

"Oh God, did I wake you?"

"Well, you were dancing with the coat rack outside my bedroom door, so it was a little hard to ignore," she teased. Maddi held her head in her hands. "Bit of a headache?"

"Mmm. Just a bit. Do we have any juice?"

"As a matter of fact, we do." She poured a large glass and handed it to her. Maddi gulped it back. "Woah, tiger Not too fast. I am *not* cleaning up spew. That's where I draw the line."

"Sorry, I'm just so thirsty."

"Yeah, that'll happen when you've been up all night, drinking." She helped herself to a glass of juice too. "Now, I know you're a lightweight, but one bottle of wine is not enough to get you off your face like that. So, who was supplying you with all the booze? A guy, perhaps?" She raised her brows with a knowing grin.

"Yeah, actually. You won't believe who it was," Maddi said, remembering the many cocktails she had consumed last night as her stomach began to gurgle. "Oh, that's not good." She held her hand to her middle, as if trying to keep the contents of her stomach from escaping.

"Don't you dare!" Rory pointed a finger. Maddi swallowed a few times, taking deep breaths.

"I think I'm okay," she said quietly.

"You sure?"

"Yip." Maddi nodded. "I might go have a shower."

"Good idea, I didn't wanna say anything before…" Rory joked, poking her tongue out at her friend.

"If I could, I'd throw something at you right now. You're lucky I'm hungover." She attempted to scowl, but her mouth betrayed her, lifting at the corners.

She dragged herself to the bathroom. The lights were too bright for her eyes, so she turned them off and left the door ajar, letting the glow of the hall light streak through. She turned the shower on and peeled her clothes off, leaving them in a heap on the floor. She stepped under the hot water, letting it cascade down her back, washing away the night before.

When she got out, she wrapped herself in a big fluffy towel and felt almost human again. She saw that Rory had left some clothes for her on the floor by the door. Her big comfy trackies, a singlet, and her favourite hoody. Definitely hangover clothes if ever there was.

A coffee and slice of cake were waiting for her when she finally emerged from the bathroom.

"You look better," Rory said, leaning on the counter, sipping from her own cup.

"Thanks, I feel it." Maddi smiled, grabbing her goodies and folding herself up on the couch.

"So, before you cleaned yourself up, you were about to tell me about the guy you were with last night." Rory followed her to the couch. "Spill." She sat facing Maddi in eager anticipation.

"Don't go getting all excited, it's nothing like that!" Maddi laughed. "We just hung out."

"Oh, that's no fun." She pouted. "You made it sound all exciting. Are you sure you didn't just misread the signs?"

"Okay, I don't know about him, but *I'm* not interested in him like that."

"What would you know? You were drunk!" Rory tried again. "The state you were in last night, I'm surprised you could even remember your own name."

"I wasn't that bad. Was I?"

"I've seen worse. But if this guy was pouring drinks down your throat, he's either keen or a creep."

"I don't think he's a creep. I didn't get that vibe off him." She scrunched her nose. "I haven't even told you who it was yet. You'll never believe it."

"Well?"

"You remember super-bitch, Sacha?"

"Yeah, of course. She wasn't there, was she? Ooh! Did you knock her out?!"

"Yeah, totally. That's what I did." Maddi snorted. "Of course I didn't! And no, she wasn't there. But Dane was."

"No way! You hooked up with her boyfriend? Gold!" Rory hooted, practically dancing in her seat.

"Firstly, he's not her boyfriend anymore, and secondly, I didn't hook up with him. But he *was* the one pouring the drinks. We hung out all night. He said we make a good team." She smiled. "If he remembers, I think he may ask me to be his dance partner."

"Not quite as good as hooking up with him, but it's a start. But rewind a bit there. They're not together anymore?" she asked.

"Nope. Turns out, she *is* Jessie's type."

"You're kidding?!" Rory gaped. "I did *not* see that coming."

"It explains why we haven't seen him lately."

"I guess. Pretty rude though, if you ask me."

"You don't know the half of it. Rachel told me Dane walked in on them… ya know… gettin' busy."

"Eww gross!" Rory stuck her tongue out, making retching sounds.

"I know. Poor Dane though. That's pretty rough."

"I reckon. More reason for you two to work together then. Show them up on the dancefloor. I bet Sacha couldn't stand to have someone else in the limelight."

"You could be onto something there. It would be nice to take her down a peg or two," Maddi agreed. "I'm gonna have to start practising if I'm going to show her up though."

Chapter 17

"So, I was thinking…" Sacha drawled as she lay across Jessie's stomach.

"Mmm?" he said, stroking her hair.

"How would you feel about entering the salsa comps with me?" She looked up, her eyes full of hope.

"You're joking, right?"

"Nope. I'm one hundred percent serious."

"I've only just started dancing. I'm not ready to compete!"

Sacha sat up, folding her legs beneath her. "Sure you are. You're picking it up really fast, and the comps are still a few months away; we've got plenty of time to whip you into shape." She grinned.

"I dunno…"

"Please?" she begged, holding her hands as if in prayer. "Pretty please. I really wanna enter with you." Pausing for effect, she added, "I'll do anything you want me to," in a sing-song voice.

Jessie laughed. "Okay, okay. If that's what you really want, I'll do it."

"Yay! Thank you, thank you, thank you!" she squealed, leaning over to kiss him. "We are gonna kick arse!" She clapped her hands together excitedly. "I've already got a heap of ideas."

"How about we get me confident with the basics first, and then we can start planning for the comps." Jessie smiled.

"Oh, alright then, spoil sport." Sacha pouted. Jessie ran a finger around her lips.

"I believe there was a promise to do anything I wanted." He waggled his brows suggestively.

"Promise? I don't recall making any such promises," Sacha said, full of innocence. Jessie lunged, pulling her down on top of him once more. She giggled in delight. "Okay! What do you want?" she asked.

"I'm sure we can come up with some sort of arrangement," he said, running his hand through her hair and kissing her.

"I like your way of thinking," Sacha said breathlessly. Jessie rolled so that Sacha was pinned beneath him. She wrapped her legs around his waist, pulling him closer to her. He held her hands and drew them up behind her head. Holding them in one hand, he used his other to trace down her arm, making her squirm. He continued down her side, until his hand was cupping her behind. Lowering his head, he kissed from her shoulder, up her neck and back to her lips.

Sacha wiggled her hips against him as she hungrily kissed him back. She wanted to touch him, but he had her hands firmly in his grasp.

"Let me touch you," she breathed. Jessie grinned against her lips.

"Oh, but this is much too fun."

"Tease," she said hoarsely.

"Oh, you think so, do you?" He kissed a trail down her neck, lifting her top to expose her creamy skin. He flicked his tongue across her stomach, slowly making his way to the waistband of her jeans. Sacha watched him with eager eyes. She lifted her hips as he skilfully removed her pants with one hand.

He ran his hand up her leg as he lightly kissed his way up her inner thigh. Sacha moaned, arching her back and drawing her knees up. Jessie paused with a wicked grin on his face.

"*Now*, you can call me a tease," he said, getting up off the bed. Sacha stared at him, mouth gaping open.

"You did *not* just do that!" she said, throwing a cushion at him. Jessie laughed.

"Hey, you called it."

"Well, now I'm un-calling it. Get over here and finish what you started!" she demanded, kneeling on the bed. She slowly peeled her top over her head as he watched.

"Seeing as you asked so nicely…" he murmured, unable to tear his eyes away as she ran her hands over her body enticingly. With one step he was tangled in her arms once more.

"That was amazing," Jessie stated, running a finger up and down Sacha's arm as she cuddled into his side.

"I know." She grinned, kissing his chest.

"Still so modest." Jessie chuckled.

"Hey, you don't get to be this fantastic without blowing your own trumpet. No-one else is gonna do it for you," she said matter-of-factly.

"That's a bit of a morbid way of looking at things, don't ya think?"

"Just saying it how it is."

Jessie pulled her in tightly, kissing the top of her head. Sacha certainly was a different breed of woman. He had never met someone so brutally honest before. There was more to her than met the eye.

"Come on, if we're gonna "kick arse" at these comps, we'd better get practising. I've got a long way to go," Jessie said, throwing the crumpled sheets off and swinging his legs over the edge of the bed. Sacha snaked her arm around his waist.

"That's why we're so good together. We're both driven." She kissed his back. "Now go get cleaned up!" She swatted his behind teasingly. "We've got a lot of work to do."

"Yes, drill sergeant!" He saluted her before marching to the shower.

Sacha stretched out on the bed, pleased with herself. She had chosen well this time. Not only was he amazing in bed, he was also ambitious and competitive—qualities she held in high regard.

His desire to be nice to everyone was his one flaw, though she had every intention of using it to her advantage. There was no way she was going to look for another place to stay, and she knew Jessie would never kick her out. She had him right where she wanted him.

Now, to keep him from learning her secret plan for the comps. What she had up her sleeve was sure to win them first place. She just had to keep him away from Dane.

Chapter 18

"Are you sure this isn't a date?" Rory asked sceptically.

"Positive. Now get ready!" Maddi replied, shoving her towards the door. "He'll be here soon."

"I don't wanna be the third wheel," she whined.

"You won't be. Go!" Maddi pointed across the hall. Rory padded back to her room to change.

Much to Maddi's delight, Dane had invited them to go to Feeney's with him this week. She hadn't seen him since the party and was looking forward to dancing with him again. Dancing with the beginners in class just didn't cut it after being flung around the room by a pro.

Stepping back and inspecting herself in the mirror, Maddi was satisfied. She brushed on a little lip gloss before sauntering into Rory's room to see if she was ready.

"How do I look?" Rory twirled, fishnet-gloved hands on hips. "Do I pass?"

"Sure do. You look great!" Maddi clapped her hands. It never ceased to amaze her how quickly her friend could get ready to go out. She was dressed in an off-the-shoulder crop-top with cut-off denim shorts. Her short blonde hair was spiked up in all directions and she had attached a thin headband over top. High-top sneakers with a built-in heel finished off her look. She could be quite the fashionista when she wanted to be.

Maddi, on the other hand, went for a sleeker look. Black leggings with diamantes down the sides, coupled with a deep purple singlet and matching heels. She wore a silver tasselled scarf around her hips. Her hair was half tied up, the rest curling around her face and down her back.

"You look pretty good yourself." Rory grinned, giving her the once over.

There was a knock at the door. Maddi and Rory quickly grabbed their bags and both went to answer it.

"Hey." Dane waved. "You two look stunning."

"Thanks." Maddi smiled warmly before gesturing to her friend. "This is my flatmate, Rory."

"Nice to meet you, Rory." Dane offered his hand.

"Likewise," she said, shaking his hand firmly. "I hear you're quite the dancer."

"That so?" Dane raised his brow at Maddi with a sly grin. "What else has she been saying about me?"

"Only that you plastered her with alcohol at the party the other night." Rory held her hand up for a high five. "Well done you."

Dane chuckled and slapped his hand against hers.

"Shall we get our dance on then?" she asked.

"Absolutely. Do you dance salsa too?"

"Me? Not really. I've been to a few classes, but that's about it."

"We'll have to change that then." He winked, ushering them out the door.

They kept up a steady banter on their way into town. Dane was a pretty smooth talker; it was clear to see why he was so popular.

"Have you guys been to Feeney's before?" he asked.

"Actually, my dance troupe performed here last week. It was pretty fun," Maddi said.

"Oh, that's right." A flicker of something crossed his face before he schooled his expression. "I'm sorry I missed it." He smiled, changing the subject. "They play the best music here, don't they?"

"Yeah. It's nice to hear new songs. I didn't realise there were so many different styles." Maddi smiled at the memory.

"Stick with me, kid, I'll show you them all! And I promise, you won't get thrown around this time." He grinned mischievously.

Maddi giggled. "I should hope not! That was a one-time-only thing."

"Okay, I'm confused. Is this some dance lingo I don't understand?" Rory frowned.

"Didn't I tell you about that?" Maddi laughed.

"Clearly not." She rolled her eyes.

"I may have picked Maddi up and thrown her around the room last weekend. Kinda like pass-the-parcel," Dane explained, "only it was pass-Maddi."

"Wait, you *literally* threw her around the room? That's kinda badarse." Rory rounded on Maddi. "I can't believe you missed that part out of the story!"

"It *was* pretty fun," Maddi admitted. Dane opened his mouth to speak, but Maddi jumped in first. "But never again!" She pointed her finger at his chest.

"Oh alright then," he huffed. "Come on, we're here," he said grabbing their hands and leading them through the doors. "You guys want a drink?"

"Sure," they chimed together.

"What'll you have?"

"Surprise us," Rory said, dragging Maddi to a table. They draped their bags over the back of a chair and sat down. "He seems pretty cool."

"Yeah. Wait until you see him dance," Maddi said. "He's amazing." She scanned the room to see if anyone from class was there. "Oh my God!" she half squealed, turning to face Rory with her mouth gaping open. "Look who just walked in," she hissed, pointing behind her.

"Is that Jessie?"

"And Sacha," Maddi whispered.

"*That's* Sacha? Wow. Not what I had pictured at all," Rory said, surprised. "She's so tiny. You could take her, easy." She narrowed her eyes with a nod of her head.

"Something tells me she would fight dirty." Maddi scowled. "Is it wrong that she irritates me this much?"

"Are you kidding? I haven't even met her and I'm irritated," Rory scoffed.

"Here's your drinks. Vodka and Red Bull. Hope you like it." Dane grinned as he placed their drinks in front of them.

"Ooh, sounds tasty," Rory said taking a big swig. "Mmm, it is. I think this will be my new favourite drink." She raised her glass to Dane.

"You okay, Maddi? You look like you've seen a ghost," Dane asked.

"Uh yeah, I'm fine." She glanced behind her with a wince. "I'm just not sure how happy you're going to be."

"Why's that?" He followed her line of sight. "Oh... I see." His smile faded momentarily. "No big deal. There's room here for all of us, right?" He chugged his drink back. "I just might go get another one of these." He stood and made his way back to the bar with slumped shoulders.

"Poor guy," Rory said quietly.

"Yeah. I feel so bad for him. Maybe we should leave."

"No! You can't let her see that she's having any kind of effect. Just pretend like she isn't even here."

"Easier said than done," she said, plastering a smile on her face as Dane approached. "Hey, you wanna hit the dancefloor?"

"Sure." He smiled back with a look of relief. He clasped her hand in his and led her to the middle of the dancefloor.

"Go easy on me." She grinned.

"Not a chance." He winked, sweeping her into a low dip. He spun her around the floor for several dances, the tension easing with each one. Maddi was pleased that she was still able to keep up with him.

"Um, wow! That was amazing! You two look so good together!" Rory whistled when they finally joined her at the table again. "I didn't know you could do all those moves!" She nudged her friend with her elbow.

"I didn't either." Maddi laughed. "He's a good teacher."

"Why, thank you. You're a really light lead, it's a nice change." He looked at Maddi with a goofy grin.

"I see you've found a new toy already, Dane. It seems we're not that different after all," Sacha said condescendingly as she came up behind him.

Dane stood to face her. "Sacha," he said. "Decided to crawl out from under your rock I see." He took a mouthful of his drink. "Have you met Maddi? My *new* dance partner?" He placed his hand on the small of her back.

Without missing a beat, Maddi held her hand out.

"Hi," she said sweet as pie. Sacha eyeballed her hand as if it were covered in mud.

"We've met," she said with disgust.

"This is Jessie. We *used* to be friends," Dane said, motioning to Jessie. He couldn't bear to look him in the eye. "Oh, that's right. You two know each other already, don't you?" He waved his drink between them.

"We do," Maddi agreed. "It's good to see you're still alive, Jessie," she said coolly.

"I deserve that. Sorry." He shifted uncomfortably. "I… I never meant to…"

"Yeah, we've heard that before," Dane interrupted, his eyes wandering around the room in boredom. Jessie looked back at Maddi.

"You look really nice," he said with a small smile. Sacha shot him a dirty look.

"Well, Jessie is *my* new dance partner," she said, drawing the attention away from Maddi. "We're going to compete this year."

"That so?" Dane asked. "Well, isn't that a coincidence? So are we," he announced, glancing sideways at Maddi.

"You two?" Sacha scoffed. "Good luck with that." She laughed mockingly, looking Maddi up and down.

Determined not to let her get to her, Maddi simply said, "Same to you."

"May the best man win then," Jessie said, offering his hand to Dane with a smile.

"Is that meant to be some kind of joke?"

"No, I… I didn't mean it like that, man," Jessie stammered, dropping his hand to his side. "Forget I said anything."

"Don't worry, I plan to," Dane spat.

"Come on, babe," Sacha said, looking up at Jessie. "Let's go have a dance. I'm tired of this now." She grabbed his hand and dragged him to the dancefloor. Jessie gave Maddi an apologetic look before turning away.

"Well, that sure was fun," Rory commented from behind them.

"You can say that again." Maddi slumped down in her seat.

"Sorry, I kinda threw you in it back there. I totally understand if you don't wanna be my dance partner. I just couldn't let her have something else over me," Dane said.

"It's fine. I'd love to be your dance partner." Maddi's face reddened as she added, "I was kinda hoping you would ask."

"Really? Great!" He beamed. "And the comps too?" he asked with hope.

"Sure. Why not? May as well go the whole hog." She shrugged. She knew it was childish, but she really wanted to wipe that smug smile off Sacha's face. Beating her at the comps would hit her where it hurt the most—her ego.

Chapter 19

"Can you believe those two?" Rory asked, disgusted. "Get a room!" she yelled across the crowded floor.

Sacha had straddled Jessie's lap and was giving him an impromptu lap dance. To his credit, Jessie appeared embarrassed by the display and kept trying to get her to stop. Sacha clearly had other ideas though.

"How can she be such a bitch? This must be killing Dane," Maddi said with a sigh. She glanced over at the bar, hoping he hadn't noticed the little show Sacha was putting on. He had.

He stood with his drink in hand, watching with a look of pure hatred in his eyes. His fingers were taught around the glass he was holding, the knuckles white from the pressure. If he wasn't careful, it'd shatter.

Maddi waved out, and reluctantly, it seemed, he tore his eyes away from the scene before him. Tipping his glass back, he slammed it on the bar and made his way over.

"You okay?" Maddi asked gently. She reached out and put her hand over his.

"Yeah, I'm fine," he grimaced. It was obvious he was trying to hold his composure, but it was getting harder to keep his cool. And rightly so. Dane had every right to be mad. He had not said one wrong word against them even though they had hurt him deeply with their betrayal. Now he was having to endure it in public too. How could they be so cruel?

"We can go if you want. I don't mind," Maddi offered.

"No, it's fine," he said through his teeth. "Let's just have a dance."

"Whatever you need." She allowed herself to be led to the centre of the dancefloor. It was a bachata playing. Maddi recognised the beat but hadn't actually tried it before. "I'm not sure how the steps go," she admitted.

"That's okay. Just listen to the music and let it flow through you. You'll pick it up easily. We don't have to do anything fancy." He smiled, pulling her in close. "Wrap your hands around my neck. Just follow my lead."

They began swaying to the music. Maddi closed her eyes, letting it flood over her. It had such a beautiful melody that she found herself getting caught up in it. Dane leaned forward, leading her through a slow, circular dip. He held her against his body and slowly went through the steps with her. As predicted, she followed without too many hiccups.

"That felt wonderful," she said dreamily. "The music just begs to be danced to."

Dane smiled. "It's my favourite style of dance."

"I can see why."

They went back to the table, and this time, Dane pulled Rory up for a salsa.

"Wish me luck!" she called back.

"Luck!" Maddi laughed. She took a quick mouthful of her drink before heading to the bathroom to freshen up. It was pretty hot out on the floor.

She splashed some water on her face and was dabbing it dry with a paper towel when the door swung open and in sauntered Sacha.

"What do you think you're playing at?" she demanded, coming up behind Maddi.

"Excuse me?" Maddi turned to face her.

"Don't act dumb. Swooping in, taking my sloppy seconds. You think you actually have a shot at the comps?" She smirked, folding her arms across her chest and jutting her hip out.

Maddi squared her shoulders. "Yeah. I do."

"He's going nowhere. Jessie is where it's at. We *will* win," she spat.

"Who're you trying to convince? Me or you?" Maddi asked, smiling.

"Sweetheart, I can out-dance you with my eyes closed," Sacha snarled, leaning in close. "You haven't got a hope in hell." She turned on her heel and stalked out.

Maddi shook her head in disbelief. How can she be so vicious to someone she barely knows? It was mind-boggling. But it set things in place in Maddi's mind. She was going to show Sacha.

She left the bathroom and joined Dane and Rory at the table.

"We are going to have to start training. There is no way I'm letting her beat us," she said.

"Did she jump you in the bathroom?" Rory asked, leaping to her feet, ready for a fight. Maddi calmly gestured for her to take a seat.

"Not quite. She *did* come and tell me she was better than me," Maddi said.

"Right. That's it." Dane stood and marched over to Sacha, tapping her on the shoulder. "You can't bear the fact that I found a better dancer than you, can you?" he demanded.

"Who? *Her*?" Sacha pointed at Maddi. "Don't make me laugh!" she scoffed.

"Look, I've held my tongue so far, but not anymore. You're so sure you can beat us? Put your money where your mouth is," Dane said.

"Alright then. If we win," she pointed a finger to his chest, "you have to find another dance partner." She raised her brows with a wicked grin.

Dane barely batted an eye. "Deal. And *when* we win—and we *will* win—you two," he pointed between her and Jessie, "have to stay away from Feeney's."

"Deal." They shook hands. "Good luck finding another partner!" Sacha called out as he walked away. He didn't bother biting back.

"What was that all about?" Maddi asked when he sat back down.

"We *have* to beat her," Dane said.

"Okay."

"No, we *really* have to beat her. Otherwise," he paused, looking sheepish, "I have to find another dance partner."

"Oh."

"You didn't seriously bet on it, did you?" Rory asked.

"Don't worry. We got this. One thing I know about Sacha—she's no good at choreography. That was always my job." He grinned.

"So, what do *you* get if we win?"

"Those two are not to step foot in Feeney's again." He took a sip of his drink.

"You didn't wanna try and split them up too?" Rory questioned.

"Nah. They can have each other as far as I'm concerned. I'm done with them."

Chapter 20

The next day, Dane showed up on Maddi's doorstep with three takeaway coffees and a bag of croissants.

"I brought breakfast." He grinned goofily. "Thought if you didn't have any plans, we could get straight into training."

"You certainly are determined." Maddi smiled, taking one of the warm cups from him and inhaling. "Mmm, coffee." She sighed, taking a gulp. "Rory! Dane brought coffee!" she called over her shoulder. She stepped aside, ushering Dane into their home.

"Did someone say coffee?" Rory mumbled as she shuffled out of her room, bleary eyed and dishevelled.

"Uh-huh. And croissants." Maddi held the bag and cup out enticingly.

"Gimme." Rory reached for them. "Oh, sweet coffee, how I love thee." She settled on the couch, her hands wrapped around the warm cup. "To what do we owe the pleasure?" she asked.

"Sorry, I came too early, didn't I?" Dane said apologetically. "I just wanted to get a jump on the training."

"Geez you're eager."

"I think it's a great idea." Maddi beamed. "I'm going to need a lot of work to get up to Sacha's standard."

Dane frowned. "You need to stop doing that."

"What?"

"Putting yourself down. You're just as good as she is."

"Hardly!" Maddi scoffed. "She's been doing this style a lot longer than I have."

"So? It's obvious you've danced before."

"Well, yeah, but it's not the same, is it?"

"No, it's not. It's better." He winked. "Sacha's all about the attention. Believe me, if she didn't think you were a threat, she wouldn't be getting this worked up about it."

"Listen to the man, he has a point," Rory agreed. Maddi rolled her eyes.

"Trust you to take his side." She finished her coffee and grabbed a croissant from the bag, peeling a chunk off and popping it into her mouth. "I guess I should go change so we can get started," she said around her mouthful, bounding back down the hall.

Sweeping her hair up into a ponytail, she rummaged through her drawer for something comfortable to wear. She settled on a pair of grey yoga pants and a baby pink singlet. After pulling on a pair of ankle tights, she grabbed her old jazz shoes down from the wardrobe shelf. They would do for training, but she was going to have to invest in some proper dance heels now that it had gotten so serious.

Serious was an understatement. The National Salsa Competition was a big deal. Add their wager into the mix, and it's even more so.

"Okay, I'm ready," she said as she breezed back into the lounge. "Where shall we start?"

"Okay, well, I thought maybe we could use this song." He pushed play on his iPod, and a beautiful guitar solo filled the room. "We could start off with a shine, and when the beat comes in, go into some combos. How are you with lifts?" His eyes shone with an excitement Maddi had never seen before.

"Ah, good, I guess. I've never really done them before, but I've always wanted to try."

"Great. We can try a few out, see what feels comfortable, and then incorporate those into the choreography. What do you think of the song?"

"It's beautiful."

"Yeah, it is," Dane said with a smile. "You wanna see what I have planned so far?"

"You've already got moves worked out?" She shook her head with a laugh. "That's impressive."

"Yeah, well…" Dane shrugged his shoulders. "I couldn't sleep last night," he admitted. "After we decided on entering, I just had all these ideas floating around in my head. Couldn't shut my brain off until I got up and started working through some steps."

"The curse of an artist," Maddi said. "Better show me what you've got then."

Dane handed his iPod to Rory and got into position. She hit play once again and he began moving his feet to the strum of the guitar. He danced with such grace, almost as if he were floating on air. His fancy footwork was flawless, his spins sharp. Maddi could hardly believe he had only just come up with this stuff.

Rory whistled from her perch on the couch. "The guy sure can move."

"He certainly can. Dane, that was amazing!" Maddi beamed as she pulled her ponytail tighter. "Can you break it down for me?"

"Of course. You really like it?"

"I really do." She put her hand on his arm. "It's fantastic."

"Thanks." He smiled, running his hand through his hair. "Okay so we'll have to come up with a starting pose, but basically, it starts like this." He popped his chest back and forth before crossing his feet one in front of the other with a twist. "This is called a Suzy-Q step. You wanna make sure you are twisting your hips to do it, rather than taking big steps. Like this." He demonstrated again. This time, Maddi did it alongside him. "Good."

They continued popping, stepping, and spinning until they were both drenched in sweat. Dane had broken down the entire guitar solo for her, and the more they practiced, the more polished they became.

Rory had filmed them a few times before escaping to her room. They watched it back to see how it looked and what needed work. Other than a few minor changes to make Maddi's moves sleeker and more feminine, they were impressed with their work so far.

"Not bad for our first day of training," Dane said with a smile. "You regretting it yet?"

"Not a chance." Maddi grinned, dabbing her neck with a towel. "That was so much fun. I haven't danced like that in years."

"I find that hard to believe. You're a natural."

A warm glow swept up her neck and cheeks. She wiped the towel across her face to try and hide it. Dane chuckled.

"You're gonna have to face it one of these days. You keep dancing like that and people are going to notice you." He pulled the towel from her hands. "I think you're pretty great, ya know?"

She was suddenly very aware of the fact they were on their own. "I… um. You wanna drink?" she asked, trying to change the subject. His close proximity made her feel a little awkward.

Dane dropped his hands to his side, a small smile on his face. "Sure, a drink would be nice."

"Water? Juice? Coffee?" she asked, walking through to the kitchen, avoiding eye contact. She didn't want him to think they were more than just friends.

"Coffee would be great, thanks," he said. "Milk and two please."

"Sweet. I'll put the jug on. Rory, you want another coffee?" she called down the hall.

"Uh does a cow go moo?"

Maddi sighed quietly in relief. If anyone could diffuse the situation, it was Rory. A long time ago, they had come up with a code for such times as these. After one too many persistent guys who couldn't take a hint, they had devised a plan to help each other out. They had decided on a few different phrases for different situations, so that they would always have an escape if need be.

Maddi locked eyes with Rory when she walked in. "Is that a new top?" she asked, brows raised. Rory frowned, looking over at Dane.

"This old thing?" she asked. "Nope, just haven't worn it in a while. Hey, can you still help me at work today?" She took a seat next to Dane, watching Maddi curiously. "We'll need to leave soon."

They hadn't used the code in years, and she couldn't see why Maddi would need it now. Dane seemed nice enough, he was a good-looking guy, and he could dance, what more could she want?

"Yeah sure, thanks for reminding me, I'd forgotten." Maddi smiled, grateful that her friend had come to her rescue. "Sorry, we'll have to cut the training short," she said apologetically. "Do you mind?"

"No, of course not. I should've checked first anyway." Dane gathered his things together.

"You can stay for that coffee, if you want. I'm sure I have time for a quick drink before I have to get ready." She looked at Rory, who gave a quizzical look.

"Ah, yeah, sure," she muttered, shaking her head. *Talk about mixed messages.*

Chapter 21

Jessie adjusted his stance, ready to try the lift again. They had been at it for an hour, and he still couldn't quite get it mastered.

"Okay, ready?" he asked a flustered Sacha.

"Of course I am!" she snapped. She hadn't anticipated it being so hard to teach a lift. She and Dane had learned together, and it had been a lot easier. Admittedly, they had been watching an instructional DVD—which belonged to Dane. Doing it from memory was proving to be difficult.

"Sorry, I've never done anything like this before. I don't want to hurt you."

"I'm not as fragile as you think. Just throw me over your shoulder like a sack of potatoes."

Jessie laughed at the image. "Okay then, if that's what you want." He bent his knees into a high squat before grabbing her underneath her thigh. Sacha wrapped one arm around his neck and held the other out for balance. "One, two, three!" He did as she asked and flung her like a sack of potatoes until she was perched across his shoulder. "It worked!"

"Easy! Don't wiggle too much or I'll lose my balance!" she said, concentrating on keeping her body straight.

"How do we get out of this?" Jessie asked, realising they hadn't discussed that part yet.

"Grab my hands and lower me down behind you." She slid gracefully down his back. "I knew you could do it!" She grinned, bounding into his arms and planting a kiss on his lips. "You just have to stop treating me like a dainty flower, cos baby, I ain't that soft."

"Yeah, I'm starting to realise that." Jessie chuckled. "You wanna try it again?"

"Sure." She unwrapped her legs from his waist and dropped to the ground. "Better make sure it wasn't just a fluke." She winked, getting herself into position. "Ready when you are."

After another hour, they had perfected both the lift and the dismount. With the comps looming, Sacha was eager to push on through with their routine. There was still a lot to cover before the big day, and she was determined to beat Dane at all costs.

So far, they had about a third of their routine done. Jessie had picked up all the combos with no problems, but the tricks were proving to be hard work. Now that he had accomplished the main lift though, she felt a slight release of pressure.

There was still so much to do; the other two thirds of the choreography for starters, and then there were costumes to organise, dance shoes to buy. All in a matter of weeks.

Sacha wasn't worried though. Things always worked out for her. It hadn't taken long for Jessie to learn the first part, and she didn't doubt he would pick up the rest without a hitch. The costumes would be easy; if there was one thing she was better at than dancing and seduction, it was shopping. She had visions of a skintight, leaving-nothing-to-the-imagination, dress. She was going to drop jaws.

For Jessie, she had planned on a simple black Latin style suit, with flared pants and V-neck top. She had already found several pairs of dance shoes for him to choose from. Her favourite was a black pair with white highlighted sides.

They would be the stand-out couple of the night, of that she was sure.

Chapter 22

"You ready to go shopping?" Maddi poked her head into Rory's room.

"You betcha." She raked a gel-covered hand through her hair, spiking it at various angles. She wiped the remainder down the leg of her shorts before grabbing her bag and throwing it over her shoulder. "Let's go!"

They were off on a spending spree. Maddi still had to find an outfit and some new heels for the comps. She hadn't had to buy dance heels before, only flats, so she was quite excited to see what was out there.

Dane had given her a list of the best places to buy Latin performance wear. He had told her to buy whatever she wanted—as long as she could move in it—and he would find something to match.

They decided to find a dress first, and then hopefully they could find some shoes to complement it.

Maddi wasn't really sure what she was looking for, that's why she had Rory with her. She had an eye for fashion and wouldn't let Maddi wear anything unflattering.

"Oh my God! You have to try this on!" Rory held up a white dress with a plunging neckline and no back.

"There's not really much to it, is there?" Maddi said, fingering the fine fabric with a scrunched-up nose.

"Nope. That's kinda the point. It'll look hot!" Rory held it out to her. "At least try it. I bet it looks amazing on." She smiled, rummaging through another rack. "Ooh, this one is gorgeous!" she squealed.

Maddi ended up with an armload of dresses in all different shades. She had to tell Rory to stop pulling any more out or she would collapse from the weight. She found a changing room and hung them on the hangers and over the door. One by one, she tried them on and paraded in front of Rory, twisting and turning to see them from every angle. She even did a few basic steps in front of the mirror to see how the dresses moved on her.

They had narrowed it down to three dresses. One black, one purple, and one emerald green. She tried each one on again, doing some of the shine steps, while watching herself in the mirror.

"I think the black one doesn't have quite enough give in it. It might be quite tricky to do some of the lifts," she said, pressing her lips together.

"Yeah, you're probably right. It's a pity though."

"I know. It's so beautiful." Maddi sighed. "I'm sure there'll be a next time." She went back to the changing room, slipping the black dress off and the purple one on.

Again, she danced in front of the mirror. This one was longer, but the skirt was cut into a V so there were splits up to her hips. She could definitely move more in this one, but the cut of the top just wasn't sitting quite right on her.

The emerald dress had a tight bodice with a halter top, leaving her back bare. The skirt was short, made of hundreds of threads of tassel in the same colour. She had the most freedom in this dress, and it looked fantastic on her.

"This is the one," Maddi said with a smile.

"You do look pretty amazing in it," Rory agreed. "I think some fishnets underneath would finish it off."

"I think you might be right. I'll grab a pair of those ones I saw by the counter." She took one last look in the mirror before changing back into her jeans.

Purchase in hand, they made their way to the shoe shops. Finding shoes to match this colour could be tricky, but there was no way they could have left with any other dress. This one was made for her.

Maddi was surprised at how many different varieties of shoes were available. There was wall upon wall, upon wall. Diamantes and sequins adorning the majority of them. She had never seen so much bling in one place before. She stared in wonder, like a child in a lolly shop for the first time.

And the colours! It was like a rainbow. Every shade imaginable seemed to be on those walls.

"It's breath-taking," Maddi exclaimed with a sigh. "Have you ever seen anything so beautiful?" she asked. Rory was just as dumbfounded as she was.

"It's like a pack of skittles exploded in here." She turned in a circle, staring at the walls. Maddi couldn't help but giggle at the awe on her face.

"You look like you're in heaven."

"Are you kidding me? I want one of every pair!" Rory clapped her hands to her cheeks. "Which ones are you going to choose?"

"I don't even know where to begin."

"Perhaps I can be of some assistance?" An older lady with greying hair pulled back into a severe bun, approached.

"Oh, yes please," Maddi gushed. "I'm entering my first competition and need some heels. I've never had any before."

"Oh, lovely. I used to compete in my younger years. Come this way." She directed them to a wall with what looked to be lower heels. "These are our one-and-a-half inch heels, which are normally what I would recommend for beginners."

"Okay, that's probably me then." Maddi scanned the shelves, eyeing up a black satin pair with emerald diamantes lining the strap.

"Good choice." The lady smiled, pulling them down from the rack. She looked at Maddi's feet. "These should fit. Give them a try."

Maddi sat on one of the stools and slid her feet out of her flats and into the heels held out to her. She had to be shown how to strap them up properly, but once they were on, they looked fantastic.

"Stand up, walk around in them, make sure they are comfortable. You want them to be firm, but not too tight. They will mould to the shape of your foot over time."

"Okay." She stood and took a few cautious steps.

"How do they feel?"

"I can honestly say, these are the most comfortable pair of shoes I have ever worn in my entire life," she said, quickening her pace. She danced down the length of the room. "It's like they're hugging my feet. I love them!" She pointed her toes at Rory.

"What do you think?"

"I'm happy if you are."

"That was easier than I thought it would be," she said, turning to the lady with a grin. "I'll take them please."

She was given a shoe brush to keep the soles in good condition and a bag to store them in.

"Now, make sure you break them in before the competition. You don't want to get blisters during a performance." The lady smiled, patting her hand. "Good luck, dear."

"Thanks for all your help." Maddi smiled back, giving her hand a squeeze.

"Well, now that that's done," Rory said, linking her arm through Maddi's, "how about some lunch? I'm starving!"

Chapter 23

By some miracle, Maddi had managed to avoid Sacha for the past few weeks. They had both been caught up in their own training schedules that their paths hadn't crossed. That was all about to change, however. No matter how much she wanted to, she couldn't hide from her forever, and they had troupe training today—the first one back since their performance at Feeney's.

Maddi was dreading seeing her. After that initial session where she first met Sacha, they had come to an understanding and just left each other alone. Now, with the competition so close, and the confrontation at Feeney's, Maddi was worried what might happen.

She dragged her feet, walking slower than her usual quick pace, trying to put off the inevitable. Pausing outside the entrance, she took several calming breaths, before marching through the door, head held high in false bravado.

She had to force herself to keep her eyes forward as she made a beeline for the seats by the window. Sitting down, she pulled her trusty jazz shoes from her bag and slipped them on. She could feel Sacha's devil stare on her but refused to be drawn into it. She moved to a clear area and began to warm up.

Thankfully, Rachel walked in before Sacha had a chance to approach her.

"Alright guys, let's get to work!" She jogged up to the front of the room. "Have you all warmed up?" Everyone nodded. "Great. I've got a few suggestions for the routine. Take your places." She waited for them to get into position, and they walked through the steps they had memorised, incorporating the new moves and styles into the old.

After going over them a few times, she switched the music on for them to try it at full speed.

"Looking good!" she yelled, bopping her head to the beat as she watched. "Sharpen those arms, ladies!"

The next time she played it through, she joined in with them, taking her place beside Maddi.

"I like the new changes. Brings it all together." She smiled.

"Thanks, I thought so too. I just felt like it was missing something."

They continued dancing for another hour before stopping for a drink break. Maddi grabbed a towel and wiped her neck and face, catching her breath. As much as she had been dreading it, she was glad she had come. Seeing the routine take on a new shape, and perfecting their moves, it was very satisfying.

"Gather round, girls!" Rachel called out. "Firstly, I want to thank you all for your hard work today. I know it can be hard to make changes this far into a routine, but you've all done such a good job of it." She smiled. "I had a lot of great feedback after our performance at Feeney's." She paused, looking each of them in the eye. "I even had people suggest we take it to the comps. What do you think?" she asked.

"Are you kidding? I'm totally in."

"I'm in."

"Me too."

"Sounds good."

"Count me in too. But I am *not* competing with *her*." Sacha glared at Maddi.

"Is that really necessary?" Rachel folded her arms across her chest, disapproval on her face. "We're a team."

"No, *we're* a team." Sacha gestured to the surrounding girls. "We've busted our arses over the last few months to get this routine down, and just like that, she gets to compete with us?" Sacha's hands landed on her hips. "Doesn't seem fair."

"That's uncalled for, Sacha. Maddi is just as much a part of our team as you are. She may not have been with us that long, but she has certainly pulled her weight."

Sacha opened her mouth to speak, but Maddi jumped in first. "It's okay, Rachel. I don't mind," she said, placing her hand on Rachel's arm. "Sacha's right. You guys deserve this. You've worked really hard for it."

"So have you," Rachel said, and the others all agreed.

"Really, it's okay. Gives me more time to focus on my own competition material." She smiled. "You guys are gonna blow them away."

"It won't be the same without you." One of the girls said, giving her a hug.

"Hey, I'll still be there cheering you on." Maddi grinned. "You can't get rid of me that easily."

"If only," Sacha mumbled under her breath. Maddi heard, but chose to ignore her. She couldn't understand why Sacha hated her so much, she was hardly a threat. Sacha had the guy, the moves, the body—what could she possibly be threatened by?

"You know what, Sacha? I had actually hoped we could be adults about all this. Obviously, I was wrong." She sighed. "I don't know what it is you want from me."

"What I want, is for you to disappear. *I* am the Queen of this domain."

"I don't know what you think I'm trying to do, but I have no interest in taking over. I just want to dance," Maddi said simply.

"If that's true, then you won't mind backing out of the comps, will you?" Sacha scowled, hands on hips.

"I'm not going to do that. I made a promise to a friend, and I don't break my promises." She gathered her gear in her arms. "Now, if you'll excuse me, I have somewhere to be." She pushed past Sacha and headed for the door.

Chapter 24

Maddi walked through the door and immediately slumped against the wall. She hated confrontations, they always made her feel flustered. For no real reason, tears filled her eyes.

Pull it together, Maddi. You're better than this.

Placing her hands on her thighs, she took three deep breaths, then made herself start walking. She didn't want Sacha to have the satisfaction of thinking she was rattled.

She retrieved her phone from her back pocket and sent Dane a text to let him know she was finished early. She didn't bother informing him of the 'discussion' her and Sacha had just had. There was no point rocking the boat even more.

They were planning on having a dress rehearsal today, to make sure that there were no costume malfunctions on the big day. After all the hard work they had put in over the past few weeks, she wasn't going to let something so simple and preventable, hinder their performance.

She was actually looking forward to seeing what it looked like all together. As per usual, Rory was going to film them, so they could go over it after. She didn't know what she would do without her.

Neither one of them had seen the other's outfit. Maddi had only shown Dane her shoes, so he had an idea of colour, but that was all. She couldn't wait to see what he was wearing. The anticipation was rather exciting.

With that in mind, she picked up her pace. It would take her a while to get organised with hair and make-up to do as well. For her hair, she would have an intricate plait on each side with glittering sequins to match her dress, plus swirls of colour down the side of her face by her eye, false lashes, and shimmering gloss for her lips - that was the plan anyway. She was putting her faith in Rory to pull it all together.

"Rory! You home?" she called out, bursting through the door.

"In here!" As per usual, Rory was in the kitchen, covered in flour. "I'm making cupcakes." She grinned.

"Perfect. We'll need them for sustenance after rehearsal," Maddi said, swiping her finger through the batter in the bowl and popping it into her mouth.

"There won't be any left if you eat all my batter!" Rory laughed, batting her hands away as she attempted another swipe.

"Fine." Maddi pouted, poking her tongue out. "You still okay to help me today?"

"Of course. I'll just get these in the oven, then I'm all yours." She busied herself scooping batter into cupcake cases, humming to a tune in her head.

Maddi went to her bedroom. She carefully pulled her costume out of her wardrobe and lay it on the bed. She still couldn't believe she got to wear something so beautiful. Even through the plastic covering it, you could see how magnificent it was.

She tore her eyes away and grabbed her dance tights and fishnets to add to the pile. She padded back to the kitchen and through to the bathroom.

"I'm just gonna have a quick shower before I get ready," she said on her way past. "Won't be long."

"I'll be here," Rory said, sliding the tray into the oven and setting the timer. She wiped her hands on her apron before untying it and hanging it on its hook. The cupcakes would take a few minutes to cook, so she ran and gathered her make-up kit, hairspray, and clips, setting them up on the kitchen counter with a mirror.

Maddi came back through, wrapped in a towel.

"Time to get pretty!" she squealed excitedly, almost forgetting that it wasn't the real deal.

While she ran to get changed, Rory pulled the cupcakes from the oven and set them on a wire rack to cool. Adorning her apron once more, she set to work making the buttercream icing to go on top.

She had just set the mixer on auto when there was a knock at the door.

"Can you get that?" Maddi called out.

"Coming!" Rory bellowed as she skipped down the hall to the door. "Hey, come on in. Maddi's just changing."

Dane stepped in, holding up his bag. "Yeah, I still need to do that. Didn't fancy walking over here in a Lycra shirt." He grinned.

"You can use my room if you want." She gestured to the door on her left. "I'll be in the kitchen."

"Thanks."

Rory knocked on Maddi's door as she passed, "Dane's here. He's just getting ready in my room."

"Thanks! I'll be out soon." She sat on her bed, pulling the fishnets carefully over her flesh-coloured dance tights, making sure they weren't twisted. Easing the dress out of its plastic sleeve, she slipped it on and studied her reflection. The brilliant emerald made her ice-blue eyes seem even brighter. Rory had been right about the fishnets too; they really did finish off the outfit.

She opened the door and peeked out. "Okay, here I come." She walked into the lounge. Dane was wearing shiny black dance pants and a Lycra V-neck shirt with emerald sequins to match her dress. "Wow. You look great!" She beamed.

"So do you," Dane managed, eyes glued to her. "You look… beautiful."

Maddi felt her cheeks flush. She ran her hand nervously through her hair. "Thanks."

"Ready for your make-over?" Rory asked.

"Uh-huh," Maddi stammered, uncomfortable under Dane's watchful gaze.

"Sit." Picking up a comb, Rory began raking it through her hair, dividing it into sections. With nimble fingers, she quickly got to work on the plaits, weaving emerald-sequined ribbons through as she went. "Done," she announced, securing the final pin. "Now, head up." She tilted her face up, brush in hand, and painted a sequence of swirls down one side of her face, applying diamantes along the edges.

"That looks great, Rory," Dane said, impressed.

"She certainly has an eye for fashion," Maddi agreed, checking herself out in the hand mirror she was holding.

"She's got a good palette to work on too." Dane grinned cheekily.

"And the award for cheesiest comment goes to…" Rory mocked, doing an imaginary drum roll.

"Yeah, yeah, sorry. Shall we get started?"

"Sure." Maddi placed the mirror on the table behind her and stood up, smoothing the tassels on her dress down. "Let's do it."

Rory took her place in the corner of the room to film, while Dane hooked his iPod up to their speakers.

"Ready?" he asked.

"Ready."

"And… Go!" Rory said, pushing record on her phone. The sound of the guitar solo flooded the room as Dane and Maddi began their routine.

They moved fluidly between their solo shine steps and their partnered combinations, throwing in a few dips and lifts to fit with the hits in the music. Maddi's tassels flicked around her body with every step, accentuating her hip movements. The plunging V-neck of Dane's shirt allowed a view of his perfectly sculpted chest. Altogether, the performance was faultless. No wardrobe malfunctions, no stumbles—pure perfection.

"You two look fantastic!" Rory gushed when the music had come to an end, and they were panting in their final position. "I'm so proud of you!" She clapped her hands together, almost dropping her phone in the process. "Come and look! You're gonna be amazed at how good you look."

Maddi clambered onto the arm of the sofa to get a look at the screen, Dane stood on the other side of Rory.

"Oh wow." Maddi sighed in delight. "I never imagined it would look like that. We really do look amazing." She smiled at Dane.

"I knew we would." He returned her smile with a wink. "Told ya we make a good team."

Chapter 25

For the next week, Maddi dragged herself out of bed every morning for a run before Dane joined her for a training session. They wanted to cram in as much rehearsal as possible before the big day. They had made a few tweaks here and there in their routine, but for the most part, it was competition ready. They knew it inside and out, and even had a few backup moves in place, for any mishaps on the night.

Despite the awkward situation that had prompted their entry into the competition, Maddi was feeling good about it all. She loved having Dane as a dance partner—he challenged her, which she liked. Of course, they had their disagreements, as any partnership does, but they always managed to work past it.

After their final rehearsal before the comps, Maddi sat in her room, wrapped in a towel, staring vacantly at the wardrobe that appeared to have nothing appealing in it. She let out a heavy sigh.

"What's up?" Rory asked as she threw herself across Maddi's bed. "You seem tense." She poked at Maddi's arms and shoulders until she swatted her away.

"I have nothing to wear!" She threw her hands up in disgust. "All of these clothes," she waved her arm about, "and nothing I want to wear. Not. A. Thing. I keep staring at it, hoping something will magically appear."

Rory laughed as she sat up and began massaging Maddi's shoulders. "You wanna raid my wardrobe? I have heaps that would look cute on you."

"I don't know. I guess." Maddi slumped down. "What's wrong with me? I feel so… emotional." She sighed, looking down at her fingers twisting in her lap.

"It's just nerves. You've been working your arse off for the last few months, and now it's almost at an end. It's natural to be emotional." She gave her shoulders a squeeze. "But you have nothing to worry about. You're gonna be great."

Maddi attempted a smile. "Thanks."

"Come on." Rory gave her a gentle push. "Get up, let's go see what we can find in my wardrobe for you to wear."

"Okay." Maddi reluctantly stood, allowing herself to be led across the hall. Rory sat her down on her bed and began pulling all manner of garments from her hangers and drawers. Within seconds, she had a large pile for Maddi to sift through and find something to her liking.

"You look through here, and I'll go whip us up a coffee and some cake."

"Cake for breakfast?" Maddi questioned.

"Damn straight! Breakfast of champions." Rory winked before bounding out the door to the kitchen.

Maddi knelt on the floor and began picking through the pile of clothes scattered around her. She chose a lilac, off-the-shoulder sweater with a pair of three-quarter length jeans covered in colourful patches.

She ran her fingers through her hair and pulled it up into a ponytail before padding out to join Rory.

The coffee was ready and waiting, along with a healthy slice of red velvet cake. She had to admit, cake did sound like a pretty great breakfast right now. Perhaps the sugary sweetness would boost her mood.

She scooped up her plate and coffee and made herself comfortable on the couch, curling her feet beneath her.

"Have I told you how much I love you?" she asked Rory, with a mouth full of cake.

"Not today." Rory grinned, wiping the frosting from the sides of her mouth. "Is it working? You feel better?"

"Mmhmm," Maddi mumbled. "Thanks."

"Anytime."

They ate in silence, barely taking a breath between mouthfuls. Maddi's shoulders loosened as the tension from earlier slipped away with every bite. Rory certainly knew how to put her at ease. It was like her superpower.

"So, what's on the agenda for today?" Rory asked after licking the crumbs from her plate.

"Something that doesn't require much thought," Maddi said. "My brain is out of order today."

"Shopping it is!" Rory announced. "You can help me find something to wear for tomorrow night."

"Ooh sounds fun!" Maddi perked up. "What kind of look are we going for?"

"Hmm," Rory considered. "Chic meets street."

"Whatever that means." Maddi laughed. "Come on then, let's get going. This could take all day." They each placed their plates in the sink, ready to wash, before running to their rooms to grab the essentials—shoes, purse, and lip gloss. Pulling the door closed behind them, they linked arms and walked down the path towards the mall.

Several hours, and shops later, the girls emerged from the brightly lit mall, blinking their eyes as they adjusted to the natural light of the day. Not only had they managed to find Rory the perfect mix of 'chic meets street', but also a pair of grungy, lace-up boots to match, a funky beret-style cap, and some hair dye to finish it off. Rory's already short peroxide blonde hair was about to have some purple streaks put through it, care of Maddi.

Rory had a style all of her own and was forever changing her hair. In the years they had known each other, she had had all manner of cuts—long with layers, braids, bobs—you name it, she'd had it. Boredom played a large part in that, as did keeping up with the latest trends. This pixie cut, however, had managed to stay the course the longest, the only change being to the colour. She was able to style it in various ways with gel, keeping the boredom at bay.

Maddi couldn't wait to see what the streaks would look like. They had chosen a deep purple colour, hoping it would lighten up once added to the peroxide already present in her hair. She was to put streaks through the bulk of it, with thick foils in the front.

It would be her first attempt at streaking someone's hair—hence the beret—just in case it didn't quite go to plan. Whatever happened, Rory was going to look fantastic. They'd covered all the bases.

Chapter 26

The following morning, Maddi was up and in the kitchen, preparing breakfast at an unspeakable hour. Nerves had gotten the better of her during the night and she had tossed and turned for hours.

Retrieving the pancake batter from the fridge where it had been chilling for the past hour, she gave it one last whisk. She placed a blob of butter into a hot frying pan and began to spoon the mixture in, swirling it to spread it out.

While she waited for the first side to cook, she flicked the jug on and pulled two cups down from the shelf. She knew it wouldn't be long before Rory stumbled out upon smelling the goings on in the kitchen. She was surprised the bacon crisping in the oven hadn't already drawn her out.

Considering her lack of sleep, she was feeling surprisingly chipper this morning. Prancing about the kitchen in her pink bunny slippers and robe, she allowed herself to feel excited about the evening ahead. They had worked so hard over the past few months; it would be great to finally show everyone what they were capable of. And by everyone, she meant Sacha.

She flipped the first pancake over, then pulled the bacon from the oven. She brought out two plates and the maple syrup. Once the jug had switched itself off, she poured their coffees and called out to Rory.

"I made you breakfast." She grinned, holding the plate out to her dishevelled flatmate. Rory's purple and blonde hair stuck out at all angles, like some sort of new era hedgehog. As if on cue, she ran her fingers through it, softening the spikes, while she yawned and staggered to the kitchen.

"Mmm, I thought I could smell bacon," she said, reaching for the plate. She poured an extra helping of syrup over her already drenched pancakes.

"Coffee's over there." Maddi pointed at the bench with one hand, while pouring the next lot of batter into the pan.

"You're up early."

"Couldn't sleep. Stupid nerves," she grumbled light-heartedly. "At least I get to enjoy the sunshine though." She smiled, looking out the kitchen window.

"Aren't nerves meant to be a good thing? Adrenalin and all that?"

"Provided I don't crash and burn before our performance."

"You'll be too wired for that to happen. Red Bull, my friend. That'll get you through." Rory shovelled a forkful of dripping pancake and bacon into her mouth. "Mmm, this is good." A trickle of syrup made its way down her chin, and she tried to lick it up with her tongue.

"I hope so, I'm starving." Maddi flipped her pancake onto her plate and piled several pieces of bacon on top, followed by the maple syrup. "I've been waiting all morning for this." She eyed her plate hungrily before scooping some into her mouth. "Oh yeah," she mumbled with her mouth full.

"Mmhmm," Rory agreed. She was licking the plate clean, making sure she got every last drop.

"I think you got it," Maddi laughed, almost choking on her food. One of the things she loved most about Rory was her childlike behaviour. How she couldn't care less what people thought of her, or her actions. In return, Maddi could also act the fool and Rory wouldn't even bat an eye. In fact, she was likely to join in.

"What time do you have to be there today?"

"The competitors have to meet at lunch to walk through stage settings. That should take an hour or so, and then it's time to get ready," Maddi said with a smile.

"So, I'll meet you there around two to get your hair and makeup done?"

"Yeah. Thanks, Rory. I don't know what I'd do without you."

"Anytime, babe. That's what I'm here for."

Down at the venue, Dane was pacing back and forth waiting for Maddi to arrive. He kept patting his pocket to check he had their music, even though he had a backup in his bag. A dream the night before had made him paranoid that they would have the wrong music playing and it would ruin their routine. The first thing he did when he got up, was to check it and make a copy so there could be no mistakes.

The door opened, and in breezed Sacha and Jessie. They looked just as nervous as he felt. Jessie saw him watching and offered a small wave. Dane simply nodded in their direction.

Maddi came bounding up behind him. "Hey."

"Hey, yourself." Dane grinned as he turned to face her. "How you feeling?"

"A little tired, but other than that, pretty good."

"Couldn't sleep either, huh?" Dane had spent the night counting the dimples on his ceiling.

"Not really, no. But don't worry, I can still do this." She grinned, her eyes wide as she took in the crowd. "Are all these people competing?"

"Yup. Some will be in teams though. They're not all our competition."

"Oh, of course." She waved at Rachel and the other girls when she spotted them. "This is quite exciting," she gushed. "I've never been to anything like this before."

"Yeah, it is pretty cool," Dane agreed.

"Alright, people! Gather round so I don't have to yell!" A man was standing centre stage holding a clip board. "We have a lot to get through, so if we can stick to the schedule, this will all run smoothly. In a moment, we are going to have all the teams come to the stage in their order of performances so we can get positioning and lighting right. After them, we will have the Beginners Couples, the Intermediate Couples and the Advanced Couples. The schedule is up on the wall." He pointed. "Let's get started!"

One by one, the teams made their way to the stage, taking up their starting positions. Maddi and Dane sat watching.

"Have you seen Sacha and Jessie?" she whispered.

"Yeah, they're back there." He pointed behind him. "I was thinking of going over there."

Maddi pursed her lips. "Is that wise? We don't need to start a fight before the comps, Dane. Let's just keep our distance."

"I was actually thinking of wishing them luck."

"Oh, really?" Her jaw dropped and she scooted back in her seat. "You've had a change of heart."

"Yeah. I guess. You do a lot of thinking when you can't sleep." He chuckled, scrubbing a hand across his chin. "I just don't want to be angry anymore."

"Good for you." She smiled encouragingly. "Do you want me to go with you?"

"If you want." He shrugged his shoulders but offered his hand as he stood up. Together they walked over to where the others were seated.

"Sacha. Jessie." Dane nodded at each of them. "I just… *We* just wanted to wish you luck tonight." He offered his hand.

"Thanks, man," Jessie said, standing to shake hands. "That means a lot."

"We're not the ones who need luck," Sacha smirked.

"Sacha!" Jessie looked at her with an embarrassed look.

"What? Don't think that coming over here and acting all nice as pie is going to change the fact that we have a bet on."

"I wasn't trying to get out of anything. I just wanted to put this shit behind us."

"Fine by me, but a bet's a bet. If we win, you still have to find another dance partner," she sneered.

"Just because I wish you good luck, doesn't mean we're giving up. We're still in this to win it." He folded his arms across his chest.

"Bring it on." Sacha held her arms out in challenge.

Maddi stepped between Dane and Sacha, looking her up and down. "Oh, we will, don't you worry."

Chapter 27

"Ladies and Gentlemen! Welcome to the annual National Salsa Championships!" There was a loud cheer from the audience. "We have a fantastic show lined up for you tonight! These dancers have put everything they have into making this a show to remember, so sit back and enjoy! First up tonight, we have the teams!"

Backstage, there were bodies running around everywhere. Two teams were lined up, ready to get on stage, while the others were busy putting on the finishing touches to their make-up or having last minute run-throughs.

Rory was applying the diamantes to Maddi's face while she touched up her lipstick.

"I'm so nervous!" she blurted, waving her hands in front of her. "I can't sit still."

"Nearly done," Rory said, her fingers pressing the last one down. "There." She held Maddi's chin between her finger and thumb, admiring her handy work. "Not bad, even if I do say so myself."

Maddi stood, checking herself out in the full-length mirror provided. Her hair glistened with the glitter hairspray Rory had used, the sequins catching the light every time she moved. It was going to look great on stage.

"I'd better head out. Don't want to miss your performance!" Rory grinned, giving Maddi a big hug.

"Break a leg!" She squeezed her tight, before planting a kiss on her cheek. She fought her way through the throngs of competitors and out the door.

The first team came barging back through the changing room, giggling and chattering excitedly.

"Oh my God! That was so much fun!"

"I know! I was so sure I was going to fall."

"I missed the turn!"

"You were great, no-one would've even noticed."

Maddi smiled as she listened to their enthusiastic banter. She scanned the list on the wall to see when Rachel and the girls would be making their way to the stage—they were the last team in their category. Maddi rushed out to find them, wanting to wish them luck before they went on.

"Rachel!" she called out, raising her hand to wave.

"Maddi, hi!" Rachel said. "Can you believe this? Who knew there were so many amazing dancers in New Zealand?" She grinned.

"I just wanted to wish you and the girls the best of luck. You're gonna be fabulous!" She beamed, pulling them in for a group hug.

The next team came running down the stairs, and their name was called out.

"This is it!" Rachel turned to the front, leading her team to the stage. Maddi cheered them on from the side-lines. They looked fantastic in their tiny black shorts, tight white tees and black suspenders. Their hair was pulled back in tight buns, with black top-hats adorning their heads.

The audience clapped and whooped as they made their way off the stage with huge grins on their faces. Sacha pushed her way to the front, shoving Maddi aside.

"Out of my way! I have to get changed."

"Rude," Maddi muttered under her breath. She brushed her hands down her dress, making sure everything was in place then went to find Dane out back.

"Where have you been?" he demanded when he spotted her.

"Sorry, I was watching the girls perform. Did you want me for something?" she asked.

"Sorry, I just freaked out. I thought you had backed out,' he admitted sheepishly.

"Dane, we're in this together. I wouldn't just leave." She touched his arm gently.

"I know. I guess I'm just a little paranoid." He ran his hand through his hair restlessly. "You look great, by the way," he added with a smile.

"Thanks, so do you." She smiled warmly. "You ready for this? We're up soon."

"Yeah, I'm ready." He let out the breath he had been holding, shaking his head side-to-side like a boxer preparing for a fight.

The beginner couples started to line up by the stage door. Some looked as though they may throw up, others chattered nervously. There were only three couples in this category, and Maddi was impressed at their courage. To be in the beginner category, both dancers had to have been dancing for a maximum of six months and had no performance experience.

Because Dane had been dancing longer and they had both performed before, they were put in the intermediate section. It was the same for Sacha and Jessie. There were four couples in their category, one on either side of them. Maddi and Dane would be performing third in line.

One by one, the beginners made their way up the stairs to the stage, each time reappearing with a look of relief. Performing in front of a crowd took a bit of getting used to, but there was nothing quite like the rush of being on stage, under the lights, and hearing people applaud for you.

"Intermediate couples to the stage door please," the man with the clipboard said as he rushed down the hall.

Maddi's face lit up with anticipation. She gripped Dane's arm and jumped up and down on the spot. Her enthusiasm was infectious, and soon he was grinning along with her.

"Come on then, let's go line up," he said with a laugh.

They stood behind Sacha and Jessie. She feigned indifference, while Jessie smiled nervously at them.

"Good luck," he whispered after the first couple took to the stage.

"You too," Maddi said back. She grabbed Dane's hand and gave it a squeeze. "I still can't believe we're really here!" she said excitedly.

"Well, believe it. It won't be the last time, I can guarantee it." He smiled down at her, patting her hand.

The doors swung open and they heard the announcer's voice. "What a lovely couple! Let's give them another round of applause!" The stage director motioned for Sacha and Jessie to move up to the curtains, ready for their entrance.

"Our next couple to the stage are a new partnership, let's see what they've got for us! Put your hands together for Sacha Barret and Jessie Jameson!"

Sacha plastered a smile across her face and strutted out onto the stage. They took up their positions, waiting for the music.

Maddi and Dane crept up to the curtains to watch, they wanted to see what they were up against.

The music blared, and Maddi could feel Dane grow tense. He was flexing his hand by his side, as if ready to throw a punch, and the look on his face was pure murder. She had no idea what had caused this sudden change in his mood, but it obviously had something to do with Sacha. The longer he watched them, the deeper the scowl on his face became.

Maddi bit her lip, her eyes darting back and forth between the stage and Dane. The song was almost over and then it would be their turn. She needed him to focus, or they would lose the bet.

Doing the only thing she could think of, she grabbed his hand and dragged him away from the stage. She reached her hands up to cup his face and pulled him towards her, planting a soft kiss on his lips.

His eyes grew wide at the shock, but then he began to kiss her back with an eagerness. He crushed his lips against hers, pulling her body in close as he ran his fingers down her back.

The music came to an end and the room erupted into applause. Maddi pulled away, giving Dane a small smile.

"What was that about?" he asked with a goofy grin on his face.

"Just because," Maddi said quietly. "Come on, we're up." She took his hand and intentionally led him to the back of the stage, away from where Sacha would be leaving from.

"Let's welcome our next couple to the stage! Give a warm welcome to Maddison Lee and Dane Rogers!"

"Let's do this!" Maddi winked. Dane offered his elbow, and they made their way to the centre of the stage. He spun her a few times, letting her go to get to her position. They stood opposite each other, hands on their hips and faces dipped down. The audience was silent as they waited with anticipation.

"Go, Maddi!" Rory called from the crowd, doing her best wolf whistle. Maddi's smile stretched even wider as she listened to her friend make all kinds of noises in the silence.

The beautiful sound of a guitar rang through the speakers, and both Maddi and Dane came to life. Out of the corner of her eye, she could see Dane was giving it everything he had. She had never seen him dance with such passion before. He flashed a smile in her direction as they turned to face each other, ready for the next part of their routine.

It all happened so fast. One minute they were dancing, and the next, they were doing their final lift, puffing and panting, listening to the cheers of the crowd. Of course, Rory was the loudest of them all.

"Woohoo!" she hollered through cupped hands. "That's my best friend!" she yelled enthusiastically to anyone who would listen.

Dane lowered Maddi to the ground, and they walked to the front of the stage for their bow. Maddi could see Rory jumping up and down, waving. She couldn't help but giggle at the sight.

Turning, they both marched off the stage and down the stairs.

"Oh, man, that was amazing! You were on fire!" Maddi could barely contain herself. She was giddy with adrenalin.

"You were pretty amazing yourself." Dane grinned, happy to see her like this. "That kiss kinda spurred me on," he admitted.

"Yeah? I'm glad," Maddi said, suddenly feeling shy. "It just felt like the right time."

"It was the perfect time. I'm glad you did it." He reached for her hand. "You're welcome to do it any time you like." Maddi smiled, feeling her face flush. "Maybe we could go on a date sometime?" he asked, his voice full of hope.

"Yeah, I think I'd like that," Maddi said, genuinely surprised at herself. She hadn't really thought it through before, it had been a spur of the moment thing, but she couldn't see the harm in seeing where it went. Dane was a nice enough guy, and they *did* make a good team.

Chapter 28

"You!" Dane's face clouded over, and he was filled with rage once more. Maddi turned to see who he was talking to—Sacha—of course, she should have known. No one else could have that effect on him.

"Me?" Sacha pointed at herself, looking side-to-side.

"Yes, you! Who else?" Dane spat as he stormed towards her. Sacha took a step back, a look of panic on her face. She held her hands up as if to fend him off, but Jessie stepped in front of her.

"Is everything okay, Dane?" he asked, placing a hand on his chest, "you seem upset."

"That's an understatement!" He shoved Jessie against the wall. "Her I expected this from, but not you! To think, I actually thought you were sorry for what you did to me."

"Woah, man! I have no idea what you're talking about!" Jessie held his arms up, palms out. He frowned.

"The hell you don't!" Dane barked.

Maddi put her hand on his arm. "Dane?" she questioned, just as confused as Jessie. "Why don't we calm down and talk about this?" She pulled his arm away from Jessie's chest, turning him to look at her. His eyes softened, and he dropped his hands to his sides. Taking a deep breath, he managed to calm himself down enough to speak without drawing so much attention to them.

"They stole my routine," he said to Maddi.

"They *what*?" She looked at Jessie incredulously.

"Now, hang on…" he started but Dane shut him down with a look.

"I choreographed that routine for me and Sacha. They used my work against me."

"Sacha?" Jessie turned to look at her. The smug look on her face told him Dane was telling the truth. "You did that?" he asked, mouth gaping open in shock.

"Don't act so surprised. What else was I going to do? There wasn't time to start from scratch, and it's not like he was going to use it." Sacha took a defensive stance.

"I can't believe you did that," Jessie said quietly. He turned to Dane. "I'm so sorry. I honestly had no idea."

Dane huffed, clearly unimpressed by the apology. "You know what? I'm glad you two found each other. Now I can see you for who you really are, Sacha. You're only out for number one." He swung his gaze to Jessie. "You better watch your back. Once a cheater, always a cheater." He draped his arm around Maddi's shoulders. "Come on, they'll be announcing the winners soon."

They walked away, leaving Jessie to deal with Sacha. Maddi almost felt sorry for him. Almost.

"Alright, ladies and gentlemen! Now for the moment you've all been waiting for! The results!" the host announced as he was handed a card from the judges.

There was a hush over the audience as the competitors filed back on stage, gathered in a large group, arms around each other.

Sacha was standing with her teammates, while Jessie stood to the back of the group. He had his hands in his pockets and was looking at the floor.

Dane wrapped his arm firmly around Maddi's waist, pulling her in close and kissing the top of her head. She scanned the audience in front of her, watching as Rory bopped up and down like a yo-yo. She wondered what the person behind her thought of all that.

Each of the teams who had placed were standing at the front of the stage, holding their medals and certificates up for all to see. Someone jumped out with a camera, snapping pics of the winners.

Maddi applauded with the audience, cheering loudest for Rachel's team who had taken out first place. They all shuffled along, so that the beginners were closest to the host. Maddi reached out and squeezed Rachel's arm as she passed her by. She winked and gave her a thumbs up.

The butterflies in her stomach were throwing a party. She was more nervous now, than she had been before performing. More than just reputations were on the line. If they didn't beat Sacha and Jessie, she and Dane would have to find new dance partners. On the other hand, if they won, she wouldn't have to see Sacha anymore.

She crossed her fingers behind her back and said a silent prayer.

"Now for the Intermediate couples! We had some fierce competition this year! The votes are in, and it was a close one!" the host bellowed through the microphone. "Coming in third place is… Nadine and Rob!" They stepped forward and accepted their awards. "With only three points between them and first place, the second place goes to… Sacha and Jessie!"

Jessie's head snapped up when he heard his name. Sacha latched onto his elbow as they made their way to the front. She gave Maddi a smug smile over her shoulder.

"And the winner of the Intermediate couples' section is… Dane and Maddi!" The audience erupted in a bout of cheers and whoops, led by Rory.

Dane pulled Maddi into his arms, lifting her off her feet and planting a kiss on her lips. "We did it!" he cried. Maddi giggled, flinging her arms around his neck. They collected their medals, and someone handed Maddi a bouquet of flowers.

Joining their fellow winners for photos, Maddi snuck a peek at Sacha. The smugness had been wiped from her face and replaced with a bitter smile as she tried to pretend it didn't matter.

When it was all over, and they were no longer in front of an audience, Dane walked up to Sacha and Jessie, towing Maddi behind him.

"Nice work," he said, "I guess we'll see you around sometime. Oh, that's right. No, we won't," he smiled from ear-to-ear. "I seem to recall that we had a bet. You'll have to find another bar to frequent. Sorry." He turned on his heels, stifling the laughter bubbling up inside.

Maddi giggled, "That was mean," she whispered.

"Admit it, you enjoyed it too."

"Maybe just a little." She held her finger and thumb together, leaving the tiniest of gaps. Dane threw his arm around her shoulder again, and together, they walked out to meet Rory.

Chapter 29

"Hurry up! He'll be here soon," Maddi said impatiently as Rory weaved her fingers through her hair.

"Shut up and sit still. I swear you're worse than a three-year old!" She had bobby pins hanging from her mouth, and a look of sheer determination. "Just this little bit here… there! All done," she said proudly.

After the plaits she had perfected for the comps, Rory had become somewhat obsessed with finding new ways to braid hair, and not having a lot of her own, Maddi was her guinea pig, whether she liked it or not.

This particular braid was made up of several small plaits, woven together in a spiral around her head. It was time consuming, but the result was worth it.

"Nice work," Maddi praised. "Will it hold?"

"There's like, a hundred pins in there and half a bottle of hairspray. That baby ain't going anywhere." Rory grinned, spinning the bottle around in her hand cockily.

Maddi stretched her arms above her, twisting her head side-to-side to relieve the cramps from holding it still for so long. She stood, brushing her hands down her front. "Do I look okay?" she asked.

"You look fine. Stop worrying so much!"

"I know I shouldn't be nervous, but I can't help it. First date jitters and all."

There was a knock on the door, making her jump.

"Eee! He's here," she said in an excited whisper.

"Well? What are you waiting for? Go get 'em!" Rory shoved her towards the door. "Have fun!" she called.

Maddi opened the door, grinning goofily. "Hey," she sang with a little wave.

Dane chuckled. "Hey, yourself," he said. "You ready?"

"Yup." She went to walk through the door, misjudging the step down. She stumbled and fell against Dane's chest, his arms circling to catch her.

"Well, I didn't think you'd be throwing yourself at me so soon," he joked, helping her to her feet.

"Ss-sorry about that," she stammered, her cheeks blushing to a rosy colour. "I'm such a klutz."

"I don't know, I think you're a real catch," he grinned, nudging her with his elbow.

Maddi burst out laughing. "That was cheesy!"

"Got you smiling though, didn't it?" He offered her his arm. "Shall we?"

"We shall," she said, looping her arm through his.

"I told you we make a good team."

Stacey Broadbent
Dancing In Circles
A Step in Time book two

He may have won last year, but Dane is not about to let his ex, Sacha, get the better of him. He will be number one again, but at what cost?
Pushing Maddi to her limits, he finds himself broken and alone, wondering what the hell happened.

Maddi finds what she's been missing in shy guy, Ricki Macavoy; an equal. Someone to share the load, win or lose.

Dane wants Maddi back and will do anything to prove his love for her. He'll make her see how good they were together. How good they could be once again.

Love and betrayal.

The rivalry continues.

Chapter 1

"Will you stop anticipating?" Dane threw his hands in the air.

"I'm not anticipating, I'm following. Maybe if you led me correctly, I would do whatever it is you are trying to get me to do!" Maddi was sick of listening to him complain about her dancing. She was every bit as good as he was, if not better.

They had competed together in the National Salsa Competitions the previous year and come out on top in their category. This year they planned on doing the same. The pressure was on though, as there was some fierce competition. Sacha and Jessie—who came a close second place—had made it known they were working on something big and had been all year. They were good. More than good, they could actually win; there had only been a few points between them. But Dane was determined to put them in their place this year. It was sweet at the top, and he intended on staying there.

"I am leading. You're not following!" He hit the bench, making Maddi jump.

"You know what? You need to cool down. I'm not dancing with you like this." She turned to walk away, but he grasped her arm, pulling her towards him.

"I'm sorry, okay? I just want to win so bad. I couldn't stand to see that smug bitch, Sacha, beat us." Maddi smiled and reached her arms up to caress his neck. He and Sacha had a history together. They had been dance partners (and more) when they first started out. They were practically inseparable from the moment they met at their first salsa class… until Sacha met Jessie that is. He had been a friend of Danes who took to dance like a fish to water. To his credit, Jessie had fought off her advances at first, she was just so damn persistent. Once she had someone in her sights, there was no way to resist her. Dane didn't blame Jessie, not anymore. He knew the powerful intoxication she possessed with her pouty lips and seductive eyes.

What he didn't expect was for her to take his routine and use it against him in the competitions. He had actually forgiven them both for their betrayal until that moment. Watching them do the routine he had poured so much of himself into, had made his blood boil. If it hadn't been for Maddi standing by his side, holding his hand and keeping him focused, he probably would've caused a scene. Instead, he'd channelled all of that negative energy and they'd pulled off the best performance of their lives. Now, just the thought of Sacha beating him was enough to get him all hot and bothered.

"Baby, we beat them last year, we can do it again," she soothed, stroking the wisps of hair at the base of his neck. "You know we'll kick arse. I mean, come on, you have me as your partner." She grinned up at him as she felt him relax into her.

"You're awesome, you know that?" His lips skimmed hers. "And gorgeous…" She felt the warmth of his breath on her neck as he nuzzled her, his thoughts clearly on other things.

"None of that. We have work to do. This routine won't come together on its own." She eased herself out of his grip.

"Slave driver."

"You know you like it. Now, where were we?"

They continued to practice through the night, but Maddi could see Dane's mind wasn't really on it. He was more than a little obsessed with the desire to win. No, not just to win, but to hurt Sacha. That was what it really boiled down to, and Maddi knew it. At first, she didn't mind his dedication, but it was starting to take its toll. There was only so much you could hear about an ex before it got on your nerves. Not to mention, Dane wouldn't let Maddi help with choreography. She had so many great ideas for the new routine, but Dane was so stubborn that he dismissed them before she even got a chance to share them. Sure, he was the more experienced salsa dancer, but that's not always what makes you the strongest dancer.

Maddi believed in learning other styles and incorporating them into your dance; blending techniques. When she was a child, she had taken jazz, rock 'n' roll, and even a little Irish—you know the kind where your body is still, while your feet are moving at

50mph? She had always liked the look of salsa, and after a messy break up, decided to give it a go. It only took one lesson before she was hooked. She went to as many classes as she could manage; even some workshops with international teachers to learn some new styles that were becoming popular. It wasn't long before she had been asked to join a ladies' troupe where they choreographed 'shine' routines—where you dance solo, but in a team—so no partners needed. She had been dancing every day of the week; training by day and social dancing by night. Her teacher had taken her under her wing and introduced her to everyone worth knowing in the dance scene. This was how she'd met Dane, and after a few dances together, they'd realised how well they gelled. From then on, they had been partners.

Their relationship didn't blossom until that night at the comps. Maddi had seen the anger flash in his eyes as he watched Sacha and Jessie execute the routine he'd choreographed. She knew that he would be too distracted to dance, so she did the only thing she could think of. She grabbed his hand, pulled him aside, and kissed him. It certainly took his mind off his ex, for a while at least. They had been together ever since. Not exactly your fairy tale love story, and definitely not the way Maddi had intended for things to happen. You work with what you've got though, right?

Secretly, she had been working on a solo routine to pull out at the comps this year. She felt confident she had a shot at placing, if not winning. Maddi loved dancing more than anything, and all she wanted was to express herself through dance. She could see that that was never going to happen with Dane squashing her ideas, and that was when she made the decision to work on her own routine as well. Maybe Dane would take her seriously once he saw what she could really do.

"I don't know about this."

"Oh, come on, how bad can it be? It's not like we don't know anyone here. We'll just try it for one night, and if you're not happy then we can go back to Latin Flava, okay?" Maddi practically dragged Dane up the stairs to the dance studio. After much discussion, she had finally convinced him to see if perhaps they could pick up some new moves for their routine. She had seen the performance troupe doing their thing at one of the social nights and had been dying to try them out ever since. "They have a unique style. I think we could really use some of it to spice things up a bit." Dane rolled his eyes at her.

"You and your 'style'. What's so wrong with the way I dance?"

"Don't be like that. You know that's not what I'm meaning. I just think we will have an advantage if we broaden our skills." She waited a beat before adding, "If you want to beat Sacha, this is the best way to do it and you know it. She's far too arrogant to take lessons from anyone else." With that, she pushed through the doors and headed towards the teacher to introduce herself. She could hear the whispers as she walked by.

"Is that who I think it is?"

"I heard they're competing again this year."

"What do you think they're doing here?"

"I guess we'll find out soon enough. Oh, I'd love it if they were going to teach!"

Maddi smiled; they were well recognised in the salsa scene after winning last year, and the attention had yet to diminish. She got such a kick out of it. I mean, who wouldn't? Knowing that there were so many girls out there who would give anything to move like her—or have the confidence to do so—and to have a dance partner who could match you. It's not easy to find someone who matches your skill level, style, *and* is the right height.

Maddi had just kind of fell into a partnership with Dane after a drunken night with a bunch of dancers that her teacher had introduced her to. Even after all the drinks, they had still been able to dance together, and well. The rest, as they say, is history.

"All right, everyone! Gather round! We are lucky enough to have some fabulous dancers joining us this evening. For those of you who don't know them, Dane and Maddi won the intermediate section at the Nationals last year." Lisa beamed at them. "Perhaps we could persuade them to do a freestyle for us after class?" There was a lot of clapping and cheering. Amusement danced in Dane's eyes. If there was anything that could bring him out of his mood, a boost to his ego would be it.

"Sure, no worries, we can bust out some moves for ya." He winked at Lisa as he pulled her in for a dip, holding her just long enough for her to get flustered. Always the ladies' man was Dane. It was one of the reasons he had started dancing in the first place—to get the girls. He loved the attention that came with being able to move in time to the beat—you'd be surprised how many guys have no idea of rhythm, and girls were only too happy to share that with him. They were enamoured with his moves and couldn't get enough of him. Of course, he was with Maddi now, but as far as he was concerned there was nothing wrong with a bit of flirting. Maddi got annoyed every now and again, but she knew it was all in fun, she was his after all. Sure, sometimes he would let his hand linger a little too long or pull them in for a cuddle and hold just that little bit tighter, but she was the only one who got to go home with him. The way he saw it, she should feel privileged that he was willing to be with her. She had been a nothing until he came along and made her into the dancer she is today. Other girls would kill to be in her shoes.

Class turned out to be better than they had expected. Dane seemed to be enjoying himself, and Maddi had done as she had set out to do—learn new material. With a bit of luck, she wouldn't have to work so hard to get Dane to come along to a class next time. As much as he'd like to think he was God's gift to dance, he didn't know all the moves. It was impossible when dance is forever evolving.

As promised, they did an impromptu freestyle performance, which was well received. Several girls came up to Maddi afterwards to ask for some tips on styling. She was more than happy to help. One of the things she loved most about them being titleholders, was that she could be an inspiration to others. She never would have made it this far, had she not been taken under the wing of her teacher, Rachel, and now it was her chance to 'pay it forward' and help other girls find their potential. She was good at it too, never making people feel silly for asking, and always finding time to help.

Lisa was watching her do this while she went about closing up for the night.

"You're good with them, you know. Have you ever thought about teaching?"

"Me? It hadn't really crossed my mind. I'm not qualified or anything."

"You don't need to be. They love you. I've seen the way you are with them. These girls would follow you anywhere." She smiled warmly.

"Oh… My… God! You have to!" squealed the brunette standing next to Maddi. "I would love to learn from you! You're sooooo good, and you make it look really sexy. I wish I could get my hips to move like yours," she gushed. Maddi's cheeks flushed as she smiled warmly.

"Well, I can hardly let down my fans now, can I?"

Lisa winked at the brunette. "That's great. When can you start? Maybe you could do a styling class for the ladies, and then you and Dane could teach some partner moves? I know a few of the guys would be keen to learn from him. The studio has had a recent influx of students, and I don't have enough teachers, you'd be doing me a huge favour."

"Sure, sounds like fun. I'll talk to Dane tonight, and we can sort out a time. I'd be keen to start up whenever you'll have me."

The brunette jumped up and down excitedly, "Yay! I can't wait to tell Piper, she's gonna go mental!"

Chapter 2

Maddi stared at her reflection as she tried to mentally psych herself up for her first ever teaching gig. With her ice-blue eyes and bouncing blonde curls, she was a knockout. While most girls would give anything to have her stunning beauty, she felt it was more of a burden. Sure, she could get into clubs at an earlier age and often had guys falling at her feet to go out with her, but it wasn't all it was cracked up to be. She'd had her fair share of guys trying to get in her pants and then some. It had led to the occasional obsessive guy who couldn't take no for an answer. Not to mention the jealousy of other girls. She saw the way they looked at her when she was anywhere near their boyfriends—as if she was trying to lure them away. It made it hard for her to make friends.

Rory was the only one who wasn't paranoid. They had been best friends since preschool, ever since Rory had come to her rescue after one of the other girls had shoved Maddi. She was headstrong and not afraid of anything. Maddi looked up to her, wishing she could be more like that herself. She cared too much what people thought of her, leaving her feeling as if she was never quite good enough.

Pulling on a crimson, merino sweater, she took one last look at herself and headed out the door. It was her ladies styling class tonight, and she wanted to be there early to go over a few things. To say she was nervous was an understatement. She hoped she had enough material to last them the full hour. Dane was going to be there, teaching men's footwork at the other end of the studio. They were to join up in the last hour to teach some partner work—a move of his choice, of course.

When she opened the doors to the studio, she was pleasantly surprised by how many people had shown up already for their classes. The place was packed! She couldn't quite believe that they were all there to see *her*. If only she wasn't so nervous.

Walking over to one of the spare seats, she attempted to calm herself. *Come on, Maddi, you can do this! They all believe in you, so now you have to believe in yourself. You got this!*

She put her dance heels on, grabbed her iPod and headed for the front of the room. She could feel their eyes watching her every move. *Don't trip, don't trip, don't trip.*

Clearing her throat, she began, "Alright, everyone. Ah, if you're here for ladies styling then gather round and we'll get started." She smiled as they moved into position. "Okay, so we'll start with a warmup, just like in class, only we'll be doing ladies steps this time—we are ladies after all." There was a smatter of laughter, and the tension fell from her shoulders. She could do this.

"We'll then move on to some styling techniques that you can use in both your solo dancing and your partner dancing. I'll show you several different options, and hopefully there will be something for everyone."

The music began, and the last of her inhibitions dissipated. She relaxed into the music, her body on autopilot. It was what she loved most about dancing—losing herself to the music. Watching her students in the mirror, she could see there were some others who felt the same way.

"Good. Feel the music, let it wash over you. You need to let go and just let it happen." She found that the more they got into it, the more they gave her. She was pushing them, and they were responding to every instruction, every movement. By the end of the session, they were all glowing.

"Well done, everyone. I hope you enjoyed it as much as I did. Keep practicing those body isolations; we'll be doing more work on that next week. If you are staying for the next class with Dane and I, then have a quick drink, and we'll get back into it."

What a rush! Maddi had never felt more alive than she did at that moment. The pure joy of dancing and sharing that with others; there was nothing quite like it. She couldn't believe she was actually being paid to do this. What more could she possibly want from life?

After a brief drink break and a few words to some of the girls, she was ready to get into the next class. Looking around, she was happy to see some new faces among the 'regulars' who graced the social floors.

"Gather round, everyone! We've got a big class tonight so split into a few rows for the warmup. Make sure you can see us. We'll rotate the rows throughout the song." Dane put on some music and called out the steps. Once he got to the more difficult moves it was easy to spot who the newcomers were. Maddi gave him a *take it easy* look, which he ignored. Any chance to show off. If he kept this up, they'd lose them.

"Alright, for those of you who haven't done a lot of shine work, just continue doing basics if you don't know the steps. Dane can get a little carried away sometimes." Maddi smiled sweetly at him. *That should bring him down a peg or two.* "Now if everyone can grab their partners and make a circle, that would be great. If you don't have a partner, you can slot in between a couple, and we will rotate around so that everyone gets a chance to try the moves." She dragged Dane into the centre of the circle. "This is the move we will be doing tonight, just watch this time, and then we'll break it down." She looked up at Dane, ready for him to take the lead. The look in his eyes told her he was not happy with her. *Oh great, what's he going to do now?* He grabbed her, a little tighter than was necessary.

Smiling, he bent down to whisper, "Don't *ever* try to embarrass me like that again." His smile never wavering, he straightened up and began the move. He changed it from what they had rehearsed, obviously trying to trip her up, but she was prepared and followed him faultlessly, which pissed him off even more. He could be so petty sometimes. Maddi was not about to let him intimidate her; she was a professional and she would teach this class with or without his help. She took the lead and began to break down the move. After each part, she would work her way around the room to make sure everyone was grasping the steps before moving onto the next stage. There were some great dancers; a few even adapted the moves to suit their own style, which really impressed her. One guy in particular stood out from the rest. He'd seemed so reserved at the beginning of class; Maddi had hardly noticed him, but once he started moving, he was beautiful to watch. She could tell he was nervous when it was her turn to dance with him, so she attempted to keep it light.

"Don't think of me as the teacher, I'm just a girl wanting to dance, like all the others." She could see a hint of a smile as he lifted his eyes to meet hers.

"Yeah sure, just a girl who could dance circles around anyone in this room. No, that's not intimidating at all." He grinned back at her, his face lighting up.

God, he's gorgeous! That cheeky grin and those beautiful brown eyes. I could just melt into them. She had to force herself to turn her eyes away and stop staring before she made him uncomfortable. Laughing, she reached for his hand.

"No need to be intimidated, I'm nothing special. Like I said, 'I'm just a girl', now dance with me."

"Yes, Ma'am."

"Ma'am?" She stood back, her hands on her hips. "How old do you think I am?" she joked, "Call me Maddi."

"Alright then, Maddi, I'm Ricki." He pulled her in to begin the move. She had never had to concentrate so hard to follow in her life. The smell of his cologne, the feel of his hands; it was all rather distracting. And he thought *she* was intimidating. She should be calling out for people to switch partners, but she was enjoying herself too much with Ricki. He had such a nice style and was eager to learn. It was refreshing to dance with someone who was in no way arrogant. Dane had been like that once. It's amazing how much a little attention can change someone.

Speak of the devil. When his eyes landed on her and Ricki, his chest puffed out. Not wanting her to be enjoying the arms of another man so much, he quickly put an end to it.

"Right, everyone, I think that's enough for tonight. You all picked that up well. We might have to come up with something trickier for next week to really challenge you. Don't forget there is a social night in town tomorrow at Feeney's Bar from 9pm. I hope to see you all out there." He was laying it on thick, like he always did, trying to charm people. It generally worked too; Maddi had seen it all too often.

"So, I guess that's it then." Ricki pulled away and automatically shifted back into shy awkwardness.

"Yeah, I guess so. Thanks for the dance, you're better than you think, you know?" She touched his arm. "Will you come tomorrow night? Feeney's is pretty cool. They play great music, and the floor is huge." She looked at him hopefully. "We could go over the move some more if you like. Or just fool around… on the dancefloor I mean." Her face was on fire as she tried to laugh it off. *Oh…My…God, could I be more embarrassing?!*

He laughed with her. "Ah, yeah, maybe we could do that." He looked as though he was about to add something, but then his face went red, and he ducked his head as he took a step back. "M-maybe I'll see you there. I should be going…" He turned and walked away.

Odd, she thought, until she too spun around to see Dane glaring. Not willing to get into an argument with him, she avoided his stare and went to grab her things. He had other ideas.

"You two were looking quite cosy over there." He was standing so close behind her she could feel him breathing down her neck. He had a wicked jealous streak, a temper too. She had found that out the hard way one night in town. They hadn't been together long, maybe three months, and had gone out with a group of friends. She had run into a friend who she hadn't seen in a few years, who also happened to be a good-looking guy. A good-looking *gay* guy, who was rather affectionate and wrapped her in a big bear hug, planting a wet kiss on the top of her head. Dane had been furious. He had ripped them apart and pushed him up against a wall, about to start throwing punches, when the bouncers stepped in. Of course, Maddi had been beside herself. She had never seen him flip out like that before, and over something so innocent at that. He had apologised and told her it would never happen again, it was just hard for him to trust after what Sacha had done to him. In the end, she had let it slide. She was not about to throw Ricki under the bus to face the wrath of Dane. She turned towards him.

"Baby," she crooned as she placed a hand on his chest, "are you a little jealous? We were just dancing. That's all." She batted her lashes, a move that always worked. "You have nothing to worry about." Sliding her hand up and around his neck, she pulled him in for a kiss.

Over his shoulder, she could see Ricki quickly turn away and walk out the door.

Chapter 3

"What do ya think? The red or the blue?" Maddi held up two dresses for Rory to see.

"Hmmm… I think the blue, it really brings out your eyes." She batted her eyes, laughing as Maddi threw a soft toy at her head. "No really, the blue is bangin', you should totally wear it."

"Blue it is then," she said as she slipped it over her head. "I don't even know why I'm so anxious, he probably won't even show." She added a necklace and some chunky bracelets.

"Which one? Dane or Ricki?" Rory teased. Maddi had given her a run-down of what had happened the night before—the chemistry with Ricki, the tension with Dane. She didn't want to hurt Dane, but lately he had been getting on her nerves, his anger towards Sacha was getting worse every day and, quite frankly, she was sick of dealing with his tantrums. She had been putting up with it because she thought it would be easier than handling the fall out—she had seen first-hand the way he was with Sacha. But now that she had met Ricki, she found she couldn't get him out of her head. There was something so appealing about him, and not just the way he moved.

"Smart arse. You know who I'm talking about." She slumped down on the couch next to Rory. "Oh, everything is so messed up. What am I going to do?" She buried her head in her friend's shoulder.

"What you're going to do is sort out if you want to be with Dane or not. Ricki shouldn't factor into it. You either wanna be with Dane, or you don't. And I'm pretty sure you don't."

"It's not that simple."

"I think it is. Don't overthink it. I've listened to you complain about how he doesn't show you any respect, keeps undermining you, and how he tries to intimidate you. I know there have been some good times, but from where I'm standing, the bad outweighs the good by far." She stroked Maddi's hair. "You deserve way better than him. I wish you could see how awesome you are, so you wouldn't let him treat you the way he does."

"Aww, you're sweet, hon. Maybe you're right." She hugged her friend tight.

"You know I am. If you were truly happy with Dane, Ricki wouldn't even be on your radar."

"Hmmm, I guess that makes sense." She sat in thought for a moment. Rory did have a point. If Dane truly made her happy then she wouldn't have even noticed Ricki. It seemed to be that Dane was more interested in getting back at Sacha than working on their relationship. Not to mention his little power play the night before. Perhaps a break was what they really needed to get some perspective. This fixation with Ricki could all be because she was frustrated with her own relationship and where it was going. How to bring it up with Dane though? It would have to wait for another night. She could hardly tell him she wanted a break when they were out socialising with friends. It could wait until tomorrow. At least it would give her the time to come up with what she would say.

"Right, enough of this moping, we have to finish getting ready. What're you wearing?" She stood up, dragging Rory with her.

"What? You don't like my trackies?" She pouted, heading for the dresser. "Fine, I guess I'll wear those cute jeans I bought then."

They were the first to get to Feeney's (just like every other week), so chose a table to stow their bags and jackets, then headed for the bar. It was always nice to get there before the crowds and have the dancefloor to themselves for a while. Rory wasn't a salsa dancer, but she could shake it with the best of them. Living with Maddi meant that she knew all the other dancers too and was happy to tag along for a few drinks. Plus, there was the added bonus of getting to scope out the guys. There's something about watching a guy who can dance, the way they are in control, the way their hips move… There was only one word for it: hot.

Sipping their vodka and Red Bull concoctions, they made their way back to the table. A few more people had started to arrive. Maddi recognised the bubbly brunette from her class, and her friend Piper. They waved excitedly.

"Ooh looks like you have some fans," Rory commented as they took a seat.

"Yeah, looks that way." Maddi smiled, "They come to my classes. Actually, it was the brunette, Charlotte, I think her name is, who convinced me to teach." She reached into her shoe bag, pulling out a strappy, silver pair of heels. "So, are you ready to get your dance on?" She winked at her friend as she quickly pulled them on.

"You know it!" Rory grinned. She may not be a dancer, but she knew how to have a good time. The music hadn't changed to salsa yet, so they were dancing *old school* as Maddi liked to call it—the kind of dancing she did before; pub dancing. They were the only ones on the floor, but it didn't bother either of them, dancing was their stress relief. It was the only time Maddi truly felt relaxed.

They had worked up quite a sweat by the time the hordes of people came in. The salsa beats were blasting now, and the floor was slowly filling up. Breathless, the girls went back to their table for a break. Dane was there with a few other dancers. He gave Maddi a brief kiss on the cheek before heading for the bar. They quite often came out by themselves to social occasions. It was nice to have a break from the constant training, and now with the classes they taught, there wasn't a lot of down time. She loved having the opportunity to dance with others and keep on her toes—she knew Dane's moves so well that she never missed a step, and dancing with different people was more challenging.

As she took her seat at the table, a familiar couple caught her eye. Sacha and Jessie were sitting at one of the corner tables.

Oh no, not tonight. This is going to cause a drama that I really can't be bothered with.

She looked around for Dane to see if he had noticed his ex. Judging by the steely look in his eyes and the way his jaw was set, he had.

Maddi slinked over to him, wrapping an arm around his. "Baby, come on, we don't have to do this. Just leave it, okay? We're here to have a good time. Save it for the comps." She attempted to pull him onto the dancefloor, but his muscles were taut with anger, and she couldn't move him.

"She shouldn't be here."

"You can't stop her from coming. It's a public place, Dane."

"Doesn't matter, she knows that we come here. It's our turf."

"Come on, let's just have a dance. Forget about them." She attempted to drag him away again, but his feet remained planted, and his eyes were locked on Sacha's.

Maddi gave up trying to reason with him and went back to Rory.

"Looks like trouble's a-brewing. You okay?" she asked.

"Yeah, I'm fine, just Dane is livid. He's going to do something stupid, I just know it."

"Ah let him, you can't control him. Let's go dance and forget him." She grabbed Maddi's hand and led her away. "Come on, shake that booty! You know you want to." She wiggled her bottom at Maddi, making her laugh. "That's more like it! Now shake it!" Rory flicked her head about to the beat, her blonde and purple streaks catching in the flashing lights. For such a petite girl, she could really throw herself about the floor. Giving in, Maddi let the music take control of her body too.

The peace only lasted for one song. Sacha and Jessie had taken to the floor and were creating quite a commotion. A circle was formed around the couple as they used showy lifts and combos.

Wow, she is a piece of work. Now I see why she and Dane worked so well together.

Maddi attempted to ignore them, but it was near impossible. A hand gripped her wrist and yanked her towards the centre of the floor. It was Dane. There was a fire in his eyes, but it wasn't directed at her. It was all for Sacha's benefit.

He couldn't take his eyes of Sacha. Every move she made, he matched. Maddi was being thrown around like a ragdoll, it was both exhilarating and humiliating at the same time. He was so angry, more so than usual. His holds were getting tighter, his fingers digging into her flesh. She wanted desperately to stop but she couldn't break free. The moves were becoming more and more daring, and the crowd loved every minute of it, cheering loudly.

Only a little bit longer and the song will end, hold on, Maddi, you can do this.

She knew it was coming, the song was building to a finish. Where was he going to go with this? A big dip?

A lift? Either way she was prepared, and then she was going to walk away. She was *not* going to get in the middle of the power struggle between those two. Not anymore. Both so desperate to be *number one* and loved by everyone.

Here it comes… and she was being thrown over his shoulder into a lift similar to that of *Dirty Dancing*. The other dancers went crazy. A thunder of clapping and cheering assaulted their ears as they panted, holding position. Maddi glanced towards Sacha to see them in a similar hold. She was glaring at Dane, and Maddi had no doubt he was doing the same. Angry that they had dragged her into their battle, she slid down Dane's back and began searching for Rory. Hot tears threatened to fall as she fought her way through the throngs of people. Bodies were pressed so close she was starting to feel faint, and then a hand grasped hers and she let herself be led outside. When they broke through, she was surprised to see that it was Ricki who had come to her rescue.

"Hey," he said shyly. "You looked like you needed to get out, I hope you don't mind."

"Uh, yeah, it was getting a bit tight in there. I get a little claustrophobic in crowds." The lie rolled right off her tongue, and he seemed to accept it. Perhaps he hadn't witnessed the whole debacle. "Thanks." She smiled at him as she realised he still had her hand in his. He must've noticed at the same time because he let his hand drop.

"Yeah, sure, no problem."

"There you are! I thought I'd lost you." Rory ran up to them, holding Maddi by the shoulders, "Are you okay?" She searched her eyes then continued on. "He's such a jerk. I can't believe he did that to you." She shook her head, rolling her sleeves up to her elbows. "You were amazing though." She nudged her then stopped when she noticed Ricki standing nervously by Maddi's side.

"Oh, Rory, this is Ricki, he saved me from the stampede. Ricki, this is my best friend, Rory."

"Hey."

"Hey yourself." She looked him up and down. *Nice* she mouthed at Maddi when his back was turned. It was a struggle to keep a straight face. "So anyways, are you okay? You looked a little pissed when you left."

"Yeah, I was. God, he was being such a dick. I've never been so humiliated in all my life." She raised her shaking hands. "He was hurting me. He's never done that before, but… I'll be surprised if I don't have bruises tomorrow."

Ricki lifted his head. "He hurt you? Let me see." He held her hands ever so gently, turning them over to see the red marks Dane had left on her. "I don't care how angry you are, you don't take it out on your girlfriend. Do you want me to say something to him?"

Whatever Maddi was expecting, it was not that. Was this the same shy guy she met the other night? Offering to defend her honour?

"Oh, no, it's okay, I can handle Dane. Thanks though." Smiling, she slipped her hands from his, their eyes locking.

"So…" Rory interrupted their moment, "You're a dancer too, huh? You certainly made an impression on this one." She pointed her thumb in Maddi's direction, grinning.

"Don't listen to her, she was dropped as a baby," Maddi said, while Rory feigned shock.

"How rude!" Laughing, she linked her arm through Maddi's. "No really, like, you like dancing with her? I'm trying to convince her to give Dane the flick." She winked at Ricki conspiratorially.

"Oh, come on, give the guy a break. He's only danced with me once. You don't have to answer, Ricki." She came to his rescue. Tempted as she was to hear what he had to say, she didn't want to pressure him. There was plenty of time for them to get to know each other first.

Chapter 4

"Are you seriously not going to talk to me?" Dane asked, frustrated. It had been three days since the showdown in town, and Maddi had barely said more than two words to him. She was still upset at the way he had acted.

"I don't know what you want me to say, Dane." She sighed as she continued to sort through her wardrobe. Anything to avoid looking him in the eye.

"I just… I just want us to be okay. Please talk to me, or yell at me if you need to. Just don't shut me out." He sounded desperate, and Maddi could feel herself giving in. She hated hearing the vulnerability in his voice. She didn't want to feel sorry for him though, he had acted like a jerk.

"You know you hurt me, right? Like physically." She pulled up her sleeve to show the marks still present on her arm. "You let your hatred take control and you took it out on me. Do you know how scary it is to be held so tight that you can't move? That you can't get away?" The shock in his eyes was obvious as he stared at the bruises on her arms. "It's horrible, Dane."

"I did that to you?" He reached for her arms, but she pulled away. His face dropped. "I'm so sorry, I didn't know. I didn't mean to. I…" His voice trailed off as he paced around the room. "I would never intentionally hurt you, you know that, right? Jesus! I'm so sorry, Maddi." He reached for her hand again, willing her to accept his apology.

"I know you didn't mean to, but you still did it. You need to get over this *thing* you have for Sacha or it's going to take over your life. It's not healthy."

"I know. I can't seem to control it, every time I see her, I see red." He paused before adding, "I'll try harder, Maddi. Really, I will, as long as you're by my side, I know I can deal with it." His eyes pleaded with her. "Please?"

Do it now. Tell him you want a break. Looking into his eyes though, she couldn't do it. She couldn't be the one to hurt him. Sighing, she agreed. "Okay, but if this happens again, I'm out. I can't take any more aggression." He pulled her in for a hug, holding her tight.

"You won't regret this, I promise."

The next evening, they were training at the studio. There was a class on, but they had gone to one of the corners to work on some moves for their routine. Maddi was still uneasy about being so close to Dane. She may have forgiven him, but she certainly hadn't forgotten what he'd done. Every time he grabbed her wrist for a lead, she couldn't help but flinch. Of course, it didn't help that the bruising was still tender. Tension was building between them, and it was making her feel even more on edge.

"You know what? I think I need a break. My arms are still a bit sore." She pulled away from him. "We can do more tomorrow, okay?" Without thinking, Dane grabbed for her, his hand landing right on top of the biggest bruise. "Ow!" she cried out as she wrenched her hand away.

"Oh shit, I'm sorry, Maddi! I didn't mean to do that. Are you okay?"

"I just told you I was still sore!" He lifted his arm to reach for her again. "Just leave me alone, okay?" She rubbed at her wrist as she started to walk towards her bag. She was fighting back tears, determined not to cry in front of everyone.

"Wait, what do you mean? It…it was an accident, Maddi."

"It's always just an accident though, isn't it?" she demanded. "I just need some time to myself, alright? Just give me some space."

"Maddi, please don't go. I wasn't thinking, it won't happen again. Baby, please."

"Actions speak louder, Dane. Just back off and give me some time. I'll call you." She turned her back and went to grab her things. Class had finished, and several people were trying to cover up that they had been watching their little tiff take place. Ducking her head, she quickly made her way out the door, trying to make sense of what had just happened.

She was so lost in her thoughts that she didn't see Ricki rounding the corner. She walked straight into him.

"Oh my God! I'm so sorry. I was away with the fairies." She looked up at him, eyes still glistening with unshed tears.

"Hey, no worries, I wasn't really watching where I was going either." He nodded to her shoe bag in hand. "Are you not coming to class?"

Was that a hint of disappointment in his voice?

"Oh, I've already been up there. I kinda had a fight with Dane so I thought I'd go for a walk and clear my head."

"Oh. Okay then." He hesitated. "Is everything okay?"

Is everything okay?

I did want a break.

"You know, I actually think it might be." She took a deep breath. "I don't suppose you feel like skipping class and joining me? Might be nice to have some company. I could even throw in a few moves, do a bit of practice with you, if you want?"

"Ah, yeah sure, why not?" He smiled warmly as she linked her arm through his.

"Excellent. Let's just walk and see where it takes us." They headed away from the studio, neither of them noticing Dane standing in the shadows, watching.

After walking for nearly an hour, they settled down for hot chocolate in a quaint little café by the river side. There were cosy nooks with cushions, well-worn couches by the fire, and a few intimate tables scattered between. They opted for one of the couches. Maddi kicked her shoes off and curled her feet underneath her.

"Ah, that feels better, those heels are gorgeous, but they are *not* made for walking in!" She laughed, her eyes shining. The fresh air and company had made her feel normal again. Unravelling her scarf and throwing it on the table beside them, she reached for the marshmallows on her plate.

"Making yourself at home, I see," Ricki joked. Maddi poked her tongue at him.

"Of course," she said matter-of-factly as she pointed at his plate. "Are you going to eat that?"

"Help yourself." He grinned as he held it out to her. Unable to help herself, Maddi grinned back. For a rough start, this was turning into a pretty good night. She felt so comfortable with Ricki, and it seemed as though the feeling was mutual now.

"So, are you still going to help me go over that move from last week?" he asked.

"Yeah, sure. We can go over whatever you want, you lead, and I'll follow." She smiled, stretching her body like a cat. "Come on, we can do it over here. There should be enough room." Jumping up and grabbing his hand, she pulled him towards the empty space.

"Here?"

"Yeah, why not? We'll give 'em a show." She winked.

"Ah, okay, I guess." He pulled her in close—careful not to touch her wrists—and began to move. She was surprised that he remembered about the bruising. They hadn't actually discussed what had taken place between her and Dane earlier. It was sweet that he cared and was being so gentle with her though. Maddi had to admit, it made her feel kind of special, like she was a fragile bird he had to protect.

She knew he was worried about dancing in front of strangers; his hands trembling in hers made it obvious. Giving them a squeeze, she willed him to continue. Someone turned the music up, encouraging them. As if a trigger had been pulled, his muscles loosened, movements becoming fluid, confident. He was feeling the music now and moving by instinct.

This is the dancing I want to do. Unplanned, unpolished, natural dancing. This is how it should always be.

She sighed, content to be led wherever the music would take them.

"You look how I feel right now," he whispered in her ear.

"And how is that exactly?" she asked, leaning into his chest.

"Happy… relaxed… at home."

"That's exactly how I'm feeling too. This is so… easy. Like we've done this a thousand times before." She smiled. "I like that. I like dancing with you."

"Yeah, I like it too. Maybe we could practice together sometimes? You know, if Dane doesn't mind, that is." At the mention of Dane's name, he broke contact, pulling them back to reality.

"It's not up to Dane who I dance with. I don't even know if I *want* to dance with him anymore. That's kind of what we argued about today." She paused, trying to find the words. "Dancing with Dane is hard work; it's his way or not at all. He doesn't *feel* the music like we do. It's all about the steps and the flashy moves." She looked into his eyes. "I *really* like dancing with you." His smile reached his eyes, making them crinkle in the corners.

"Come on then, let's give it another go." He spun her into him, making her laugh.

"Oh, go on then." They continued dancing and entertaining the patrons for another hour or so until Maddi's feet were aching. Reluctantly, they gathered their belongings and headed out the door together, hand in hand.

Chapter 5

Maddi skipped up the path to her door, a goofy smile plastered on her face. Ricki had walked her back to the studio and then given her a ride home from there. She had nervously said goodnight, unsure whether he would make a move or not. He hadn't. Just a quick hug before he headed on his way. To say she was disappointed was an understatement, but she understood why it had to be that way. Things were still kind of up in the air with her and Dane. She could hardly expect the guy to throw himself at her.

The lights were off inside, so Maddi moved silently through the house to her room, trying not to disturb Rory. She was a light sleeper and did *not* like to be woken. Maddi's room was at the other end of the house and looked out over the backyard. Pulling her curtains closed, she grabbed some clean pyjamas from her drawer and headed for the bathroom. Her phone vibrated in her pocket. Looking at the screen, she saw Dane's name come up. Not ready to talk to him yet, she hit 'ignore' and left it on her nightstand.

A glass of water, teeth brushed, pyjamas on. Maddi padded back to her room. She picked up her phone and saw six missed calls from Dane.

"Extreme," she whispered to herself, climbing into bed. She switched off her bedside lamp, and a figure appeared outside her bedroom window. She screamed then clamped her hand over her mouth.

What do I do? What do I do?

Her heart was pounding in her ears.

Get up, get up, get up!

She threw her sheets back and crept over to the window. Taking a deep breath, she ripped the curtains open. Dane was standing outside, not moving, just staring back at her, his eyes dark and menacing.

"What the fuck, Dane?! Are you out of your mind? You scared the shit out of me!" she yelled, forgetting about her sleeping flatmate.

He studied her face with a scowl. "Is he here?"

"What? Is who here?" Maddi asked, confused.

"You know exactly who I'm talking about. The guy you've spent all night with."

"Excuse me?"

"Cut the crap, Maddi. I saw you with him outside the studio."

"You've been following me? What's wrong with you? I'm allowed to have friends outside of you, Dane!" Guilt swam through her veins as she said it, knowing full well she'd wanted more with Ricki. She took a calming breath. "Go home. I'm not talking to you like this." She pulled the curtains closed and turned her back to the window. Her phone began to vibrate again. Walking slowly towards it, she saw Dane's name flashing, and anger leapt to the forefront once again. She stabbed a finger at the button and held it to her ear. In a calm but stern voice, she said, "I told you, go home. It's late."

"I just want to talk to you, Maddi. I'm going to keep ringing and banging on the door until you talk to me," he threatened.

"That's really mature. This is crazy, Dane. I don't want to talk to you right now, so please, just go." She hung up on him and switched her phone off.

"Is everything okay, hon?" Rory asked, pulling on her robe.

"Oh shit, I'm sorry, I didn't mean to wake you." She was pacing, her body shaking from adrenaline. The landline began to ring. Maddi looked at her friend, "Don't answer it, it's Dane."

"Okay… This sounds interesting. Since I'm up, you want a hot chocolate?"

"Yeah, actually that sounds good. I don't think I'm going to be getting much sleep tonight."

After a restless night, Maddi had come to the conclusion that Dane was out of control. The harassment had lasted for quite some time. In the end, Rory had had enough and threatened to call the cops. He'd left after that, though his text messages remained constant throughout the night. When Maddi switched her phone on in the morning she had been bombarded with messages:

Dane: *I just want to talk.*

Dane: *Please call me.*

Dane: *I love you, Maddi, take me back.*

Dane: *You can't do this to me! Talk to me!*

Dane: *Or maybe you're too busy with your new boyfriend. Is that it? Talk to me damn it!*

Dane: *I'm sorry, baby. I love you. Call me.*
Dane: *Please?*
Dane: *TALK TO ME!!!!!!!!!*

She had to admit, it was a little scary. She hadn't seen this side of him before. It made her wonder what really happened with Sacha and what he was really capable of. Would he hurt her? *Seriously* hurt her? Something had to be done before it was too late.

Grabbing her bag, she made her way to Dane's place. She left a note for Rory, letting her know where she was… just in case. She wanted to believe that he would be calm, but after last night, she wasn't going to take any chances.

When he came to the door, it was obvious he hadn't slept. He was wearing the same clothes as the night before, his eyes were bloodshot, his hair a mess.

"Maddi! You came! Thank God!" His eyes darted around, checking to see if she was alone. He reached for her. She took a step back. "You still think I'm going to hurt you?" he asked, disappointment evident in his eyes.

"Dane, you really scared me last night. It's not okay what you did, you know that, right? Following me, showing up at my house…" She let her voice trail off. There was a flicker of anger in his eyes, and she took a step back. "I just came to make sure you were okay. I care about you, but I meant what I said. I need some space to work things out. I think we both do."

"Don't tell me what I need! I know what I need, and it's you!"

Maddi sighed, running her hand through her hair. "I'm sorry, Dane. I just don't know what I want anymore. Things have gotten out of control. You're not the guy I thought you were and to be honest, it's kinda scary."

"Don't bullshit me. I know what you *really* want. You want to toss me aside so you can get it on with *him*," he spat at her, suddenly disgusted.

"Believe what you want to, Dane. All I'm saying is that I need a break. No contact. For a week at least, so that I can clear my head and work out what I want."

"What about what I want?" He was trying a different tact now, almost whispering and reaching for her hands again. "Doesn't it matter what I want?"

"Of course it matters, Dane, but you can't force me to stay with you."

"What about our dancing? How will we practice if I can't contact you? We've got the comps…"

"Well… I've got to think about that too. I'm not sure if dancing with you is such a good idea for me. I feel like we both want different things out of it. This business with Sacha is just too much for me to deal with."

"I told you I'm working hard to be better at handling it. I know last night things got a bit crazy, but it's just cos I love you so much. You know that, right? That I love you?"

"Yeah, I do," she whispered. "But it's not enough."

"What more can I do? I need you, Maddi."

This was harder than she thought it would be. Fighting back tears, she turned to walk away.

"I'm sorry, Dane. I just need some time."

He grabbed for her arm, swinging her back to face him. "You don't get to come here and call all the shots and then just walk away! I need you to tell me what you want. You have to choose. Me or him, Maddi? Who's it going to be? The champion dancer or the beginner? You know we could win again. We *will* win. Just pick me!" A mix of anger and desperation in his voice. "Me or him? Just answer and then you can leave." He was crowding her, blocking her path with his arms.

"You're not listening to me! I don't even care about winning anymore. I just want to dance!" She took a breath, meeting his eyes. "If this is how it has to be, and you won't give me the week, then my answer is him." She turned and strode down the drive, trying to get as much distance between them as she could.

Chapter 6

Dane couldn't believe what had just happened.

Surely she doesn't mean that? She doesn't really want to end it with me. She can't. We're meant to be together. I just need to make her see that.

He grabbed his coat and, pulling the door closed behind him, he began to walk.

With no real plan in mind, he found himself heading for the studio. No one would be there at this time of day so he would have the place to himself with no distractions. Once inside, he walked slowly around the room, looking at the trophies and medals the studio had won over the years. He studied the picture of Maddi and him, taken last year, holding their own medals with pride.

He remembered how she had grabbed his hand and kissed him that night. He hadn't expected it at all, but it had felt so right. She had the softest lips, and when she smiled … she took his breath away. If he was honest, she was well out of his league, with her clear blue eyes and drop-dead gorgeous smile, she could have any guy she desired. For a brief moment there, it had been him. And now, he may never get to feel the warmth of her kiss again. The anger slowly built up inside at the thought of not having her in his life. She was the best thing to happen to him, and he had ruined it.

No, *he* had ruined it. If *he* hadn't been involved, she never would have left.

Dane now knew why he had ended up at the studio. All the records of the dancers were stored in the office.

Yes, that's what I'll do. I'll sort him out, man to man. What was his name again? Robbie? Ronnie?

Rifling through the files, he finally came across the one he was after.

"Ricki Macavoy. That's gotta be him. I think I might just pay him a little visit." He scrawled the address down on a piece of paper and shoved it in his pocket. Haphazardly throwing the files together on the desk, he made his way out the door.

"Ricki? You there?" Dane called out as he thumped on his front door. "Ricki!" He stalked around the side of the house, checking for his car. It was still sitting in the driveway. "Come on, man, I know you're in there!" He pounded on the door again, peering through the window. He heard footsteps approaching, and the door swung open.

"Dane?" Ricki glanced side-to-side. "What's up? Is everything okay?"

"Yeah, man, of course. My girlfriend just told me she doesn't want to be with me anymore and she wants to dance with you. So, yeah, everything's fucking fantastic." He raked his hand through his hair as he glared at Ricki.

"Oh… ah… sorry? I guess if that's what she wants…"

"It's what she *thinks* she wants. You must've put it in her head. What did you say to her?"

"I didn't *say* anything. We just talked. That's all. She was upset. You really hurt her, man. She deserves to be treated better."

"And you would know, huh?"

"I know I would never hurt her like you did. Only a coward takes his anger out on the one he loves. She's way too good for you." There was a flicker of pain in Dane's eyes.

"She loves me, and I love her. We're meant to be together," he whispered, as if trying to convince himself.

"I thought you just said…" Dane pushed Ricki up against the wall before he could finish.

"*She's mine.* You got it? I don't want you sniffing around thinking you can score, cos she's going to be with me. Back off, alright?" He was in Ricki's face, breathing heavily, spit glistening on his lips. A manic look in his eyes. Ricki held his hands up to placate him. He spoke calmly.

"I wasn't trying to steal her away, Dane. Like I said, we were just talking. We're just friends."

"It better stay that way then." With one final shove, Dane let him go. "I'll be watching you." He continued to stare as he slowly backed off the porch and strode down the drive.

"Pick up, pick up, pick up!" Ricki had been trying to reach Maddi since Dane had left. It worried him that she wasn't answering her phone. Dane had been acting crazy, but surely he wouldn't have done anything stupid. Would he? There was no way he could have made it to her place on foot by now, but Ricki wasn't taking any chances. He had to see her, and it had to be now. He couldn't bear the thought of her being hurt again. Tucking his phone in his back pocket, he rounded the corner to her house.

"Ricki, hi." Maddi smiled as she answered the door. "This is a surprise."

"Sorry to just show up, you weren't answering your phone, and I was worried that something might've happened to you." He looked up at her. "Are you okay? He hasn't hurt you?" Maddi groaned.

"Oh no. My phone was charging in the other room. I didn't hear it. Sorry to worry you like that." She paused. "I take it you've seen Dane then?" Ricki nodded. "God. He just won't leave things alone." She rubbed at her face. "I'm so sorry you've been dragged into all this." She stepped aside. "You should probably come in and I'll fill you in on everything." Closing the door, she led him to the kitchen where Rory was making coffee. "Better make another cup." She smiled at her friend.

"Ah, let me guess, the cray cray has come visiting you too?" She grinned at Ricki, her brow raised in question.

"Yeah, you could say that."

"You should've been here last night. That boy's not right in the head." She handed him a steaming cup. "Milk and two?"

"Yeah, perfect. What happened last night?" he asked, full of concern.

"Long story short, he saw us talking outside the studio and followed us. He was waiting for me when I got home."

"Yeah, but in a creepy way; you missed out the part where he was standing outside your bedroom window. What a perv!" Rory added.

"Firstly, what part of that isn't creepy? Secondly, he was outside your window? That's a bit stalker-like, isn't it?" He looked at Maddi as she nodded.

"Just a touch."

Ricki frowned. "Wait, I still don't understand why he came here. If he followed us, it's not like he would've seen anything. All we did was talk and dance. We did nothing wrong."

"Yeah, to you and me it would seem that way. But he gets a little jealous. Sacha, his ex, left him for his best friend last year."

"A *lot* jealous you mean. He once bailed a guy up for giving her a hug! And he was gay!"

Maddi nodded as her friend recounted the ordeal. Thinking about it now, it should have been a sign of things to come. She just never would have guessed that it could get so bad, so quick. Maddi wanted to believe the best in people and naively thought that if she was good to others, they would be good to her. Clearly that was not the case for some people.

She looked over at Ricki as he listened to Rory's tale. She was surprised he hadn't run a mile after encountering Dane; others would have. He noticed her watching and gave her a sympathetic smile.

"You've had a pretty rough go of it with him, huh?"

"You could say that. It wasn't always like this though. He used to be sweet and kind, but now his ego and obsession with his ex has taken over." She sighed. "He got it in his head that you were *with* me last night. That's why he was here. I don't know what he would've done if you had been. He's never been quite like this before." She dropped her face into her hands. "Everything is so messed up."

Ricki moved to sit next to her. "Hey, it's gonna be okay," he soothed, awkwardly patting her knee. "We'll work this out."

"Real smooth, Romeo," Rory whispered on her way past.

Ricki, confused, pulled his hand away and stood; clearly uncomfortable.

"I ah… I wasn't trying to crack onto you. I just wanted to make sure you're okay." He looked to the door. "I can go if you want. I don't want to make things difficult for you."

Maddi huffed. "How would you be making things difficult for me? You've been a great friend. It's really sweet that you wanted to check on me." She smiled up at him.

"I just… I mean, you and Dane… I don't want to be in the way. Just tell me to leave, if that's what you need me to do."

"No. That's not what I want at all. I told Dane if I had to choose," she looked into his eyes, "I choose you."

Chapter 7

Maddi didn't see Dane for the next few days, much to her relief. After Ricki had left, she and Rory had spent the day in the kitchen baking cupcakes and cookies. Rory had a flare for cooking, and it helped to keep her mind off all the dramas. Chocolate chip cookies, red velvet cupcakes complete with cream cheese frosting, and of course, the ultimate in guilty pleasures—a huge chocolate mud cake with ganache. Aprons dusted with flour, the girls sat back to admire their hard work.

"Thanks, chick, I really needed the distraction," Maddi said as she swiped a cupcake off the counter and swiftly took a large bite. "These are fantastic," she mumbled with her mouth full.

"No worries, hon, any excuse to bake, you know that." Rory grinned, also helping herself to a healthy slice of cake. "Coffee?"

"Mmmm, sounds good." She grabbed two cups down and began scooping coffee and sugar into each cup while Rory boiled the jug. "I know I shouldn't, but I'm totally having some cake next. You're a damn fine cook. You'll make someone a good wife one of these days," Maddi teased, dodging the tea towel being flicked in her direction. "You love me really." She laughed, grabbing her friend and pulling her into a hug.

"Yeah, yeah, someone's got to." Rory hugged her back. "Speaking of…" She deliberately trailed off, pulling away. "What are we going to do about Ricki?"

"What do you mean?"

"Well, it's obvious how into you he is. And you are clearly smitten by him." She poked her friend in the arm. "Don't deny it, you two are made for each other." She paused for effect. "If I have to choose, I choose you," she mimicked playfully.

"Oh, ha ha, you're hilarious," Maddi retorted.

"I know." Rory grinned, chocolate ganache over her teeth. "Seriously though, I'm just worried that he won't make any kind of move with Dane hovering in the background. You heard what he said, he didn't want to get in the way."

"Yeah, he did seem a little more awkward being around me, and who can blame him? I'm surprised he even came over after dealing with Dane's tantrum."

"The important thing is, he *did* come. You just might have to be the one to make the first move." Rory flicked frosting in Maddi's direction. "You could always cook for him. The way to a man's heart and all that."

Wiping her face and licking the frosting from her fingers, Maddi agreed. "That's not actually a bad idea. I do cook a mean roast."

After the confrontation with Ricki, Dane had needed to cool off. The anger was burning him up inside and he hated the fact that it made him feel so out of control. He had considered going to see Maddi and trying to get her to see sense but thought better of it. If he was going to win her back, he needed to keep his cool. He had already forced her to make the wrong decision once and he was not about to make the same mistake again. No, he had to play it smart this time, show her what she was missing. The hard part was going to be getting her to hear him out. What he needed was a plan, one that would give her no option but to listen.

"He just messaged me and asked me to come over tomorrow to practice." Maddi squealed with delight.

"Chill, hon, I wouldn't exactly call that a date."

"I know, I know. But he must be thinking of me though, right? That can't be a bad thing. And it's the perfect opportunity for me to cook for him," she singsonged as she danced around the room.

"Very true, just don't be upset if he doesn't do anything. I mean, you did only just break up with Dane, remember? And he seems like a decent guy—one who probably won't want to rock the boat."

"Talk about buzz kill. I thought you wanted me to 'make a move'." She held her fingers in the air as quotation marks.

"Of course I do, ya big baby. I just don't want you to get your hopes up and get hurt. I'm just looking out for you. It's part of my duties as your best friend." Rory grinned at her. "That and beating the crap outta anyone who does hurt you." She punched the cushions on the couch to make her point. Maddi giggled.

"You're such a dork."

"Yeah, but it's part of my charm. You know you love it."

"It's true, I do. What would I do without you?" she asked, her giggles turning into laughter as she watched Rory continue her torment on the upholstery. "You'll bust a seam if you're not careful. What did that cushion ever do to you?"

"It looked at me funny," she puffed, her face glowing with a sheen of sweat from her workout.

"And that is why you're my best friend. I'd rather be on your side, than against it."

"And don't you forget it." With a mischievous look in her eyes, she quickly grabbed a discarded cushion and hurled it at Maddi's head. She managed to dodge it just before it made contact.

"Right, it's on now!" she cried, as she leapt up to fend her off. "You're going down, my friend." Grabbing a cushion each, they proceeded to pummel each other until they both collapsed on the floor in fits of laughter.

Chapter 8

Maddi was so nervous getting ready for her 'date' at Ricki's place. She had changed her outfit three times, trying to get the perfect look. Something that would be sure to make him notice her as more than just friends, but in a tasteful way. She settled on her favourite pair of dark skinny jeans with ballet flats—to emphasise her long, lithe dancers' legs, topped with a baby pink singlet and black, lacy shawl. Other than a few stray curls which she clipped back, the rest of her blonde mane was left to frame her face. She added a silver locket and a dab of lip gloss to complete her look.

Twisting and turning in front of the mirror to check herself out, Maddi gave one final twirl before grabbing her purse and phone.

"Well, I'm off then. Wish me luck!" she called out to Rory on her way to the door.

"Luck!" Rory came running out of her bedroom to get a glimpse of Maddi. "Ooh someone looks flash," she sang.

"Is it too much?"

"No, you've got it perfect, hon. Just the right amount of girl-next-door meets seductress." She winked. "Go get 'em, Tiger!"

Maddi laughed. "Grrr!" She made a claw with her free hand as she pushed the door open to leave. "Oh!" She stopped short when she saw that Dane was standing sheepishly on the doorstep, hand up, ready to knock.

"Ah, hi. You look nice," he said awkwardly. "Are you going somewhere?"

"Ah, yeah. I'm out for the day sorry. Did you want something?" She could feel Rory coming up behind her for moral support.

"I was hoping we could go for a coffee or something. Just to talk, ya know?" he stammered. Maddi hadn't seen him quite so nervous before, it was a little endearing. She shifted uncomfortably, unsure what to say to him.

"Well, you're too late," Rory jumped in. "She's on her way out, like she said." She moved to stand slightly in front of Maddi, arms folded defensively.

"Yeah, of course. Where are you going? M-maybe I could come with you? Walk you there?"

"I don't think that's a good idea."

"You'd be kind of a third wheel, if ya get my drift," Rory sneered. Dane looked at his feet then into Maddi's eyes.

"You're going to see him?" His voice broke as he tried to hold it together. The pain in his eyes was hard for Maddi to see. She hated that she was hurting him so much.

"Dane… I…" Her shoulders sagged as she let out a sigh. "Don't make this harder than it already is, okay?" she pleaded with him. "It just wasn't working for us. You know that." She paused. "For what it's worth, nothing has happened with Ricki. I don't even know if it will. We're just friends."

Rory rolled her eyes. "Don't go getting any ideas though. She told you it's over, so you have to deal with it. Give her some space, man." She held her ground in front of Maddi, ready to jump into action, if need be.

"I… I have to go now," Maddi whispered, avoiding eye contact as she made her way down the steps.

Full of anguish, Dane took a step towards her. "Maddi, please…" His voice trailed off as he watched her walk away. Dropping his head in defeat, he let her go.

It took every ounce of willpower for Maddi to keep walking and not turn back. She felt like the biggest bitch in the world. She liked to make people happy, and this was torture for her. Her lips trembled as she fought back the tears that wanted to fall.

I will not cry. I am stronger than this. Just keep walking.

By the time she had arrived at Ricki's place, the tears that threatened had dissipated, and she was back to feeling excited. The butterflies in her stomach were going crazy as she walked up to his door. She puffed out her breath before knocking politely. "Here goes nothing," she whispered to herself.

When he opened the door and smiled that beautiful smile at her, all her nerves went out the window. She couldn't explain it, but he just put her at ease. He stood back, allowing her to walk through to the hall.

"Just down the hall and to the left." He ushered her in the direction of the kitchen. "I didn't know what you needed…" He waved his hand in the air. "The kitchen is at your disposal."

"Right, well let's get started then." She clapped her hands before removing her shawl and throwing it on a chair in the corner. "Do you have a large roasting dish?" she asked while washing her hands in the sink. She set to work, seasoning the lamb leg with salt and pepper and a few sprigs of rosemary. Ricki scrubbed the potatoes, while she chopped the rest of the vegetables. They worked side by side, in a comfortable silence, as if they had been doing this forever. Once everything was in the oven and the dishes were cleared, they sat down with a drink.

"So I thought, if you want to, maybe we could get some movies to watch, ya know, after dancing and eating and stuff." He raked his hand through his hair, something Maddi had noticed him do when he was nervous. She found it adorable, like so many other traits he had.

"Yeah, sure, that sounds great." She smiled at him, trying to make him comfortable. "Did you wanna have a dance before dinner? It'll be a while before it's ready."

"Good idea." He stood up, offering her his hand. "I don't know if I can remember what you showed me the other day…"

"You'll be fine. Believe in yourself. You're better than you give yourself credit for." She moved in close, looking into his eyes. His hands shook as he wrapped them around her. "Just take a deep breath and do whatever comes to mind. I'll follow, no matter what."

Exhaling, he slowly began to move. Cautiously at first, then with more confidence. He was brilliant really. Maddi was impressed with the speed at which he learned and adapted moves. He only needed to be shown once and then he made it his own. His hands were no longer shaking, but strong and steady in his lead. He guided her through lengthy combos and spins, their bodies moving as one at times. Their eyes locked on each other's.

They were interrupted by the sound of clapping. "Wow. Dude, I didn't know you could move like that. That's awesome!"

Maddi inspected the newcomer. He was shorter than Ricki, with dark brown hair spiked up at the front. His eyes were an almost yellowy green; they looked her up and down as he let out a whistle. "Damn, brother, she's a looker." He winked at her.

Laughing, Ricki made the introductions; "Maddi, this is my flatmate Damon, Damon, this is Maddi—the one I was telling you about."

"Nice to meet you, Damon. I'm interested to know what he's been saying about me." She grinned, offering her hand for him to shake.

"All good, I promise you." He chuckled. "Is it you who's responsible for those delicious aromas coming from the kitchen?" He took a deep breath in through his nose. "My stomach's grumbling just smelling it."

"Guilty. I hope you like roast lamb and lots of veggies." She couldn't help but grin at him.

"She cooks, she dances, and she's smokin'—if you don't mind me saying—she's a keeper." He winked at her again.

Maddi laughed. "Thanks, I like to think so." She was distracted by the sound of her phone ringing. "Excuse me, I'd better go see who that is." She jogged into the kitchen where she had left her things. Flashing on her screen was the name 'Dane'. She groaned, pushing the ignore button.

"Everything okay?" Ricki asked when he saw her face as she walked back in.

"Yeah, it's just Dane. I don't feel like dealing with him right now."

"Has he been hassling you again?"

"No, not really. He made an appearance this morning, asking me to go for a coffee to 'talk'. I was on my way over here though, so…" She gave him a shy smile. "I turned him down of course. Rory couldn't wait to tell him that I was coming over here for the day." As if on cue, her phone buzzed again. Having a quick glance at it, she put her phone aside once more.

"He's persistent, I'll give him that. I take it he's the ex?" Damon asked, stretching out on the couch.

"Yep, that's him. He doesn't seem to understand the concept of giving someone space." She wrinkled her nose. "Anyways, I should check on dinner. It should be ready soon." She busied herself in the kitchen, turning the vegetables, basting the lamb, all the while ignoring the buzzing that went off every few minutes. Ricki could see how agitated she was getting.

"Hey, do you want me to answer it? I can tell him to give it a break, see if that helps?" His offer was sweet. Maddi wasn't sure it would work, but she didn't really know what else to do to get through to him.

"Thanks. That might at least get him to stop for today." She handed her phone over, their fingertips brushing lightly, sending a shiver up her arm. "Hey." She reached out. "I'm really sorry you've gotten stuck in the middle of this. I... I really appreciate you being here with me." She leaned in to give him a quick peck on the cheek, making him blush.

"Anytime you need me, I'll be here." He gave her hand a gentle squeeze. "I'd better answer this, put him out of his misery." He held the phone to his ear. "Dane, it's Ricki... No, she doesn't want to talk to you right now... I understand, man, but she just wants to relax for the day without any stresses, ya know? I know you want to talk to her, but you have to give her some space... I don't think that's any of your business... No... We're friends, hanging out, dancing and eating, no big deal... Look, man, you have to let it go. She'll talk to you when she's ready, but it's not going to be today... I'm hanging up now." He pushed the end button and handed the phone back to Maddi. "I don't know how much good it did."

"Thanks for trying anyways." She switched her phone to silent and put it under her shawl. "Out of sight, out of mind." She attempted a smile. "You hungry?"

"You bet." Ricki retrieved the plates from the cupboard and called out to Damon, "Grubs up!"

"Finally! I'm starving in here!" He came running into the kitchen. "Mmmm, smells good. You can come visit anytime you like, Maddi." He swung an arm around her shoulders playfully.

"Be careful what you wish for, I just may take you up on that." She beamed as she dished up a huge plateful of food for him. Lamb, roast potatoes, pumpkin and kumara, along with peas and corn smothered in gravy. The boys were in heaven.

"It's so good," Damon murmured between mouthfuls. "So, so good."

"It really is. I haven't had a meal like this since I left home. I'm with Damon, you can totally cook for us anytime you like," Ricki said, scraping the last of what was on his plate, onto his fork.

"Aww, thanks guys. I'm glad you like it." She smiled contentedly. "Maybe we could do this every week," she suggested.

"I'm totally down with that," Damon said, "Seriously, man, you gotta put a ring on this one. If you don't, I will." He nudged Ricki, chuckling. "I'll take care of the dishes tonight. Leave you two in peace." He gathered up the empty plates and made his way to the kitchen.

Chapter 9

After filling their stomachs, Maddi and Ricki took a stroll to the local DVD store to hire out some movies. The sky was just beginning to darken, and the air was a little crisp, but it felt good to be out. Maddi had checked her phone before leaving and discovered several more missed calls and text messages. Did he not realise how much stress he was putting her under? How much he was pushing her away? All she wanted was to be free from dramas, even if for just one day. Was that too much to ask?

"You okay? You seem far away," Ricki asked, studying her face. Turmoil weighed heavily on her shoulders, and it showed in her eyes. "We don't have to get movies if you don't want to, we can just talk or whatever. Up to you."

Maddi gave a tight smile. "No, a movie is just what I need." She gave him a sidewards glance. "Just promise me, no love stories."

"Aww really? I was so hoping for a good romance," Ricki joked, jostling her with his elbow.

"I knew it! You're a big softy." She latched onto his arm, "You're just a big teddy bear inside, aren't you?"

"Hey, I can be manly when I need to be." He puffed his chest out, strutting like those body builders whose muscles are too big for their bodies. Maddi laughed as she watched him strike a pose in the middle of the street.

"Oh wow, that's super manly." She giggled, once more grabbing his arm and dragging him along the path towards the store.

"Anything to hear that laugh." He looked down at her, his eyes crinkling in the corners as he smiled. She lifted her face to meet his gaze. They were close enough that she could feel the heat radiating from his body. She let out an involuntary shiver.

"Are you cold? Do you want my jacket?"

"Then *you* would be cold. We're almost there, I'm okay." She slipped her hand into his and put it in his jacket pocket, their arms pushed up against each other. "This will keep me warm enough until then."

Once they had selected their movies and made their way back to his flat, Ricki set about making popcorn and grabbing blankets to keep them cosy. The curtains were pulled to keep in what little heat was left in the room. Maddi curled up on the couch, a blanket draped over her legs as she waited for the movie to begin. Ricki sat down next to her.

"Ready?" he asked, fingers poised over the remote control.

"Almost," she said as she sidled in closer. "It's a little chilly, I hope you don't mind." She swung her legs over his lap and leaned her head on his shoulder, pulling the blanket tight around them both. Ricki wrapped his arm around her shoulder.

"Not at all. This is nice." He pressed the button to start the DVD and rested his free hand on her leg. Maddi found it hard to concentrate on anything other than the closeness of their bodies and the smell of his cologne. The realisation that she was within kissing distance made her heart hammer in her chest and her mouth go dry. She tried her best to focus on the film.

"Don't mind me, I'm just going to pick at the leftovers," Damon said as he strolled past. "You guys want anything from the kitchen?"

"A water would be great, thanks," Maddi answered, lifting her head, "Oh and the popcorn! We left it on the bench." She resumed her position, snuggling just a little bit closer still.

There was rustling from the other room, and then quiet voices. Footsteps and then a clearing of the throat.

"Ah, guys? You have a visitor." Damon stood sheepishly in the doorway, with a grief-stricken Dane beside him. His eyes were darting back and forth between Maddi and Ricki, taking in the scene before him.

"I… I just want to talk to you, Maddi, you weren't answering your phone. Can we go somewhere? Please?"

"Oh my God, Dane." Maddi swung her legs from Ricki's lap. "I wasn't answering my phone for a reason. I already told you, I don't want to talk to you. Not today." She waved her hand towards Ricki. "I know Ricki told you too." She folded her arms across her chest. "Showing up here isn't exactly doing you any favours." Her voice shook with wariness as she massaged her temples. "I'm not going anywhere with you, so you may as well leave."

Damon stepped aside with a nod of his head. "I'll show you out then."

"No, I don't want to go yet. I just got here and I'm not leaving until she speaks to me. She owes me that much." He pointed an accusatory finger at her.

Damon placed a hand to Dane's chest. "Mate, this isn't your house. You don't get to decide who stays and who goes. Maddi is our guest, and she clearly doesn't wanna see you, so I suggest you make this easy and leave."

Dane looked down at the hand on his chest then up to meet Damon's eyes. He squared his shoulders, his fists held at his side.

"Guys, stop." Maddi stood up. "There's no need for this. Dane, you have five minutes to say your piece and then you have to go. No more calls, no more texts. I'm done. Okay?" She touched her hand to Damon's chest, holding him back. "Thanks." She smiled.

"Is that a good idea, Maddi? Do you want me to come with you?" Ricki asked gently.

"It's okay, Ricki, thanks. Dane won't hurt me, will you?" she asked, touching his arm to draw his attention away from Damon.

"Of course I won't hurt you! I've apologised for that, and I swear it'll never happen again." He raked a hand through his dishevelled hair. "I just want to talk."

"Damn right it won't happen again. Five minutes and then I'm coming to get her, and you will get off my property." Ricki spoke evenly, holding his hand up, palm out. "Five minutes," he said again.

"I'll be okay," she soothed, "I'll be back soon, you go get the popcorn ready." She forced a smile, trying desperately to calm the situation. A fight was the last thing she wanted. Everything seemed to be escalating out of control. She grabbed Dane by the arm and pulled him to the door. "This better be good," she muttered.

Outside, Maddi stood on the step above, staring blankly at Dane. For someone who only had a brief time allowance, he didn't seem to be doing much talking. He paced back and forth, stopping to look at her before beginning again.

"I thought you wanted to talk?"

"I thought you said nothing was going on with you two?" he finally said.

Sighing, Maddi responded, enunciating every syllable to ensure that it sank in this time. "For the last time, Dane, nothing is going on with *us*," she pointed between the two of them for emphasis, "or with me and Ricki, *not* that it's any of your business. What you saw in there, was two friends watching a movie together. It's cold. I cuddled in for body heat. Oooh big deal." Sarcasm dripped from her lips as she waved her hands in the air.

"Okay, okay." He held his palm up to calm her. "You just looked so cosy, and I miss that. It used to be me that kept you warm. It seems like you've moved on straight away and I meant nothing to you." His eyes glistened with tears.

"Don't you dare try to lay the guilt on me. I've done nothing wrong here." She pointed a finger at his chest. "*You* were the one who was obsessed with Sacha, *you* were the one who used me to get to her and bruised my arms at the same time, *you* were the one who followed me home and harassed me." Her voice was rising with every point she made. "And then you have the audacity to show up here, after being told to leave me alone, and try to ruin my night! Didn't anyone ever tell you, no means no?"

"Maddi, please, I know it's my fault. And I'm sorry. You know I can't think straight around you though. This isn't what I wanted to happen." He dropped his head in his hands.

"Oh really? Tell me, *Dane*, what did you think would happen? Huh? Did you think I'd come running back into your arms because you showed up? Or were you hoping to catch me doing something so that you would have an excuse to start a fight?"

"No! That's not what I want… I just… I don't know! I just went crazy when you wouldn't talk to me, so I had to see you. We were good together once. I miss you." He reached for her hands, begging her, a tear spilling over.

She pulled away from him. "Don't. Touch. Me," she seethed.

The door opened behind her, making her jump. "It's been five minutes. You want me to get rid of him?" Ricki stood in the doorway, his body rigid, hands balled into fists.

"Thanks, I think we're done here." She looked at Dane "You can leave now." Folding her arms, she stood her ground, waiting for him to move. His body sagged in defeat. With one last look at them, he turned on his heel and slowly loped down the drive.

When she could no longer see him, Maddi twisted around to face Ricki. He hadn't moved except to look down at her. She brushed her fingers lightly over his fists and up his arms, feeling each part relax with her touch. When she reached his shoulders, she stepped towards him, leaning her head against his chest. He wrapped his arms around her, cradling her as she cried.

"Sorry." She sniffed, her voice muffled in his shirt. "I didn't realise how angry I was." He stroked her head gently while the other hand slowly rubbed circles on her back. "Did you hear me screaming at him? I kinda lost control for a bit there." She looked up at him, mascara smeared under her eyes. Using his thumb, he softly wiped it away.

"He deserved all of it and more. Damon had to hold me back. It wasn't easy leaving you out here with him, knowing what he's capable of. I don't trust him, Maddi." He felt her shiver against him. "Shit, you must be freezing. Come on, let's get you back inside." He gathered her in his arms and led her back to the lounge where Damon was waiting.

"Everything okay? Do we need to break some bones?" he said, standing when he saw them enter.

Maddi smiled. "Everything's fine now, Damon. Thanks." She gave him a hug. "I can't believe you were going to jump in there for me when we've only just met."

"Purely selfish reasons I'm afraid." Maddi frowned, so he continued, "Well, I could hardly let someone hurt you after you cooked such a mean feed now, could I? Not when you've promised to do it again." He winked.

Maddi laughed, playfully whacking his arm. "I guess it's a good thing I didn't burn dinner then, eh?" She grinned. "So, are we gonna watch the rest of these movies or what?" She plonked herself down on the couch, clutching the bowl of popcorn in one hand, patting the cushion next to her with the other. "What are you waiting for?" Ricki took up his spot beside her again, while Damon lounged on one of the recliners in the corner. The corny jokes on screen had her laughing again, the tension slowly draining from her body.

Chapter 10

When Maddi awoke the next morning, she blinked slowly, taking in her surroundings. She was still on the couch in the lounge, where she must've fallen asleep during the movie. Ricki's arm was draped casually around her middle as he lay peacefully behind her. Her head was resting on his chest, and their legs were intertwined. Sighing contentedly, she snuggled in, taking full advantage of the warmth of his body. She slid her hand over his, careful not to wake him, and closed her eyes once more.

I could get used to this.

She was wearing a beautiful, flowing, white gown and she was dancing a waltz with Ricki. They were circling the dancefloor, their audience captivated. It was almost as if they were dancing on air, their movements were so fluid. He looked impeccable in his suit and tie, and she felt like a princess in his arms.

When the music came to an end, they looked into each other's eyes. He brushed his hand down her cheek, ever so softly, whispering how beautiful she was. He cupped her chin, tilting her face towards his, as he slowly lowered his lips to hers...

"Son of a bitch!" Damon came crashing into the room, waking them from their sleep. "Shit, sorry, I didn't mean to wake you. I stubbed my toe on the door. You would not believe how much it hurts!" He hopped over to the recliner.

Maddi stretched her arms above her head, hoping no one noticed her flushed cheeks. Ricki was still lying behind her but propped up on his elbow, his other hand lightly stroking her hip.

"How did you sleep?" he asked.

"Really good actually. You're quite the hot water bottle." She smiled up at him, her eyes drifting to his mouth as he smiled back.

"Oh good, glad to know I have a purpose." He chuckled. He didn't seem to be in any hurry to get up, which suited Maddi just fine. She couldn't help but think about how different he was from their first encounter. He had been so shy and quiet, barely making eye contact. Now, he lay beside her, joking around, as if it was the most normal thing in the world.

"What's the plan for today?" he asked, brushing a stray hair behind her ear.

"Ah, I hadn't really thought about it. Do you have to work?"

"Not till this afternoon. Are you teaching tonight?"

"Oh shoot. Yes, I am. I guess I'll be working on a class plan then." She flopped her head back onto the couch, her brow creased. Ricki pushed himself up and climbed over her, much to her disappointment.

"Well, I'd better get to work on your breakfast then," he said, as he made his way to the kitchen. "You can't concentrate on an empty stomach. I hope you like eggs!" he called out.

Maddi swung her legs over the side of the couch and padded to the bathroom to freshen up. Borrowing a squirt of toothpaste on her finger, she hastily 'brushed' her teeth to be rid of any morning breath. She splashed water on her face and combed her hair with her fingers. "You'll pass," she said to herself, looking in the mirror.

In the kitchen, Ricki was busy whipping up scrambled eggs on toast, and a pot of coffee was brewing. He was humming to a tune on the radio, unaware of Maddi watching. She was tempted to walk up behind him and wrap her arms around his waist but decided against it. Even though the signs were there, she still wasn't a hundred percent sure he was interested. Unlike other guys she had known, Ricki seemed content to just hang out with her as a friend. It was both refreshing and frustrating.

"Mmmm, smells good," she said, settling on standing next to him at the counter. "Anything I can do to help?" she asked, helping herself to a cup of coffee.

"Nope, all done. Here, I hope you like it." He smiled, handing her a steaming plate.

"Are those chives I see?"

"Of course. I'm not a complete dud in the kitchen, you know." He winked at her. "Damo, eggs are ready if you want 'em."

"Hells yeah!" he bellowed from the lounge. Sauntering in, stubbed toe forgotten, he grabbed a plate and joined them at the table. "Mate, you have outdone yourself." He clapped his hands before digging in. "You know, if you two get hitched, I'm totally gonna live with you, eh? You're cooking is mean." Maddi and Ricki laughed. "You think I'm joking, but I'm not. You're stuck with me forever."

After breakfast, Maddi said her goodbyes and headed back home to prepare for class. She switched her phone back on as she walked and saw a text from Rory asking how her night had been and when she would be home. She quickly scrolled through the other messages before replying. Most were from Dane before he had shown up, she was pleased to see that he hadn't bothered her again after her little temper tantrum.

Starting a new message, she clicked out a text for Rory.

Maddi: *Hey chick, great night with Ricki. He's so adorable. Fell asleep on the couch watching movies. Had a visit from Dane though! Can you believe he showed up there? How rude is he? He was calling non-stop and texting. Ricki even answered and told him to back off, it was sweet. Then he shows up when we're snuggling on the couch. I could've died! I did my nut at him, went a bit mental actually, but he makes me so angry! Anyways, I'll fill you in more when I get home. See you soon!*

"Sending to Dane" came up on the screen. "Oh shit! Oh no!"

Within seconds, her phone was buzzing in her hand. A text flashed up on the screen from Dane.

Dane: *What the fuck Maddi?*
Maddi: *Sorry, that wasn't meant for you.*
Dane: *You spent the night with him?!*
Maddi: *That's none of your business.*

She groaned in frustration. *Way to ruin a great morning, Maddi. Stupid, stupid, stupid!* She switched her phone back on to silent and hurried the rest of the way home. Rory would know what to do.

Rounding the corner, she could see Dane already on her doorstep, arguing with Rory. He must've been on his way there when she had sent the text.

"Un-fucking-believable!" she hissed to herself.

"I told you already, she's not here!" Rory's voice carried across the air.

"Don't bullshit me, Rory! She must be home by now, I know she left his place already. Maddi! *Maddi*!" he yelled, as he attempted to force his way past.

"I'm going to call the cops if you don't back off!" She shoved his chest. Maddi quickly ran up the path before it could escalate any further.

"What the fuck is going on here?" she demanded, staring Dane down. "It's bad enough you showing up last night, now you're harassing my flatmate too?"

"I'm not harassing anyone!" He held his hands up defensively.

"The fuck you're not!" Rory spat. "Coming here, trying to push your way in. You're a fucking joke!"

Dane narrowed his eyes. "You watch your mouth, little girl." He pointed his finger in her face.

"Hey! You keep away from her! This is between you and me, leave her out of this." Maddi stepped in front of her friend. "Now, I suggest you go and cool off, before I call the cops and get a restraining order on you."

"That's a little dramatic, don't you think?" He scoffed, folding his arms across his chest.

"Oh really? I've got plenty of witnesses who will testify that you're stalking me."

"You think I'm stalking you?"

"You don't? What would you call it then?" Maddi asked sarcastically.

"I keep telling you, I just want to talk. I know we could work through this if you would just hear me out."

"Do you hear yourself? You're like a broken record! You keep saying you want to talk, and then when I actually give you the chance, you don't say anything! You're trying to control me, telling me who I can and can't hang out with. You need to get it through your head—I'm not yours to control. I never was!" She took a step back, running her hand through her hair. "Please, just go, okay? I don't want to see you anymore." She felt Rory's hands holding her steady as she swayed with emotion. Determined to make her point, she forced herself to continue her cold stare. His face crumpled. He wiped at his eyes as he backed away.

"Okay. I get it," he whispered as he left. Maddi watched as he broke down when he reached the path. His sobs were destroying her. She turned to her friend and buried her face in her shoulder as she wept. Rory continued to rub her back soothingly as she led her inside and closed the door.

Chapter 11

Allowing herself some time to cry and let out all the anger and sadness she was holding in, Maddi curled up in a ball on her bed. Rory kept popping in to check on her every half hour, bringing coffee and chocolate. After two hours, she'd had enough. Something needed to be done.

"Okay, hon, I know things are shitty at the mo, but you have to pick yourself up. You have class tonight, remember? Don't you have to practice or something? You know it always makes you feel better."

Maddi sniffed. "Yeah, you're right. I don't know why I'm letting him get to me so much." Wiping her eyes, she stood. "I might get some practice in now before I have a shower. Thanks." She gave a small smile. Heading to her iPod, she caught a glimpse of herself in the mirror. Red, puffy eyes, hair dishevelled, still in last night's clothes—she looked a right mess. Ignoring her reflection, she turned on some music, and let it wash over her, cleansing away the negativity of the last few days. Her hips began to sway, her feet soon following the beat. It wasn't long before she was drenched in sweat, puffing. It felt good to be moving. Within an hour she had perfected her lesson plan for the evening and even added some new moves to her choreography.

Satisfied with her afternoon's work, she showered and dressed in a pair of black leggings with pink leg warmers and heels. Her long pink tee hung off her shoulder and she pulled her hair to the side in a messy plait. Her eyes were still a little puffy around the edges, but it was nothing a touch of makeup couldn't cover. At least she no longer resembled a zombie.

Grabbing her bag and dance shoes, she headed for Rory's room to say goodbye.

"Hey! You look much better. See? I told you dancing would help." She winked, a grin twitching at her lips.

"Thanks, I *feel* better. I've made a decision too. I'm going to try and keep things civil with Dane. I don't need all this stress, and I don't want you to be stuck in the middle of it either."

"Fair enough. You know I'll back you up, though, no matter what." She pulled Maddi in for a hug, "But if you change your mind, you just say the word and I'll kick his arse." She sprang back into a fighting pose, waving her arms through the air.

Maddi laughed. "Of course. You'll be the first to know if that happens."

Up at the studio, Maddi was busy setting up when Lisa walked in.

"Okay." She drew out the word as she glanced behind her. "I wasn't expecting you in tonight. Dane rang to cancel. Any idea why?" She folded her arms across her chest.

"Oh, ah. That's probably my fault. We broke up a few days ago." Maddi winced. "Things have been a bit tense between us," she said sheepishly. "I honestly thought he'd still come to class though, sorry. I can still do the partner work without him though, it's just his styling class that will be effected."

"I'm sorry to hear that, Maddi. If you're not up to classes, I understand if you want to cancel too."

"No, no. Really, I'm fine." She smiled to prove her point. "I'm not going to let my personal life get in the way of work. You have nothing to worry about."

"Okay, well, if you ever need to talk…" Lisa squeezed her hand, then she walked back to the desk to get ready for the students who would be arriving any minute.

Maddi turned back to her music, unsure how to feel about Dane not coming. Before she had had too much time to think about it, her students started flowing through the doors, excited babble filling the room.

"I have been waiting for this all week! I love your classes," Piper gushed.

"Yeah, totally! What are we doing tonight? I've been practicing my body rolls," Charlotte added eagerly.

"That's great, guys, I'm glad you like my class. Good to get some feedback." She winked, "You're in luck, Charlotte, body rolls make a feature in the move tonight." The two girls beamed as they took their places in the front row. Maddi called the others to attention and took them through their warm-up. She watched in the mirror, pleasantly surprised at how well the girls were moving compared to the last lesson. "Awesome, guys. I can tell you've been practicing, which is a good thing cos tonight's move is a tricky one." She quickly ran through the combo she had prepared, and then bit by bit she broke it down.

While the girls went through each part, she walked around, giving pointers where needed. "Great work. Make sure you don't roll your shoulders forward when you do your body rolls. You should feel it in your core. Are you feeling it?"

"Yes," they chorused, clearly enjoying themselves. There was a lot of chatter and laughter as they perfected their rolls.

"Alright, let's put it all together. One, two, three… five, six, seven." They rolled and shimmied to the beat, their bodies glistening with sweat by the end. "Nice work, guys. We're almost out of time, so we'll try it to the music and then you can film it to practice at home." She pushed play, and counted them in. "Five, six, seven!" She did it with them the first time, and then stepped aside to watch. Every one of them managed to pull it off, and Maddi beamed with pride.

"You guys rock! I love it! In fact, you're giving me an idea." She smiled, looking at each of them. "I've been working on a choreography for the comps which I was going to do solo, but now I'm thinking, maybe I should have a team. What do you think?" Several girls jumped up and down, their eyes wide.

"Oh my God, yes, yes, *yes*! That would be sooo cool!" Piper was the first to comment.

"Well, anyone interested, send me a text or leave your details with Lisa, and I'll organise a plan for rehearsals. It'll be a lot of work, but it'll be rewarding too."

As the girls flittered about the room or chatting with Lisa, Maddi spotted Ricki walking in. She smiled at him, beckoning him over.

"You're a sight for sore eyes. I couldn't ask a huge favour, could I?" She peered up at him, eyes pleading.

"Oh, I see how it is." He pointed a finger at her. "You don't play fair. How can I turn down that face?" He grinned.

"Oh!" She clapped her hands. "Thanks so much. Dane cancelled on me, and I need you to fill in for him."

His smile waivered.

"Just to demonstrate a move. You don't have to say anything. I'll do the talking. I just, you know, need a body to show them how it looks, and I can't do it by myself." She stood on tiptoes, pressing her hands to his chest. "Please?"

"I… ah… I guess so. Where is Dane?" he asked. "Why did he cancel?"

"Ah, long story short, I had a bit of a run in with him after I left your place this morning, I may have told him I'd get a restraining order on him," she replied awkwardly.

"Are you okay?" He studied her face, noticing the bloodshot eyes.

She nodded. "Yeah, I'm fine. I'll tell you all the details later if you want."

He pulled her in to him, wrapping his arms around her waist and resting his chin on her head. "I'm glad you're okay. We can go for a coffee after class if you want. I have no plans."

"Thanks, that would be good," she said, enjoying the warmth of his embrace. But it couldn't last. They had work to do.

Reluctantly, she pulled away. "We should probably go over that move before everyone arrives." She took his hand. "Come on."

The class went off without a hitch. Ricki had been shaking when they did the demonstration, but once that was over with, he loosened up—even offering help to the men in class. Maddi was glad she had roped him into it.

After packing up, they walked through town discussing the evening's happenings, heading for that same little café by the river. They ordered and looked for a table this time, one a bit more secluded where they could talk in private. They each draped their jackets over the backs of their chairs, talking animatedly until their drinks arrived. Maddi wrapped her cool hands around the steaming mug of hot chocolate and inhaled. The sweet smell instantly reminding her of their last visit to this place. She smiled at the memory.

"What?" Ricki grinned back at her, taking a sip of his drink and leaving a foamy moustache above his lip. "Do I have something on my face?" he deadpanned. Maddi couldn't contain her laughter.

"No, not at all." She smirked as he wiped his mouth with a napkin. "I was just thinking about the last time we were here. It was the first time you seemed to relax with me."

He chuckled. "Yeah, I was pretty nervous when I first met you." He stretched his arms above his head, his shirt lifting slightly. "Not now though." He grinned. Maddi's eyes drifted to the section of bare skin showing under his shirt. Defined abs and a dusting of hair leading a trail under the waistband of his pants. She blinked her eyes back up to his, her cheeks colouring when she met his gaze. Busted.

Ricki shifted forward, resting his elbows on the table between them. "I don't want to distract you from the pleasantries, but you were going to tell me what happened today." Maddi was thankful for the change of direction.

"Yeah, that's right, I was." She slowly recounted the whole ordeal from the miss-sent text to the restraining order threat.

"Wow, that's pretty ballsy of you. I'm impressed. You did the right thing, though." He reached across and placed his hand over hers. "If he shows up again, you can call me, you know that, eh? Anytime of the day or night. If you need me, I'll be there." His thumb was tracing circles around her hand, making it impossible for her to concentrate. He was staring into her eyes with such intensity, she had to look away.

Should I? Shouldn't I?

Taking a deep breath, Maddi looked up at him once more. "Ricki, I… ah… I just don't know what I would do without you. I know we haven't known each other long, but I feel a connection with you that I've never felt before."

"Yeah, me too. And don't worry, I'm not going anywhere." He smiled.

"Good. Because… I was… I mean to say… um, I really… like you." She looked down at their hands and then back to his eyes. "Like, a lot."

Ricki pulled back, his brow furrowed. "I… I really like you too."

"You do?"

"I do, but I think… we're better as friends, don't you? I mean, I wouldn't want to ruin what we have."

"Oh. Okay. I understand." She bit her lip, shaking her head. "No, you're right. Why ruin a good thing, eh?" She forced a smile on her face as she sat back in her seat. Twisting her fingers in her lap, she averted her eyes. How did people do this? Put themselves out there, only to be rejected? It wasn't something she'd really had to deal with in the past, and it hurt more than she cared to admit. Tears welled in her eyes, but she fought them back, determined not to show him how much she was hurting.

"Well, I guess it's time to head home then. I've gotta plan my next lesson anyway…" She stood up, desperate to put some distance between them.

"Maddi, wait. You don't need to rush away."

"No, I'm not rushing. I'm okay. I really do have stuff to do." She offered a small smile.

"Okay then, if you're sure?" His eyes searched hers, and she nodded. He stood with her. "Are we still going to dance this week?"

"Yeah, of course. Maybe we could check out my old studio or something." She wrapped her scarf around her neck and put her jacket on. "Well, I guess I'll just text you tomorrow then." She turned and walked away, head held high, when all she really wanted to do was curl into a ball and hide.

Ricki watched her walk out the door.

I'm such an idiot.

I can't believe I just turned down the most beautiful woman I've ever known.

But how could I possibly begin to explain to her how much she means to me? I'd rather have her in my life than not, and a girl like that will always have guys after her. She'll see eventually. She's way too good for me.

Chapter 12

Maddi didn't text Ricki for a few days. She had been too embarrassed to face him again. It was Rory who had convinced her to persevere with him.

"Maybe he's just scared. He is totally into you. I can see it in his eyes, and from everything you've told me, he's definitely keen. I think you should just forget about that conversation and pretend it never happened. Who knows, maybe he's one of those guys who has to do the asking."

"I guess…" Maddi was unsure, but she didn't really have any other options if she wanted him in her life—which she did. "Okay, I'll text him and see if he wants to dance tonight."

"Good idea."

Maddi: *Hey, you wanna go dancing tonight? I thought we could try a different studio for a change.*

Ricki: *Hey yourself, I was starting to worry that you'd forgotten about me.*

Maddi: *Sorry, I've had a busy couple of days. I'm here now.*

Ricki: *Great! Name the time and place and I'll meet you there.*

Maddi: *7pm, Latin Flava.*

Ricki: *It's a date.*

Maddi smiled at his last message. She knew he didn't mean it that way, but it still made her heart skip a beat. They had so much fun when they were together, and even though she had been mortified at his reaction, she still couldn't wait to see him again. Even if it was just as friends.

Eager to see Maddi and ensure she really was okay with him, Ricki arrived at the studio ahead of time. He paced nervously outside the doors, not ready to go in alone.

Even after helping Maddi with her class the other night, he was still wary of dancing in front of others—especially a whole bunch of people he had never met before.

This was his first time at Latin Flava, and he wasn't sure what to expect. Others were milling about, nodding as they passed. He recognised a few faces from Feeney's Bar, but it didn't help his unease.

"Well, who do we have here?" Sacha drawled, chewing gum loudly and twirling a strand of dark hair around her finger. She looked him up and down with an appreciative grin.

Ricki glanced side-to-side before pointing a finger at his chest. "Ah, are you talking to me?" When she nodded, he stammered, "I… I'm Ricki." He recognised her from the bar. She was the one who had caused the friction between Dane and Maddi that night.

"Hi, Ricki, I'm Sacha," she purred, "You waitin' for someone?" She leaned in close, her minty breath assaulting his nostrils.

"Ah, yeah. Maddi. I'm waiting for Maddi." He stepped back, trying to put some distance between them. She laughed, a deep throaty laugh, and took his hand.

"What's the matter? You scared of me? I don't bite… not unless you want me to." She winked, a wicked gleam in her eye. "Come on, I'll introduce you to everyone." She dragged him through the doors, ignoring his protests.

"I really should stay outside and wait for her…"

"Oh, come on. She's a big girl. I'm sure she can find her way in. This *is* her old studio after all." Sacha threw her belongings on the table. She flicked her jet-black hair over her shoulder and pulled Ricki behind her. She had quite a strong grip for such a petite person.

After circling the room and introducing him to everyone, Sacha escorted him back to the front. She still had hold of his hand and wasn't showing any signs of letting go. Ricki was feeling more and more uncomfortable, but he didn't know how to get rid of her. Standing up to Dane was one thing, but Sacha was different. It didn't feel right to tell her to back off; she was just being friendly after all.

"Hey, you wanna have a dance?" She wiggled her hips in front of him.

"Ah, thanks, but I think I'll just wait for Maddi." He managed to squeeze his hand out of hers and take a step back.

Sacha pouted her full, red lips. "Please?" She pushed herself up against his chest. "Just one little dance?" She walked her fingers up his chest with each word she spoke, her free arm snaking around his back.

She was peering up at him, her eyes wide, and her finger still caressing his chest.

"I… ah… haven't warmed up yet… so… maybe later?" he said, removing her hand and hoping she would accept his excuse.

"The dance would be a warmup, silly." She giggled playfully. Reaching up, she cupped the back of his head and pulled him closer, whispering, "You won't regret it, I promise." Her hips grinding up against him, she slowly moved to look him in the eyes, her mouth grazing his jaw. Licking her lips, she leaned in, tilting her head up.

Panic set in.

"Woah!" Ricki pulled out of her grip. He glanced up, seeing Maddi standing in the doorway, her mouth dropped open and eyes glistening with tears. She quickly turned on her heel and strode out of the studio before he could stop her.

"What the hell was that?" he demanded of Sacha.

"What? Just a friendly peck." She grinned impishly as she watched Maddi disappear. "Oops. Are you two, ya know? Together?" She held her hand to her mouth, feigning guilt.

"That's none of your business, Sacha. Stay away from me," he seethed, gathering his gear as he ran out the door.

Maddi couldn't believe her eyes. This certainly wasn't what she expected when she organised for them to meet at her old studio. If she had known Sacha would be there, she never would have suggested it. And now, here she was, watching Sacha fawn all over the man she had feelings for. Clearly he was quite taken by her too. She was draped across him, holding him close, and he certainly wasn't pulling away.

Is that why he doesn't want to be with me?

Why does it have to be her?

What is it about her that drives men so crazy?

Tears clouded her eyes as she witnessed Sacha lean in to kiss Ricki. She couldn't watch anymore. She turned and blindly ran out the door, only stopping once outside. Her back against the wall, she sank down, dropping her head in her hands.

"Maddi? Is everything okay?" She looked up to see Jessie crouching beside her.

Jessie.

This affected him too. Maddi sighed, shaking her head.

"I just saw something I wasn't prepared for, even though I probably should've seen it coming." She sniffed, hugging her arms around her legs.

"What happened?"

"I don't think you're going to want to hear this." She frowned, looking up at him.

He let out a sigh. "What's she done now?" His brow furrowed. She could see his jaw tighten, bracing himself for the answer.

"I just walked in on her throwing herself at Ricki. She was all over him, Jessie. I'm pretty sure she kissed him." She looked at him apologetically. If it was hurting her this much when she wasn't even with Ricki, it was bound to be tenfold for Jessie. "Sorry."

"Maddi!" Ricki came running from the studio, Sacha trailing behind, chewing her gum with a grin. "Maddi, it's not what it looks like, nothing happened," he panted.

Jessie stood, chest puffed out. "You kissed Sacha?" he demanded, blocking Ricki's view of Maddi.

"What? No!"

"Oh really? Because Maddi saw it happen." He squeezed his hands into fists at his side. "Are you calling her a liar?"

"No, I mean, I can see how it would look that way…" Jessie's fist connected with his mouth, and he stepped back, hands held up. "Shit, man!" He spat blood from his mouth. "I didn't kiss her, I swear! She tried to kiss me, but I pulled away." He looked at Maddi, his eyes pleading, "I backed away, I swear it. I wouldn't do that to you."

She could see Sacha leaning against the door, a smug look on her face as she inspected her perfectly manicured nails. She was enjoying this. "Even if you didn't kiss her, you still let her think she could. She was all over you." Maddi swallowed the lump in her throat, trying to keep her voice steady. "I get it, okay? You don't want to be with me. I just wish you could've chosen someone else to make your point with." She gathered her things and got up off the ground.

"You want me to walk you home? I don't really feel like being here anymore either," Jessie said, still glaring at Ricki.

"Thanks, but I think I want to be by myself right now." She squeezed his hand before walking away. She turned her head to look at Ricki one last time. There was blood trickling from his nose, and he looked as though he might cry—she wasn't sure if that was from the punch or from being caught out. Either way, she hated seeing him like that. It took every ounce of her strength to keep on walking.

Chapter 13

"He did what?!" Rory gasped. "Well, I definitely didn't see that coming." She quickly covered the ground between her and Maddi and pulled her in for a hug. "What a jackarse!"

"I know, right? I feel so stupid," she mumbled into Rory's shoulder.

"What? Why? You haven't done anything wrong." She pulled her friend out in front of her. "This isn't your fault."

"I know. I just wish I hadn't thrown myself at him the other night. He must think I'm so pathetic."

"Are you kidding? You are a beautiful, fun, loving, warm person, and any guy would be lucky to have you. He's just too stupid to see what he had right in front of him." She paused. "If he can't see how amazing you are, he doesn't deserve you." She brushed the hair off Maddi's face, tucking it behind her ear.

"Have I told you how awesome you are?" Maddi smiled.

"It does sound like something you would say…" Rory joked. "I'm happy to hear it again though, ya know, if you feel you need to." She grinned. Maddi giggled, playfully swatting her arm.

"You are the most awesome person in the history of awesome people. Is that what you wanna hear?"

"Well, if you say so, it must be true." She stood, addressing an imaginary audience, "I'd like to thank my

Mum and Dad for making me this awesome. I never could have done it without you guys!" She fanned her face with her hands. "I promised myself I wouldn't cry!" Holding her hands up as if she were examining an award, she continued. "It's nice to be recognised for my awesomeness, and I thank my best friend, Maddi, for bringing that to everyone's attention. I have worked really hard… hey!" She dodged the cushion flying towards her head.

"You're such a clown!"

"An awesome clown though." Rory winked. It was good to see Maddi laughing again. She hated to see her upset and lately it seemed to be that way more often than not. Something would need to be done. It was time to call in the big guns.

As it happened, Damon had had the same thoughts. After Ricki had arrived home with a fat lip and looking sorry for himself, he knew it was time to step in and take action. Someone needed to get these two in line. It was obvious to everyone how crazy they were about each other and how good they were together. Talk about stubborn.

Once Ricki had left for a run the following morning, Damon searched his room for Maddi's address. It wasn't hard to find. Lucky for him, Ricki had been using it as a bookmark. Pocketing it, he made his way to her place.

When Maddi opened the door, she was surprised to see Damon standing there.

"Hey, gorgeous. You got a minute?"

Maddi couldn't help but smile. "Yeah, of course, Damon. What's up?" she asked, opening the door wider for him to walk through.

"Well, I've got this hankering for a roast, and I was hoping maybe you'd be kind enough to rustle one up?"

Maddi frowned. "What? Right now?"

"No, no, no. That would be rude of me. I mean tonight." He winked.

"I don't know if that's a good idea."

"Aww, go on. No one cooks a feed as good as you," he whined, giving her the ultimate puppy dog eyes. "I've got all the food at home. You don't even have to bring anything."

Laughing, she swiped at his arm. "You do not play fair, Mr. How am I supposed to turn down those eyes?"

Damon beamed. "So that's a yes?"

"It's a *maybe*. Does Ricki know you're here?"

"Nah. I thought I'd surprise him. Let him see what's he's missing, if you know what I mean. You two are made for each other."

"Hey, it's him you need to talk to about that, not me. I told him how I feel, but he turned me down." She plonked herself down on the couch. Damon followed suit. "Did he tell you he kissed Sacha?" She screwed her nose up.

"First up, he didn't kiss her. She was getting all up in his face, and when he realised what she was doing, he pushed her away. He was pretty bummed when he came home last night." He paused, meeting her gaze. "He really turned you down?"

Maddi nodded. "Yup. He said we should just be friends. I mean, I get it. I *am* just out of a relationship and all…"

Damon whistled, shaking his head. "That crazy dumbarse! He never told me *that*." He sat back, looking to the ceiling. "That must've been why he was so quiet the other day. He's a sad sack when you're not around." Sitting up and grabbing her hand, he said, "You gotta come tonight. I know he's been a bit of a dick, but he's so into you. I've never seen him as happy as he is when he's with you."

She smiled sadly. "I thought so too, but what am I supposed to do? I can't make him want me."

"Come tonight. *Show* him. Hell, flirt with me—that ought to do it." He chuckled. "I'll happily make him jealous if it gets him to see sense."

Maddi couldn't help but giggle. She lucked out when she met Ricki, gaining Damon as a friend too. "It might be worth a shot." She thought for a moment before adding, "Okay, I'll come. On one condition. I get to bring Rory with me. She's my flatmate."

"Yeah, of course, whatever you need." He stood, "Yes! Roast for dinner!" Maddi laughed and pushed him towards the door. "Alright, alright, I'm leaving," he said, palms up defensively. He pulled her in for a big bear hug, kissing the top of her head. "We'll sort this out, beautiful." He let go and gave a little wave as he sauntered out the door. "Later!"

"So, what's this Damon like?" Rory asked as they rounded the corner on their way to Ricki's. She had jumped at the chance to tag along and meet the burly guy who was playing match maker. Maddi was glad to have the company; she was anticipating a lot of awkwardness tonight. Even with all that Damon had said, she was still hurting from seeing Ricki with Sacha and didn't really know what to say to him. That was one of the main reasons she wanted Rory with her, to keep her calm. It was her superpower.

"You'll love him. He's like a big teddy bear. And he gives the best hugs."

"Ooh, just the way I like them." She rubbed her hands together before looping her arm through Maddi's. They walked up to the door and knocked.

"Hey, beautiful." Damon grinned at Maddi as he opened the door. "You must be Rory, another looker I see," he said behind his hand to Maddi, making her laugh.

"I like this one." Rory pointed her thumb in Damon's direction as she made her way inside. "Nice place you got here," she added, giving the place the once over.

"You were expecting otherwise?" He clutched at his chest, a mischievous grin on his face.

"Well…" She looked him up and down before grinning. "Nah, just kidding."

Damon chuckled. "I see why she's your best friend. You got a good one here."

"I sure do. We've been besties since pre-school." She smiled at her friend. "I guess I'd better make a start on dinner."

She started rummaging through cupboards, pulling out everything she needed. "You two get acquainted, I've got this." She pushed them out of the kitchen and got to work.

As promised, Damon had provided a chicken to be roasted, along with a selection of veggies. Maddi turned the oven on and began seasoning the bird, humming to herself. She then peeled and chopped potatoes, kumara and yams to add to the pan. She found a can of corn kernels in the cupboard, which she tipped into a saucepan with some water, ready to go on later. The only thing left to organise was the gravy, which she would make while the chicken was resting. Feeling pleased with herself, Maddi turned to join her friends in the other room but came face-to-face with Ricki.

"Oh! I didn't hear you come in. You scared me." She held her hand to her chest, catching her breath. He stood awkwardly in the doorway, rubbing his hand through his hair.

"Sorry, I didn't mean to scare you." He offered a small smile. "I heard the commotion in here and came to investigate. Damon didn't tell me you were coming, but I assume he organised this?"

"Oh, um yeah. I guess it's my turn to apologise then."

"No, I didn't mean… I'm glad you're here." He cleared his throat and shuffled his feet, then shoved his hands in his pockets.

Maddi walked over and wrapped her arms around his shoulders. He sighed and circled his arms around her waist, pulling her in close. "I was worried you wouldn't want to see me anymore." He buried his head in her hair, inhaling her scent.

"You can't get rid of me that easily." She pulled away.

"I hope you know, I never meant to hurt you. You mean too much to me."

"I know. It's forgotten. Come on, let's go see how Rory and Damon are getting on."

Ricki raised his eyebrows. "You left them alone together? That should be interesting." He grinned, rocking back on his heels. He threw an arm around her shoulders as they headed for the living room.

Maddi smiled, leaning into his touch. She hated being mad at him. She hadn't realised how tense she had been until they had embraced. In that instant, all her anger had faded away and she realised something. She wanted Ricki in her life. And if it meant they could only be friends, then that's what she would have to do.

They sat down and enjoyed the meal Maddi had prepared, complete with homemade gravy and all the trimmings. Light banter went back and forth across the table as they each devoured their food and raised their glasses to the chef. Rory and Damon monopolised the conversation, each trying to one up the other with witty comebacks. It was all very entertaining.

Maddi caught Ricki watching her a few times. Not wanting to read anything into it, she just smiled and turned her attention back to Rory, laughing at the jokes she was telling. It made it easier to be around him, having Rory there as a buffer. The light-heartedness of the evening was just what they both needed to get back on track.

Once the table had been cleared, and dishes washed and put away, Rory and Maddi wrapped themselves up in their coats and scarves and said their goodbyes to the boys. They linked arms once again and began their trek home. The air was crisp and they could see their breath, but that didn't dim their moods. Rory kept up an endless chatter—she seemed rather taken by Damon, even if she couldn't see it herself.

Maddi smiled as she listened to her best friend talk. Things were going to be okay. Regardless of what type of relationship she had with Ricki, she just knew that they were meant to be in each other's lives, and she was willing to accept it in any state.

Chapter 14

It was quiet in the studio when Maddi arrived for rehearsals with her girls. She had held try-outs the other night and was pleased with the turn out. This was to be their first rehearsal together, and she was planning on pushing them to their limits. The comps were just around the corner, and she wanted them to be performance ready. Competition would be tough, but she knew what her girls were capable of.

Music filled the room as she went through some stretches and warm-ups. Watching herself in the mirror, she slowly went through the routine she had worked so hard on. If the girls could pull it off—and she had every confidence they would—they had every chance of coming out on top. It hadn't been easy picking the team—she hated to disappoint anyone—but she was happy with her choices. The girls who showed dedication and potential stood out to her, and it was clear to see they had been practicing the steps in class. She needed that kind of effort if they were going to compete against the likes of Sacha.

They all began filing in as she continued to rehearse, each taking out their dance shoes and pulling them on before joining her in the centre of the room. Some did their own warm-ups and others attempted to follow her moves. She smiled, glad to see the initiative they had taken. She had chosen well.

"Alright, girls. We'll do a quick warm-up and then start going through the choreography. I will be working you hard today, so be prepared to sweat. We have a lot to get through before the comps, but I have faith in you." She smiled warmly. "Let's get started, shall we?"

After the warm-up, she broke down the first half of the routine. They went over and over it, perfecting each part before moving onto the next. Once Maddi was satisfied they had it well enough, she put the music on for them to try it at speed.

They had been hard at work for two hours before they stopped for a break, each girl dripping with sweat. Even as tired as they were, there were still plenty of smiles and happy chatter. It pleased Maddi to know they were enjoying it as much as she was.

While they were resting, Maddi described her costume and make up ideas and asked for their opinions as well. They decided on a black leotard with cut-outs around the waist and diamantes of different colours, swirled around the centre and up to the neckline. It would have tassels attached to the lower part to create a skirt, of sorts. Fishnet stockings, and glittery make up would finish the look. As the comps were coming up fast, they would have to do a lot of the work themselves, but they were all eager to help.

They continued to dance for another hour, making the most of their studio time. Maddi had them each take turns at standing down and watching everyone else so they could offer support and suggestions. She had them film what they had done so far, and then did the whole performance to the music for them to watch.

The girls invited her out for a coffee afterwards, which she gratefully accepted.

"Okay, girls, great first practice. Now for the hard part… We need a name!" Maddi declared as she sat down at the table with her hot chocolate.

"Hmmm, how about Sexy Senoritas?" Charlotte suggested.

"Ooh yeah, that sounds good!" Piper agreed. "Or Saucy Salseros?" she added with a giggle.

"Latin Divas."

"Salsa Sweethearts."

"What do you think, Maddi?"

"Hmm, it's a tough one, but I'm leaning more towards Latin Divas."

Piper stood up, holding an imaginary microphone, "Ladies and Gentlemen! Presenting the one and only… Latin Divas!" she bellowed. "Yeah, I like it."

Chuckling, Maddi agreed. "It does have a nice ring to it. Latin Divas it is." She raised her cup in the air. "To the Latin Divas." They clinked their cups together, giggling as droplets of hot chocolate and coffee fell to the table.

Grabbing some napkins, Maddi mopped up the mess. She sat back down and looked around at the girls who would be her shadow for the next month. They were such a charismatic bunch, so full of life—it was easy to get caught up in their energy. Even though this was originally to be a solo piece, she couldn't imagine doing it without these girls now. It felt right to have them be a part of it. They added a completely different feel to it, a different element. As if it was always destined to be this way.

Over the next few weeks, the Latin Divas met every second day for two hours at a time, to go over their competition piece. They all seemed determined to make it flawless, much to Maddi's delight. Not once did they complain about the rigorous schedule, some even still managing to make it to Maddi's shine classes on Tuesdays. To say she was proud was an understatement. These girls had come to mean a great deal to her, providing a much-needed distraction from her feelings towards Ricki. They still spent an awful lot of time together, but it was easier to remain friends alone, now that she was pouring her energy into grooming her Divas for the comps.

There had been many evenings spent blinging their costumes with rhinestones of various colours and patterns. They were beginning to look the part. Even their dance heels had had a spruce up with the shiny stones.

Charlotte had perfected their make-up now too, and that, along with their new and improved costumes, made quite an impression. Maddi had to admit, they looked stunning. She couldn't wait to see how it all looked under the glittering lights of the stage.

The morning of dress rehearsal—full make-up and everything—there was a nervous buzz in the air. They all primped themselves in front of the mirrors, excited to see how it all looked once put together. Charlotte was busy applying black and gold swirls around each of their eyes, dabbing glitter and tiny rhinestones into the paint. Piper was clipping everyone's hair back and spritzing them all with a shimmering hairspray.

Maddi pulled her black fishnets up over her long legs, making sure not to twist them. Her leotard had purple, pink and gold rhinestones in the shape of a star right in the centre, with swirls of each colour around it. She gave herself one final look in the mirror before walking out to the studio to get the music set up. Rory and Ricki were both out their waiting—she had asked them to film it and give some critical feedback.

Rory whistled. "Damn, girl! You look fine!" She drew out the last word, adding a finger snap for emphasis. Maddi chuckled, crossing her leg behind her and lowering into a curtsy.

"Why, thank you." She strutted over to where her iPod was set up, flicking through the playlist until she came to the song she wanted. Turning back to Rory, she pointed at the back of the studio. "I'll get you guys to set up over there, that way the mirror is behind us." Rory nodded, slinging her camera over her shoulder. "Hey, thanks heaps for this, eh?"

"No problemo." Rory saluted before marching to the back of the room. Ricki tagged along, tripod and bags in hand.

Maddi watched them go, her teeth tugging at her bottom lip. She had poured her heart and soul into this choreography and other than her girls, no one else had seen it yet. Even Rory had only been privy to small sections of it. She really hoped they liked it.

The 'Divas' were now in the studio with them, all eager to get moving. During rehearsals, they normally danced in front of the mirrors to ensure their timing was perfect. Maddi had wanted them to do it with the mirrors behind them tonight so they would be prepared for the comps. Bad habits start when you rely on what you see in front of you, and it can be off-putting the first time you face a different direction.

"Alright, girls, you ready? Let's show 'em what we got." She grinned, leading them to their positions. "You ready, Rory?"

"You betcha."

She motioned for Ricki to start the music. The girls, already well-rehearsed, didn't miss a beat; they shimmied and rolled their bodies in perfect unison. Every formation change was flawless, every beat hit with gusto. Maddi had never been prouder.

When they had finished, the air was alive with energy as they bounced about. Gathering around behind Rory, they waited eagerly for her to play back what she had recorded. It looked even better than they had imagined. The costumes and make-up glimmered with every move they made, emphasising the fluidity of their movements.

"I don't care what anyone else says, we rock! We're totally gonna win!" Piper jumped about enthusiastically. She and the others all high-fived one another. Ricki wrapped his hand around Maddi's wrist, pulling her towards him.

"Wow. I don't even know what to say. That was… incredible. You're one hell of a dancer." He looked at her with awe. "And that outfit… you're breath-taking." His eyes raked over her body with appreciation, making her feel both exposed and excited all at once. She knew he only wanted friendship, but his eyes were telling a different story.

"Ah, thanks." Her cheeks warmed, and she glanced at the girls to avoid the way he was making her feel. "I should probably get back to them." She nodded her head in their direction.

"Oh, yeah, of course," he stammered.

Maddi turned and walked awkwardly away, as if she had forgotten how to. Suddenly the Divas seemed as though they were miles away.

Breathe, you idiot.

She could still feel his eyes on her as she finally joined the others. Smiling, she offered her congratulations to them all.

"You guys were great! Absolutely ready for the comps. I'm so proud of you!" She beamed. "One week to go!"

Chapter 15

The next night was another social night out at Feeney's Bar. Maddi and Ricki were going together—as they had been for the last few weeks—and they had managed to convince Damon to come along too; his only condition was that Rory came to keep him company. She was only too happy to oblige.

Ricki and Damon were meeting them at their flat and then they were going to leg it to town. As per usual, the guys arrived on time. Both Rory and Maddi were still applying the finishing touches to their hair and make-up, all the while dancing to a 'Hits of the 80's' CD and singing as loud as possible. Not hearing them enter the room, the girls both squealed when the boys appeared behind them, belting out the words to *Girls Just Wanna Have Fun* and gyrating their hips towards them. They collapsed in fits of laughter.

Once they had composed themselves, Maddi and Rory continued primping themselves, with the boys mimicking them in the background.

"Does this colour suit me?" Ricki asked Damon in a high-pitched voice.

"Oh yeah, totally, it like, makes your lips soooo kissable." He puckered his lips and blew a kiss.

"Oh stop! We're not that bad!" Maddi laughed.

"Nah, I guess not. You know you guys don't need all that crap though, eh?" Damon picked up a handful of cosmetics. "You're stunners just the way you are. Either of you could have any guy you want." Maddi looked at him in the mirror with an eyebrow raised. *If only*, she thought. He shrugged, looking sheepish as he realised what he'd said. "Sorry" he mouthed.

"Any guy, huh?" Rory asked. "That sounds like a challenge." Damon chuckled, throwing his arm around her shoulders.

"Hey now, no need to go crazy. They have to get through me first." He gave her arm a wee squeeze before tickling her ribs. Rory pretended to struggle against him, but the contentment in her eyes and the flush of her cheeks made it obvious how she felt. Maddi would put money on the two of them ending up together.

Feeney's Bar was just starting to get busy when they arrived. Rory and Maddi grabbed their usual table by the dancefloor, while the boys went to the bar to order their drinks. There were a number of people milling about but no one actually dancing yet. Rory liked to watch people and wager who would brave the floor first. Feeling bold, Maddi strutted up to Ricki and slipped her hand in his. Nodding to the dancefloor, she raised her brow in question.

"Shall we dance?"

"Yeah, sure." He allowed himself to be led to the empty space. It was one of their favourite songs playing, so he could hardly turn her down. He was getting used to dancing in front of others now, in fact, he didn't even notice them anymore. He had eyes only for Maddi.

Even amongst all her troupe training, they had still managed to find time to practice together, and they always made it to Feeney's for a night out. They were living and breathing salsa and loving every minute of it.

After dancing for four songs straight, they headed back to the table for a breather and a drink. Rory and Damon were deep in conversation.

"Seriously? Any superpower in the world, and you would choose speed?"

"Yeah, you know, like *The Flash*. That'd be awesome!"

"No, I'd much rather be able to fly."

"Boring! Come on, Rory, think about it, I could get the shit jobs done super-fast, and then have more time to do what I wanna do. Hell, I could run to Dunedin and back, just to get you a coffee!" Rory rolled her eyes, but she couldn't help but laugh.

"Okay, that would be pretty sweet," she conceded as she turned towards Maddi and Ricki. "Hey, guys, having fun?"

"Clearly not as much as you two," Maddi said with a smirk on her face. "You gonna get up and have a dance too? You should drag this one with you." She poked Damon in the arm as she took a seat. "You could show him a thing or two."

"You know, I just might." Rory stood and, latching onto Damon's hand, she pulled him out of his seat. "Come on, let's see what you can do, Speedy." Maddi could hear her giggling as they made their way out to the middle of the packed dancefloor. She swivelled back to face Ricki, her eyes alight with glee at the thought of those two together. Ricki laughed.

"I know that look. What are you planning?" He leaned in conspiratorially. As he bent his head towards her, she caught a glimpse of the door and sucked in a breath. Dane had just entered the bar with a group of dancers. She shouldn't have been surprised; they had both frequented the place before everything went to custard, she just hadn't seen him in weeks. True to his word, he had in fact left her alone—not even coming to their classes. Maddi had welcomed the break from him. The classes with Ricki as her partner ran smoothly, and her dance troupe was gaining momentum. Things had been great without his overbearing presence in her life.

As her smile waivered, Ricki followed her gaze. He too had relished the respite from all the aggression Dane had caused. He had quite enjoyed hanging out with Maddi free of stress and interruptions. It was selfish of him, he knew, but he had been hoping Dane wouldn't return.

Reaching across the table, he held her hand, rubbing circles around her wrist with his thumb.

"You okay? We can leave if you want." He looked at her with such concern, she thought she might burst into tears if she didn't look away.

"No, it's okay. I'm not going to let him ruin our night." She forced a smile on her face. "You want to dance again?"

"Of course." He smiled warmly, trying to ease the tension emanating off her. They made their way to the middle of the crowded floor, hiding among their peers. Ricki pulled her in close and, with his thumb and finger, he tilted her chin upwards.

"Forget about him. We're here to have fun, remember?" He kissed her forehead before spinning her out to his side. Maddi squealed, grinning. It worked every time. Spinning her back into him, he took her through several long combos, keeping her on her toes. She was puffing and bright-eyed by the end of the song.

"Thanks for that. I needed it." She smiled, walking back to their table once more. Rory and Damon were at the bar getting more drinks. The bartender placed a round of shots on a tray and handed it to Rory.

"I, ah, thought you could use one of these." Rory gestured to the drinks as she placed the tray on the table. "Bottoms up!" They all downed their Sambuca's in one go, slamming the glasses on the table after.

"Aagghh! I forgot how much I hate that stuff!" Maddi waved her hands in the air and jumped up and down. She shook her head, reaching for another. "Salute!" They lifted their glasses in the air before shooting them back.

"Woo! I feel good!" Rory stuck her black tinged tongue out. "We should dance some more!" She grabbed Maddi's hand and proceeded to bump and grind right there on the spot. The boys were only too happy to watch, even yelling out encouragement.

"Yeow! Shake it, baby!" Damon whistled, clapping his hands together, enjoying every second of the show. Maddi and Rory exchanged a knowing look. Grinning, they both pounced on him until he had no choice but to join in.

"If I'm dancing, so are you!" He gripped Ricki's arm and dragged him up too. They continued dancing in their own little circle, trying to out-do each other. It wasn't long before they were collapsing on their chairs, cheeks sore from laughing so much.

"That… was… so… fun!" Rory panted, clutching her knees as she tried to catch her breath. Maddi was rubbing her face.

"I haven't laughed so much in ages!"

"Me neither!" Damon added, gulping back the rest of his vodka. "You guys want another?" He shook his glass in the air. There was a chorus of yes, so he stumbled to the bar.

"I'll go help him," Rory offered.

"You wanna get some air?" Ricki yelled over the music.

"Sure, that'd be good." Maddi stood, seizing his hand. The burst of fresh air on their faces felt amazing, instantly cooling them down. Maddi dropped her head back, closing her eyes as she let the wind blow over her.

There was a little cough from beside the entrance. Dane stepped out from the shadows.

"Ah, hi." He waved. "How've you been? You look good." His eyes raked over her body and back to her face. "Real good."

Maddi's skin crawled. It was as though he was undressing her with his eyes. He had a hint of a smile on his lips, enjoying her discomfort. "I was hoping I might run into you tonight. Thought maybe we could have a drink, ya know, for old times' sake."

Maddi didn't want to do *anything* with him, let alone have a drink, but what could she do? It would be rude to turn him down.

"Um, yeah, sure," she mumbled. Still holding Ricki's hand, she could feel his body tense up against her. She gave his hand a gentle squeeze, looking up at him over her shoulder. "One drink." She mouthed before turning her attention back to Dane. He rested his hand on her lower back to guide her through the doors and to a table away from the busy crowd. Glancing around, she saw Rory with a look of loathing on her face, her hands balled into fists. She marched towards them, but Maddi shook her head. She needed to do this.

Chapter 16

He pulled a chair out for her. She perched on the edge of it, her hands in her lap.

"Still drinking vodka and Red Bull?" he asked, pulling his wallet out of his pocket.

"Um, yeah thanks." She smiled weakly. Fidgeting in her seat, she kept looking back to her friends. Rory was glaring at the back of Dane's head as he ordered drinks at the bar. Ricki was pacing beside the table, glancing up at her every few steps. Damon looked as though he was trying to calm him down. As nervous as she was to be here, she was relieved to know that her friends all had her back if anything went down.

Dane, ignoring Rory's stare, carried their drinks back to the table. Ordinarily he would have stopped and chatted to others, but tonight he had his eyes fixed on Maddi. It unnerved her. She had to keep breaking eye contact; it was just too intense and confrontational. There was something about the *way* he watched her that put her on edge.

Handing Maddi her drink, he took his place opposite her, pulling his chair in close. He reached for her hand across the table. Slowly stroking her thumb with his.

"I'm so glad you're here, Maddi. You look amazing, as always."

Shifting uncomfortably, she glanced up at him. "Thanks," she said. She shifted her hand, but he held firm.

"I never told you enough how beautiful you were… *are*. You should be told every day how brilliant you are." He continued stroking her hand and staring into her eyes. Unsure what to say, Maddi gave a little shrug and smiled. "Never were good at taking compliments, were you?" He chuckled.

"Your compliments usually required an expectation on my part," she said calmly, lifting her eyes to meet his once more. He pulled his hand away, leaning back on his chair.

"Ouch." He held his hand to his heart. "I deserved that, though. You're right. I've done a lot of thinking these past few weeks, and I realise what a dick I was being."

"I'm listening." She folded her arms across her chest.

He grinned. "You're gorgeous when you're being stubborn, ya know?"

"Quit it with the compliments, it's weird. You said you wanted to talk about something?"

His brow furrowed. "I wasn't a complete jerk, was I? I mean, you *were* happy with me at one point, weren't you?" His eyes pleaded.

Sighing, Maddi replied, "There were good times, in the beginning at least. I was just so tired of being compared to *her* all the time and treated like my opinions didn't matter."

"Who?"

"What?"

"You said you were tired of being compared to *her*. Who was I comparing you to?"

She rolled her eyes. "Oh, come on, Dane. Like you don't know." He stared blankly. "Um, your ex, Sacha. Ring any bells?"

He sucked air in through his teeth. "You thought I was comparing you two? Maddi, she cheated on me and stole my work. Why would I compare you to *her*?"

"You didn't trust me because of her. You didn't let me have any say in our dancing because of her. She was the third party in our relationship, and I let it go on too long. Constantly hearing about your boyfriend's ex and how good a dancer she is eventually takes its toll."

Dane rubbed his hands over his face and through his hair to rest on the back of his neck.

"I don't know what to say. I guess I just never thought about it that way. I was so scared of losing you that I got a bit too controlling, I guess. I'm so sorry, Maddi. I never meant to make you feel that way."

"I know you didn't."

"I'd like to make it up to you." He rested his elbows on the table, tapping his fingers to the beat.

"That's not necessary. Let's just put it in the past."

"I think it is necessary. We'll never get past it if I don't make amends."

"Wait, what?"

"Well, we can't move forward in our relationship if you still hold it against me, can we? So, I have to do something to make it better." He continued drumming his fingers on the table, watching them as he did so.

"What relationship, Dane?" She swallowed, the hair on the back of her neck standing as she waited for his response.

"What do you mean? You and me." He motioned between them. "I did what you asked and gave you space to think, and I did the same. I think we can still make it work. We can go back to where we left off." He smiled and reached for her hand again.

She pulled away, flicking her eyes to her friends' table to check they were still there. She could see all eyes watching their every move. "Ah, I think you are a bit confused. We can't go back to where we left off."

"No." He shook his head. "You're right, we want to move forward not backwards."

"No, that's not what I mean." She looked him in the eye to make sure he really heard her this time. "I don't want to go back at all."

"I gave you nearly a month to think about things, and I'm willing to work on stuff, so what's the problem?"

"Dane, I don't want to be with you. That's kind of a big problem, wouldn't you say? This space that I've had has been a welcome change. For the first time in ages, I feel like *me* again. I've got other things going on in my life now. And… I'm happy." She whispered the last part, afraid of hurting him.

"No. That's not right. You said you just needed space and time to think. You didn't say we were over for good." He frowned.

"I told you I didn't want to see you anymore. Remember?"

"Yeah, but I… I went away. I gave you what you needed." He was speaking slowly and clearly, making sure she heard what he was saying.

"I think maybe you got the wrong idea. I'm sorry, Dane. I don't think we're good together. Please accept it." She stood on shaking legs. "I have to go."

"That looked intense," Rory said as Maddi sat down.

"You could say that." She glanced over at Dane, who was still staring after her with a confused look on his face. "He seems really mixed up. I don't know if he's talked himself into thinking we're still together or what."

"He thinks you're still together? Oh, that's fucked up."

"Hmmm," Maddi agreed. She was worried about him. Something didn't seem quite right about him. It was as though something had snapped. She hoped he would be alright.

"You okay?" Ricki asked as he joined them at the table.

"Yeah, I'm fine." She smiled. "I could really do with another drink though."

"On it!" Damon called on his way to the bar.

"That bad, huh? How about a dance to make you feel better?" Ricki offered his hand, which she accepted.

"You read my mind." She allowed herself to be led to the dancefloor, wanting to forget what had happened.

Dane looked on with a sadness in his eyes. He stood up and strode out the door.

Chapter 17

After an hour of letting loose on the dancefloor, Maddi and Ricki sauntered towards their table, ready for a much-needed break. They dripped with sweat and panted as they tried to catch their breath. The discussion with Dane was a distant memory now.

Their table was empty, save for a few scattered shot glasses from earlier. Maddi noted that Rory's bag was missing, and so was Damon's jacket.

"I think we've been ditched," she stated with a grin, waving her hands at the empty spaces.

"I think you might be right. Do you think they hooked up?" Ricki asked, returning the grin.

"I'd bet money on it." Maddi laughed. "About bloody time too!" She threw herself into one of the chairs. "I'm knackered."

"Yeah, me too. You want another drink, or you want to go home?" he asked, reaching for his wallet.

"Maybe one more before we hit the road."

"Okay, be right back," he said as he walked up to the bar once more. Maddi watched him go, thinking about how much she enjoyed being with him. His friendship meant the world to her. She knew she was probably setting herself up for heartbreak, but there was something intoxicating about him—she couldn't give him up. As if he could feel her watching, he turned and smiled back at her, that lop-sided, sexy grin she loved so much. She grinned back, wiggling her fingers in a small wave.

He casually strolled over with their drinks in hand, never taking his eyes off her. Surely he felt the chemistry between them? The way he looked at her—as though there was no one else in the room—undid her. Her heart fluttered in her chest the closer he got. She would give anything to feel his lips on hers, even just briefly. Trying to calm her heart and head, she rummaged through her bag, looking for something to distract herself with. There was no telling how much longer she could sit idly by and not throw herself into his arms.

"Here you go, Maddi." He handed her a drink, which she happily accepted, taking a large gulp.

"Thanks, I needed that." She bent down to untie the straps on her dance shoes. She put them into their bag and reached for her street shoes. She wiggled her toes. Street shoes always felt so foreign after she'd been dancing. Dance heels mould to the shape of your feet, so the fit was as close to perfect as you could get. She could dance for hours on end with them on and not bat an eye. Sitting up again, she took another mouthful of the cool liquid.

"You okay?" Ricki asked.

"Yeah, I'm fine. Just tired I guess."

"You want to head off?" Ricki stood, gulping down the last of his drink and offering her his hand.

"Um sure, if that's okay." She quickly sculled back the rest of her vodka and grabbed hold of his hand. She found herself admiring those strong hands of his. They were much bigger than hers, the perfect size for hers to fit into. The rough calluses on his palm were a contrast to the softness of the rest of his hand. She couldn't help but wonder what they would feel like on her body.

"Shall we go?" he prompted. Maddi nodded, snatching up her bag and shoes before following him to the door.

They walked hand-in-hand—as they did so often now—all the way home. Anyone could be mistaken for assuming they were, in fact, a couple. The way they interacted with each other screamed intimacy.

Maddi giggled as they discussed their missing friends and their whereabouts.

"Do you think they're at your place or mine?"

"Who says they even made it that far?" Ricki joked. Maddi swatted his arm.

"Ewwww! Mental pictures!" Ricki chuckled at the face she was making. "God, I hope they're actually in a bedroom and we don't walk in on them." She shook her body in disgust. Ricki tipped his head back, laughing even harder. Maddi frowned at him, the corners of her mouth lifting slightly as she fought off the bubbling laughter inside, until she could no longer contain it. She clutched her stomach as she laughed, tears forming in the corners or her eyes. Every time she stopped, she'd look at Ricki, and they'd both burst into yet another fit of laughter.

"Oh God. I haven't laughed that much since… since I don't even know when." Maddi swiped the tears away as she began to laugh again.

Ricki smiled, nudging her with his elbow. "Shall we carry on? I'm sure they'll be done by now." He winked.

"They better be." She grinned up at him. She ever so elegantly, straightened, reaching for his arm to steady herself as the ground swam before her eyes. "I may have had a little more to drink than I thought." She giggled.

"Come on, you." Ricki swung his arm around her shoulder to hold her up as they continued their trek home. Taking advantage of the opportunity, Maddi snuggled in closer.

"Mmm, you're warm." She wrapped one arm around his back and the other around his waist to meet. His grip tightened, securing her in his embrace.

"Let's get you home to the fire." He quickened his pace. They continued walking in silence, the cold making their breath visible. Ricki slowly rubbed his hand up and down Maddi's arm, keeping her warm. A part of her wanted to slow down, so that she would have an excuse to cuddle into him for longer. It was so nice and comforting being in his arms. He wasn't a big guy, but she felt safe when she was with him. Something she had never felt with Dane.

"Almost there. I'll come in and stoke the fire for you, if you like," he offered. Maddi smiled; she had lived there with Rory for a while now and they had managed fine by themselves, but the sentiment was nice anyway.

"Sure, that would be great. I could even rustle us up a hot chocolate while you do that."

"Sounds great. That should be enough to keep me warm before I head back to mine." He smiled down at her. Tempted as she was to offer for him to stay over—on the couch of course—she thought better of it. Things had been ticking along nicely between them and she was scared to put herself out there again. Instead, she just returned his smile.

The house was dark with no signs of life. Maddi rummaged through her bag for the keys.

"Looks like they made it to your place after all." She grinned at him.

"Looks like it." He followed her in, closing the door behind them. "Lucky me," he deadpanned. They walked into the lounge where the fire still had a faint glow. "I'll get this baby pumping. Can't have you catching a cold so close to the comps now, can we?" He got to work bringing in some large logs of wood and stacked them beside the fire for her. She switched the jug on and grabbed two cups down off the shelf, scooping some cocoa into each one. Hunting through the cupboards, she triumphantly brought out a bag of marshmallows that had been hiding in the back.

"Look what I found." She waved them in the air before dropping several on top of their steaming mugs. She joined him on the couch in front of the fire, the flames flickering light on their faces. She handed him his mug.

"I had a really good night tonight."

"Yeah, me too."

He pulled his lips to the side, peeking sideways at her. "So… Do you want to talk about the whole Dane thing? It looked kind of intense."

"Um, yeah, it was." She frowned. "He was acting as though we were still a couple. Like he was just giving me space and then we'd be good as new."

Ricki whistled low. "Wow. That *is* weird." His brows furrowed. "You think he got the message and he'll leave you alone now?"

"I don't know. I hope so." She paused, staring into her drink. "I do feel sorry for him though. He seemed so confused. It's like his brain won't let him process that we broke up." She blew on her hot chocolate before taking a sip.

"Hmm. I don't like it. You need to keep your doors locked, just in case. I don't really like the idea of you being alone." He looked into her eyes, concern all over his face. It was the perfect opportunity to ask him to stay, but again, she couldn't bring herself to do it.

"I'm sure it'll be fine. He didn't hang around at the pub after our talk so maybe it has sunk in now." She nodded as if agreeing with herself. "Anyway, it's late, I'm sure he went home already. And Rory is generally here with me. I'll be fine." She stared into the fire, deep in thought.

"If you're sure?" He placed his hand on her knee, once again looking into her eyes. "You can text me or call anytime, okay? Even if you just get scared." He squeezed her knee. "Promise me you'll call me if you need me."

"I promise." She smiled, placing her hand over his.

Taking advantage of the dark night, Dane huddled down in a bush outside Maddi's place. He had wandered aimlessly through the streets after they had had their talk and eventually found himself at her house. The lights were off, so he knew she wasn't home yet.

He couldn't shake the feeling that something was going on between her and Ricki. They looked far too cosy at Feeney's. Determined to get to the bottom of it, he stalked around the outside of her home, looking for any signs of his presence. He tried each of the doors and windows to see if he could get in, but they were all shut tight. In the end he had settled for hiding in the bushes, waiting for her to come home.

When he saw them arrive, all cosy in each other's arms, his blood had boiled. He positioned himself behind a bush outside the lounge window. He needed to see for himself if there was anything there. He needed to see what he was up against. She had said she didn't want to be with him anymore, but he wasn't going to accept that. He needed her. She *belonged* to him.

From his vantage point, he could see them happily playing house; getting the fire cranking and having hot drinks on the couch—the couch where he and Maddi had shared many drinks together—how cosy. It all looked innocent, until he saw Ricki put his hand on her.

And the look in her eyes was one that he was all too familiar with. He should know; it was the way she used to look at him, back when they first got together. It was a slap in the face. The sudden stabbing pain in his heart made him catch his breath. He clutched at his chest, unable to turn away from what he was witnessing. They sat that way, holding hands, for quite some time before Ricki finally stood up to leave. He watched as Maddi walked him to the door and saw them embrace before saying goodbye.

Dane waited until he was sure Ricki would be far enough away, then he slowly, silently stepped out of the shadows and walked calmly to the door.

Chapter 18

Ricki unlocked the door to his place, jingling the keys loudly to prepare anyone in the house of his arrival. The lights were on, and empty wine glasses sat on the table, with an open bottle of wine between them. Rory's jacket was draped across one of the chairs, and her heels had been discarded by the couch.

He threw his jacket on the coat hook and switched the jug on to make a coffee. Taking a cup down from the shelf he then searched the drawer for a clean spoon. After coming up empty, he rinsed one that had been sitting in the sink. Scraping the last of the coffee into his cup, he scrawled himself a note on the whiteboard to buy both coffee and spoons.

The sound of giggling came from Damon's room as he walked past. Ricki had a little chuckle to himself as he retrieved his phone from his pocket to ring Maddi and let her know they were there and check that she was okay on her own.

He walked into his room, shutting the door behind him as he punched in her number. She didn't answer. She must've gone straight to bed after he left. He sent her a message, filling her in so she wouldn't be worried. He sat on his bed, sipping his drink and kicking his shoes off. The walk home had woken him up, so he grabbed his book from his nightstand, turning to the marked page.

He settled back against his pillow, but before he could get too comfortable, his phone began to vibrate.

Maddi's picture flashed up on the screen. Grinning, he answered.

"Hey, did you get my text? … Maddi?" The sound was muffled as if in a pocket. She must have butt dialled. "Maddi?" he said louder, hoping she would hear his voice and pick up.

"…Dane, please don't. You're scaring me…"

"Maddi?" he asked again, sitting up. His heart thundered in his chest.

"…Don't touch me!"

"Oh shit!" He quickly hung up the phone and grabbed his shoes, banging on the wall to alert Damon.

I never should have left her.

He thumped the wall again.

"Kinda busy, man!" came Damon's response.

"Sorry, but this is an emergency!" he yelled. "Maddi's in trouble. We need to get over there now!" He heard them scurrying around as they threw clothes on and ran out to join him.

"What's going on?" Rory demanded, pulling her heels on once more.

"I don't know. I just got a call from Maddi, and all I could hear was her pleading with Dane, she sounded really scared. We've got to go!"

"Oh my God! Maddi!" Rory's face went pale.

After Ricki had left, Maddi had started getting herself organised for bed. She had just changed into her nightie and was heading for the bathroom when she heard a knock at the door. Smiling to herself, she quickly ran to open it, her robe flowing open behind her.

"Okay what did you forget?" she asked before realising it was Dane at the door and not Ricki. "Oh, hi," she said. A wave of unease washed over her. She clutched her robe around her, shifting from one foot to the other.

"Hey, Maddi." Dane raked his hand through his hair. "I was in the neighbourhood…" He drifted off, his eyes wandering until they rested on the small spot of bare skin he could see at the top of her robe. "I really had to see you. I didn't like where we left things at Feeney's, you know?" He stepped towards her, looking into her eyes.

Backing away, Maddi said, "Dane, it's late. Can this wait? I really just want to get to bed." She reached for the door, but his hand flew out and stopped her.

"It won't take long, Maddi." He took another step forward, blocking the doorway with his foot.

"I… ah…"

"I need you, Maddi. I always have. You need me too." He was staring down at her, slowly easing his way further into the house.

"I'd like you to leave please," she said, raising her chin in defiance.

"I'm not ready to leave yet. We have things to sort out." He looked back to where her robe was loose, a hint of a smile playing on his lips.

"Dane, please don't. You're scaring me. I'd like you to leave."

"I would never hurt you, you know that, Maddi. I just want to love you." He reached a finger out to stroke down the side of her face. Maddi froze in fear. He continued to drag his finger down her neck, towards the top of her robe.

"Don't touch me!" she screamed, swatting his hand away. His face twisted in pain.

"I need to show you, Maddi. Would you just stop fighting me and let me show you?" He was breathing down on her, one hand grasping her wrist, while the other pushed the door closed behind him. "I just want to love you," he whispered again, cupping his hand behind her neck, leaning in as if to kiss her. He grinned as he began dragging her towards her bedroom.

"Dane, please. Don't." She fought against him, trying frantically to get out of his grip, but he was much stronger than she was. He kicked the door to her room open and led her inside. Tears were streaming down her face as she continued to beg. "You don't have to do this."

"Yes. I do. You need to see. I have to show you. We were made for each other." He pressed on her shoulders, making her sit on the edge of the bed. He grabbed the collar of her robe and slipped it off her shoulders, revealing her silky nightie. "God, you're so beautiful," he whispered, leaning down to nuzzle into her neck. Maddi closed her eyes.

"I love you so much, Maddi. You'll see." He kissed her neck and up towards her mouth. She turned her head away. Sighing, he stood and pulled his shirt off over his head. Maddi scrambled up the bed, away from him. "Now, now." He crawled up to follow. "Don't be a little cock tease." He slammed his fists against the mattress. Panting, he grabbed her ankles and yanked hard, bringing her back to the edge of the bed and underneath him. "Stop fighting me, goddamn it!" He pinned her wrists above her head with one hand, while the other was busily undoing the zipper on his pants. Maddi squirmed beneath him, but his grip was too tight. She was trapped.

This is it. This is actually happening right now.

"Dane, please, don't do this," she begged once more, looking into his eyes, hoping to see a glimmer of empathy.

"I'm not going to hurt you. I promise." He smiled, lowering his body onto hers, making it impossible for her to move. She turned her head to look out the window, trying to shut her brain off so that she didn't have to be present while this was going on. Her silent tears were pooling on the bed sheet as she gave up fighting.

"Look at me, Maddi," he whispered into her ear, but she couldn't hear him anymore. "I said, look at me!" He clutched her face in one hand and pulled her to look at him. Her eyes had glazed over. She was no longer present. There were voices in her head, calling her name. They kept repeating it over again.

"Maddi!" It was Rory. It sounded so real, like she was in the room with her.

"Get off her!" Dane was lifted and thrown up against the wall. She could see Ricki holding Dane by the neck, he reared his hand back and punched him in the face, again and again until Damon grabbed his arm and pulled him away.

"Ricki, stop! He's had enough."

"Oh God!" she cried, her hands covering her mouth as she shook her head. Rory rushed in and jumped on the bed, wrapping Maddi in her arms, rocking her back and forth.

"Shhhh, hon. It's over. You're okay," she kept repeating through tears of her own. "You're okay." Maddi gripped onto her friend, scared to let go. She stared at the limp body of the man who had only moments before been tormenting her. His face was slick with blood from his nose. It looked broken.

"Is… is he dead?" she whispered.

"No. He should be, but no," Damon said, finally releasing his friend. "Let the cops sort him out now, Ricki."

"Yeah, yeah." Turning to Maddi, he asked, "Are you okay?" Those three little words were enough to let loose another onslaught of tears. Her face crumpled, and her body sagged with the weight of what had just happened. Ricki ran to her, enveloping her in his arms, holding her up.

"I'm here now. I won't let anything happen to you. You're safe." He kissed the top of her head, resting his cheek against her. "You're safe now."

"I'll call the cops before he wakes up. Damon, keep an eye on him," Rory said as she ran from the room.

"Of course." Damon stood over Dane's body, watching for any signs of movement.

"How did you know?" Maddi sniffed.

"What?"

"How did you know he was here? That I needed you?" She lifted her head to look up at him.

"Your phone. You rang me. I could hear you… him…"

"But I didn't…" She looked at her discarded robe. "I must've knocked it. It was in my pocket."

"Good thing you had it on you."

Rory walked back into the room. "They're on their way." She sat next to Maddi. "I'm so sorry."

"What for?"

"If I hadn't disappeared on you, you wouldn't have been here alone." Rory looked down at her hands as she twisted them together on her lap. "I'm so selfish."

"You couldn't have known this would happen. You're allowed to have a life," Maddi said, slipping her hand into her friend's. "I knew something wasn't right with him. I just never thought he'd do… something like this. I just can't believe it." Her eyes glistened with fresh tears at the thought of what very nearly happened.

"You're safe now. I won't let him near you again," Ricki said tightening his grip.

Dane came to but was kept under the watchful eye of Damon. Ricki had led Maddi out of the room and to the warmth of the lounge, while Rory made her a hot drink.

Damon held Dane hostage until the police arrived quarter of an hour later.

Maddi had given her statement, and Dane had been taken away. He had attempted to apologise to her as he was being escorted to the awaiting vehicle, but she had turned her back on him. He had had enough chances as far as she was concerned.

Damon joined Rory in her room, and Ricki curled up beside Maddi on the floor in the lounge. She couldn't face her room. Ricki held her in his arms all night. She clung to him, calling out in her sleep as she re-lived her nightmare, and every time, he would whisper that she was safe, stroking her face to calm her. It pained him to know that this could have been avoided if he had just insisted on staying with her like he'd wanted to.

Chapter 19

The day of the comps was looming, and Maddi was only just recovering from her ordeal with Dane. She was fine during the day, but the evenings were when she found it hard. The sight of her bedroom would send her into a panic attack, so she barely went in there anymore. Rory decided that a change was in need, and after recruiting the boys to help, they moved all her furniture out and into the spare room. She bought new bed sheets and duvets and rid her drawers of any reminders of Dane. When they were finished, she felt much better.

The boys stayed again. Maddi didn't seem to be able to sleep without the extra company. As a thank you to her friends for all their help, she shouted fish 'n' chips and beer for tea. Rory and Damon had gone out to pick it up and stop at the DVD store on the way back. They were planning on just a quiet, relaxing night at home, before the pressure of the comps the next day.

Maddi was a little nervous about how she would go with her performance—she wasn't exactly feeling sexy. Far from it in fact. The thought of prancing around in front of all those people, in an outfit that leaves little to the imagination, was more than a little daunting. She wasn't sure she could do it, but her girls were counting on her. They had worked so hard to get here, she couldn't let them down now. The Divas didn't know what had happened, and unless she wanted to divulge that information, she had no choice but to go on.

After the movie, Damon and Rory retired to her room for the night—they had become virtually inseparable these days. Maddi was so happy for them; she had never seen her friend like this before.

It must be love, she thought with a smile.

Ricki and Maddi headed for her room. They climbed into bed and assumed their usual position—Ricki on his back, with Maddi tucked in under his arm, her head resting on his chest. Just having him near her was enough to make her feel safer. Even though Dane had been arrested, she couldn't shake the fear that he would return, and Ricki seemed more than happy to keep her company each night. He gently stroked her arm.

"Are you ready for tomorrow?" he asked.

"Mmm, I guess so. I'm a bit… I don't know…" She paused, trying to think of the words to say. "It feels weird to be dancing in those clothes, and in that way. You know, after…" She trailed off.

"What do you mean? You're a fantastic dancer and you look great in that outfit."

"I feel very exposed in it. You don't think it's a bit… provocative?" She looked up at him.

"Maddi, you don't think what happened was your fault, do you? Because I can tell you right now, it wasn't. You did nothing wrong. You can't shut yourself away and hide. He wins then." He lifted her chin. "You are gorgeous, and the best dancer I know. You and your girls have put so much into this. You deserve to show everyone your routine and how hard you've worked. Don't let him take that away from you."

She smiled a sad smile. "It's just. I'm scared. What if he gets out? What if he shows up?" Her eyes welled up, tears spilling over her lashes and onto his chest. Ricki sat up, pulling her with him.

"That's not going to happen. I won't let him come near you again. Okay?"

"Okay." She sniffed, nodding. "Thank you."

"Hey, I told you, any time you need me, I'll be there, and I meant it. You're stuck with me." He smiled down at her.

She smiled back. "You're so good to me."

The next morning, Ricki snuck out of bed early and prepared a massive feast of scrambled eggs, sausages, and hash browns for everyone. He had a pot of coffee brewing and had even set the table up with placemats and cutlery. The whole shebang. When Maddi walked out to see what he was up to, she was pleasantly surprised.

"What's all this?"

"It's the day of the comps. I thought you could use a decent feed to help get you through the day." He grinned at her. "Coffee?" he asked, holding the pot in the air.

"Mmm, please," she said, taking a seat at the table.

"Is that coffee I smell?" Damon stumbled out to the lounge wearing only a pair of boxers.

"Yeah, it is. Get it while it's hot," Ricki said, "And put some clothes on, man." He laughed. Damon gave him the finger as he made his way to the bathroom.

"Here you go, beautiful." Ricki placed a plate down in front of Maddi and one for himself. "I hope you're hungry." He ran back to the kitchen to retrieve the coffee and milk. "Can't forget that now."

"Something smells A-Maze-Ing!" Rory called as she bounced out of her room and into the lounge. "Did you do this?" she asked Ricki as she swiped a piece of toast from the table, taking a bite.

"Sure did. Help yourself, there's plenty."

"Mmm, don't mind if I do." She helped herself to a plate and proceeded to load it up. Ricki whistled.

"Damn, girl, you can eat. You are perfect for Damo." He laughed. Rory just smiled and threw her crust at him.

"Hey, a girl's gotta build up her strength for all the bedroom gymnastics going on in there." Ricki almost choked on his coffee.

"Too much information." He laughed. Damon came out of the bathroom, scratching his head.

"Babe, have you seen my shirt?" He searched around the lounge. "Never mind." He dragged a tee out from under the couch, pulling it over his head before joining them at the table.

"Rory's just telling us about the bedroom gymnastics." Maddi grinned.

"Oh yeah? You should see it. Damn, my girl can bend." He winked and blew a kiss in Rory's direction.

"Thanks, babe," she said, catching his kiss and holding it to her heart. She jumped up and sat on his lap, dragging her plate with her. Damon circled an arm around her waist and then reached over to steal one of her hash browns. She promptly smacked the back of his hand with her fork. "Hey, I need that. This," she motioned to her body, "doesn't bend without sustenance."

Chuckling, Damon grabbed his own plate and started piling food on it. "Fair call," he said.

"So, Maddi, I had an idea I wanted to run by you," said Ricki.

"Yeah, what's that?"

"Well, I thought that maybe we could dance together. Tonight." He looked at her, a twinkle in his eye.

"At the after party? I wasn't planning on going to that."

"Okay, firstly we need to address that. Why wouldn't you go?"

"You know why."

"When you guys win—and you will—your girls are going to want to celebrate. With you, their leader. You have to go. Even if it's just for an hour. And of course you'll dance with me there." Maddi put her fork down and clasped her hands over her plate.

"I guess…"

Ricki rested his hand on hers. "I know." He looked at Rory for support.

"You guys are totally gonna nail it tonight, hon. We'll be there to watch and cheer you on too, won't we, Damo?"

"Wouldn't miss it."

"What I actually meant though, is that maybe we could enter together?" Ricki stared into her eyes, waiting for her reaction.

"We have nothing prepared though," she said.

"That's not entirely true. We've been working really hard, and I know we can do it. You and Dane were registered to compete already, so…" He winced, bracing himself for her reaction. "I changed the names on the form," he said hesitantly.

"You entered us already?"

"Ah, yeah." He looked down at his plate, suddenly not hungry anymore. This was not the reaction he'd been hoping for. "I thought it would be a nice surprise for you. I asked Lisa if we could change the names, a few weeks ago."

"I… I don't know."

"Maddi." He pulled his chair closer to hers and clasped both her hands in his. "We can do this. Do you trust me?"

"Yes." She nodded, biting her lip to stop the quivering.

"Hey." He lifted her chin. "We can do this," he said again.

"You guys will be great!" Rory added. "We can go shopping and find you a new dress to wear if you want. We still have a few hours before you need to head down there." Maddi smiled at her friend. "Oh, this is so exciting! Shopping!"

"Thanks, Rory. That would be great." She squeezed Ricki's hand.

"So, that's a yes?"

She nodded. "I mean, I guess." She bit her lip, nodding. "Yes. It's a yes."

Down at the auditorium there was a hive of activity. Groups were rehearsing on the stage to get their positioning, while others were backstage putting their make up on and slicking their hair back. Rory had tagged along to help with the preparations before she had to head back to her seat with Damon. With her help, Maddi had found the perfect dress for her performance with Ricki. It was a fitted, royal blue halter dress with a plunging backline. There was a split up each side, revealing her long, muscular legs. It didn't have the bling of her troupe's costume, but she looked stunning all the same. Rory was busy applying her false lashes and then all she needed was a splash of lipstick. She had decided to wear her hair loose for her dance with Ricki, before pinning it up for the Divas performance.

She had to admit, she was glad Ricki had entered them, she was even starting to feel excited. The thrill of being on the stage again—she'd forgotten how that felt. She hadn't thought about entering with Ricki before; he'd shown no interest in competing, so it had come as quite a surprise when he'd announced it this morning. Their category was meant to be choreographed, but she trusted Ricki to lead her through.

"Ten minutes to curtain time!" came a call from off-stage somewhere.

"That's my cue to leave," Rory said, jumping up and down. "Knock 'em dead, hon!" She gave Maddi a quick hug before running out the door to where the audience was sitting. Maddi peered out through the tiny window in the door to the auditorium. It was a full house. Every year, more and more people came to see the show.

"There you are," Ricki said, reaching for her hand. "Wow! You look… amazing." He stood back to admire her.

"Thanks." She blushed. "You look pretty good yourself." She brushed some fluff off his shoulder, smoothing his top.

"Shall we head to the stage? I think we're third up." He offered his arm.

"Sure." She smiled, sliding her arm into his. She took a deep breath to calm the somersaulting butterflies in her stomach.

"What are *you* doing here?" Sacha stepped in front of them. "I didn't think you'd be competing this year, what with you and Dane going your separate ways." She looked back and forth between Ricki and Maddi, her eyes settling on Ricki's chest. "You look good, baby," she crooned, running her hand down his arm. "This look suits you."

"Who said she wasn't competing?" he said, removing her hand.

"I guess I just thought that maybe you'd be tired of her by now." She pouted, leaning into him. "Ready for a real woman, ya know?" She winked.

"Maddi's more woman than you'll ever be." He glared at her. Sacha threw her head back, laughing.

"Oh please. Her? Come and find me when you get bored with little Miss Girl Next Door." She turned on her heel and sashayed away from them.

"God, I hate her," Maddi said through her teeth.

"You and me both," Ricki replied. "Don't let her get to you. We got this." They stepped up to the stage doors.

"Five minutes to curtain! Can I have Sacha and Jessie, Nicole and Rob, and Maddi and Ricki up to the stage first. The next three couples line up down here." He pointed to the space beside the stairs. Everyone rushed around, applying the final touches to their costumes. Some were still rehearsing in the changing rooms, while others sat against the wall, psyching themselves up for their turn on stage. "The list with your order is on the wall over there. Make sure you are ready to go on ahead of time."

"Ladies and Gentlemen! Welcome to the annual National Salsa Championships! I'm Lisa, and I'll be your host tonight. We have three fabulous judges from around the country who have come to watch all our talented performers. Please give them a round of applause!"

Lisa carried on making introductions and listing the order of the show. "Right, so without further ado, it pleases me to announce the first competitors in the advanced section; Sacha Barrett and Jessie Jameson!" The crowd applauded as they took to the stage. Sacha, in her ruby-red dress and fishnets, took up her starting position, giving one final look over her shoulder at Maddi before the intro to their music came on. Maddi recognised it as the same song that they had danced to at Feeney's when Dane had dragged her onto the dancefloor. In fact, the moves they were doing were very much the same. She couldn't believe it. She nudged Ricki, pointing.

"It's the same," she whispered excitedly.

"What do you mean?"

"Their routine. I've seen it before—I practically danced it at Feeney's with them." Ricki watched more closely.

"Oh my God, you're right." He grinned. "We have this in the bag." He rubbed his hands together in glee. He already had a fair idea of what he was going to do when they got out on the stage, including a few surprises he had up his sleeves. While Maddi had been training with the girls, he had been doing some solo practice himself. He had allowed some gaps in the music where he figured they could just freestyle it—they had a great connection after all, but the majority was all planned out. He couldn't wait to see the look on her face when the music started.

"Give it up for Sacha and Jessie!" Lisa called out as she walked across the stage, clapping. They made their way off stage, Sacha brushing up against Ricki as she went past.

"Beat that," she said smugly.

"Please welcome our next competitors! Nicole Marshal and Rob Burdett!"

"Good luck!" Maddi said as they rushed past. They had been in the intermediate section last year. She remembered thinking they were good enough to be in advanced. She cheered them on from the side.

"What are you doing?" Ricki asked.

"Being a good sport." She smiled. "Quite frankly, I don't care where we get in this competition, as long as Sacha doesn't win."

He chuckled. "Sounds good to me." The closing notes of the song rang out. "You ready?"

"As I'll ever be."

"Let's hear it for Nicole and Rob!" The audience clapped and cheered. "And now we have Maddison Lee and her partner Ricki Macavoy!" Lisa bellowed into the mic.

"This is it!" Maddi took a deep breath, plastered a smile on her face and walked out onto the stage. Ricki spun her out and back in to their starting position. The music started. Maddi looked up at Ricki when she realised it was her favourite song. He winked at her.

They began to dance, moving through various combinations and even breaking away to a solo shine. They quite regularly did that when they were dancing at Feeney's, so she was well prepared for it. Ricki pulled out some slick moves she'd never seen before, then pointed at her for her turn. Without hesitating, she threw herself into a deep lunge to the ground, then straightening her legs she rolled her body upwards, followed by an intricate footwork shine. The audience whistled and whooped. Rory hollered, "That's my friend!" which made her smile. They finished off with a lift they had been practicing, where she went up and over his shoulders, sliding down and around his body like a snake. She landed on the floor, her arm extended as she beamed out at the room full of people. She'd done it.

"Make some noise for Maddison and Ricki!" Lisa cried out as she took to the stage once more. Ricki pulled Maddi up and walked her backstage.

"Oh my God! That was amazing!" She threw her arms around his shoulders, and he lifted her in the air.

"I know! What a rush!"

"Nice work, guys!" Piper came running up. "We were watching from the curtains. Did you hear us yelling?"

"I thought that was you." Maddi grinned. "You guys all ready for our section?"

"You betcha! You should probably get organised, though. I don't think there's a lot of time between sections."

"I'll meet you back here after, okay?" Ricki said, squeezing her hand once more before she took off for the changing rooms. "Break a leg!"

The Divas huddled in a circle backstage, waiting for their name to be called.

"Okay, girls, I want you all to know that no matter what happens out there, I'm so proud of you guys. You have made my dream a reality, and I can't thank you enough." She smiled at each of them. "Right, hands in."

She held her hand in the centre of their little circle, and they all placed theirs on top. "Gooooo Divas!"

They strutted out from behind the curtain into their formation. The music began. For a lot of them, this was their first time on stage—not that you could pick it. Just like in rehearsals, they were flawless.

There's something about being under the lights in front of an audience that makes you want to perform to the best of your ability. It gives you such a rush. Hearing the audience cheer and whistle is such a confidence booster.

And then, as quickly as it began, it was over. The Divas held their final positions as the audience continued to clap. Maddi gestured for them to stand, and they strutted back off the stage, hips swaying as they went.

"Alright. Can we have all competitors back on the stage please?" the stage manager yelled. Everyone excitedly moved to the stage door, and up through the curtains, gathering in their groups or couples. Maddi stood between Ricki and the Divas, an arm draped around Piper, and her other hand holding tightly onto Ricki.

The curtains pulled open, and Lisa took centre stage.

"And now, for the moment you have all been waiting for! The results! Judges, have you made your final decisions?" She looked to the judging panel, and they all nodded in agreement. The piece of paper that held their fate was delivered to the stage. "Before we announce the winners, can we have one last round of applause for all our wonderful competitors?" Lisa clapped, turning to smile at everyone behind her.

"And, of course, to our lovely judges for travelling to be with us today, and for being the ones to make the tough decisions." More applause from the audience.

"First up, the teams! We had so many entries for this category, and such variety. I don't envy the judges having to decide this one! In second place, we have…" She paused for effect. "The Latin Divas!"

"Oh my God!" Maddi exclaimed in shock. Her hand flew to her mouth as she looked up at Ricki.

"I knew you could do it!" He smiled at her. "Go get your medal." Piper was almost pulling her arm off as she clung to her, bouncing about excitedly.

"We did it!" she kept screaming.

"Come on up, girls," Lisa said, smiling warmly at Maddi. They shook hands with each of the judges and received their very own medals. They stepped to the side, waiting to hear who had won.

"Congratulations, girls!" Lisa turned back to the audience to announce the winners for the teams' section. Maddi was barely paying attention. She still couldn't believe that her girls had placed. With her routine, no less. It was what she had been working so hard for, and now it was a reality. She was already starting to think about what they would do next when the girls shuffled her back towards the others. They were about to announce the winners of the next section.

She clapped and cheered on her fellow comrades, watching each step forward and take their medals. When it came time to announce the advanced section, Piper grabbed her arm.

"Coming in third place in the advanced section, is… Sacha and Jessie!" Maddi heard Rory boo from off stage and stifled a giggle. She may have placed, but at least she hadn't come in first. It was clear from the look on Sacha's face that she had not been expecting third, and she was *not* happy. She plastered on a fake smile as she and Jessie went up to accept their medals.

Ricki gave Maddi's hand a squeeze, smiling down at her as they waited for the next names to be called out.

"In second place in the advanced section, we have… Nicole and Rob!" Maddi clapped and congratulated them. She made a mental note to catch up with them at the after party. Perhaps they could collaborate for next year.

"And… the winner of the advanced section is… Maddison and Ricki!"

"Yes!" Ricki yelled out as he picked Maddi up and swung her around. She laughed in delight. Two years in a row! And to think, she hadn't even planned on entering. It was all thanks to Ricki, her knight in shining armour.

They went up to accept their medals and a huge bunch of flowers. Rory and Damon were standing right in the front row, cheering them on. Maddi gave a little wave and blew them a kiss.

All the winners gathered around for photos with their medals. Maddi made sure to get some with her girls and promised them all a round of coffee the following morning when everyone had recovered.

Looking around at all her friends, it was easy to forget all the dramas of the past few months. She had been through a lot, but she had come out on top.

Chapter 20

Rory and Damon met them out the front of the auditorium, all ready to party. Rory rushed up to Maddi, sweeping her into a crushing hug.

"You were great!" she cried, the biggest smile across her face. "And you looked so hot in that dress." She nudged her arm.

"Thanks."

"She's right, you're a knock-out. Well done, eh," Damon said, shaking hands with Ricki. "Fucking awesome, mate."

"Thanks, man. It was a bit nerve-wracking, but we made it." He grinned at Maddi.

"Did you see the look on Sacha's face when you won? Priceless!" Rory giggled, imitating her. "I'm surprised she didn't trip over her bottom lip!" Maddi laughed at Rory's re-enactment.

"So now what? You guys wanna go to the party?" Damon asked. Maddi and Ricki exchanged glances.

"Sure, why not?" Maddi said, swinging her arm around Rory's shoulder. "Lead the way."

The after party was bigger than they had expected. It seemed as though every audience member, competitor and their families had turned up to congratulate the winners and join in the celebrations.

Maddi and Ricki had a lot of people coming up to talk to them, asking if they would teach them, or be part of their team for the following year. They caught up with Nicole and Rob and organised to have coffee later in the week to discuss plans for a collaboration.

After a few hours, Maddi had had enough of the festivities, and all she really wanted to do, was go home and hang out with her friends. Once she had sought out Rory and Damon, they made a move for home.

When they got back, they put on some music and Ricki and Maddi attempted to teach them some basic steps. Rory had seen it enough times to pick up the first few moves without any trouble. Damon, on the other hand, had two left feet.

"You know what? How 'bout I just do this?" He bopped up and down. "And you can do your salsa steps around me." He tickled Rory as she swished her hips side to side in front of him.

"That works too." Ricki laughed. He pulled Maddi in, lowering her into a dip. "It's just not as smooth as this though, bro."

"I'll never be as smooth as you, mate." Damon patted his friend on the back. "Who's up for a drink?"

"Ooh I could go for a hot chocolate," Rory piped up.

"Okay, Nana. I was meaning something a little stronger."

"Actually, I could go for a hot chocolate as well," Maddi agreed with a grin. "With marshmallows!" She ran to the cupboard, retrieving the bag she had stowed away.

"Ooh, yes please." Rory snatched them out of her hand, shoving one in her mouth. "I'll put the jug on," she mumbled as she pulled four mugs down from the shelf.

"Alright, hot chocolate it is then," Damon said with a sigh.

"You know you want it," Rory said, shoving yet another marshmallow in her mouth, and then one in his. "Give us a kiss?" She winked at Maddi as she puckered up, gooey marshmallow sticking out. Damon just grinned and kissed her.

"Now that's love," Maddi said, laughing.

"Sure is," Ricki agreed, helping himself to a marshmallow as well. "Give us a kiss?" he said, turning towards Maddi.

"I thought you'd never ask." She grinned, jumping into his arms. She leaned in, their lips almost touching.

"Wait!" cried Rory. "You forgot your marshmallow! Get it right!" She giggled, offering the bag to Maddi.

Without taking her eyes away from Ricki, she reached for the sweet, popping it into her mouth before wrapping her arms around him. They grinned at each other before Ricki slowly lowered his lips to hers.

Stacey Broadbent
Dancing
with
Destiny
A Step in Time book three

Another year, another clash at the Nationals. Ricki and Maddi have teamed up with friends to compete this year, only this time, Ricki has something secret up his sleeves. The only problem is, he's not very good at keeping things from Maddi.

On a path of self-destruction, Sacha is on a downward spiral. With no one to turn to, and no idea how to fix things, she finds comfort in the bottom of a bottle. Like mother, like daughter.

In the blink of an eye, their whole world is shattered as friends fight to make things right.

One night is all it takes...

Bitter rivals to the end.

Chapter 1

"Get out of my kitchen!" Rory yelled, shooing Damon away with a tea towel.

"Oh, baby, don't be like that," he cooed, circling his arms around her waist and planting a kiss on her neck.

Rory giggled. "Stop! You're distracting me! This needs to be perfect." She reluctantly pulled away from his grasp, huffing as she did. "What if it isn't good enough?" she asked, a frown creasing her brow.

"Are you kidding me?" Damon grabbed her by the shoulders, turning her to face him. He curled his finger under her chin and tilted her face up so she couldn't avoid his eyes. "Babe, you're the best cook I know. That culinary school is going to be lucky to have you. Don't stress so much, okay? You got this." He kissed her forehead before turning her towards the bench and smacking her bottom lightly. "Now, get back to work, woman." He grinned and darted away before she could reach him, but it'd had the desired effect. She was smiling again.

He'd never known a woman to look so hot covered in flour before, but somehow, Rory did it. Her apron was splattered with various shades of colouring from all her fondant mouldings, her hair sticking every which way, and her face dusted with flour, but damn if she wasn't still beautiful to him.

When they'd first met a year earlier, he'd fallen for her instantly. Her wild sense of humour had him hooked right from the start, the fact that she could cook almost anything she put her mind to was an added bonus.

He watched her potter about the kitchen, her petite frame almost gliding—she really was in her element. He was so proud of her for enrolling in the most prestigious culinary school in Christchurch, *Gastronomie*.

For as long as he'd known her, cooking had been her passion. She'd been working for catering companies and had the occasional shift in one of the local restaurants when they were short staffed. But what she really wanted was to own her own café come bookstore. She envisioned having scatter pillows and bean bags for people to sit and read while sampling her tasty treats. There would be poetry nights and book signings, and it would be the place for all the hipster generation to be. She even had the perfect name picked out, *Bon-appetête-à-tête*.

"I can feel you watching me," she said, carefully placing the fondant flowers around the top tier of the wedding cake she was making. Selection for entry into *Gastronomie* was one of the most challenging things she'd ever had to do. There were several stages to it; the first had been a selection of appetisers; the second, a dish using a specific ingredient that was only disclosed on the day—Rory had been given duck; and the third, a dessert.

You had to pass each stage to move on to the next, and so far, Rory had excelled. Of the 200 students who had enrolled, only 100 remained. There was one dish left to prepare. Only 40 students could go through, so in a way, this was the most important of all.

The fourth and final stage in the selection process, the students were given free reign, where they could showcase their best dishes. There were no limits to what they could do.

Rory had chosen to make a four-tier wedding cake, each tier a different flavour and theme. Damon had happily accepted the title of 'official taste-tester'. Each flavour blend she tried went past him first. Together they had come up with some winning combos. The bottom tier was a twist on the traditional fruit cake, with hints of cardamom, nutmeg, and ginger; the next, a dark chocolate mud cake with a sweet-chilli buttercream; the third layer was raspberry and white chocolate with a cinnamon swirl, and the top tier, a light vanilla sponge with a blood-orange syrup drizzled over top before a layer of buttercream and fondant was added.

Each layer was a different colour, representing different emotions. White for purity, baby blue for faith, lilac for romance and finally, pink, for love. She had spent hours forming flowers and ribbons out of fondant, and even more time painting swirls and bursts of colour with edible paints. She was nearing the end and she was exhausted. Exhilarated, but exhausted.

"Oh my God! Rory, that looks amazing!" Maddi gushed as she and Ricki joined them in the kitchen.

"You really think so?" Rory asked, wiping her hands down the front of her apron. "I thought maybe it needed something else." She motioned her hand around the middle of the cake. "Maybe something here?"

"No! Don't you dare touch it, it's perfect the way it is," Maddi scolded, taking Rory's hands and leading her out of the kitchen. She turned her back around so she could see her cake from afar. "See? It's beautiful." She hugged her friend from behind. "Now, go and sit down and I'll make you a cup of coffee. No offense, but you look like you've been dragged through a bush backwards."

"I'd pretend to be shocked by that comment if I weren't so knackered. Who knew it would be this hard to get in." She threw her hands in the air.

"Well, I think you've done an amazing job. We're all super proud of you, no matter what happens."

"Hell yeah, we are, babe." Damon scooped her up in his arms, spinning her around in circles before collapsing on the couch with her. "Maybe I could show you how proud I am of you later…" He buried his face in the crook of her neck, kissing the sensitive spot just below her ear and making her giggle.

"Ahem," Ricki cleared his throat. "There are other people in the room," he whispered behind his hand.

"Like you haven't heard it before." Damon snickered.

"Don't I know it. The walls are pretty thin, man." Ricki placed his hand on his forehead, shaking his head. "Sometimes, I can't sleep for all the noise you two make."

"Oh rubbish!" Maddi said, playfully nudging him with her elbow. "We don't hear a thing."

"Sure we don't," he said before mouthing "we do" and nodding behind her back.

"Guess we'll have to try harder then," Damon said with a grin.

Maddi rolled her eyes, chuckling. "Who else wants a coffee?" Everyone nodded their heads eagerly as she filled the jug and got some cups down from the cupboard. "You want two scoops of coffee, Rory?"

"Mmm, please. I can barely keep my eyes open. Do we have any toothpicks or match sticks or whatever it is you use to prop them open?" She yawned loudly, covering her mouth with the back of her hand.

"Why don't you go and have a rest? You've been at it for hours," Damon suggested.

"No, I'm good. I've still gotta clean up my mess and then get it down to *Gastronomie* before the deadline."

"Don't be silly, we can clean up for you. Can't we, boys?" Maddi placed her hands on her hips in a no-nonsense way.

"Of course," Ricki said.

"Ain't no way I'm getting on your bad side, Maddi." Damon pretended to look scared. "We know how good we have it here, there's no way I'm gonna jeopardise my chance of having another one of your supreme roasts, or my girl's red velvet cakes." He jumped up from the couch, pushing his sleeves up. "I'll wash, you dry," he said to Ricki.

"You got it."

Maddi set their coffees on the counter for them before carrying hers and Rory's through to the lounge. "Here ya go, hon."

Rory closed her eyes and inhaled deeply. "Mmmmmm. Coffee, how I love thee."

"And I'm sure it loves you too." Maddi grinned. "So, when do you find out if you've been selected?"

"Like, 7PM I think. We have to have it in no later than five, which gives me just over an hour to get showered and presentable." She stared off into space, her eyes glazing over.

"Hey," Maddi said, snapping her fingers to get her attention. "You're gonna be fine." She lay a reassuring hand on her knee before standing up. "Now, what are you going to wear?"

Chapter 2

"You're what?" Sacha asked, folding her arms across her chest.

"I'm moving out," Jessie said, raking his hand through his hair. "It's just not working. I can't do this anymore."

"No."

"No?"

"No. That's a lame-ass excuse and you know it. Tell me the real reason." She started tapping her toe up and down. "There's someone else, isn't there?"

"No, Sacha. I swear. There's no one else. I just…" He looked around the room as if searching for something to say.

"You just what?" she said, putting emphasis on the 'T'. He could see she was angry, not that he'd expected anything else from her. How do you tell someone you love that you feel like they're dragging you down? That they're like a poison, slowly eating away at your insides.

"I just need a break from all this…" He waved his hand between the two of them. "From us."

"Are you seriously pulling the "we need a break" bullshit? What does that even mean?"

"I don't know what you want me to say, Sacha!" Jessie wasn't normally one to raise his voice, but she could always bring that side out of him, and he hated it.

"Just say it."

"Okay, you want to know why? Because… Because I can't take it anymore." He raked a hand through his hair.

She huffed out a laugh. "I can't take it anymore," she mimicked.

"This is exactly what I'm talking about. The sarcasm, the nastiness. The constant looking over my shoulder to see if you've got your claws into someone else."

She opened her mouth to speak but he held his hand up to stop her. "Don't even try to deny it, Sacha. I'm not blind, and I'm not stupid. Or are you forgetting about that little episode with Ricki last year?"

"Ricki? What would I want with that loser?" she spat.

"Right. Of course. He's a loser because he didn't fall under your spell like I did."

"What's that supposed to mean?"

"Come on, I know you only used me. You thought you'd picked a winner, but you were wrong. You backed the wrong horse. You don't need to pretend anymore, Sacha. I can see it in your eyes when we dance. You don't love me. I don't even know if you ever did."

Sacha blinked, taken aback by his words. Her eyes narrowed and she pointed a manicured finger in his face. "You will never find anyone else like me."

"You know what? I'm actually fine with that." He picked up his bag and turned towards the door. "I'll be back to pick up my stuff tomorrow. Maybe you could be elsewhere when I do." And with that, he opened the door and walked away.

Sacha just stood there, watching, and waiting for him to come back through. This isn't how things worked. She was the one who did the leaving, not the other way around. Her hands kept balling into fists by her side, and she felt the tiniest of pinpricks behind her eyes.

No.

Crying? Over a boy? What was wrong with her? She didn't do that.

She quickly wiped her arm across her face in the hopes that it would stop the tears from falling, but it only made them fall faster.

He left.

He actually left.

And now I'm all alone.

Chapter 3

"Stop pacing."

Rory flicked her hands up and down in front of her as she treaded back and forth down the hall. "I can't, I'm too nervous."

"It's out of your hands now, just relax," Maddi said. "Come on, let's get out of the house for a bit. Why don't you come to Feeney's with us? Let your hair down."

Rory stared at her as if she were crazy. "I can't leave! They could ring any minute!"

"And you'll have your phone with you, so it's not a big deal." She turned to Damon. "A little help, please?"

He took hold of Rory's hands and led her reluctantly down the hall and into the bedroom. "We'll be ready in fifteen," he called over his shoulder.

"Fifteen? I'm gonna need at least half an hour to get ready to go out," Rory piped up from behind him. "It's like you don't even know me."

"Oh, I know you better than you think," he said with a smirk. "Don't worry, I'll have her primped and primed and ready to party in no time." He winked at Maddi then closed the door. She could hear low murmuring, followed by the unmistakeable sound of

Rory giggling. She could always count on Damon to get her out of a slump.

Padding back to her own room, Maddi wondered where Ricki had got to. He'd disappeared around the same time as Rory had taken her cake down to the school, and she hadn't heard from him. She checked her watch, 6:55PM. He was cutting it fine if they were to make it to Feeney's before the crowds.

She opened her wardrobe and pulled out her favourite blue strapless dress, slinging it onto the bed along with a pair of dance tights and some silver heels. She stood in front of her mirror, tapping her chin as she contemplated how she would wear her hair.

"You will look beautiful no matter what you wear," Ricki said from behind her. He wrapped his arms around her waist and pulled her into him. "Sorry I'm so late, I lost track of time."

"You're here, that's the main thing." Maddi smiled at his reflection. "I've convinced Rory and Damon to come with us tonight too."

"Yeah? We haven't done that in a while."

"Yeah. I thought Rory could do with the distraction. She was wearing the carpet thin in the hall with all her pacing." She chuckled. "Come on, we should get organised. I wanna have that dancefloor to ourselves for a bit before all the girls come flocking to take you away."

"I think you have that around the wrong way. You're the one everyone wants to dance with, not me." He grinned at her. "I don't blame them either."

"You know, if you keep saying sweet stuff like that, I just might have to keep you on."

"I'm gonna hold you to that." He stepped away, pulling his shirt over his head and dumping it in the basket before searching through the wardrobe for another one. Maddi took a moment to admire his strong physique; something she could never quite get enough of. His perfectly sculpted abs mesmerised her, and no matter how often she saw them, she found herself wanting to run her fingers over the ridges.

She'd never been with another man. Ricki was her one and only, and she hoped it would always be that way. Sure, she'd dated other guys, but none that she had felt comfortable enough to share something so intimate with.

After everything that Dane had put her through, Ricki had been the perfect gentleman, never once putting pressure on her. He had waited until she was ready, and even then, he was tentative. He treated her with a gentleness she had never experienced before, making her sure that her decision had been the right one.

"Maddi?" Ricki asked, eyeing her with a cocky grin on his face. "You gonna get ready?"

"Mmhmm," she murmured under her breath, slightly embarrassed to have been caught staring. She quickly undressed, then slipped her dress on over her gentle curves. "Could you zip me up?" she asked, holding her hair in a pile on top of her head.

Ricki stepped in close, grasping the zipper in his hand and slowly pulled it up. The warmth from his fingers caused shivers to run up and down her spine. He rested his hands on her hips and kissed the back of her neck. "You look beautiful," he whispered, his lips brushing lightly against her.

"Mmmmmm," Maddi moaned, leaning back into him.

"Oh my God, oh my God, oh my God!" Rory burst through the door, making them jump apart.

"What is it? What's happened?" Maddi asked, running to her friend.

"That was one of the judges! They loved my cake! I got in! I'm going to culinary school!" she screamed, jumping up and down. Maddi grabbed her hands and joined in.

"Oh my God! I'm so proud of you! I knew you could do it!"

"Oh-em-gee, me too!" Damon said in his best attempt at an excited teenage girl voice as he bounded into the room with them. "We should totes take a selfie to celebrate!" He pretended to flick his hair behind his shoulder and puckered his lips into something resembling 'duck face'.

Rory swatted his chest, giggling. "Geez, Damo, you're such a clown."

"That's why you love me, though, right?" He grinned at her, wiggling his eyebrows up and down suggestively.

"Yeah, yeah. I love you, ya big teddy bear." She reached up on her tippy toes to kiss him.

"I knew it!" He palmed her bottom and lifted her into his arms, wrapping her legs around his waist. "I don't know about you lot, but I'm ready to party!"

Chapter 4

Feeney's was a bar downtown, situated on one of the busiest streets. It got a lot of foot traffic, and the salsa nights were always a hit. The music was already blaring by the time they rounded the corner, and the girls couldn't help but start bopping to the beat as they walked. Now that Rory had her confirmation, she had lost her anxiety and was back to her usual bubbly self, ready to kick her heels up.

"God, I feel like it's been forever since we came out dancing!" she cried as they entered the bar. "Hurry up and change your shoes. I wanna get my dance on."

"All right, keep your shirt on," Maddi said with a grin.

"How about some drinks, ladies?" Damon asked.

"You even have to ask?" Rory raised her brow at him. "We're celebrating, remember?"

"So, two vodka and Red Bull's then?"

"You know it!" The boys made their way up to the bar to get their orders, while Rory continued to shake her body to the music. "Maaaddddiiiii, I wanna dance," she whined, tugging on her arm.

"Two secs, I've just… gotta… get this… clasp… done!" She stood up and let Rory lead her to the empty space in the centre of the room. They had the whole floor to themselves for now, and they were going to take full advantage of it.

"Let's show 'em what we got," Rory said, waving her hands at the few people still seated at their tables finishing off their meals. She broke into some sort of shimmy-type move, where she would shake her shoulders and wiggle her butt, then jump around to face another direction and repeat the process. Maddi couldn't contain her laughter as she watched her friend circle the room. She had the most intense look on her face, as if it was taking all her concentration to co-ordinate her body.

Out of the corner of her eye, she saw that the boys had put their drinks on the table and were heading out to join them. Damon immediately joined in on Rory's circular dance, mimicking her every move, but going in a counter-clockwise direction. They were the perfect match for each other—just the right amount of crazy.

"Can I have this dance?" Ricki asked, offering his hand.

"Of course." Maddi placed her hand in his and they began to sway, going through some of their favourite moves. Now that they were both teaching full time, it was nice to have these nights where they could just enjoy the music and the dance together, without it having to be about performing. This year had been rather busy preparing for the Nationals. Instead of entering as a couple though, they were focusing on their teamwork. They'd become fast friends with Nicole and Rob, the second-place winners from last year's competition, and had put together a salsa routine with them and a few other couples who'd auditioned. If they placed this year, they were planning on taking it to the World Champ's in Singapore. They had been practically living and breathing salsa for the last six months.

Of course, Maddi also had her ladies shine team to train too. They had been working on a saucy bachata number to take up to Auckland for Nationals and it was fast approaching. The Divas had been pulling some long hours, but it was all coming together nicely. In fact, they had been talking about combining the two troupes and making one big mixed team for the next year. They would just need to find a few extra men to join in to even it up.

"Don't look now, the bitch has entered the building," Rory said as she sidled up next to Maddi and nodded her head towards the door. "Looks like someone's been hitting the bottle a bit too hard." She made a drinking motion with her hand. Maddi turned to see Sacha staggering in.

"I see what you mean."

"Don't let her get to you. Just ignore her." Ricki took hold of her hand, planting a kiss on her palm.

"Sorry, she just puts me on edge."

"I know."

"The way she looks at you…"

Ricki cocked his head. "Maddi, you have nothing to worry about. She can look at me however she wants, it's not going to make me change how I feel about you."

He tilted her chin up, touching his forehead to hers. "I'm not going anywhere."

Maddi sighed, letting her body relax into his. "I know. She just rubs me the wrong way. And what about Jessie? If *I* see the way she watches you, you can bet he does too."

"It's his choice to stay. He must see something in her that we don't." He shrugged. "Anyway, let's not let her ruin our night. We came here to celebrate, didn't we?" He peered down at her with a grin.

"Yes, you're right. Forget about her!" she said loudly, waving an arm in the air dismissively.

"Already forgotten." He pulled her in tight before throwing her into a series of spins around him. Their record was twelve before she began to lose balance.

"Oops," Sacha said as she stuck her foot out, making Maddi stumble. If Ricki hadn't had a hold of her still, she would've ended up in a heap on the floor. "My bad, ssooorry," she slurred.

Maddi could see Rory gearing up to cause trouble. She quickly shook her head, telling her friend not to bother with her. She then turned to Ricki and, taking his hand, she led him to another spot on the dance floor, away from Sacha's writhing body.

"We can go if you want," he said, watching her with derision in his eyes.

"No, we're not going to let her ruin our night, remember?" She reached up and pressed her lips to his. "I won't let her think she's getting to me."

"And that's why I love you."

"I love you too."

Chapter 5

Maddi scrolled through her playlist, searching for the song she wanted to use for their warm-up in class tonight. She liked to keep it interesting for her students and vary the music so they didn't get sick of hearing the same old songs. Of course, she would always have her favourites—the ones she would play every chance she got—and tonight was one of those nights. She needed to hear that familiar rhythm pumping through her veins.

The sound of cow bells filled the room as the music began to play. Without even having to think about it, Maddi began to move to the beat, her feet taking over. She and Ricki took turns running the warm-ups each week, that way they could keep it fresh and play to their strengths.

A blast of air rushed in as the door opened behind her. "Oh, sorry."

"Jessie?" Maddi pressed pause and ran over to him, throwing her arms around his neck. "How are you? Are you here for our class?"

Jessie pulled back, smiling. "Yeah, I thought I'd come and check it out, see what all the hype is about." He chuckled, looking around the room. "Where's Ricki?"

Maddi threw her arms up in the air. "I have no idea. He was meant to meet me here to go over tonight's combo." She pursed her lips, a frown creasing her forehead.

"You wanna practice with me?" he offered.

"Would you? I just need to decide what styling I'm going to add in."

"Of course. Let me get my shoes on." He sauntered over to the chairs at the edge of the studio. "It'll be nice to dance with you again, it's been a while." He looked up at her with a sadness in his eyes. Ever since he and Sacha had begun dating, it had been abundantly clear she didn't want him getting too close to Maddi.

"Yeah, it has." Maddi watched Jessie. Something wasn't quite right with him. "Are you okay?" she asked.

With a sigh, Jessie ran his hands through his hair. "That obvious, huh?" His shoulders dropped as if he was holding a huge weight on them.

Maddi walked over and sat in a vacant chair beside him. She placed her hand on his knee, peering up into his eyes. "You want to talk about it?"

He smiled at her, though it didn't quite meet his eyes. "Do I want to talk about it? Not really. Should I? Probably." He laughed nervously before meeting her gaze. "I left Sacha." He exhaled, lifting his head to stare at the ceiling.

"Aww, Jess, I'm so sorry. What happened?"

"I just couldn't be there anymore, you know? All the negativity, the cattiness." He turned to face her again. "The way she looked at other guys."

Maddi nodded her head, looking down at her lap. "Yeah, I noticed that too. I'm so sorry, Jess. I know how much she meant to you." She gave his knee a squeeze.

"Yeah, well… I can't force her to want me, so…" he trailed off, staring across the room.

"Ahem, am I interrupting something?" Ricki cleared his throat as he strolled toward them.

"Oh, hey, I didn't hear you come in. Where've you been?" Maddi asked, jumping up to greet him.

"I just had some stuff to do. Everything okay here?" He eyed Jessie warily. They'd come to an amicable friendship of sorts, though he hadn't forgotten the punch to his face a little over a year ago.

Maddi pulled him towards the front of the room. "Everything's fine. Jessie just needed a friend to talk to." She peered over her shoulder at him before whispering, "They broke up."

Ricki's eyebrow shot up. "Sacha and Jessie?" Maddi nodded. "I guess that explains her drunken state last night then."

"Mmmm, yeah I guess." She chewed the corner of her lip. "Maybe they both meant more to each other than they thought."

"Maddi," Ricki said with a warning tone. "Don't get involved. You know that Sacha will only turn it against you."

"But they're hurting," she said, looking up at him with her bright blue eyes. "And he's my friend."

Ricki let out a sigh, running his hand through his hair. "You care too much for your own good, you know that, right?" The corner of his lip curled up into a small smile.

"I know," she said, kissing his cheek. "Now, I'm going to go and have a dance with Jessie, while you get your shoes on. Class starts soon and we haven't even had a run-through." She poked a finger at his chest and attempted to give him a stern look but failed.

Ricki saluted with a grin. "Yes, ma'am."

She turned back to Jessie, who was pretending to play on his phone. "You ready for that dance?" she called, holding her hand out to him.

He looked up at her with a smile. "Just try and stop me."

Chapter 6

Rory heaved into the porcelain bowl, emptying the contents of her stomach. "I am never drinking again," she muttered, gulping in the air as she sat back against the bath, lowering her chin to her chest.

Having been so stressed out over the last few weeks while the tutors decided her fate, Rory had finally let her hair down while they were at Feeney's the night before, and she was now paying the price.

"It was those damn shots," she murmured. "Why didn't you stop me?" She squinted up at Damon who was crouching beside her.

"Baby, you only had one shot, and you were having fun, I didn't want to ruin your night for you. It was a celebration." He smiled, brushing her hair away from her face.

"Mmmm, I feel so joyous right now," she mumbled sarcastically. "Oh God…" She scrambled back to the toilet, her head hovering over the edge. "Alcohol is the devil." Her body began retching once again, ridding her stomach of whatever still remained. Damon rubbed circles on her back soothingly.

"Aaaaarrrgghhhhh," she groaned as she finally caught her breath. "Kill me, kill me now."

Damon chuckled. "I think you'll live."

She glared at him. "*You* might not."

He kissed her forehead. "Have I ever told you you're cute when you're angry?"

Rory raised an eyebrow at him, running a hand down her body in the least sexy way possible. "Are you trying to tell me you want a piece of this?"

To his credit, Damon held her gaze. "I always want you, baby." He scooped her up in his arms. "But maybe a shower wouldn't go amiss."

"Any excuse to get me naked," she said with a tired grin before running her tongue along her teeth and pulling a face. "Urgh, I need to brush my teeth too."

"Well, I didn't wanna say anything…" Damon chuckled as she slapped his chest. He set her down on the stool in the corner of the room. He opened the shower door and turned the faucet on to hot, then retrieved her toothbrush. "Here," he said, holding it out to her. "I'll go grab you a towel."

Rory slumped on the stool, slowly running the toothbrush back and forth in her mouth. She leaned her head against the wall, letting the coolness of the tiles seep through her.

"Come on, babe, let's get you into the shower," Damon said as he re-entered the room. He had a large fluffy towel and her robe draped over his arm. He set them down on the vanity, then grabbed her toothbrush from her, putting it back in the drawer. He took hold of the hem of her shirt and gently lifted it over her head, then helped her to step out of her jeans. Taking her hand, he led her to the shower and watched as she cautiously stepped under the hot stream.

"Ahhhhh," she moaned, letting the water cascade over her back as she leaned against the wall.

"You okay in there? Need any help?" Damon asked hopefully, making Rory giggle.

"You're crazy, you know that? Any other guy would be running for the hills, not rubbing my back while I blow chunks."

"Such a way with words," he said through his laughter. "Anyway, ain't no other guy gonna be watching you blow chunks but me. I'm the only one who gets that privilege."

Rory poked her head through the shower door. "Like I said—crazy." She twirled her finger by her ear and stuck her tongue out at him.

"The extremely hot kinda crazy though, right?" He put his hands on his head and began to roll his pelvis seductively at her, adding a few hip thrusts for good measure.

"Mmmhmm, definitely the hot kinda crazy," she said, her eyes dancing as she watched his little display. "Come on then." She opened the door, summoning him to join her.

"I knew you couldn't resist my charms," he said, wiggling his eyebrows at her as he tossed his clothes on the floor.

"Yeah, your 'charms'. Is that what we're calling them now?" She grinned up at him, wrapping her arms around his neck.

"You can call them whatever you want, baby." He smiled against her lips, his hands gripping onto her waist. Rory sighed, resting her head against his chest. "How you feeling now?" he asked, gently kissing the top of her head while bringing his arms around her further.

"Mmm, better, thanks."

"How much better?" he asked, going back to his hip rolling. He could feel her lips pull up into a smile.

"Trust you, Damo." She slapped his chest again.

"Hey. You can't blame a guy for trying." He ran his hands down to her bottom, palming her soft flesh and giving a squeeze. "I mean, we are naked…"

"Mmmm, yeah, we certainly are…"

"And it would be a shame to waste it…" He thrust his hips again, his length sliding across her stomach.

"Mmmm, tis true. I mean, you are getting older, and erectile dysfunction is just around the corner for you…"

"Hey!"

"Maybe you should take matters into your own hand…" She grinned up at him. "Because it ain't happening with me I'm afraid." She pressed her lips to his chest. "I would hate to blow chunks all over this here hotness." She ran her hand up and down his body.

Damon sighed. "So, I'm not getting any?"

"Not this time, buddy. Sorry," Rory said, turning around to press her body against his. "You stay in here and… ya know… do your thang." She wiggled her bottom before stepping out of the shower and grabbing her towel.

"Woman, you do not play fair sometimes," Damon complained, a groan escaping his lips as she sashayed out of the bathroom.

Chapter 7

"And five, six, seven!" Maddi called out, signalling the beginning of the move. "Basic… cross body lead, flare and booty… bring her across… switch hands as you turn…" she continued to call out instructions as they all moved to the beat. It wasn't a particularly difficult move, but putting it together with the music always proved challenging when learning a new combo.

"Break back… and comb your hands over her head…" She kept careful watch of her students, making sure that each one understood the move. She hated to move on when someone was struggling. "Good! And high five. Ladies move to the left!" They continued doing their basic step back and forth in the centre of the circle, waiting for everyone to switch partners. "From the top! And five, six, seven!"

Ricki led her through the combo, a smile on his face as he listened to her calls. His confidence had sky-rocketed after the comps the previous year, but he still wasn't as natural in front of people as Maddi was. Without her, the classes would fall apart.

One-on-one lessons with the guys was more his forte. He didn't feel so much pressure to perform in those instances and was able to relax more. In fact, he had been in discussions with a select few to form an all-male shine team. He and Rob had hit it off immediately, and between them, they had found another three guys to join them. The girls had no idea. They were planning on surprising them at the Nationals. Ricki had very nearly let the cat out of the bag on a number of occasions—keeping anything secret from Maddi was difficult, but so far, she was none the wiser.

"And high five. Ladies move to the left!" Ricki led her across so that they were facing the opposite direction. "Ladies, don't be afraid to add in your own styling. If you feel the need for a shimmy," she demonstrated against Ricki, "or a body roll, then by all means, add them in! Make it your own." She grinned, pulling herself through another cross body so she could play it up. Hoots and hollers came from around the circle as everyone cheered her on.

At first, Ricki just let her do her thing, but when he saw his chance, he broke off into his own shine steps. He may not be confident speaking to everyone, but he had the skills on the dancefloor, and he wasn't afraid to bring it. Maddi's eyes lit up as she watched him with pride.

What had begun as a demonstration had turned into a mini shine battle. "Yeow! Work it, Ricki!" one of the girls yelled out, clapping.

As the song came to an end, Ricki took charge once more and spun her over and over as he walked in a straight line through the circle, finishing by throwing her into a dip right on the final note. The class erupted into claps and cheers as they panted, smiling at each other.

Ricki pulled her back up and they took a bow. "All right let's put some music on for you guys to practice," Maddi said, walking over to where her iPod was docked. "I wanna see some originality in there, show me what you got!"

The couples all spaced out around the room, going over what they had been taught and adding in their own personal flares. Maddi and Ricki watched on from the side, checking that everyone had the move down.

"I think they've got it," he said. "Shall we?" He offered her his elbow, nodding his head to the dancefloor.

"I thought you'd never ask," she said, linking her arm through his. "Let's show 'em how it's done."

They walked out to an empty space and began to dance. "So, are you going to tell me where you keep disappearing to?" she asked, the corner of her mouth tilting up into a half-smile, as if she knew something he didn't.

"I told you, I just had some jobs to do." He avoided her eyes, knowing she would see straight through him. He wasn't sure how long he could keep lying to her.

"Oh… okay," she said, pressing her lips into a straight line. They kept dancing, but her movements became tense and mechanical. She wouldn't meet his eyes when he smiled at her.

The last thing he wanted was to upset her, but short of blowing their cover, he was out of ideas. He glanced around the room, spying Jessie sitting to one side. "Hey, why don't you go have a dance with Jessie? He looks a little lonely."

Maddi turned to see Jessie sitting on the outside, scrolling through his phone. "Okay." She dropped her arms and walked away. Something was going on with Ricki, but she couldn't figure out what. He never kept things from her.

She plonked down on the seat beside Jessie, forcing her mind to shift gears. "You know, I'm much better company than your phone," she said, draping her arms across the backs of the seats.

Chuckling, Jessie clicked his phone off and shoved it into his pocket. "Subtle, aren't you?" he said.

"Who, me?" She placed a hand to her chest, a mock look of shock on her face. "Whatever do you mean?" She held his gaze until he broke, looking away.

"I don't really wanna talk about it," he said, looking down to his feet.

"That's okay, neither do I." She winked. "I thought you might like to dance." She stood up and held her hand out to him. "Come on, you can take it out on the dancefloor."

Jessie sighed. "You never give up, do you?"

"When my friends are involved? Never." She grabbed his hand and pulled him up. "Now, let's go and help you forget about her."

Chapter 8

Rory padded down to the kitchen in the boxers and singlet she had worn to bed the night before. Her stomach was still feeling a little funny after their big night in town, and she was hoping it would settle down with a little water and some Panadol.

She was surprised to find Ricki up and dressed already. She glanced at the clock and saw that it was only 7AM. "Where are you off to this early on a Saturday morning?" she asked, stifling a yawn behind her hand.

"Just thought I'd go for a run. Couldn't sleep." He finished tying his shoes then grabbed his phone and keys off the counter. "Catch ya later," he said as he breezed past and out the door.

"Weird," she mumbled to herself as she rummaged through the drawer to find what she was looking for. Pulling an open packet out, she pressed two tablets into her palm then grabbed a glass down from the cupboard. She tipped her head back, swirling the water around her mouth as the pills slipped down her throat. She put her cup into the sink and stood, holding onto the counter with her head bowed and her eyes closed. She'd never had a hangover last so long before.

"You okay, baby?" Damon asked, coming up behind her. He placed a hand on the back of her neck and trailed it down her back.

"Yeah, I just feel a bit off still."

"You think you're coming down with something?" he asked, spinning her around to look at him. He put the back of his hand to her forehead. "You don't feel hot or anything."

"No, I'm sure I'll come right. I think I just can't handle drinking like I used to anymore. Apparently two drinks is my new limit." She attempted a weak smile.

"Maybe you should go lie down some more."

She shook her head. "No can do. My first day at *Gastronomie* is on Monday, and I need to make sure I have everything ready."

"At least let me make you some breakfast," he said. "You need a good old greasy feed of bacon and eggs. It's the perfect cure for a hangover."

"If you say so." The thought of bacon had her stomach grumbling. The eggs, not so much. "Maybe some toast too, and I have to have coffee."

"Don't you worry, I've got it covered. You go and relax." He shooed her away, busying himself with pots and pans.

Rory hovered by the counter. "I could help if you want," she offered. The kitchen was her domain usually.

"Nope, I got this. Let me look after you." He kissed the tip of her nose, then with his hands on her shoulders, he turned her towards the lounge. "Now, go and put your feet up. Read a magazine or something."

"Okay." She sighed. It wasn't easy to let go of the reigns. She liked to be the one in the kitchen feeding everyone. Let's face it, she liked being the one in *control* of the kitchen. She knew just how to make things to her liking, and she found it hard to let someone else take over. "Do you know where everything is? I don't mind helping," she tried again.

"Rory, I've lived here for almost a year. I think I know where things are by now," he said, a grin forming across his face. He knew how hard it was for her to let anyone help, but damn it, he wanted to be able to look after her too.

He had the jug boiling, the bacon in the oven and the frying pan heating by the time Maddi came out to join them.

"What's going on in here?" she asked, tying her robe around her middle.

"Damo's cooking breakfast, and he won't let me help." Rory rolled her eyes. She kept flicking through her magazine, not really paying attention to what was on the pages. Her eyes kept wandering back to the kitchen.

"Okay, I give up," Damon conceded. "Where the hell is the whisk?"

"I thought you knew where everything was?" Rory teased, her eyebrow raised.

"Third drawer down," Maddi said with a grin.

"Of course! I knew that!"

"Sure you did," Rory said.

"Quiet in the cheap seats. Breakfast will be ready soon." He brandished the whisk in the air dramatically.

"Hey, have you seen Ricki? He's not in our room," Maddi asked, joining Rory on the couch.

"Oh yeah, he was out here when I got up. Said he couldn't sleep and was going for a run?"

"Really?" Maddi screwed her nose up. "That doesn't sound like him."

"Mmm, that's what I thought too. I'm sure he'll be back soon."

Maddi leaned in closer. "Yeah. Has he seemed a little strange to you lately?" She looked at Rory, worry clouding her eyes.

"No, why? You think something's going on?"

She sat back against the couch, blowing a whoosh of air out as she did. "I don't know. He seems to be disappearing a lot. And he never tells me where he's going."

"I'm sure it's nothing. You want me to quiz Damo? Do some digging?"

"Nah, you're right. It's probably nothing." She got up from the couch, leaning on the breakfast bar. "How's breakfast coming along?"

Chapter 9

Walking along Stanmore Road to meet up with Nicole and Rob, Maddi couldn't help dragging her feet. Her thoughts kept wandering to Ricki and his behaviour of late. Disappearing at random times of the day with no explanation—this wasn't the Ricki that she knew. He loved her, of that she had no doubt, but something wasn't right. She hated to act like the jealous girlfriend who didn't trust her man, but it was getting harder and harder to ignore.

The door leading up to the studio was open when she got there. Aside from her and Lisa, Ricki was the only other one who had a key. As far as she was aware, Lisa was away for the weekend, and she couldn't think why Ricki would come down here by himself. She checked for signs of a break in, but there appeared to be none.

Cautiously, she climbed the stairs, careful not to make a sound. She peered through the window at the top of the door. Ricki was there, playing with the sound system. Maddi breathed a sigh of relief. He must've come down early to open up and crank the heaters. The studio could be freezing at this time of year.

She placed her hands on the door, about to push it open when a voice stopped her in her tracks.

"Thanks, baby," came the unmistakable drawl of Sacha.

Maddi's heart jumped into her throat as she silently watched on. Ricki turned to the right, where the bathrooms were. Sacha sauntered towards him, straightening what she was obviously trying to pass off as a skirt, but really it was more like a belt. She glanced over at the door and Maddi quickly ducked down, not wanting to be caught spying. Not when she didn't really know what she was witnessing.

Could he really be seeing Sacha behind her back? The thought made bile rush up the back of her throat. Taking a deep breath, she forced her eyes back to the window. She had to see what was going on.

Sacha was trailing a finger along the barre between her and Ricki, her ruby-red lips turned up into a sly grin. She licked her lips as she approached him, saying something that Maddi couldn't hear, no matter how much she strained her ears. She watched as Sacha ran her hand down Ricki's arm, her other hand snaking around the back of his neck, drawing him closer to her. Ricki directed his gaze to where her hand rested, but he didn't move out of her grasp. Before their lips touched, Sacha glanced back towards Maddi, winking at her. Then she smashed her lips into his, holding his face between her hands to keep him where she wanted him.

Maddi had to look away. Her throat felt constricted as she leaned her back against the wall, her head tilted back as she fought to breathe, gasping for air. When she closed her eyes, all she could see was the two of them together.

Calm down, Maddi. You've been here before. She's just trying to hurt you. He wouldn't do this.

Would he?

She didn't know what to think anymore. She needed to get out of there. She couldn't face him right now. Grabbing her bag from the floor, she quickly ran down the stairs and out into the brisk morning air. Throwing her bag over her shoulders and tucking her hands in her pockets, Maddi began to walk. She had no idea where she was going, all she knew was that she needed to get as far away from them as she could.

"Maddi?" Jessie said as he opened the door. "Is everything okay?"

"Can I come in?" she asked, her voice small and catching, as if her throat didn't want her words to escape.

"Of course." He stepped aside, ushering her into the warmth of his apartment.

"Sorry to just show up unannounced like this. I know you're still getting settled, I just didn't know where else to go." She stood awkwardly in his sparse living room.

"No, it's fine. You're always welcome here, Maddi. I'm glad you thought of me." He folded his arms across his broad chest. "I'd offer you a coffee, but I haven't bought a jug yet. It's on my list of things to do today…" A blush ran up his face, giving him a boyish look. "Here, have a seat." He rushed to pull the boxes off the couch.

"God, how rude of me. You're not even finished unpacking, and I show up crying on your doorstep," Maddi said, her face pulled into a frown.

"Seriously, Maddi, it's not a problem. You're actually doing me a favour. I was starting to go a little stir crazy. It's been so long since I've had my own place. There's so much I need to get."

"Didn't you, um, I mean, wasn't everything yours in the first place?" She couldn't bring herself to say Sacha's name. Not yet.

Jessie laughed, though the sound lacked humour. "Yeah, it was. I just didn't feel like fighting over a bunch of stuff. It was just easier to leave it there."

Maddi nodded. Sacha certainly had perfected the art of getting what she wanted.

"That's not why you're here though. Do you wanna talk about it?" he asked, repeating the same words she had said to him the night before.

"I don't know. I'm not even really sure what to say." She sighed, twisting her fingers in her lap. The sound of her phone ringing in her pocket made her jump. She pulled it out and saw Ricki's face pop up on her screen. She hit 'ignore' and shoved it back into her pocket.

"How about we start with why you're ignoring his calls, and why you came here instead of going to Rory?" He quickly added, "Not that I mind."

"I didn't want him to find me," she whispered, turning her head away as she blinked away the tears.

Jessie clenched his fists by his side. He liked Ricki, but Maddi was his friend, and he didn't like to see her hurting. He took a calming breath and crouched down in front of her.

"Maddi, what did he do?"

She sniffled. "It's like last year all over again. I saw them together."

Jessie's jaw tightened at her words. "You mean Sacha?" She simply nodded. "Where was this? What did you see, exactly?" he asked gently. He understood her anxiety all too well. It had all been a misunderstanding last time, but even knowing that, it still didn't stop it from hurting.

"Ricki was at the studio early. I was about to walk in when I heard Sacha's voice. She called him *baby*." She paused, clearing her throat. "She kissed him. And this time, it really happened. He didn't pull away."

Jessie blew out a breath. "Shit, Maddi. I don't know what to say. I mean, you know what Sacha's like. Are you sure there isn't any way you could be wrong?"

"I know what I saw, Jessie. She held his face and kissed him."

"There has to be some sort of explanation for this. I've seen the way he looks at you. There's no way he would cheat. I can see it in his eyes, he's in love with you."

"I'm not so sure anymore," she whispered. "He's been acting strange with me lately, all love and flowers one minute, and then disappearing for long periods of time without any explanation. He's hiding something from me, and I guess this is what it is."

He took hold of her hands. "I've never seen a man more in love before. Trust me, there has to be some other reason." He pulled her in for a hug. "He would never choose Sacha over you."

Chapter 10

"Sorry guys, she's not picking up. I'm not sure where she is," Ricki said, staring at his phone. He'd tried calling her three times, but each time he was sent straight to voicemail. She was avoiding him for some reason, and he wasn't sure whether to be worried or not.

"It's all right, I think we're pretty ready for Nationals anyways. We can go over our part at home, eh, Rob?" Nicole said, slinging her shoe bag over her shoulder.

"Yeah, no problem. I'm knackered after our extra rehearsal this morning anyways." Rob smiled, placing his hand on Ricki's shoulder. "She'll be right, mate. Maybe she just forgot."

Ricki nodded, though he knew she would never forget training. It meant too much to her. That, and she hated to let people down. It was one of the many things he loved about her. "Yeah, you're probably right," he said, not wanting to give them any reason to worry.

"You want a lift home?" Rob asked.

"Nah, I might just hang here for a bit, see if she shows up."

"No worries, we'll see ya Friday?"

"Yeah, of course."

"See ya then." Nicole gave him a hug and kissed his cheek. "Everything will be fine," she said quietly. "She probably just needed some time to herself. That girl does too much." She rubbed her hand up and down his arm a few times, offering a little comfort.

"Right, let's do this," Rob said, grabbing her hand and leading her out the door. "Have a good one," he called over his shoulder.

"Yeah," Ricki muttered under his breath. He checked his phone again. Still no reply to his messages. He'd give her another ten minutes and then he'd try calling again. He couldn't shake the feeling that something was wrong. It was so unlike Maddi to ignore his calls. Even more unlike her to completely disregard her friends.

"So, she hasn't been home?"

"For the last time, Ricki, no. Why would I lie?" Rory stood with her arms folded across her chest, one hip jutted out.

He looked at her incredulously. "Um, maybe because you're her best friend?" He ran his hand through his hair, grabbing the back of his neck. "Sorry, I'm just really worried about her. She's never done this before."

Rory's expression softened. "I promise you, I don't know where she is. And in all honesty, if she was trying to avoid you, she'd hardly come back home. Obviously that's the first place you're gonna look."

Ricki sighed. "Yeah, I know. I guess I just hoped I was wrong about her avoiding me."

"What'd you do anyway?" she asked.

"I have no idea. She just didn't turn up, and now her phone is switched off."

Rory pursed her lips. "Well, I know she was heading to the studio, so maybe something happened while she was on her way there?"

"Wait, so she actually said she was on her way?"

"Yeah, like two hours ago."

His mind began racing as he thought of all the possibilities. Two hours ago. Right around the time…

"Shit." He put his hands on the top of his head, his fingers threading through his hair and taking hold. "I know why she didn't show." He began to pace. "Shit!"

"Care to enlighten me?"

Dragging his hands down his face, he turned to look at her. "Sacha was there." He winced.

"Sacha? As in, bitchface, Sacha?"

He nodded his head slowly. "Yeah, her."

"Well, I mean, I know she doesn't like her, but that wouldn't stop her from training. They've faced off before." She put her hands on her hips, raising an eyebrow. "What aren't you telling me?"

"She might've kissed me."

"She what? What the hell were you thinking? Why would you let her do that?"

"I don't know! She came in saying she needed to use the bathroom, then before she left, she grabbed me and kissed me!"

"And you didn't think to push her off? Typical bloody male!" she yelled.

"She took me by surprise!"

"Oh yeah, I'm sure," she said sarcastically. "Her lips just happened to fall into yours."

"You know what she's like."

"Yeah, I do, and so do you. You never should've let her in in the first place."

"Don't you think I know that?" He paced back and forth. "What am I going to do?"

"I'll tell you what you're going to do. You're gonna go out there and look for her, and when you find her, you're going to get down on your hands and knees and beg for her forgiveness." She blocked his path, forcing him to look at her. "Don't screw this up."

"Thanks for the vote of confidence," he replied acerbically.

"I mean it. You go about this wrong, and you will lose her. You didn't see her last time. She was devastated. Now that you two are together, it is ten times worse. Be very careful what you say to her." She grabbed his arm before he could walk past. "And stop with the sneaking around. You're not doing yourself any favours."

Chapter 11

After roaming the streets for an hour, Ricki was nearly ready to give up. She obviously didn't want to be found. He'd tried calling the girls from her dance troupe, but no one had seen her. He stopped on the corner, leaning up against a lamp post while he scrolled through his phone again, hoping for a name to jump out at him.

"Jessie, of course," he mumbled to himself as he put the phone to his ear.

"Ricki," came Jessie's abrupt voice.

"Jessie, hi," Ricki began, suddenly nervous. "I… ah… don't suppose you've seen Maddi? She didn't show up for practice today, and she won't answer my calls." He hung his head, hating to have to admit that to him.

"Yeah, I've seen her."

"Oh, thank God! Is she okay? Can I talk to her?"

"She's not here. She left about fifteen minutes ago."

"Oh, okay. Umm…"

"Why'd you do it, man?"

Unsure what she had told him, he answered, "Do what?"

"You know what I'm talking about. Why'd you kiss Sacha?"

Ricki sighed, running his hand through his hair. "I didn't mean for it to happen. She caught me by surprise."

"Well, Maddi thinks you're cheating on her. She saw you kiss, and she didn't see you pull away. She said you've been sneaking around too. What's that about?" Jessie demanded.

"I haven't been sneaking…"

"Look, if you're not going to be honest with her, then just end it," he interrupted. "Take it from me, Sacha only looks out for number one. She doesn't care about anyone else. Maddi is one of the sweetest girls I've ever met. Don't string her along. She deserves better than that."

"She deserves the world! I swear to you, Jessie, I am not cheating on her. I would never do that to her. I love her."

"I want to believe you, man. I do. But it's not looking good."

"I was going to propose!" Ricki blurted out.

"Wait, what?"

"The sneaking about? I've been planning to propose when we go up to Auckland for the Nationals. I've got this whole routine planned out around it. I thought it would be romantic. I never meant for any of this to happen. Please, Jessie, you've gotta help me. I can't lose her," Ricki pleaded.

"Shit," Jessie huffed down the phone. "Well, at least *that* I can believe." He paused, thinking. "Does it have to be done in Auckland?"

"No, I guess not."

"Okay, it's Saturday night, there will be dancing somewhere. Let me check around and I'll get back to you. Be ready to propose tonight."

"She won't even talk to me, Jessie. How is this going to work?"

"I'll make sure she's there, you just worry about this routine you've got planned. Please tell me Sacha isn't involved in it?"

"Of course not!"

"I just had to check. I may be able to get her to hear you out, but I'm no miracle worker," he joked.

Ricki couldn't believe what Jessie was doing for him. They'd had their moments, but when it came down to it, Jessie really was a good guy. It was no wonder Maddi thought so highly of him.

"Hey, Jessie?"

"Yeah?"

"Thanks. I know we never really got off on the right foot… I just really appreciate your help."

"Hey, it's like I said, Maddi is the sweetest girl I've ever met, and she deserves to be happy. If I can be a part of that, then I'm happy to help. Now, I'm going to head out. I'll text you with the venue."

Disconnecting the call, Ricki shoved his phone back in his pocket, a nervous thrill running through his body. He was going to propose tonight.

He was going to propose *tonight*. Holy shit.

Drumming his fingers on the table while his knee bobbed up and down nervously, Ricki sat watching the door, waiting for Jessie to show up. He had text him the venue and had even spoken to the manager to arrange their little presentation.

Ricki had spent the afternoon with Rob and the guys, rearranging their routine to fit with the smaller space. He had pulled the little square box out of his pocket so many times, just to check that it was still there. He wanted everything to be perfect.

"You look like you could use one of these," Rob said, placing a bourbon in front of him.

"Thanks," Ricki said, wrapping his hand around the glass. "I've never been more nervous in my life."

"You two are crazy about each other. What are you so worried about?" he asked.

"That she doesn't show up, that she says no, that I forget the ring…" He palmed his pocket once more just to be sure.

"You've got the ring, I've seen you staring at it all day, and she's going to say yes, so don't worry, man. Have a drink, it'll calm your nerves."

Nodding, Ricki lifted the glass to his lips, taking a large gulp.

"Better?"

"Mmhmm," he murmured, turning his attention back to the door. He had given in and told Rory what was going on so that she and Damon would convince Maddi to come out tonight. *God, what if she's so mad at me that she doesn't show?*

He checked his watch; half an hour until they were on. Where were they? He could feel the sweat beginning to form on his brow as he considered the thought that she might not come.

He grabbed his drink and finished it in one mouthful. Standing, he muttered to Rob that he was going to the bathroom before staggering across the room. He pushed through the door and was relieved to see that he was alone. He went to the sink and turned the tap, cupping his hands underneath. Splashing the cool water on his face, he lifted his head to stare at his reflection in the mirror. "Get a hold of yourself. She'll be here." After a beat, he pulled a paper towel from the holder and held it to his face, soaking up the moisture. With one last look in the mirror, he crumpled the paper into a ball and threw it in the bin.

Stepping out of the bathroom and back into the bar, he couldn't stop his eyes from travelling to the door once more. His breath caught in his throat when he was met with the icy-blue gaze of Maddi. She was finally here.

Chapter 12

"It wasn't easy, but I convinced her to come. Don't worry, I haven't let the cat out of the bag. She thinks we're here to see Nicole perform her solo," Rory said as she sidled up to Ricki's side.

"Thanks, Rory. It means a lot." He smiled nervously at her. "You want a drink?"

Screwing her face up, Rory quickly shook her head. "Not for me thanks. I'm still recovering from the other night." She rubbed her stomach as if the thought alone made her queasy. "Can't be showing up to class all hungover anyways."

"Yeah, probably not the best look on your first day." Ricki blew out a breath, wiping his hand across his brow before patting his pocket once again. "God, I'm so nervous."

Rory slapped her hand on his shoulder. "I know she's pissed at you right now, but she'll get over it. She loves you, man."

"I hope so. I don't want to lose her."

"Just work your magic. I know she can't resist your bangin' moves on the dancefloor." She turned her body, leaning her back against the bar. "I'd better get back to her. Can't have her getting all suspicious now, can we?"

Ricki nodded his head, bringing his drink to his lips for a bit of Dutch courage. It was almost time.

"Bitch alert," Damon said as he came up to the bar.

"You've got to be kidding me."

"Nope, sorry. She looks wasted again, too."

"Son of a bitch. Just what I need right now," Ricki huffed. "Has Maddi seen her?"

"Not yet, but it's only a matter of time."

Plastering what he hoped was a charming smile on his face, Ricki stepped away from the bar.

"Where are you going?"

"Damage control." He stalked over to the table where Maddi and Rory were sitting, watching the dancers on the floor. "Ahem, Maddi?" he started. "Would you like to dance?" He held his hand out to her, silently praying that she would accept.

"Ricki…"

"Please? Just one dance? You don't even have to talk to me if you don't want to." He wasn't above begging if it meant she would be in his arms again. "It's our song," he said softly. She sighed, gingerly placing her hand in his.

"One dance," she said, avoiding his eyes.

He led her to the dancefloor and pulled her into a closed position, careful to leave a little space between them. Just the fact that she was allowing him this dance made him feel more at ease. Maybe, just maybe, she would forgive him. But would she say yes? Part of him felt like it was silly to ask her now, while she wasn't talking to him. The rest of him wanted to do anything to have her back in his arms for good.

As the song went on, Maddi slowly relaxed into him as she pressed her cheek to his chest. A contented sigh left her lips, and he took that as a sign that things would be okay. He pressed his arm into her back, pulling her against him. She didn't resist.

One song led into another, and Maddi made no move to leave. She even managed a smile as she broke into a shine.

"Woooh! My turn," Sacha slurred as she twirled through the dancefloor, colliding with Maddi and sending her crashing to the floor. Before Ricki could help her up, Sacha had latched onto his arm for balance.

"What the fuck are you doing, Sacha?" he cried incredulously.

"Taking what's mine," she snarled, slamming her lips into his. Ricki gripped her shoulders and pushed her off him.

"Jesus, stop!"

"What? You don't wanna piece of this?" She ran her hands up and down her body, pursing her lips seductively.

"No, Sacha, I don't want any piece of you! I want Maddi!" He spun around to grab her from the floor, but she was gone. "Fuck!"

"Whassa matter, big boy? Your girl can't handle a bitta competition?" Sacha sneered.

"What the hell is wrong with you? There *is* no competition! Even if there was, Maddi would win hands down every time! She's the one for me. Get it through your head!" He turned on his heels and marched off the dancefloor, his eyes scanning the crowd for Maddi.

"She's gone, mate," Damon said from behind. "Come on, I'll help you look for her."

"Don't you ever get tired of messing with people?" Jessie said as he came up beside Sacha.

"What? I'm juss havin' some fun. 'snot my problem if they can't handle the jandal." She erupted into a fit of giggles. "Handle the jandal," she repeated with a snort.

"You're drunk," he stated with a sigh.

"So? What's your point? Why d'you even care?" she slurred, stumbling into him. She relaxed into his chest for a few seconds before pushing away. She turned her eyes brimmed with tears to his. "We're not together anymore, remember?"

"I still care about you, Sacha. You know that. But what you just did? That was beyond cruel. You're toying with their relationship."

She waved a dismissive hand. "Pfft, whatever. She'll get over it."

"I don't know if she will. After that stunt you pulled this morning, and now this little display, you can't blame her for being upset."

"An' this is my problem because…" She folded her arms across her chest defiantly.

"You made it your problem when you decided to play your games. She thought he was cheating on her, but he was going to propose tonight," he said softly. "You can't keep doing this to people."

"Wait… He… He was going to propose?" she whispered, her hand flying to her mouth as she blinked away the tears that sprang to her eyes. No one had ever wanted her enough to propose before, except maybe Jessie, and she'd pushed him away. Her stupid antics to make him jealous had backfired, and short of throwing herself at him, she didn't know what else to do. "I didn't know…"

"I know you didn't. But this is why you can't go around messing with people's heads."

"I can fix it…" She scanned the room, hoping to find Maddi so she could explain. "Lemme fix it."

"You need to leave them alone. Give them their space." He paused, his earlier anger now replaced with pity. "I know you, Sacha. Even though you tried to hide it, when we were together, I saw glimpses of the real you, the vulnerable you." He cupped his finger and thumb under her chin, tilting her head up to look at him again. "Find what makes you happy. Maybe then you'll stop hurting others." He brushed his lips across her forehead before walking away.

No longer able to conceal her tears, they slowly slid down her cheeks as she watched him leave, her fingers held to her lips. "You made me happy," she whispered.

Chapter 13

"Same 'gain," she said, slamming a twenty down on the bar. Her sorrows were slowly dimming as the alcohol took over her system, numbing the pain.

"I think you've had enough, Miss," the bartender replied, pushing her money back.

"Nope, I don' thinkso." Sacha pursed her lips in an attempt to be sexy. "Jus' one more." She held her finger in the air.

"Sorry, I can't serve you any more alcohol tonight."

"Fine. I'll fin' someone who will." She stumbled away from the bar, falling into a group of guys. She giggled, grabbing a muscled bicep to hold herself up. "Sorry." She giggled again. Her mother's words from long ago, rang in her ears, *"You, my girl, have been blessed with boobs and a booty that men will find irresistible. Show 'em a bit of skin, a good time in the bedroom, and you'll want for nothing..."* Puffing her chest out, she leaned into her muscular friend and gave him a wink. "Buy me a drink?" she purred, licking her lips.

"Sure thing, baby. What are ya drinking?"

"Whateveryou're buyin'."

"That's my kinda girl." He palmed her arse, giving a squeeze on his way past. "Don't you go anywhere."

Sacha stood there, swaying out of time to the music. Her vision was starting to blur, and she was finding it harder to stand up straight. Staggering backwards, she caught hold of a chair to steady herself while she waited for her new friend.

"Here ya go, sexy," he said, holding a tall glass out to her.

Sacha took hold of the drink, her tongue darting out to find the straw. She drew in a few quick mouthfuls.

"Mmmm, delishishis…delishish…delicious," she slurred, again breaking into giggles. "Oops!" She fell against the chair that had been holding her up, tipping it into the table and in turn, spilling several drinks.

"Here ya go." One muscular arm wrapped around her waist, helping her to stand, while the other retrieved the teetering chair before it clattered to the floor. "Maybe we should sit down." He swung the chair away from the table and sat, bringing her onto his lap. "That's better."

"Mmmmm, much." Sacha leaned into his hard chest, nuzzling her head into the crook of his neck, pretending it was Jessie. She brought her glass up, this time deciding to do without the straw, and took a big gulp.

"You like that?"

"Mmmhmm," she murmured, her lips still wrapped around her glass.

"Plenty more where that came from." He ran his hand down from her waist to her thigh, resting it there.

"'Sat right?" she asked, tipping her head back to finish it off. She held the glass up in front of her, wiggling it side to side. "Finnnnissshhhhed," she sang.

"Hey, Mike! Grab us another drink, would ya?" He handed his friend some money. "Make hers a double." He winked, edging his hand further around her thigh, his fingertips trailing back and forth.

"'snuffa that," she muttered, picking his hand up and moving it back to her waist. "Don' wanna giveyer frien's a show," she garbled, waving her hand about in front of her. "'saint no peep show." Her hand dropped down onto her lap as she fell back against him, her eyes struggling to focus. "I don' feelsogood."

"You'll be right. You just need something to drink, that's all." Mike had returned with their drinks, and he promptly thrust one in her face. "Drink up, love."

"Jus' a lil bit." She tried to reach for the glass, but the room was beginning to spin and she couldn't see straight. Her hand just flailed about in front of her.

"Here." He put the straw into her mouth. "Suck."

"Mmmhmm." She did as she was told, though it wasn't making her feel any better. What she really wanted to do was go home to bed. Pushing the glass away, she attempted to push up off his lap.

"Woah there. Steady on, let me help you."

"Immmmmokay, I candoit," she said, but his grip around her waist tightened.

"I said, let me help you." He quickly stood up, still holding her against his side. "Sure you don't want more of that drink?" he asked.

She wrinkled her nose. "Nope," she popped the P, letting her eyes close and her head lean into him. "I jus' needta…" She fluttered her eyes open again, trying to stay focused. "I… think…I needagohome… ta'bed."

"Sure thing, sweet cheeks. Lead the way."

She let him hold her up, taking the majority of her weight as she stumbled through the crowd. When they burst through the doors and she was hit with the cool night air, she started to feel a little better. She looked up at the hulking guy beside her. He seemed nice enough, but did she really want to be going home with him? She'd been with Jessie so long, it seemed strange to be in this situation again.

Jessie.

She turned her head, searching for his face amongst the throngs of people, unsure if she wanted to find him or not. The thought of him seeing her in this state didn't sit well with her. Despite what he thought, she really did love him. *God, please don't let him have seen me like this.*

Her mind made up, she placed her hand on his chest to stop him. "I'm jus' gonna calla taxi," she said, pushing away from him.

"No need, babe. I can drive us back to mine." He pulled a set of keys out of his pocket and jingled them in front of her.

Frowning, Sacha poked her finger at him. "You can't drive."

"Sure I can." He grinned at her, his arm snaking around her waist and drawing her back into his side. "Trust me." He kissed the top of her head, giving her middle a squeeze, his thumb brushing back and forth against the underside of her breast.

Sacha waited for the feeling of self-worth to fall over her as it so often had in the past when she had the attention of a man, but it didn't come. Instead she was left feeling disgusted. A chill ran down her spine as she realised what a mistake she was making.

"I don'wanna…" she said, prying his fingers away from her.

"Come on now. I'm just having some fun," he taunted, placing his hand further up so he was now cupping her.

Panic began setting in, sobering her somewhat. "I said don't," she managed, as she tried to wrench his hand off her, but he only held on tighter, hurting her. She looked around for someone who could help her.

"We're all alone here, sweet cheeks. Come on, let's have some fun." He smirked as he dragged her around the corner into darkness.

"Sorry, mate. That was Rory. Maddi's going home and… she doesn't want to see you."

"Of course she doesn't. I've really fucked things up this time, Damo. I don't know why I tried to do something so over the top. It's not who I am." Ricki ran his hand through his hair in frustration. "I should've just proposed when I had the chance, without all the theatrics."

"You'll get through this. Maddi's a reasonable girl, and she loves you. She'll hear you out once she's calmed down."

"I hope you're right." Shoving his hands in his pockets, Ricki stopped to suss out their whereabouts. "May as well head back. Do you think it'd be okay if I sleep on the couch?"

"It's your place too," Damon said, shrugging. "And mine. I'm sure she'll be over it by the morning."

As they rounded the corner to take them back to Feeney's, a movement in the shadows caught his eye. Nudging Ricki, he nodded toward the darkness. "Is it just me, or does that look like a couple making out?"

Ricki followed his gaze, squinting his eyes to focus. "Is that… Sacha?"

"You know, I think you may be right."

A crease formed on his brow as he continued to watch. "I don't feel good about this. She's not moving,

I don't think she's conscious. And who is that guy she's with?"

"Certainly not anyone we know." Damon flexed his hands into fists.

Ricki turned to Damon with a look of concern. "I'm probably going to regret this, but we should do something."

"You don't have to ask me twice." He tilted his head side-to-side, cracking his neck. "For the record, this is why Maddi will come back to you. Even after all the shit Sacha has caused you, you're still willing to help her when she's in need. You're a better man than most." He squared his shoulders, pushing his shirt sleeves up. "Now, let's go sort this shithead out."

Chapter 14

"He was going to propose?" Maddi stopped walking, turning to face her friend. "Seriously?"

Rory nodded her head. "Yup. That's what all the sneaking around was about. He had this big elaborate thing planned for in Auckland, but you know, shit happened today, so he brought it forward. Jessie helped him organise it."

"I had no idea," she said softly.

"You and me both. The only reason he told me was so that I would make sure you came tonight." She reached out, grasping Maddi's hands. "What you saw in there? That was just Sacha being Sacha. Ricki is head over heels in love with you, girl. Always has been."

Maddi searched Rory's eyes, knowing she would never lie to her. Letting out a sigh, she brought her hands to her face, then slowly peeled her fingers open to peer through.

"Okay, maybe you're right. We need to go back and find him."

Rory beamed. "That's my girl!" She let out an excited squeal. "I'm gonna be a bridesmaid!" She latched onto Maddi's elbow, practically dragging her down the road and back into town.

"Hey!" Damon roared as they approached the couple in the shadows.

"Sacha?" Ricki called out. "You okay?"

"She's fine, mate. We're just leaving."

"Sacha?" Ricki tried again.

"Back off and get your own date," the guy growled.

"We're not letting you take her anywhere," Damon spat. "What's the matter, *mate*? Can't get a sober girl to go home with you, so you have to resort to dragging a comatose one down a dark alley?" He puffed his chest out as he stepped in front of the guy.

"Who the fuck do you think you are, tough guy?" the guy snarled, letting go of Sacha and moving to within an inch of Damon's face. They both stood there glaring at each other, daring the other to make the first move.

"Sacha? Can you hear me?" Ricki asked, cradling her head against his chest. "Sacha? Come on, I need you to wake up now."

"Mmmmmhmmmpffff," she mumbled.

"That's a girl, open your eyes for me," Ricki said, gently rocking her in his arms. Looking over at Damon and the guy's stare off, he cleared his throat, directing his next words their way. "What did you give her?"

"I didn't give her anything."

Damon narrowed his eyes. "Try again, mate. What did you give her?" He spoke slowly, articulating each word.

"I told you, I didn't give her anything. I just bought her a couple drinks. It's not my fault if she can't handle her alcohol," he sneered, shoving Damon, whose large frame barely even moved.

"Tut tut," Damon said, shaking his head with a glint in his eye. "Everyone knows you don't make the first move." Flattening his hands against the guy's chest, he pushed, sending him backwards. "Now you're fair game. Self-defence and all that." He stalked towards him, fists clenched at his sides.

Meanwhile, Ricki had one arm wrapped securely around Sacha's back, holding her up while he cupped her face in his other hand. "Come on, Sacha. Talk to me. What did he do to you?"

Her brow furrowed and she whimpered, bringing her arms up between them as if to push him away.

"Shhh, Sacha, it's me. It's Ricki." He began to stroke her face, trying to calm her. "I'm not going to hurt you."

"Ricki?" she mumbled, her eyes fluttering as she tried to open them. "I'm so sssorry," she slurred before passing out. Ricki scanned the area for a place to sit her down. Spotting an empty doorway down the road, he quickly walked her over, leaving Damon to sort out the douchebag.

"Here we go, let's take a seat." He eased their bodies down to the step, cushioning her body against his, her head resting on his shoulder. He wrapped an arm around her, pulling her shaking body in close to keep her warm. With the light from the lamp post beside them, he took a moment to scan over her, searching for any signs of harm. Her dress was torn but still intact, and her hair had matted in a sticky mess to one side. As gently as he could, he brushed her hair aside to find a large gash just above her ear. "Shit." A shudder ran through him at the thought of what might've happened. "Sacha, I need you to wake up for me," he said again, rubbing his hand up and down her arm. "Come on, open your eyes."

A scuffle to the side caught his attention as Damon hauled the guy over, his hands twisted behind his back. His eye was swelling shut, and a trickle of blood ran down from the corner of his mouth. "You got your phone on you? We should call the cops and report this guy," he said, barely even out of breath.

"Yeah, hang on, it's in my pocket." Ricki shifted his weight, Sacha's head lolling forwards. "Shit," he cussed under his breath, trying to hold her up and reach for his phone at the same time.

"Ricki?" Maddi's small voice came from across the road.

"Maddi?" he called out.

"What's going on?" she asked as she made her way over to them, eyeing up the battered man in Damon's arms. "What did you do?" It was then that she saw Sacha practically in Ricki's lap. Her eyes went wide as they darted between the three of them. "What happened? Is she okay?"

"Is that Sacha?" Rory asked, squatting down beside Ricki to get a better look. "She doesn't look too good."

"No, she's not. We need to call an ambulance and the cops, do either of you have a phone on you?" Ricki's voice sounded calmer than he felt.

"On it," Rory said, snatching her phone out of her purse. "What am I telling them?"

"We caught this guy dragging her off down that alley over there," he nodded down the street a bit. "She wasn't moving, and I think maybe he drugged her. I can't get her to wake up."

Maddi clasped her hands to her mouth, shaking her head side-to-side as tears came to her eyes. Her breath came out in pants as she stumbled backwards.

Ricki knew how hard this must be for her to see after what Dane had put her through the year before. "Maddi, it's okay. She's going to be okay. He didn't have a chance to… ya know… He didn't… We got to her in time." He held her gaze, willing her to stay with him and not regress back to the shell of a woman she had been for a time after her attack.

Sacha's body began to twitch in his arms, causing him to look away. Her jaw clenched tight as her eyelids fluttered open, her eyes rolling backwards. A thin trail of spittle ran down her chin as her body started convulsing fiercely.

"Shit! She's having a seizure!" Ricki yelled, struggling to keep her from falling to the concrete. "Maddi, I need your help!" When she didn't move, he shouted again, "Maddi! Help me!"

As if a switch had been turned on, she blinked once, then ran to his side, cradling Sacha's head in her arms as they lay her jerking body across both of their laps.

"Ambulance is on the way!" Rory called, settling herself on the step below them to help. "Don't hold her too tight. I read somewhere that you're not meant to try and stop them, or they can hurt themselves." Placing a hand on both their knees, Rory formed a barrier so that Sacha couldn't fall from her perch, and they could loosen their hold. Within minutes, the seizure had subsided. "We need to get her onto her side and check her airway. I think she's better off lying on the concrete."

Between the three of them, they eased her down to the ground and into the recovery position while they waited for the ambulance to arrive. Damon continued to hold her attacker, twisting his hands just that little bit further up behind his back, making him cry out in pain.

"What's that? Am I hurting you?" Damon said, dragging him closer to Sacha. He grabbed him by the hair and forced him to look at her. "See what you did?" he demanded. "She's half your size, you worthless piece of shit. Did that stop you?"

"I'm sorry," he stuttered, wincing as his arms were bent even more.

"Damon," Ricki cautioned, nodding towards the girls who were trying to make Sacha comfortable by rolling a jacket up and sliding it under her head. The distant sound of sirens let them know that help was finally on the way, so Rory got to her feet and jogged out to the corner to wave them down.

"You're going to be okay, Sacha," Maddi crooned softly while stroking her hair. "You're going to be okay."

Chapter 15

"Where is she?" Jessie ran up to the reception desk. "Sacha Barrett, she was brought in here, I need to see her."

"Jessie," Maddi called, beckoning him over to the waiting room. She stood, her arms held out in front of her, offering comfort. Without hesitation, Jessie threw himself into her arms, grasping onto her as if his life depended on it. She just held him, slowly running her hand up and down his back soothingly. Little by little, he felt the tension begin to wane. Pulling back, he looked into her eyes, searching for some kind of solace.

"What happened? Is she... is she okay?" he whispered.

"Come and sit down," Maddi urged, taking hold of his hand and leading him to one of the seats away from prying eyes. "They haven't really told us much, I guess because we're not family. All we know is that she has been rushed into surgery. She had bleeding on the brain, and they needed to do something to relieve the pressure."

The colour drained from his face as he stared at her in disbelief. "This can't be happening," he murmured, swiping his hand across his eyes. "I was talking to her not long ago, she was fine. A little drunk, but fine. How did this happen?" he asked.

Ricki cleared his throat. "We found her," he motioned to Damon, who was sitting to his left, his arms wrapped around Rory. "This guy had been feeding her drinks, maybe something else too, we're not sure. He was trying to drag her down an alley when we saw them. She was out to it." He paused, not wanting to overwhelm him any more than needed. "She had a cut above her ear," he pointed to his own head, "probably from trying to get away. At least that's what the cops thought."

Jessie hunched over, his elbows planted on his knees and his face in his hands. "I shouldn't have left her," he muttered. "She was upset and drunk, and I left her to fend for herself."

"This isn't your fault, Jessie." Maddi knelt in front of him, making him look at her. "No one could have known. The main thing is that they got to her before he had a chance to take it any further."

His head snapped up. "So, she wasn't…"

Maddi shook her head. "No. It didn't get that far."

Turning his tear-filled eyes to Ricki, he nodded his head. "Thank you," he managed. "Both of you. I don't know what I would've done…"

"Shhh, don't do that to yourself," Maddi soothed. "She's safe now. That's all that matters."

"If it makes you feel any better, I got a couple of punches in before the cops arrived," Damon said, a smirk on his face as he recalled the satisfying crunch of the guy's nose.

Jessie scoffed, his lips pulling up in the faintest of smiles. "Thanks, that actually does make me feel a little better."

"He's lucky I can control my temper. It wasn't easy though."

"You're a stronger man than I. I would've ripped his fucking head off," Jessie spat the last part out, his jaw locked in a grimace.

"Believe me, if I didn't have this one to go home to," he pulled Rory in close, "I probably would have." He kissed the top of her head. "I just didn't fancy being locked up while he got off scott free."

"He won't, will he?" Rory questioned. "Get off scott free I mean." She peered up at Damon, a shudder running down her spine. "Just the thought of him out on the streets gives me the heebie jeebies."

Maddi, who had gone back to her seat, was staring at her hands in her lap.

"You okay?" Ricki asked softly, placing his hand on top of hers.

"Mmhmm." She nodded, but he could see the tears slowly trickling down her cheeks. Bringing his hand up to cup her face, he gently brushed them away with his thumb.

"You're thinking about Dane, aren't you?" he said knowingly.

A small sigh escaped her lips as she glanced up at him. "I know it's wrong, we're meant to be here for

Sacha…" she trailed off, looking back down at their hands entwined.

"It's okay to feel this way, Maddi. What you went through was traumatic, and there are definite similarities here. It's no wonder it's brought those memories back to the forefront."

Nodding her head, she said, "I guess." Frowning, she added, "I was so scared. For a minute there, I thought you and her were… and then when I realised… I just kept having flashes of his face above me."

"Come here," he said, pulling her onto his lap. "It's okay. You know I will never let him get close to you again, right?"

"I know," she whispered.

"And, for the record, you're the only girl I want in my arms." He tilted her chin up, pressing his forehead against hers. "It's always been you." Those words alone were enough to open the floodgates. Unable to hold back any longer, she buried her face into the crook of his neck, sobbing while he cradled her against him.

An hour later, a short, balding man garbed in blue scrubs came barrelling through the doors and into the waiting room. "Mrs Barrett?" he asked.

Jessie jumped up. "I haven't been able to get hold of her."

"And you are?"

"Jessie, sir." He held his hand out. "I'm her… she was my… we're best friends," he said, stumbling through his words.

Ricki strode over to join them. "You're the doctor who worked on her?" he asked.

"Yes, I am. Is anyone here related to Miss Barrett?"

Jessie shook his head. "No, we're not. She hasn't seen her father since she was a baby, and her mother, well, let's just say they're not really on speaking terms," he explained. He motioned to the group around him as he said, "We're really all she has."

Nodding, the doctor said, "Well, it's not normally how we like to do things around here, but I can see how much she must mean to you all, and I'd rather she had some support while she recovers." He paused, looking each of them in the eye before continuing. "The bleed was more severe than we first thought and the amount of alcohol in her system hasn't helped. Her brain has been through a considerable amount of trauma this evening, so we've had to put her into an induced coma. She's being taken through to recovery as we speak."

"Can we see her?" Jessie asked, folding his arms across his broad chest.

"Not just yet. I'll have a nurse let you know when she's been moved into a room. I'd prefer that you limit it to one person at a time to start with. She's going to be under for at least 24 hours, maybe longer."

"But she'll be okay though?" Jessie asked.

"It's really up to her now, son. We've done all that we can for her for now." He clapped a hand on his shoulder. "She's a fighter, and she's got some great support with you here. Just try to stay positive. Talk to her, let her know you're all here for her."

"Yes, sir," Jessie said, nodding his head. "Thank you, for everything."

"No need to thank me. I'm just doing my job."

"Even so, I'm glad you're here to do it." Jessie shook his hand again. "I couldn't bear to lose her."

The doctor gave a sympathetic look. "She's still got a long road to go. Hang in there."

Chapter 16

"Why don't you guys go home and get some rest?" Jessie suggested as Rory curled up in a ball on the couch, her head tucked into her chin. "The doctor said she'll be under for a while, no point in all of us losing sleep."

"Nah, we're good," Rory said with a yawn.

"Look at you, you can barely keep your eyes open." Turning to Damon, he said, "Just take her home, honestly, I'm fine to stay here with Sacha."

"You sure?"

"Absolutely. You guys have already done so much for her. I can't thank you enough for what you did tonight." He shook his head in disbelief. "I still can't believe this has happened. It's like some sort of nightmare, you know? You hear of these stories, but you never expect it to happen to someone you're close to."

Ricki and Maddi exchanged a look. She knew he wanted to say something, but now wasn't the time. She gave a small shake of her head, letting him know how she felt. She saw his shoulders lift and fall as he suppressed a sigh.

When Dane had forced himself on her last year, she hadn't wanted anyone to know. Other than Ricki,

Damon and Rory, who had come to her rescue, no one else had been told. Word had spread through the dance community of Dane's arrest, but the details had been vague. Of course, there had been whispers, but Ricki had been quick to shut them down, knowing how Maddi wanted to keep it quiet.

He couldn't understand it really. When he'd walked in and seen her pinned to the bed with a vacant look in her eyes, he'd very nearly lost it. As far as he was concerned, Dane deserved to be dragged through the wringer. He felt that the dance community needed to know what kind of person he was. Maddi, on the other hand, just wanted to forget it had happened in the first place. She couldn't bear the thought of people pitying her or feeling as though they needed to tip-toe around her.

Directly after the attack, she had hidden herself away, only feeling comfortable around the three of them. It hadn't been until the night of the comps when she had finally stepped out of her comfort zone and gone out. It had taken some convincing, but once she was immersed into the dance world once more, it was as if a weight had been lifted from her shoulders. She had blossomed, becoming an even stronger dancer and mentor for others. What she'd been through, he wouldn't wish on anyone, but he had to admit, it had made her a stronger person. The change had been subtle, and only those close to her had really noticed it.

Maddi had this light inside her that shone brighter than anything he'd ever seen before. People were drawn to her. Not only was she mesmerizing to watch, she was also humble, and that made people want to be around her. It was inevitable that they would begin teaching their own classes alongside Lisa.

Watching her now, he knew she was hurting from the reminder, but he could still see that light behind her eyes. He would do anything to keep that light shining bright, and if it meant he had to keep it in and not divulge her secret to Jessie, then so be it.

Turning his attention back to Jessie, he acknowledged what he'd said. "Yeah, it was pretty scary to see." Shoving his hands in his pockets, he caught Maddi's eye, trying to convey his understanding to her. "I'm just glad we could help. She's going to need a lot of support to get through this."

Rubbing the back of his neck, Jessie glanced up from the floor, an odd expression on his face. "Look, I know you guys haven't always seen eye to eye," he raised his hand to stop them from saying anything before he continued, "and I know that it's her doing. I just… what you're doing, by being here? It really means a lot. It's no excuse, but she hasn't had an easy life. I know she puts on this tough front, but her folks aren't really around, and as you know, she's not the best at making friends or letting people in." He toed the ground, taking a deep breath. "I know you don't have to be here…"

Maddi put her hand on his arm. "It's okay, Jessie. We want to be here. For both of you."

His shoulders sagged with her words. "You have no idea how much that means to me."

"It's what friends do." She smiled. "And even though you both won't admit it, I know you love each other." She looked over at Ricki with a grin. "It's kinda something we know a bit about."

Reaching out to take her hand, Ricki added, "You know she's right; she always is."

"I think maybe, when you go in to see her, you should tell her how you feel. I mean, it's the perfect time, don't you think?"

"At least she can't run away," Damon added as he scooped Rory into his arms.

"Damo! That's not what I meant," Maddi scolded.

"It can't hurt though, right?" Ricki said with a tip of his head. "Don't they say that you can still hear everything going on around you while you're in a coma? Might give her some incentive to wake up."

"Exactly," Maddi said, nodding.

"Or…"

"Damo!" both Maddi and Ricki said.

"Okay, okay! Just trying to lighten the mood." He walked towards the door. "I'm going to head home and get this one into bed." He waggled his eyebrows suggestively.

"Go!" Maddi giggled, pointing out the door.

"Fine, I'm going." He looked at Ricki, holding his hand up and wiggling his thumb around as if typing. "Let me know if you need anything."

"Will do."

As soon as he'd passed through the door, a nurse poked her head into the room. "Sacha has been moved into her own room now if you would like to sit with her for a little while."

Jessie practically ran to the door. "Yes please, I'd like to see her."

Smiling warmly, the nurse stepped aside, allowing him to join her. "Okay, follow me."

Chapter 17

Standing at the edge of the room, Jessie watched Sacha's chest slowly rise and fall. He had never seen her look more vulnerable than at this moment. Along one arm, a handprint was visible in shades of blue and purple. The stark white bandage adorning her head stood in sharp contrast to her jet-black hair, making her seem almost angelic.

Struggling to hold back tears, Jessie cautiously stepped into the room, edging closer to the bed. His hand hovered above hers tentatively, scared he might hurt her.

"You can touch her," the nurse said from the doorway. "You won't break her, I promise. It might even help her to feel you with her."

Jessie nodded appreciatively. Turning back to Sacha, he eased her hand into his, giving a gentle squeeze to let her know he was there.

"Hey, beautiful," he whispered. "I'm so sorry I wasn't there for you." He sat down, burying his face in her sheets and pressing kisses to the back of her hand. "I'd do anything to take it back. I never should have left you." His resolve shattered and he was no longer able to hold back the tears. A sob escaped as he raised a hand to stroke her face, committing every detail of her features to memory. "I can't lose you, Sacha. You have to come back to me. I'm so sorry I left you alone. I'm so sorry…"

Ricki leaned his head against the wall, resting his eyes for a moment. Jessie had been in with Sacha for a little over an hour and he wanted to be awake when he came back. He knew all too well the feeling of helplessness after someone you care about has gone through something as traumatic as this, and he needed Jessie to know that he was here for him if he ever needed to talk. It was the least he could do for him after he'd tried to help him win Maddi back.

Maddi.

She was curled into his side, one hand on his chest, the other wrapped around his back. He could tell from her steady breaths, that she had been asleep for a while now. Just that alone was enough to bring a smile to his face. She was back in his arms, resting peacefully. For now, at least.

He wasn't naïve enough to believe that everything could go back to the way it was. He knew he'd hurt her, albeit accidentally. He was so used to her being around, that he'd taken it for granted she'd always be there. What happened with Sacha tonight was a reminder that anything could happen. You can't plan for everything.

He had thought that he needed to make some grand gesture to prove how much he loved her, when really, all he ended up doing was pushing her away. He realised now that all he'd really needed to do was to be with her. Actually *be* present in the moment with her.

One thing was for sure, Ricki was prepared to do whatever it took to make her happy, for as long as she would let him.

"You're still here?" Jessie's voice came from across the room, interrupting him from his thoughts.

"Yeah, of course. I didn't think you'd want to be here alone," Ricki said quietly so as not to disturb Maddi. "Nobody should have to be on their own at a time like this."

"Thanks, man. I appreciate it." Jessie slumped down in one of the chairs opposite. He looked exhausted. His eyes were red-rimmed and bloodshot. He could barely keep them open.

"Why don't I drive you home? You can catch some sleep and then come back when you're fresh," Ricki offered.

Scrubbing his hand down his face, Jessie bobbed his head up and down in the smallest of movements. "Sleep sounds great." He glanced up with a look of guilt in his eyes. "But I shouldn't leave her. What if she wakes up?"

"Then she'll have nurses to keep her company until you're able to be back here." Before he could protest, Ricki added, "You're no good to her if you're dead on your feet." He cringed at his choice of words. "Sorry."

"I just don't want her to feel like she's been abandoned again," Jessie said in a pained voice.

"She won't, I promise. By the time she gets out of here, she'll be sick of the sight of us." Ricki grinned.

Jessie managed a laugh despite his fatigue. "I don't want to be gone long," he said, giving in.

"Okay, well I'll set my alarm, and I'll be back to pick you up around 9AM. That gives us almost five hours of sleep."

"You don't have to drive me," Jessie said through a yawn. "I have my car."

"And you will fall asleep at the wheel. We don't need another friend in the hospital, thank you very much. I'll drive, and you can take your car home later, okay?"

Nodding his head in agreement, Jessie pushed himself up to stand. "Thanks, Ricki. You're a good guy. I can see why she loves you so much." He gestured to the sleeping Maddi in his lap.

"The feeling is mutual," he said, grinning down at her.

Chapter 18

Rory shuffled down the hallway, her robe hanging loosely. She rubbed at her eyes but couldn't get rid of that scratchy feeling of tiredness. "Coffee," she muttered, moving through the kitchen on auto-pilot.

They'd spent a good chunk of Sunday at the hospital with Sacha and it had been another late night. Probably not the best thing to do the day before her first day at *Gastronomie.*

She had set her alarm nice and early so she would have plenty of time to get organised and pick the perfect outfit. This was the only chance she would get to make a first impression with her classmates, and she wanted it to be a good one.

After adding an extra scoop of coffee to her cup, she quickly inhaled the delicious aroma, allowing it to wake her up a little more. "Mmmm, coffee. How would I survive without you?"

Taking a sip, she instantly pulled the cup away, staring at it as if it were offensive. "What the?" she muttered, grabbing the milk and checking the use-by date. "Nope, still good." She turned back to her cup and tentatively brought it up to her lips. "Oh God, not again!" She slammed the cup down, sploshing the hot liquid everywhere before racing to the bathroom.

"This… can't… be… happening," she gurgled as she retched into the toilet.

She sat back, swiping a handful of toilet paper across her mouth as she tried to catch her breath. With as much effort as she could muster, she slowly pulled herself up to her feet. The basket of supplies in the corner caught her eye, and a sinking feeling hit the pit of her stomach.

"No," she whispered, counting back on her fingers. "Shit!" she hissed under her breath. "Fuck!" Tears sprang to her eyes as she began to pace back and forth. "What am I gonna do?"

"About what?" Damon asked, poking his head into the bathroom. Seeing her tear-streaked face, he quickly closed the gap between them. "What is it, babe? What's wrong?"

At a loss for words, Rory simply brought her hand to her stomach and nodded towards the toilet.

"Oh, you're still sick?" Rory bobbed her head up and down, not trusting herself to speak without breaking down further. Pulling her into his chest, he ran a soothing hand down her back. "It's okay, babe. I'm sure they'll understand that you can't make it."

Frowning, Rory stepped back. "I have to go," she said. "If I don't, I'll lose my place." Of that she was certain.

"But you can't be rushing off to the bathroom every few minutes. And what about the other students? You could make them sick too," he tried to reason.

Shaking her head firmly, Rory said, "No. I have to be there. I'll be fine. It always clears during the day, you know that."

Pressing his lips together, he didn't look convinced. "Rory…"

"I'm going, Damo. I worked too hard to get in to throw it all away on the first day." Stepping around him to the sink, she turned the cold tap on and held her hands underneath before splashing some water in her face. Bracing her hands on the edge, she looked up into the mirror, seeing the concern in his face staring back at her. Sighing, she turned back to face him. "I promise, if it doesn't go away, I'll come home, okay?" She brought her hand up to his forehead, smoothing out the crease.

"Rest as much as you can, and drink lots of water," he said, knowing there was no way he could stop her once her mind was set. "And call me if you need me to come get you."

"Aye aye, Cap'n," she said with a tired grin and a salute.

"Maddi?" Rory whispered, sneaking into her best friend's room.

"Mmmm?" a voice murmured from under the covers.

"Maddi, I need to ask you a favour." She tip-toed around the bed to Maddi's side, careful not to wake Ricki. Stroking her hair from her face in an attempt to wake her up, she tried again. "Maddi?"

One eye flickered open. "What time is it?" she mumbled. "It feels early."

Glancing at the alarm clock on the bedside table, Rory felt bad for waking her. "Um, it's 6AM."

"Rory," she whined, rolling over.

"Maddi, please. I need your help. It's important." She held her breath, waiting for Maddi to tell her to leave.

Instead, she rolled back over to face her. "Okay, what is it? This better be life-threatening."

"Um, well it's not life-threatening per se. More… life-altering." She sighed, this was harder than she thought. "I… um… I need you to get me something. I have course today, so I can't do it myself…" *Just spit it out already!* "I… um… I need," she lowered her voice even more, "a pregnancy test." She winced.

Maddi blinked, her eyes darting side-to-side. "Are you serious?" When Rory nodded her head, she reached a hand out to cup her cheek. "Really?"

"Maybe? I don't know. I've been so busy with getting into *Gastronomie* that I don't remember the last time I had my monthly, and I've been so sick lately. It's the only thing that makes sense," she said in a hushed voice, really not wanting Ricki to find out before Damon. "Maddi, I'm scared. I don't think I'm ready to be a mum, and what about Damo?" Her voice cracked as tears began to slide down her face for the second time today.

"Are you kidding? You and Damo would make great parents."

"We haven't even discussed children yet," she sobbed, burying her face in the sheets.

"Hey." Maddi lifted Rory's chin to face her. "He will be over the moon."

"You think?" she asked, wiping her eyes with the back of her hand.

"I know."

Rory smiled. "Thanks."

"Of course." Rory stood up to leave, but Maddi grabbed her hand. "Don't worry. We'll get through this."

Chapter 19

It was coming up 48 hours that Sacha had been under. They kept telling Jessie it was normal for it to take a while under such circumstances, but he couldn't help feeling that they were humouring him. He'd barely left her side, except for the few hours when Ricki had made him go home to sleep that first night. They'd all tried to convince him that she would be okay, but he didn't want her waking up without him there. Instead, he'd taken to dragging the over-stuffed chair in the corner to the side of her bed and sleeping there.

Maddi and Ricki had not long left. They'd been in to see her several times, talking to her and letting her know that they, and the whole dance community were all there for her. The large bouquet of flowers they'd brought in stood on a table to her side with a card attached, signed by the dancers.

Jessie was overwhelmed by the generosity of the community he'd grown to love over the last few years. They really were like a family. Which she was going to need when this was all over.

He'd tried on numerous occasions to get her mother to come and visit, but she flat out refused, using the excuse that she didn't like hospitals. He had heard the slurring of her words and knew she was really too wasted to give a shit. She'd never shown an interest in Sacha the entire time he'd known her, so he didn't know why he'd expected any differently this time around. Still, he gave it another shot.

"Hi, Mrs Barrett? It's Jessie. Sacha still hasn't woken up. I thought maybe you could stop by and talk to her? See if your voice might help bring her back to us?" His voice caught in his throat as he said that last part. He was so scared that she would never wake up, hence the reason for his continued perseverance with Barbara.

He held his breath, waiting for her to say something. After a long silence and a drawn-out sigh, she finally responded. "Honey, what makes you think I'm gonna come? You think if you keep callin', I'll come runnin'?"

"She's your daughter. Don't you even care what happens to her?" he asked, unable to comprehend what kind of mother could treat her daughter that way.

"She stopped bein' my daughter the minute she up an' left me high an' dry. Do me a favour. Don't call again." The phone clicked signalling the end of the call, and Jessie sat there staring at his phone in stunned silence. Sacha had told him they had a strained relationship, and that she'd left when her mother began expecting more than she was willing to give, but he'd still never imagined that she could be so cruel. He was beginning to see why Sacha was the way she was.

"Dude, you have a minute?" Damon asked, poking his head into Ricki's room.

"Sure, what's up?" Damon stepped inside, looking around the room to check that Maddi wasn't around before closing the door behind him. "You okay? You seem a little tense?" Ricki asked with a look of amusement.

"Ah, yeah. I saw something earlier today." He lowered his voice, moving closer. "Something that I think you might want to know about."

"Okay?" Ricki sat up, a frown creasing his brow. "What is it?"

"I went to go get Rory some chocolates to celebrate her first day at course, and I happened to walk past the pharmacy on the corner." He paused, taking a breath. "Maddi was in there." He looked up, concern all over his face.

"And?"

"She was looking at pregnancy tests."

Ricki went white as a ghost. "Pregnancy tests? Are you sure?"

Damon nodded. "Yeah, I'm sure. I didn't know if I should say anything or not, but I figured you had a right to know if she was, ya know," he held his hands out in front of him as if rubbing a pregnant belly. "I know I'd want to know."

Ricki sat back, raking his hand through his hair. "Wow. This… This is big. I can't believe it. I could be a father," he said under his breath. Slowly a smile spread across his face. "I could be a father," he said again.

Chapter 20

"Did you get it?" Rory practically pounced on Maddi as she walked through the door. Swivelling her head side-to-side, checking they were alone, Maddi nodded her head, retrieving a brown paper bag from her purse.

"I got two, just in case." She held the parcel out for Rory to grab. Biting her lip, Rory hesitated, almost too scared to accept it for fear it may make it real. "I can hold onto them until you're ready, if you want," Maddi offered.

"No!" Rory said, reaching for the bag. "I… I need to know." Peering inside, she sucked in a breath. "What if I do it wrong?"

Placing her hands over Rory's, Maddi smiled at her. "I'm sure they have instructions. Do you want me to read them with you? With both of us, I'm sure we'll get it right."

"Would you?"

Tilting her head to the side, Maddi shrugged. "Of course. That's what friends are for, isn't it?"

Fighting back tears for the fourth time that day, Rory simply nodded, an appreciative smile on her face. "Thanks, Maddi. For everything."

Waving her hand dismissively, she said, "Stop, I haven't done anything." She walked over to the bathroom door, her hand poised over the handle. "You wanna do it now?"

"Mmmhmm. I need to know. I spent all day worrying about it." She looked down at her hand resting on her belly and smiled. "It's funny how just the thought of a baby inside makes you start doing this."

"It just shows how great you'll be as a mother. You're already protective of the little thing." Maddi grinned, taking hold of Rory's hand and leading her through to the bathroom. "Now, let's have a look at these tests."

"And it wasn't until I went to the bathroom that I realised I had flour all through my hair!" Rory ran her hand through her short crop, sending another dusting of flour into the air. "I guess there was more floating about than I thought." She shrugged.

"All from a burst bag?"

"Yeah, well, I *did* drop it on the bench. It kinda went poof into the air." She moved her hands in arcs above her to demonstrate. "Not exactly the best start to the course."

"Hey, at least they'll remember who you are." Maddi grinned, giving her leg a playful shove.

"I'd rather they remembered me for my cooking, not my fuck-ups."

"They will, sweetie, give it time. Everyone has off days, yours just happened to be on the first day of course. Tomorrow, it'll be someone else. You'll see." Maddi paused to check her watch. "It's time," she whispered, glancing at the two sticks balanced on the edge of the vanity. They had been sitting on the bathroom floor for the past five minutes, discussing anything but the reason they were in there.

Inhaling deeply, Rory pulled her knees into her chest. "I'm scared."

"I know." Maddi scooted over to sit beside her, resting her head on her shoulder. "We can give it a few more minutes if you want."

"I want to know, but I don't at the same time, you know? Like, once I see the results, everything changes."

"Not necessarily. It could be a false alarm," Maddi offered.

"True, but…"

"But you think it's positive," Maddi finished for her.

"Yeah. I do."

"We'll get through this. No matter what the results, we'll work this out."

Puffing out a breath, Rory slapped her hands on her thighs before pushing herself up to stand. "Okay. Let's do this." She reached down to help Maddi up. Holding hands, they stepped up to the vanity and each took hold of a stick. "Two lines," Rory whispered.

"Yup. Two lines." Maddi gave her hand a squeeze.

"I guess I'm pregnant."

Chapter 21

"What do you think they're doing in there?" Damon asked, his arms folded across his chest as he eyed the bathroom door.

"Considering what you saw, I think it's pretty obvious, don't you?"

"I guess. It's taking them a while though."

"You ever taken a test before?" Ricki asked, one eyebrow cocked.

"No." Damon scoffed, turning his attention away from the door.

"Well, then you don't know how long it takes, do you?" Ricki made his way into the kitchen. "Coffee?" he asked, switching the jug on.

"Sure." He watched Ricki as he pulled two mugs down from the cupboard. "How can you be so calm?"

Sighing, Ricki braced his hands on the counter. "How am I supposed to be? We don't know anything yet. No point in stressing over something that may or may not happen." He shrugged, turning back to his task.

Shaking his head, Damon said, "I don't get you sometimes, man. Only a few days ago you were stressing over her not talking to you, and now that she might be," he lowered his voice, "pregnant, you look like you couldn't care less."

"Yeah well, it only takes one day to change your perspective." He ran his hand through his hair, grabbing the back of his neck. "What happened to Sacha scared the shit out of me. What if it had been Maddi? I mean, I was scared when she took off, but the thought of anything happening to her terrifies me. So, as long as she's safe and willing to have me in her life, I'm happy." Dropping his arm, he looked out the window, a grin spreading across his face. "And honestly, the thought of raising a baby with Maddi? I couldn't think of anything better."

"When you put it that way…" Damon trailed off, his eyes travelling back to the bathroom. "It would be kinda nice to have a little bundle of joy with Rory."

"We're the lucky ones, Damo." Ricki handed him his cup. "I can't imagine what Jessie is going through right now."

Damon's face dropped. "When I think about what that bastard did…" He clenched his fists by his side. "I don't care how fucked up she was, Sacha didn't deserve that."

"No, she didn't." Maddi stood in the doorway, her phone in her hand. "That was Jessie. Sacha just had another seizure."

"Jessie." Maddi ran into her friend's arms, pulling him firm against her. "Shh, she'll be okay. She'll get through this," she soothed as she ran her hands up and down his back. He clung to her as if she were the only thing holding him up, his hands grasping her shirt. With his face buried in the crook of her neck, he sobbed, his whole body shaking. "Just let it out." She continued to stroke his back and neck, trying to stay strong for him.

"She opened her eyes," he whispered when he pulled back. "She looked at me and smiled, before…" His face crumpled as fresh tears trailed their way down his cheeks. He shook his head. "I'm sorry," he whispered.

"Aww, Jessie," she said softly, cupping her hands around his face. "You have nothing to be sorry for." She gently wiped his tears from his cheeks. "Maybe she's trying to come back to us," she offered with a hesitant smile. "It could be a good sign. You just have to stay positive."

"Maybe," he whispered, but she could tell he didn't believe his own words.

Sliding her hands down his arms, she grasped his hands. "Come and sit down, you look like you've barely slept." His face was drawn, his eyes lined with a shadow that hadn't been there before.

"I haven't."

"Jessie, I know you want to be here for her, but you need to look after yourself too. You're no good to her if you fall apart." She led him to one of the couches in the corner, gently pushing on his shoulders to get him to sit. "Why don't you rest for a bit? We'll wake you if there's any news." She gestured to the others who had settled down the other end of the room.

"I don't know if I can," he said, all emotion gone from his voice.

"Please try." She sat next to him, running her fingers through his hair attempting to relax him. "Just close your eyes for a minute." She began to hum softly.

As much as he wanted to fight it, his eyes began to flutter as she kept up her gentle massage of his temples. When she was sure he was asleep, she slipped off the couch, and over to the others.

"Poor guy," Rory said with a sympathetic look. "He looks exhausted."

"Yeah. He's been staying here. I doubt he's had any sleep at all since that first night when we made him go home." Maddi wrapped her arms around herself. "I just wish there was something we could do."

"You are doing something," Ricki said, coming to stand beside her. He tipped her chin up to look at him. "You're here." Nodding, Maddi leaned into him, needing his strength. He ran his palm in soothing circles on her back, until she finally stepped away and joined the others on the couch.

A throat cleared in the doorway. "Are you here for Sacha Barrett?" the woman in scrubs asked, her hands clasped in front of her.

"Yes, we are." Maddi looked over at Jessie, wondering if she should wake him or let him sleep. "Is she okay? Can we see her now?" She made her way over to the door, her arms folded across her chest as if warding off the cold.

"I'm so sorry," she began, "the seizure caused a clot in her brain, and it travelled to her heart." She paused, her eyes flitting to the floor and back again. "I'm so sorry, there was nothing we could do."

"No," Maddi whispered, shaking her head. Ricki came up behind her, wrapping his arms around her shoulders.

"I'm afraid so. Is there anyone you'd like me to call?"

"No, her family… they're not…" She couldn't wrap her head around what the doctor had just said. *She's gone?*

"They're not around? I understand."

Maddi couldn't believe what she was hearing. Her eyes flicked to Jessie curled in the corner. "Jessie…" A sob escaped her lips. "Jessie," she said a little louder, shaking Ricki's hands from her shoulders. She walked over to the couch, gingerly perching on the edge. She reached up to touch his face. "Jessie."

"Hmmm?" he mumbled, stirring. When he saw the looks on his friends' faces, he sat upright, as if he'd forgotten where he was. "What is it? Is it Sacha?" he asked, turning to look at Maddi. "Is she okay?"

"Honey, I'm so sorry," she said, fresh trails of tears teeming down her face. "There was a blood clot… she didn't make it."

"She didn't…" he stared into her eyes, hoping that it was some sort of sick joke.

"No, I'm sorry, Jess." She shook her head, hating the pained look in his eyes. "I'm so sorry."

"She can't be gone," he said, his voice catching in his throat. "I never got to tell her how I felt. I never got to tell her I made a mistake." He closed his eyes, forcing the tears to fall. "I love her," he whispered, turning his face into Maddi's hand.

"She knew, Jess. And she loved you too," Maddi said, trying to hold it together. Sliding her hand to the back of his neck, she slowly pulled him into her arms. "She knew," she repeated, cradling him against her.

Chapter 22

The next few days flew by in a daze. Sacha's mother wasn't interested in saying goodbye, and she refused to offer any kind of help to Jessie. In the end, Maddi, Rory, and the boys had rallied around, helping him to organise the funeral and wake.

Maddi and Rory stood by the door, handing out memorial cards to all the people who had come to celebrate the life of Sacha. The salsa community had come out in full force, filling the room with their vibrant colours, rather than the traditional black; something Sacha would have done had she still been here. The sound of cow bells could be heard from out on the street as some of her favourite salsa songs were played.

"I still can't believe she's gone," Nicole said softly as she pulled Maddi in for a hug.

"I know. I keep expecting her to barge through that door and tell us all to harden up." Maddi smiled, though it didn't quite reach her eyes. "Is Rob with the boys?"

"Yeah, they shouldn't be too far away. They were almost ready to head over when I left."

"How'd Jessie look?" Maddi's face was lined with worry. Despite her encouragement, she knew he'd barely eaten or slept since the attack. Not that she could blame him; it hadn't been easy for any of them.

"Not good to be honest. He looks dead on his feet." She gasped, her hand covering her mouth. "Sorry, that was in bad taste. It just slipped out."

Maddi dismissed the comment with a wave of her hand. "Don't worry about it." As she watched Nicole make her way into the hall, the hairs on the back of her neck stood on end and she knew without looking, that they had arrived.

Swallowing back the lump in her throat, she placed the leftover cards on the table and, taking Rory's hand, she walked down the steps to join her friends by the hearse.

"Jessie," she whispered, reaching out and wrapping her arms around him. She rubbed her hands up and down his back, fighting back the urge to cry. When she pulled away, she could see the glisten in his eyes and offered a sympathetic smile. "You ready?"

With a longing look at the coffin, he nodded. "Yes."

Jessie and Ricki each took hold of the front, Maddi and Rory stood in the middle, clasping the cool metal handles, while Rob and Damon took hold of the rear.

"On the count of three. One, two, three." They lifted the mahogany box from its holder, and with slow steps, they made their way across the lot and entered the hall.

One by one, the guests stood, a silence falling around the room as the soulful voice of Garth Brooks singing "The Dance" played over the speakers. Once at the front, Maddi placed a picture of Sacha on top of the box, a white rose beside it. They each held their palms to the wood in a final goodbye before taking their seats.

"Please be seated. On behalf of Jessie, I would like to thank you all for coming to celebrate the life of Sacha Barrett. A life taken far too soon." The celebrant paused, looking out across the room. "It is heart-warming to see so many friends here, not only to say goodbye to such a charismatic woman, but to support Jessie in this difficult time. He will continue to need your love and support over the coming weeks."

Jessie nodded his head, his eyes fixed on the photos flashing on the screen behind the celebrant. The photos of him and Sacha. Hot tears slowly trickled down his cheeks as he remembered each and every moment spent with her.

"As many of you know, Sacha was well known in the Latin dance community, and Rachel would like to say a few words on their behalf."

The redhead walked down the aisle and took her place at the podium. "Hi. For those of you who don't know me, I'm one of the dance teachers in this community. I was lucky enough to teach Sacha and Jessie." She looked over to where Jessie sat, her voice faltering. "Right from the beginning, I knew she was going to be something special. She had this fire inside that wanted to come out. You could see it every time she danced." She shook her head with a smile. "She certainly had the fiery attitude to go with it. No one could ever say she didn't put her all into everything she did. She had a lot of potential, and I wish she could have had more time to show the world." Looking down at the casket, she said, "We're going to miss you, Sacha. I hope you're still dancing up there, showing them how it's done." She stepped down and made her way over to Jessie, placing her hand on his shoulder. Looking up at her, he patted her hand and thanked her for her kind words.

"Thank you for that, Rachel. I'm sure she will be dancing up a storm." The celebrant smiled. "Maddi, would you like to come to the front?"

Maddi nodded, taking hold of Jessie's hand as they stepped up to the podium together. Clearing her throat, she began. "Jessie has written a few words down and asked me to read them out." She reached back for his hand, giving it a squeeze. "Sacha, you took my breath away from the first moment I saw you dance. And even though you were with a friend of mine at the time, I couldn't help but be drawn to you and your stubborn, strong-willed fierceness." She smiled at his choice of words; Sacha definitely was all of those. "We had our ups and downs, but no matter what, I never stopped loving you. I only wish I could have told you that one more time." She paused, taking a breath as she felt the tears brimming.

"To everyone around us, you put on a show, never letting them see your softer side, but with me, there was no hiding. I was lucky enough to have a glimpse into your vulnerability, your kindness, and your dreams. I wish we'd had the time to show the world what you were really capable of. You were my friend, my mentor, and my lover. I love you more than words can say. I'd give anything to be able to hold you one last time." Unable to stop the tears, she brought her hand to her face, brushing them away. "Sorry," she said, trying to compose herself.

With a shaking voice, she managed to get out the last few words. "Sacha, I hope you know how much you mean to me. I will always hold you in my heart. Keep on dancing, wherever you are. Love you, babe."

Turning to face Jessie, she flung her arms around him as they both fell apart, crying over the woman who had driven them both crazy.

Chapter 23

Carrying Sacha back to the hearse and watching Jessie say his final goodbye had been one of the hardest things Maddi had ever had to do. She couldn't begin to imagine how he must've been feeling, knowing that Sacha would never be in his arms again.

One by one, people began to move forward, offering their condolences. Jessie stood rigidly, his hands clasped in front of him and a vacant stare in his eyes, his body moving on autopilot whenever someone pulled him in for a hug.

With Maddi and Ricki on either side of him, he slowly made his way up the steps and back into the warmth of the reception hall. Rory and the other students from *Gastronomie* had transformed the room in a matter of minutes. Long trestle tables were draped with bright cloths, and a myriad of nibbles were scattered across each table. To the side of the room was a drinks bar, complete with fancy barista-style coffee and flavoured teas.

When Rory saw them step into the room, she quickly strode over, her black apron strings streaming out behind her. "Can I get you something to drink? Coffee? Tea?"

"Um, no. Thanks though. You've done a wonderful job in here, Rory." His voice cracked and his eyes flew to the ceiling as he composed himself.

"Jessie, you need to have something. How about a sweet tea to warm you up?" Maddi nodded to Rory, and she scurried away to get it before he could protest.

"I'm fine, Maddi."

"I know you are. Humour me, okay? Let us take care of you in the way we know how."

The tiniest hint of a smile appeared on his face, and Maddi finally felt like she was getting somewhere with him.

"Believe me, it's easier to just let her have her way," Ricki said out of the side of his mouth.

"Hey! I heard that." Maddi slapped him playfully on the arm. "He's right though," she said with a wink.

Jessie turned to her with an exaggerated sigh. "If it will get you to stop pestering me, I'll drink the tea."

"Good, and it will… after you eat something as well." She grinned up at him, batting her lashes. "Please? Just something small."

"Oh all right then."

Maddi clapped her hands together before making her way to the food. Grabbing a small plate, she carefully selected a ham, egg and mayo sandwich, a piece of red velvet cake, and some chocolate fudge.

"Here you go," she said as she thrust the plate towards him.

"Something small, eh?" He raised an eyebrow as he took the plate from her hands.

"Just giving you choices. How's your tea?"

"It's good. Thank you." He smiled, the first genuine smile she'd seen from him since Sacha's passing. "And thank you for organising all of this." His eyes travelled the room. "It's perfect."

Placing her hand on his forearm, Maddi nodded her head. "It was our pleasure."

"I know things weren't great between you two, and for you to go to all this trouble for her… It would mean a lot to her."

"I'm just doing what anyone else would do."

"No, I don't think anyone else *would* do this. You're a good person, Maddi. And for what it's worth, she had a lot of respect for you, she just didn't know how to show it. Most people would bend over backwards to keep her happy, but you challenged her. You pushed her to be her best, even if it didn't seem that way to anyone else."

Maddi's eyes brimmed with tears as her thoughts turned to all the times she'd gone up against Sacha. "I wish I'd tried harder to get to know her better."

Jessie shrugged. "It takes two to tango. She was just as stubborn as you, if not more." He stared into his cup of tea, swirling the liquid around. "I'm really going to miss her."

"I know. I think we all will."

Jessie scoffed, raising his eyes to meet hers. "You don't have to say that."

"No, really. All competitiveness aside, she was an amazing dancer. She brought a fire to the dancefloor that not many possess."

Nodding his head, Jessie agreed. "You're right, she did."

"And let's face it, there was never a dull moment when she was around." Maddi nudged him with her elbow.

A slow smile spread across his face. "Yeah, she was a firecracker."

"She certainly was," a voice came from behind Maddi, making the hairs on the back of her neck stand on end.

"Dane, I didn't expect to see you here." Jessie held his hand out to his old friend. "It's been a long time."

Maddi stood frozen to the spot, her heart pounding in her chest as they continued talking beside her as if her world weren't crashing around her ears.

"I wasn't sure if I should come, but I wanted to pay my respects." Dane shoved his hands in his pockets, his eyes flicking over to Maddi.

"Of course you should be here, you were a huge part of her life too." Jessie raked his hand through his hair. "Sorry, I should've called and told you."

"Hey, don't stress about it. You had other things on your mind. It's understandable." Turning his eyes to Maddi, who still hadn't moved, he reached out to touch her arm. "Maddi?" he said softly when she shrugged away from his touch. "It's good to see you. You look good."

The slight brush of his fingers on her skin had her wanting to scream. Her eyes filled with unshed tears and her breath came out in sharp pants. She couldn't be here with him. She needed to get away, but no matter how hard she tried, her legs wouldn't obey her. She was paralysed with fear, her brain unable to cooperate with her body.

"Maddi, are you okay?" Jessie moved to stand in front of her, a look of concern on his face.

"Oh hell no!" A crash across the room drew his attention as Rory stormed towards them, her nostrils flaring and her finger pointed at Dane.

In a flash, Damon grabbed her around the waist, her arms and legs flailing as she tried to get out of his grasp. "Not here," he hissed in her ear. "Not now."

"Maddi?" Ricki moved to stand beside her, coaxing her into his arms, shielding her from the man who forced himself on her. "Come on, let's go outside and get some air." Pinning Dane with his eyes over her shoulder, he mouthed the words, *Stay away from her.*

Dane held his hands up, palms out; trying to convey his acquiescence. "Perhaps I should go, I don't want any trouble."

"I don't understand. What's going on? Is it because of the break-up?" Jessie stood between them, confused. "Maddi?"

With a shake of her head, she buried her face in Ricki's chest, clutching onto him.

"It's complicated," he said, ushering her towards the door.

"Don't leave. I'm sorry, I shouldn't have come. I thought…" He broke off, shaking his head. "Never mind. You guys stay, I'll go." Dane skirted around them, one final nod at Jessie. "I'm sorry for your loss."

Chapter 24

"He had no right to be there!" Rory paced back and forth in the lounge, her hands on her hips. "I mean, what did he think was going to happen? She'd welcome him back with open arms?"

"Easy, tiger." Damon took hold of her shoulders, making her stop and look at him. "It was a funeral, and he used to date her. It makes sense that he'd want to say his goodbyes."

"Yeah, but he could've done that from afar. He didn't need to come anywhere near her." Her eyes flicked down the hall to where Maddi was. "Did you see the look on her face? She was terrified."

"Yeah, I saw." His fists clenched at his sides. "Believe me, I wanted to deck him just as much as you did, but a funeral is not the place to be doing it."

With an exaggerated sigh, Rory threw herself onto the couch. "I know, you're right. I wasn't thinking straight. When I saw him reaching out to her…ugh! I just wanted to…" She mimed ripping something apart with her bare hands. "You know?"

"Yeah, I know. He'll get his, don't you worry. Karma has a way of catching up on people like that."

"It bloody well better." Folding her arms across her chest, she stared off down the hall again. "What do you think they're doing in there?"

"She'll be fine. Stop worrying. Ricki's got this." Offering his hands out to her, he nodded his head towards the kitchen. "Come on, let's get some of those leftovers packaged up for Jessie. I doubt he feels much like cooking."

"You're a real softy sometimes, you know that?" Taking his hands, she allowed him to pull her off the couch.

"Don't act so surprised. You know that's why you love me so much." He winked, leading her into the kitchen. "Seriously though, it's put things into perspective." Turning to rest his hip against the counter, he pulled her into his arms, resting his chin on her head. "I would be a mess if anything ever happened to you. I feel really sorry for the guy."

Squeezing her arms that little bit tighter around his middle, she nodded against his chest. "Yeah, it's pretty scary how quickly things can change." Tucking her head down, she stared at the flat expanse of her stomach, picturing how it would look in a few more months. She knew he had a right to know that he was going to be a father, but the timing felt all wrong. How could they celebrate when Jessie's life was crumbling around him? It didn't seem fair.

Not to mention Dane being back on the scene threw a spanner in the works. It hardly felt like the time to drop the baby bomb on everyone. She still had to figure out what she was going to do about *Gastronomie*. For the past few years it was all she'd dreamed of, and she'd be damned if it was going to be taken away from her. There had to be a way to have both.

"Hey, guys," Maddi said from the doorway, her fingers tangling together. "I'm sorry about before. I kinda freaked out a bit."

"*You* freaked out?" Rory stepped around Damon to give her friend a hug. "Please. I was the one who smashed a plate and had to be hauled out of there. If anyone is going to be apologising for freaking out, it's me."

Maddi chuckled lightly. "You smashed a plate?"

"Oh yeah, like full-on judo chop!" She pulled back, displaying some over-dramatic karate moves, complete with sound effects. "I would've gone all Daniel-san on his ass if Damo hadn't stepped in."

"Believe me, it was tempting to let you go all *Crouching Tiger* on him, but I didn't think Jessie would appreciate the sentiment." Damon chuckled as he began shovelling various slices into containers. "It would have made for a great show though."

"I'd pay to see it," Ricki said, giving Rory a high five on his way passed. "He deserves all that and more."

"Oh yeah. And I'm happy to be the one who dishes it out."

Ricki grinned. "I think we all would, Rory. Though, I think you'd be quite the worthy adversary." He held his hands in front of him, palms facing each other. "Compact. And quick."

"Mmhmm," Damon agreed. "You've gotta protect the twig and berries from this one, she's sneaky and just the right height to surprise punch 'em."

"That was one time, and I said I was sorry." Rory pouted. "I only meant to tap them." She shrugged her shoulders. "Apparently I don't know my own strength."

"Just a tap," Damon muttered under his breath. "Damn near had me on my knees with tears in my eyes."

"Oh, stop! It wasn't that bad!"

"Wasn't it? I may never be able to have children," he said mockingly while he flapped his hand in front of his face like a damsel in distress.

Rory's face dropped. How wrong he was.

Knowing exactly what her friend was thinking, Maddi took hold of her hand and gave a squeeze before joining the boys in the kitchen. "Let's get all this food sorted out so we can take it to Jessie."

Chapter 25

"Thanks for letting me stop by. I probably should've done this from the start instead of causing a scene back there." Dane hooked his thumb over his shoulder as he rocked on his heels in the doorway.

"No problem. It's good to see you again. Come in, have a coffee." Jessie stepped back from the door, allowing room for him to pass.

"That would be nice, thanks." As Dane followed Jessie down the hall, he took in the barren walls and boxes filling the open space.

"Sorry about the mess. I only just moved in here when…" He cleared his throat before continuing. "I've only been here a little while." Averting his eyes, he made a beeline for the kitchen, switching the kettle on, while Dane wandered around the room aimlessly.

"Where's all her things?" he asked quietly.

With his hands gripping the counter, Jessie took a shaking breath. "Still at the old place," he whispered. "We'd… we were having a break…"

"Oh sorry, I didn't realise. I just assumed…" Dane trailed off, silently kicking himself for sticking his nose in where it wasn't needed. "It's a nice place," he said, desperately trying to appease the situation.

"It's all right. Does the job." He shrugged then set to work on their drinks, if only to distract himself. It didn't work though, instead sending a jumble of thoughts through his mind about Sacha. Here was Dane offering an olive branch, when really it should be the other way around. He was the one who'd done Dane wrong and broken the number one rule: bros before hoes.

"I, ah… I don't think I ever apologised for what Sacha and I did to you," Jessie said as he carried their coffees through to the dining table. "I honestly never meant for any of that to happen… I don't know what came over me that day. I never thought I'd be 'that guy' but then Sacha… she could be real persuasive when she wanted to, and to be honest, I don't think I tried hard enough to stay away. She was…" he breathed out a sigh. "God, she was something else."

"Don't I know it?" With a shake of his head, he continued. "You don't have to apologise. It's water under the bridge now." Dane clasped his hands together. "I mean, if that hadn't happened, I never would have found Maddi." He took a sip of his coffee.

"That didn't exactly go well either though, did it? I'm not sure I did you any kind of favour." Jessie leaned forward. "If you don't mind me asking, what happened between you two? I thought it was mutual, but after what I saw today…"

Dane ran his fingers through his hair. "I'd rather not talk about it. Let's just say, it wasn't my finest moment." He gazed out the window, his fingers gently drumming on his cup. "I didn't mean to upset her, you know. I only wanted to clear the air."

Jessie eyed him wearily. "Whatever went down between you two is your business I guess, and I'm sure when she's ready to, she'll hear you out." He paused, leaning back on his chair. "You know, she was probably just surprised to see you again. What's it been? Eighteen months? That's a long time."

"Mmmm." Dane nodded. "It really is."

"Do you think you'll come back to dancing?"

"I'd like to, but…" He turned to look at Jessie. "I don't want to make Maddi uncomfortable. This is her domain now."

"There's other studios, you don't have to dance at hers." Jessie shrugged. "Maybe it's time to branch out?"

"Yeah, maybe." Pushing his chair back, Dane stood up, bracing his hands against the table. "I should let you get back to it. It was really good seeing you again." He smiled though Jessie could see the hurt in his eyes.

"Yeah, you too. And I'm sorry I didn't call… I…there's really no excuse for it. I was just lost."

"I understand. I would've been the same way." His voice caught in his throat. "I still can't believe she's really gone. I thought she'd outlive all of us." He laughed without mirth.

"If only that were true." Jessie shoved his hands in his pockets, staring at his feet. "Goes to show, nothing in life is guaranteed. It only takes the act of some arsehole to ruin everything."

Swallowing the lump in his throat, Dane could only nod, unable to think of anything to say. How could he, when he was no better than the scum who attacked Sacha? Bile roiled in his stomach as he thought about what he almost did to Maddi, what could have been if Ricki hadn't busted the door down and pulled him off her.

He'd come back to town, not only to say his goodbyes to Sacha and make amends with Jessie, but also to ask for Maddi's forgiveness. But now that he was here and listening to Jessie talk, he realised something.

He didn't deserve her forgiveness.

Chapter 26

"Are you fucking kidding me right now?" Rory roared as they rounded the corner and came face to face with Dane. Dropping the bags of food to the ground, she automatically took up a defensive stance in front of Maddi, her fists balled by her sides as she stared him down with nostrils flaring. "Why are you back?" she demanded, pointing one finger through the air.

Taking a step back with his hands up, Dane stuttered, "I-I don't want any trouble. I only came to see Jessie." He couldn't stop his eyes from straying over Rory's head to meet Maddi's. "I never meant to upset—"

"You don't get to address her," Rory interrupted. "You've put her through enough already, don't you think?"

Averting his eyes, Dane shoved his hands in his pockets, kicking a toe into the ground. "I'm sorry," he whispered. "You're right. I just..." He looked up apologetically. "I just want her to know how sorry I am... for what I did... I never should have done that." Tears brimmed his eyes as he pleaded. "I really did love her..."

Rory scoffed, putting her hands on her hips. "You've got a funny way of showing it."

"I know. I screwed up and lost the best thing that ever happened to me. Don't you think I know that already?" With a sigh and a shake of his head, Dane tried to calm down before he made matters worse. Closing his eyes, he counted backwards from ten until his breathing evened out, just like he'd been taught. "I wish I could say or do something to prove to you how truly sorry I am." Taking a chance, he peered at Maddi once more, who was watching him with a mixture of fear and understanding. "You really were the best thing to ever happen to me, and I wish to God I'd seen it sooner. Maybe things wouldn't have played out the way they did… You deserve happiness, Maddi. I hope Ricki makes you happy." After a beat, he turned on his heels and began walking away.

"Can you believe that guy?" Rory asked, hooking a thumb over her shoulder as she swivelled on the spot to retrieve the bags.

"Dane, wait!" Maddi called out, hesitantly stepping forward.

"What are you doing?" Rory watched as she took another shaky step towards him.

Dane stood with his back to them, unsure what to do. He didn't want to scare her again, not when this was the first time she'd spoken to him in over a year.

"A-are you o-okay?" she asked, stopping a safe distance behind him. They had been happy once, and even with everything he'd put her through, she still couldn't get herself to hate him. Fear him, yes, but not hate.

Nodding his head, he slowly spun to face her, keeping his hands securely in his pockets so as not to frighten her. "I am. I'm seeing things much clearer now. After… you know… I started seeing a counsellor." Pulling his hand up to his face, he rubbed his jaw. "I've been diagnosed with borderline personality disorder. Not that it's any excuse for what I did. It's never okay, and it kills me that I was able to do that to you, Maddi." He reached his hand out to her, forgetting how fragile she was. When he saw her flinch, he dropped his hand to his side. "I hate that I've hurt you. That you can't bear to be near me. I'd give anything to take it all back."

"I know," she whispered as a silent tear rolled down her cheek. She looked away, straightening her top and clearing her throat. "I hate it too, but it *did* happen, and we can't change that. All we can do is move forward, right?"

"Maddi?" Rory took her hand, offering what little support she could.

"I'm okay." She smiled through her tears. "I don't know if I'm ready to forgive you yet, Dane, but I'm going to try. It's going to take some time though."

Letting out the breath he'd been holding, Dane gave a nod of his head. "Thank you, I understand," he stammered. "You have no idea what this means to me."

"I'm not just doing it for you, I'm doing it for me too. It hurts in here." She pointed to her chest. "Every time I see you, I'm reminded of that night, and it hurts like it did back then." She shook her head of the images.

"I don't want it to hurt anymore. And I don't want you to hurt either." She gestured between herself and Dane. "We can never go back to what we once were, but I'd like to try to put this behind us and maybe, one day, we could be friends again."

"Maddi, are you sure about this?" Rory asked.

"I am," she said with finality. "If Sacha's death has taught me anything, it's that everything can change in an instant, and I don't want to waste my life holding onto negative feelings. We can't change the past, but we *can* change how we feel about it." Turning back to Dane, she said, "I can see the regret in your eyes. I can feel the sorrow inside you. I knew something wasn't right back then and I should've been more receptive instead of pushing you away."

Shaking his head, Dane disagreed. "No, Maddi, don't take the blame for it. It's all on me. All of it. I didn't have a hold of my emotions back then. I was overwhelmed, and I put you in danger. I've accepted that now, and I have strategies in place so that it never happens again."

"You're damn right it won't happen again," Rory said vehemently. "Because if it did, I would hunt you down and castrate you myself." She held her fingers in the air, making a cutting motion. "Snip, snip."

"And I would willingly let you do that. I don't ever want to be that person again. You have my word, Rory, I won't hurt her again. I promise."

"Yeah, well, just know that I'll be keeping my eye on you." She pointed two fingers at her own eyes, before swinging them around to point at his. "Eye. On. You."

"I would believe that too," he said with an uncomfortable chuckle. "Anyway." He rocked back on his heels, bringing his hands together in front of him. "I don't want to hold you ladies up any longer." Side-stepping around Maddi, he gave her a smile reminiscent of their earlier days. "Thank you for hearing me out."

She watched as he walked away, the heavy burden of holding onto that hate lifting from her shoulders with each step.

Closing her eyes, she held her hand to her chest, sighing. "I can breathe again."

"At least someone can. You could warn a girl before you go all philosophical and lovey dovey."

"I'm sorry, I know you wanted to go all mini mafia on him, but it just felt like the right thing to do. Couldn't you see the pain in his eyes?"

"I mean, I guess…"

"And I love that you jump to my defence, but are you forgetting that you have someone else to think of now?" She nodded towards Rory's stomach. "That little bean doesn't need to be in a fight before he's even born."

Placing her hands on her belly, she grinned. "You think it's a boy?"

Shrugging her shoulder, Maddi gathered the bags from the ground. "I don't know, maybe."

"I kind of think it's a boy too. I keep having dreams about a blue-eyed boy with olive skin just like his daddy."

They strolled down the street in silence, counting the houses as they went by. When they reached Jessie's mailbox, Maddi stopped and faced Rory. "You know, you're going to need to tell him. He has a right to know."

"I know. It just hasn't felt like the right time, you know? With Sacha… and then Dane showing up…"

"It's as good a time as any if you ask me. People need something good to hold on to in times like this. Give him something to look forward to." Maddi walked down the path and up the steps to the door. Glancing over her shoulder, she could see Rory was rooted to the spot. "That's my view on it anyway. It's just an opinion. I mean, I'd understand if you were scared to—"

"I'm not scared." She shook her head, dragging her feet up to meet Maddi. The look of sympathy on her face made her cry out in frustration. "I'm not!"

"Okay, whatever." Maddi grinned, knowing her words would eventually grate on her friend's mind until she had to do something about it.

"I'm going to tell him when it feels right."
"Mmhmm."

With a dramatic sigh and roll of her eyes, she threw her spare arm in the air. "Fine! I'll do it tonight."

Chapter 27

"Do you think… I can't believe I'm about to say this but, do you think maybe I'm not meant to ask her to marry me?" Ricki leaned his back against the counter next to Damon.

"Not meant to ask her? Like the universe is giving you signs or something?" he retorted with a smirk.

"I knew you'd turn it into a joke. Don't worry, I shouldn't have said anything." Sighing, he pushed off from the counter. "I'm gonna go for a walk."

Before he could get out the door, Damon stopped him with a hand to his chest. "Dude, I'm sorry, I didn't realise it was that serious. You okay?"

"Yes… no… I don't know. It just feels like every time I get close to proposing, something else crops up." Clasping his hands behind his neck, he looked up to the ceiling. "Shit, I sound like an arsehole."

"Well…" Damon grinned at him with a raised eyebrow. "Maybe a little bit." He held his finger and thumb in the air with a small gap between them before clamping his hand on Ricki's shoulder. "You're allowed to think of yourself once in a while. It's not against the law."

"No, but it's insensitive. We just buried Jessie's girl, and all I can think about is how I want Maddi to be my wife."

"Funerals affect everyone in different ways. There's no right or wrong. I can totally get why it would make you think that way." He made a show of looking around to make sure they were alone, even though he knew the girls had not long left. "Has she mentioned the pregnancy test yet?"

He shook his head. "No. But I saw the stick in the trash the next day." He lifted his eyes to meet Damon's. "It was positive. I'm going to be a dad." A small smile played across his lips at the thought.

"Even more reason to pop the question, don't you think?"

"It's all I've wanted to do for the last few months, but with everything going on, it feels like maybe it's not meant to be."

"Sounds like you're taking an easy out to me." Damon folded his arms across his chest. "You nearly lost her. Twice. Man, she is the best thing that ever happened to you, and you know it. Why are you making excuses? What are you afraid of?"

"I don't know—"

"I call bullshit," he interrupted with narrowed eyes. "This is because of Dane, isn't it?"

Knowing he wouldn't let it go, Ricki decided to lay it all out. "Maybe it is." Balling his hands into fists by his side, he began to pace. "He just shows up like what he did wasn't a big deal. Like he didn't nearly destroy her." Raking his hand through his hair, he turned back to Damon. "We were making progress, she was coming back to me, and then he shows up and crushes her all over again."

"Then be the man who puts her back together. Don't back off when she needs you the most. Show her what she means to you, what *they* mean to you." He holds his hand in front of his stomach. "Man up and show her you'll be there for her, no matter what."

"It's not that simple."

"It *is* that simple. You love her, don't you?"

"Of course I do."

"You want her to have your baby, don't you?"

"You know I do."

"Then what's the problem?"

"Why hasn't she told me yet?" he whispered. "If she wanted me to be a part of their lives, why wouldn't she tell me?" The hurt in his voice was undeniable. "She's the first person I want to tell when anything good happens in my life. I thought… What if she hasn't told me because it *isn't* a good thing in her eyes? What if she doesn't want to have my baby?"

"And what if she's just scared? Have you thought about that?" Damon perched on the arm of the chair, bracing his hands on his knees. "Cut her some slack, man." He counted on his fingers. "She thought you were cheating on her, she's worried about Jessie, and now her stalker ex-boyfriend shows up out of the blue. She's had a lot to process this past week."

Sighing, Ricki nodded. "You're right. She *has* had a lot to process."

"Just be there for her. I'm sure she'll tell you when she's ready." Slapping his hands on his thighs, he stood up. "Right, now that we're done talking about our feelings," he batted his eyelashes and tilted his head to the side, "I'm gonna make a sandwich out of those leftovers. You want one?"

Chapter 28

"How're you doing?" Maddi asked as she stepped into Jessie's kitchen, making herself at home.

"As good as can be expected." He followed her in, watching her unload the containers into his fridge. "Thanks for bringing those around. I don't think I could face cooking today."

"We thought that might be the case." Rory hoisted the remaining bag up onto the bench. "I hope you like slices and sandwiches, you'll be eating them for days." She smiled, giving his arm a squeeze. "In fact, have you eaten? I can rustle a plate up for you now, if you like."

"Thanks, but I'm okay at the moment. You guys have already done so much. I can't thank you enough for all the help over the last few days."

"Oh psshh." She waved her hand dismissively. "It was the least we could do."

"Exactly. We're happy to help." Maddi handed her empty bag to him. "Pass that lot over, would you?"

"You don't have to do that. I can put them away later."

"I know you can, but like I said earlier, food is our way of helping, so just let us do it." She grinned, taking the bag from Rory's hands. "And don't think we won't be coming around to check on you. You're stuck with us I'm afraid."

"Two beautiful girls checking up on me, however will I cope?" he deadpanned with a shake of his head. "I really do appreciate it."

"We know." Maddi pushed the fridge door closed. "Right, is there anything else you need done?"

"Seriously, stop fussing. I'd rather we just hang out. It's amazing how quiet a place can get." He gazed out the window with a faraway look.

"We can do that," Maddi said, taking his hand and pressing a kiss to his cheek. "Whatever you want."

"Why don't you come back to our place? We could grab some takeout and watch a movie," Rory offered. "I'll even let you pick the movie." She said it as though it was a huge privilege she was bestowing upon him.

"I *could* use the company…"

"Then it's settled." She looped her arm through his, nudging Maddi out of the way. "We'll swing by the DVD store on the way home. What's your fancy?"

With a firm grip, she led him towards the door but not before Maddi could whisper in her ear. "You don't fool me. I know what you're doing."

"I'm inviting our friend over to spend some quality time with us. That's what I'm doing." Pretending to mull it over, she gasped. "Oh! You mean the thing I was going to disclose tonight? Oh well, I guess it'll just have to wait. What a bummer." Her voice dripped with sarcasm as she shrugged her shoulders nonchalantly.

"If you've already got plans—"

"Nope, no plans. Free as a bird." Rory practically pushed him out the door.

"Should I even ask?" Jessie raised an eyebrow at Maddi who couldn't help but chuckle.

"Probably not. It's easier if you just run with it."

"That has got to be one of my favourite movies! Melissa McCarthy is a badarse!" Rory jumped to her feet, executing her version of the fight scene they'd just watched in *Spy*. "I could totally be an agent."

"You'd nail it, babe." Damon chuckled, grabbing hold of her hips and pulling her down onto his lap. "I could see you all in leathers, roundhouse kicking some evil mastermind."

"You could?"

"Oh yeah, in fact, maybe we could play that out later on." He nuzzled her neck, sending her into a fit of giggles.

"Ignore them. We do," Ricki said as he reached for the remote to drown out their smooching.

With a sad smile, Jessie found himself mesmerised by them. It hadn't been so long ago that he and Sacha had been the ones canoodling through a movie. What he wouldn't give to go back to one of those nights, snuggled up on the couch with her in his arms.

"You okay?" Maddi asked, noticing the wistful look in his eyes.

Forcing himself to look away, he offered her a weak smile. "Yeah, I'm okay. Just missing her is all."

"Aw, honey." Wrapping her arm around his neck, she gently pulled him in for a hug. "We'll get through this."

"I know. It feels weird to be sitting here as if nothing's happened, you know?" Slipping out of her grasp, he rested his head on the back of the couch. "I keep thinking she'll walk through that door any minute now."

"I know what you mean. It's hard to get used to the idea of not seeing her." Turning her attention back to the screen, she chewed her lip, unsure whether to say what was on her mind. He had to be getting sick of hearing everyone's opinions on how he should handle things. With a quick glance out the corner of her eye, she could see how restless he was. Deciding to speak up, she nudged him gently with her elbow. "You're allowed to enjoy a movie with friends. It doesn't have to mean anything. No one's… judging you."

"Nothing gets past you, does it?" he mumbled under his breath.

"Not when my friends are involved." She gave his knee a pat. "I know you probably feel like you're betraying her by enjoying yourself, but you're not. It's okay to try and find some peace, even if only for a moment."

Nodding his head slowly, Jessie mulled it over. What she said made sense, he knew that, but putting it into action wasn't easy. Every time he felt himself relax, her face would hover in his mind's eye and guilt would override everything. Perhaps, over time, it would get easier, but right now, he wasn't ready to let go of those feelings.

"We're all here for you, Jessie. In whatever way you need us, we're here." Her hand found his, squeezing ever so softly, a silent promise of support.

The movie all but forgotten, Jessie looked around the group surrounding him, thanking his lucky stars he still had them in his life.

Chapter 29

"Okay everyone!" Maddi clapped her hands, ushering the couples to come in closer. "I know things have been a little disjointed lately, but the comps are coming up fast and we really need to knuckle down and perfect our routine." She paused, looking to Ricki for his nod of approval. "We wanted to run something by you before we get started. As you know, the community has been dealt a hard blow with Sacha's passing, and we thought that maybe, with your permission, we could dedicate our dance to Sacha and Jessie. Sort of a homage to her passion for the dance. Maybe throw in a few of her signature moves?" She held her hand up to stop anyone from jumping in. "I know it's late in the game to be changing things up, but it just feels like the right thing to do. So, what do you think?"

"Yeah, of course. It sounds like a great idea. You know she would've been up there competing against us if she was still here. It's only fair that a bit of her comes with us," Nicole said, stepping forward. "I'm happy to do extra training sessions to get it right. I'd planned on stepping it up a notch anyways."

"It goes without saying that I'm in if she's in." Rob grinned, taking her hand and kissing her palm.

"Thanks, guys. I know Jessie will appreciate the sentiment, and you can bet your arse, Sacha will be watching us from above." Maddi grinned, turning her eyes skyward.

"No doubt about it," Ricki added.

"What I had in mind was a slight change to the intro, and in the centre shine piece, we'll incorporate some of the moves she was known for, without taking away from our original piece. Sound good?" When they'd all nodded their agreement, she continued. "This is what we've come up with so far, but feel free to throw some ideas out there. We want to make this into something spectacular."

Ricki took his place beside her and, pulling the remote from his pocket, pressed play. The haunting voice of Sarah McLachlan singing *Angels* filled the room as Maddi began to step slowly around Ricki, her hand rolling across his body until it fell into his grasp. Pulling her into him, he lowered her into a slow dip, bringing her body back up in an arc, before they moved through a series of steps Sacha had once favoured, finishing on a gentle lift. It was only a brief intro, but it was moving.

"That was beautiful," Nicole said, wiping a finger under her eyes before any tears could slip out. "Beautiful and powerful. Just like Sacha was."

Ricki placed Maddi back onto her feet. "I'm so glad you think so. It's what we were going for."

"Well, you nailed it. You want to walk us through it again?"

"Sure. Everyone take your places and we'll break it down for you."

"Okay, how does this taste?" Rory held a wooden spoon out, her other hand cupped underneath to catch any drops.

Leaning forward, Damon opened his mouth, allowing her to feed him. The heat of the chilli hit him instantly, setting his mouth on fire. He quickly grabbed for a glass, filling it with water before gulping it down.

"Damn it, too hot?" She frowned, giving the pot another stir. "I thought I'd balanced it right this time."

Flapping his hand in front of his mouth, he huffed out a few quick breaths. "I mean, it's good, it's just blow-your-head-off good. So, if that's what you were going for, then you hit the nail on the head." A light sheen of sweat had formed on his top lip and his eyes were watering. "Do we have any milk? Milk's good for spicy food, isn't it?" He didn't wait for a response, pouring himself another full glass and downing it.

"Gah! I've made chilli a thousand times before, why can't I get it right now?" She stomped over to the cupboards, wrenching the door open to see if she could find anything that would cut through the heat. "I just wanted to make a nice meal for everyone to share, and now it's ruined!" She sniffled, hating that her automatic response to anything lately was to cry.

"Babe, it's not ruined." Damon stood behind her, his large hands kneading her shoulders. "I'm sure you can come up with something amazing to go with it. And you know I'm going to end up slapping it between two slices of bread anyway."

Rory scrunched her nose. "Philistine. You're just as bad as those people who put tomato sauce on everything."

"Don't knock it till you try it. Chilli sandwiches are the shit." She tilted her head back to frown at him, and he pressed a kiss to smooth out the lines. "You know what else? My tongue is going numb, so I probably won't even notice the heat when we eat it later." He grinned, ducking out of her reach before she could swat him.

"You're lucky you're cute," she grumbled, slamming the cupboard closed again.

"Damn right, that's how I scored your fine little self." He winked, resting his hip against the counter. "Admit it, you love me."

With the hint of a smile on her face, she moped towards him, leaning her forehead into his chest. Damon's arms wrapped around her, pulling her close.

Sighing, she mumbled, "I *do* love you." And the truth was, she loved him more than she cared to admit. The thought of him fleeing when she dropped the baby bomb on him scared the crap out of her. Every time she went to do it, her voice would catch in her throat and she'd falter. It'd been a few days since she'd agreed to tell him, and she hadn't missed the disapproving looks Maddi had been firing her way.

Her shoulders shook as she fought the tears that were always so close to the surface.

"Hey." He cupped his hand under her chin, lifting gently. "Are you really this upset about a bowl of chilli?"

Biting her top lip, she closed her eyes. *It's now or never.*

"Damon, I—"

"Mmm, is that chilli I smell?" Maddi and Ricki strolled through the door, throwing their dance bags on the couch. "Smells divine."

Slipping out of Damon's arms, Rory swiped her tears away, coughing to clear her throat. "Ah, yeah. It's not ready yet. This big baby," she hooked a thumb over her shoulder, "thinks it's too spicy. I thought I might whip up a lime granita to serve with it."

"Ooh, that sounds delish." Maddi flopped down on the couch, kicking her feet up underneath her.

"Mmhmm, hopefully." Rory chewed her lip, avoiding Damon's eye as she pulled her blender out of the cupboard.

"Rory?" He stepped in behind her. "What were you going to say?"

"Hmm? Oh, um, never mind. I'll, um, tell you later." She waved her hand, shooing him from the kitchen while she went about gathering the ingredients she needed. Her heart was pounding in her chest, her fingers fumbling with the cord as she attempted to plug it in. Placing her hands on the bench, she lowered her head and closed her eyes, inhaling a deep breath through her nose and huffing it out her mouth. She would tell him tonight. Maybe.

Chapter 30

Ricki watched as Maddi went through her solo shine for what had to be the twentieth time. They'd had an extra training session with the team earlier on, and now it was just the two of them in the studio. She had always been a perfectionist when it came to her routines, and he knew she was adding extra pressure on herself with this performance being a dedication. But he was worried that she was overdoing it. He didn't really know a lot about having babies, but he was pretty sure that stress wasn't something she needed right now.

"Maddi, don't you think you should take a break? You've been at it for hours." He switched the music off, holding the remote firmly in his grasp.

"I've almost got it, just one more run through." She stood in front of the mirror, her arms positioned above her head. When he folded his arms across his chest and raised an eyebrow at her, she huffed out a breath, turning to face him. "What's the problem? You know how important this is."

Walking towards her, he gestured the length of her body. "Look at you, you're exhausted. It's okay to take a break, you know?"

She cocked her head, placing her hands on her hips. "Thanks for the vote of confidence," she said drily. "I'm fine. I just want to get this right. We've only got a few more weeks until the comps, and it needs to be perfect."

Tucking the remote into his back pocket, he ran his hands down her arms, taking her hands in his. "I know, and it will be." He kissed the tip of her nose. "It already is." His eyes dropped to her stomach and back up again. "I'm just trying to look after you. I don't want you overdoing it. You'll burn out."

"One more time, then I promise I'll stop and we can go back home, okay?"

Shaking his head with a chuckle, he held the remote over his shoulder, pressing play. "So damn stubborn."

Padding out of the bathroom in a comfy pair of trackies and a singlet, Maddi flopped onto the couch, tucking her legs beneath her. Pulling her hair over her shoulder, she dragged a brush through her mane.

"How was your bath? Feeling better?" Ricki asked as he settled in beside her with their hot chocolates.

"Mmm, it was just what I needed." She set her brush down, stretching her arms above her head with a satisfied sigh. "I didn't realise how tense I was."

"You really need to start looking after yourself, Maddi." He pursed his lips, deciding to just lay it all out there. "It's not just you you've got to think about now."

Turning to face him, she scrunched her nose. "What's that supposed to mean?"

In one fluid movement, he dropped to his knees in front of her. "I know." He waited a beat to gauge her reaction. "About the baby."

Her eyes widened as she chanced a glance in Rory's direction. "Ricki, I—"

He held his hand up to stop her. "It's okay, I understand why you didn't say anything. But I want you to know that I'm here for you and our baby. I won't let you go through this alone. We're a team, and a pretty good one, I think." He smiled, rummaging in his pocket for the box he'd been carrying around for the last few days, waiting for the right moment to present itself. "I messed everything up when I tried to go big and showy, so this time, I'm keeping it simple." With shaking hands, he held the tiny box out to her, opening the lid to reveal a rose-gold band with diamonds set in the shape of a flower on top. Maddi's hand flew to her chest, and her eyes welled. "Maddi, I love you more than anything. You're the most kind-hearted, beautiful soul I've ever met. You light up the room with just your smile, and when you dance… the whole world stops. I can't imagine my life without you in it, and I'm so excited to start our family together. Would you please do me the honour of being my wife?"

"Oh my God," she whispered. "I don't know what to say."

"Well, yes would be the preferred answer," Ricki joked with a nervous laugh.

"I have to tell you something, and I don't know if that will change things or not, but you need to know before I answer you." She looked at Rory, who had tears running down her face, whether from joy or fear, she wasn't sure.

"Okaaaay. You can tell me anything, you know that." He took her hand in his.

"Um, there's no easy way to say this. There's not… there's no baby. I'm not pregnant."

His face paled. "You…you lost the baby?" His words were barely audible. "Oh, Maddi, I'm so sorry. I can't believe you had to go through that on your own."

"No!" She shook her head, dropping to her knees to cradle his face. "That's not what I meant." She glanced over at Rory again. "I was never pregnant."

"But Damo saw you buy the test, and I found it in the trash. It was positive." He stared at her, confused.

"It was mine," Rory whispered, a sob catching in her throat. Turning to Damon, she broke down completely. "It was my positive test. I'm pregnant."

Chapter 31

"You're… You're… and we're… I'm going to be a father?" Damon stuttered, trying to wrap his head around what she was saying.

"Yes," she hiccupped, peering at him through her tears. "I'm s-so s-sorry I didn't tell y-you. We haven't t-talked about having children, and…" She took a deep breath to get the words out. "I was afraid you'd leave," she said quietly, lowering her head to stare at her fingers.

He tilted her chin up, wiping her tears from her cheeks. "Baby, look at me." With a trembling lip, she raised her eyes to meet his. "I'd have to be some kind of arsehole to get up and leave you because you're carrying my baby." He paused, pulling a face. "Wait, it *is* mine, right? I'm the baby daddy?"

"Of course you are!" she cried, punching his arm.

"Okay, okay!" He held his hands up in defence. "I was only joking. I know you've only got eyes for the D-man." He puffed his chest out. "Got you to stop crying though, didn't it?" His eyebrows waggled up and down, making her grin.

"I guess."

"Seriously though, why would I leave? You're drop-dead gorgeous and a phenomenal chef who will one day own her own café, earning us the big bucks, while I become a house-husband and look after the children. Sounds like a pretty sweet deal to me." He flexed his fingers, placing his hands behind his head as he stretched his legs out in front of him.

"You want to be a house-husband?" She quirked an eyebrow.

"Hell yeah! I'm not going to stand in the way of your dreams, and let's face it, I'm a big kid at heart, it makes sense for me to be the one who stays at home with them."

"So… we're doing this? Together?" She couldn't keep the hope from her voice.

"We're doing this. It would take a lot more than that to get rid of me."

With a squeal, she flung her arms around his neck, planting kisses all over his face.

"You keep that up and we'll be having twins!" He chuckled, wrapping his arms around her.

"I don't think that's how it works, Damo," Maddi said with a laugh. She knew in her heart he'd come through for her.

"Ah." Ricki cleared his throat. "I, um, don't want to take away from this heartfelt moment, but, um, you're kind of leaving me hanging here."

"Oh my God!" Maddi clamped her hands to her cheeks, turning to face him. "Sorry, I got caught up in the moment. Of course I'll marry you." She reached out to trace a finger along his jaw. "If you'll still have me, that is. I'm sorry there's no baby."

"Are you kidding? That just means we get to have fun trying." He winked, holding the ring up. "May I?"

"You better!" She giggled, extending her hand towards him so he could slide the ring on. "It's so beautiful," she gushed, staring at the glistening gems.

"Not nearly as beautiful as you."

Epilogue

"Good evening, ladies and gentlemen! And welcome to the National Salsa Championships!" The crowd erupted, hooting and hollering. "We have a fabulous group of performers lined up for you tonight, including a special tribute performance for one of our fallen stars. As many of you will know, the community was rocked only a month ago, by the death of one of our up-and-coming dancers, Sacha Barrett. Her presence will be sadly missed, and I ask you all to honour her with a moment's silence."

As everyone lowered their heads, the auditorium fell into silence. Backstage, Maddi grasped Jessie's hand, knowing how much this meant to him. She really hoped he liked the routine they'd put together in Sacha's memory. It would be the first time he'd seen it, and she was a little nervous.

"Thank you, everyone. Now, without further ado, let's get this show started! First up, we have the groups section!" A round of applause rang out as the groups gathered round behind the curtain. "Our first act comes all the way from Christchurch! Please welcome, the Southern Stars!"

"This is for you and Sacha," Maddi said, pecking Jessie on the cheek before taking Ricki's hand. Nicole and Rob were waiting in the wings on the other side of the stage, along with the rest of the team. Ricki took his place centre stage, with Maddi behind him. There was a hush over the crowd as the music began, and to the back of the stage, projections with images of Sacha lit up the darkness while Maddi did her slow walk around Ricki.

One by one, the other couples joined them on the stage, each weaving a tale with their bodies. When the song transitioned into their original piece, they picked up the pace, throwing their all into the routine. Behind them, the images continued to scroll through, showcasing Sacha's salsa journey, and of course, her relationship with Jessie.

When it was time for their solo shines, Maddi moved with fluidity across the stage, stopping in front of Ricki, with her back to the audience. Confused as to why she wasn't in the correct position, he raised his head to see if she was okay. What he saw, brought tears to his eyes. The other dancers faded into the background as she stood before him, holding her suit jacket open with a message sewn into the red satin:

You + Me = Three

Before he could respond, she'd spun away to join the rest of the girls for their ladies' shine. With the biggest grin on his face, he shook his head, falling into step with Rob.

The crowd went wild as the final beat was played and the dancers stepped forward to take their bows. Maddi clapped towards the side of the stage, beckoning Jessie to join them. He poked his head out from the curtain, giving a wave to the audience, before darting back again. He had tears in his eyes as he mouthed *Thank you* to her.

"Thank you, Southern Stars! What a fantastic performance! Give them one last round of applause before our next act comes to the stage!"

Jessie shook each of their hands as they made their way backstage. "Thanks, guys, that was amazing."

"You really liked it?" Maddi asked, ignoring his outstretched hand and pulling him in for a hug.

"It was perfect. She would have loved it."

"Maddi." Ricki tapped her on the shoulder. "Sorry, Jess, can I borrow her for a minute?"

Chuckling, Jessie unpeeled her arms from around him, handing her over. "By all means."

Taking her hand, he led her to one of the empty changing rooms. Closing the door behind him, he turned slowly. "Did that mean what I think it means?" he asked, searching her eyes.

A small smile graced her lips as she nodded. "Yeah, I think it does. It appears there *was* a baby after all."

"Really?"

"Really."

A knock on the door interrupted them, and Rory burst through the door. "Did you tell him yet?" She bounced up and down as Damon watched her with amusement.

"Sorry, guys, I tried to keep her out there as long as I could."

Maddi laughed. "It's okay, I told him already."

"We're gonna have twin bellies, and our kids will be the best of friends too!" She ran and tackle-hugged them both. "This is going to be so much fun!"

"Oh, I know!" Damon squealed and clapped his hands like an excited teenager before jumping in on the hug. He clamped a hand on Ricki's shoulder. "Congratulations, man."

"Thanks."

"Hey, what do you say we celebrate with a little drink?" He produced a bottle of sparkling grape juice from his pack, holding it in the air. "Non-alcoholic, of course." Popping the cork, he swiftly poured four cups, handing them out. "To shitty diapers and sleepless nights!"

They clinked their polystyrene cups together. Maddi glanced around at her best friends. It had been one hell of a year, and it was only going to get more interesting as their lives moved on to the next stage. Their destiny stretched out ahead of them, but if Maddi knew one thing, it was that they could make it through anything, as long as they had each other.

A Note from the Author

Thank you so much for reading A Step in Time, the complete series. I hope you enjoyed reading it as much as I enjoyed writing it. I'd love to hear what you thought.

If you'd like to keep up to date with my new releases, you can sign up to my newsletter <u>here</u>. I promise I won't spam you!

Thanks!

Other books by Stacey Broadbent

Standalone

Never Judge a Book
Deep Heat

A Step in Time Series

Dancing Through the Storm
Dancing in Circles
Dancing with Destiny
A Step in Time: the complete series

Hollywood Novels

Emma

Flesh-Eater Series

Fear the Fever
Fight the Fever

Dark Sins Novellas

Sins of the Flesh
Mine

Ink-Slinging Sisters

Awesome Applesauce

Super Mum Series

Frazzled
Frazzled and Frumpy
Frazzled, Frumpy and Fabulous!
Super Mum: the complete series

Short stories and poetry

Musings, Mournings, and Misadventures

Anthologies

The White Ribbon Collection
Scars to your Beautiful
Witching Hour: Vices and Virtues
Key to my Heart
A Touch of Inspiration
No Place like Home
Serendipity

Connect with Me

http://www.staceybroadbent.weebly.com

https://www.facebook.com/StaceyBroadbentAuthor

Broadbent's Bookish Babes: https://goo.gl/FY9wQN

https://www.amazon.com/author/staceybroadbent

Goodreads: https://goo.gl/YJ6dXa

https://www.instagram.com/authorstaceybroadbent/

https://www.bookbub.com/authors/stacey-broadbent

https://vm.tiktok.com/ZSJBb5bhL/

Sign up for my newsletter:
http://eepurl.com/cULu_f

About the Author

Stacey resides in Ashburton, New Zealand with her husband and three children. She is a qualified proofreader, author, wife, mother, and self-proclaimed culinary goddess. When she's not busy writing or editing books, she enjoys reading and procrastinating on TikTok.

She absolutely loves hearing from readers, so please feel free to reach out via email, Instagram, or join her reader group, Broadbent's Bookish Babes. You can also sign up to her <u>newsletter</u> for up-to-date info on releases.